GRASMERE COTTAGE MYSTERY TRILOGY

DAHLIA DONOVAN

Grasmere Cottage Mystery Trilogy © 2018 by Dahlia Donovan

For information, contact the publisher, Hot Tree Publishing.

www.hottreepublishing.com

Editing: Hot Tree Editing

Cover Designer: Claire Smith

Formatting: Justine Littleton

ISBN: **978-1-925853-10-0**

OTHER BOOKS BY DAHLIA DONOVAN

If you loved The Grasmere Trilogy, you might enjoy the other witty, real, and romantic stories and books Dahlia has published.

LIST OF BOOKS

*For all my fellow lovers of Poirot, Miss Fisher,
and the like.*

For the quiet ones who the world underestimates.

For Olivia, sorry about the cliffhanger.

DEAD IN THE GARDEN

CHAPTER 1

"That is a body." Valor stared stupidly out the window over the sink where he'd been rinsing his coffee mug, his hazel eyes glued to the obviously dead man at the corner of their garden. He dragged his fingers shakily through his mussed-up red hair. "Bish?"

"Yes, it is." Bishan joined him with their fawn-coloured, long-haired cat, Staccato, perched on his shoulder, playing with his wavy inky hair.

"That's a dead body in *our* garden." He risked a glance at his long-time boyfriend to find him mesmerised by the sight. "I mean, it's a corpse."

"Very astute of you. Very. Astute. Quite astute. Incredibly so, actually." Bishan had a tendency to repeat words when he enjoyed the way they sounded to him. He claimed it was one of his many autistic superpowers. "Ahhh—stute."

"Yes, I grasp the concept. Why's a body in our rose bushes?" Valor carefully set the mug into the sudsy water, drying his hands off on his jeans and ignoring the indignant huff from Bishan. "Right. I'll call the police, and you put Staccato in the bedroom."

Their cat enjoyed climbing up on anyone who came into their cottage. Valor didn't think the local constables would appreciate their uniforms being covered by their feline's orange-sherbet-tinted hair. She also loved to disappear into the garden, something that wouldn't be helpful either.

"Why are you calling the police?" Bishan had his phone out already.

"They hate you." Valor fumbled with his iPhone for a second.

"Only because I set fire to cotton wool. And they think I'm a terrorist." Bishan shuddered, obviously thinking about the offensive white fluff balls that he hated with a passion. "Val? It's a body. Out there. In our garden."

"Maybe stop looking at it?"

The police didn't actually think Bishan was a terrorist. They'd had one unpleasant run-in with one of their neighbours when they moved into the small cottage in Grasmere in the Lake District. The older gentleman hadn't appreciated Bish's Indian heritage, their out-and-proud relationship, or the Tamboli family who'd come en masse to help the two move into their home.

Everyone else in Grasmere had been lovely to them. They'd welcomed the couple with open arms. Valor had needed the encouragement after falling out with his own family.

Ironic, in some ways, considering they'd always assumed Bishan's traditionalist parents would be the disapproving ones. It seemed being gay and dating an Anglo-Indian had been one step too far for the son of an earl. Valor Tarquin Scott had been struck from the family; his father, mother, and elder brother hadn't spoken to him in over a decade, not since a year after his graduation from Harrow.

By contrast, the Tambolis had embraced both their son and his boyfriend. Valor had been relieved. He didn't honestly know how they would've gotten through without their support—and the help of the old boy network from Harrow.

We take care of our own.

Valor drew his attention back to his still muttering boyfriend. "Cotton wool is an inanimate object, Bish. It can't hurt you."

"It's evil and must be purged with fire." He gently set Staccato into their bedroom and closed the door. "Wicked stuff."

"Overly dramatic twit." Val rolled his eyes.

"It squeaks when you pull it apart. That's not natural." Bishan gave a full-body shudder this time. Hypersensitivity to sound was yet another of his autistic superpowers—or maybe more of his kryptonite. "Well? Call the police."

"They don't think you're a terrorist, you know." Valor left Bishan to his thoughts when his boyfriend waved him away.

How does one tell the police they've discovered a body?

What would Poirot do?

Aside from attending the same school, an unhealthy obsession with Agatha Christie was another thing they had in common. They'd watched every episode of *Poirot*, multiple times. Bishan tended to see his favourite shows over and over.

And Valor didn't complain when it came to detective shows.

Stop dithering, Valor, and call the police, or they'll think you put it off for some reason.

Why does my inner voice sound like our house matron?

Twenty minutes later, their small cottage seemed even tinier with so many people crammed inside it. He and Bishan had been pulled into separate places to be questioned. *Have you ever seen the man before? When did you notice the body? Can you account for your whereabouts for the last twenty-four hours?*

His simple, mildly sarcastic answers didn't do much to endear him to the detective. Valor found it hard to focus on the questions while also keeping an eye on Bishan across the room. He knew his boyfriend would be mortified if the looming plainclothes policewoman triggered a shutdown.

The thought had barely crossed his mind when the woman in question frowned at Bishan then stepped over to whisper into the ear of the detective who'd been speaking to Valor. He could barely make out the muffled words. *"He's refusing to talk."*

Daft cow.

"He's not refusing to speak. He can't," Valor interjected. The twin glares sent his way didn't faze him; he'd spent a lifetime being scowled at by the master of the disapproving frown, Bertram Valor Scott IV—the seventh Earl of Dorset. "He happens to be autistic. You might consider giving him a moment. He's overwhelmed, and it'll be a bit before his brain starts allowing words to filter in to him again."

"But—"

"We'll step into the garden to check on the progress out there. We've gotten enough from you both for now in any case." Detective Inspector Reggie Spurling had been kind to them during the kerfuffle with their neighbours, and proved once again to be an understanding sort of man. "If he needs a break, why don't you take the cat out for a walk?"

"Hilarious." Valor left the detectives to argue amongst themselves. He found Bishan wrapped in a blanket in his favourite armchair, trying to disappear into himself from the looks of it. "Bish? Why don't we see how many of our nosy neighbours are watching the excitement?"

Bishan shook his head, curling further in by pulling his feet up onto the seat.

Right.

Time for a bit of violin.

Valor had found over their years together, going back to being roommates as shells—new boys—at Harrow, that Bach on the violin did wonders for Bishan. He retrieved his instrument from the corner where all their various musical toys were kept. It didn't take long for him to get into the flow of one of their favourite pieces.

Poirot would definitely not be playing the violin with a mystery to solve. Sherlock might.

I'm not a detective, though.

Just obsessed with them, and now we've got our own mystery to solve. Or, no, we should probably leave the police to handle it.

We're not in a show on the telly.

A bit of snooping can't hurt, can it?

He continued to play his violin while stepping toward one of the open windows in their living room. *Calm Bish, and eavesdrop on the police while figuring out how to keep us out of their suspicions. Easy-peasy.*

Well, mostly.

"Val?" Bishan spoke twenty minutes into Valor's violin concert for one. "Don't you think the police might find the 1812 Overture an odd choice of music when we've a corpse in the bushes?"

"Found your words for you, didn't it?" Valor couldn't be bothered to worry about what strangers thought. His concern would always go first to helping Bishan cope in a world that never seemed to consider struggles of day-to-day life for autistics. "You all right?"

"Going to make tea. Lots of tea."

Turning his attention to putting his violin away, Valor allowed Bishan the time he needed to recover his composure. Despite all his assurances, his boyfriend always came out of a shutdown feeling embarrassed. *As if he's done it on purpose. Wish I could help.*

"Mr Scott?"

Valor set the case carefully onto the shelf and turned to find Reggie Spurling waiting for him. "Detective Inspector. What can I do for you? More politely pointed questions?"

"You said you'd never seen the deceased before? Either of you?"

Valor had gotten a fairly good look at the poor soul in the garden. "Not that I can recall. Bish's better with faces than I am. He'd definitely have remembered. Have you identified him? I'm good with names."

"We'd rather not disclose any information just yet. We'll be in touch, but please stay out of the garden for today at least. We're not finished back there." Detective Spurling paused to narrow his dark eyes on Valor. "I'd appreciate you remaining in the county if at all possible. With your family connections—"

"My family wouldn't lift a pinkie to offer me any sort of assistance, Detective Inspector. In fact, they'd probably do their best to help your case against me if they thought I'd done something." Valor managed not to sound as bitter as he often felt when it came to his parents, elder brother, and younger sister. "Is there anything else?"

CHAPTER 2

"Oh, my darlings. It's dreadful. Awful. How are you coping? You must come round— Oh, hello, Reginald. How's your Nan?" Lottie Wright swanned into the cottage without even knocking on the door. "My Wilfred sent me right over to make sure you hadn't gotten yourself into trouble."

"Mrs Wright." Detective Spurling appeared completely resigned to being treated like a young boy.

"Tell your Nan she owes me a tea. Now, get on with yourself, Reginald, get to work. You always were a bit of a lazy lad." Lottie bustled the detective out into the garden, shutting the door as though she were the queen of the universe. "Right. That's handled. How's your Bishan doing?"

Lottie Wright and her husband, Wilfred, ran the ginger biscuit bakery that Valor had started upon moving to Grasmere. He'd known them his entire life. They'd worked at his family estate through much of his youth; Lottie had cared for him and his siblings until they'd gone off to boarding school, while Wilfred managed the grounds.

The couple had moved back to their home in the Lake District while Valor was at Harrow. After his family disowned him, they'd invited him to come to stay with them and treated him more like their son than his own father did. Now in their seventies, they both ran around with more energy than Valor could imagine having.

"All right, Dame Lottie," Valor teased. "Bishan's making tea. Want to join us? Where's Wilfred?"

"Opening the shop."

After finishing his education, Valor had floundered for what to do with his life. Without his family's support, he'd relied on the old boy network for advice and support. One of the many benefits of attending Harrow: they had a broad group of former students who always stood by their fellow Harrovians.

His gift, if Val had one, tended toward a brilliant head for marketing, sales, and business. He'd known he wanted to start something himself. It had only been after a casual conversation with the Wrights that things came into focus for him.

With investments from several old Harrovians, the Ginger's Bread, the name a play on the biscuits and his hair, opened a year after Valor graduated from university. Wilfred and Lottie made the ginger biscuits while he handled everything else attached to the business. Two of Lottie's nieces helped out in the shop, and one of Wilfred's nephews dealt with deliveries to the local teashop and grocer.

He was proud of how the little biscuit shop had grown over the last seven years.

They'd done it.

He'd done it despite his father's insistence that he'd come crawling home to beg for money.

"Valor?" Lottie looped her arm around his. "Did you know the poor man in the garden?"

"No." He narrowed his eyes at the petite woman. "Did *you*?"

Her bright blue eyes sparkled up at him. She led him through his own cottage into the kitchen where they found Bishan sitting on the counter. His tall frame caused his head to bump against one of the cabinets.

"You doing okay, love?" Lottie immediately took over the making of the tea. She had a way with Bishan that only endeared her more to Valor. "We'll get it all sorted. All these bumbling coppers, trampling the garden. I'll get my Darren to come over to straighten it up for you once they've finally finished."

Valor leaned against the counter next to Bishan. He took the slender musician's fingers into his slightly larger ones. His boyfriend was tall and slender; he was shorter and had a stocky frame. "Want some toast?" he asked.

Opposites.

We've always been opposites.

From day one as roommates at school, the two had been so different from one another. The wealthy son of an earl whose name had been on the register at Harrow practically from birth, and the son of a doctor and accountant who'd gotten into the school on scholarship. *The prince and the pauper. The sporty toff and the musical Indian.* They'd had all sorts of things thrown at them teasingly by their fellow West Acrians —West Acre had been their home away from home, one of the twelve boarding houses at the school.

Your house is your family.

They stayed in touch with many of the lads from their years at Harrow. *Many, not all.* Every family had their problems. Valor had tried to put the few not-so-good memories from school behind him.

"Valor, love?" Lottie pressed a fresh cup of tea into his

hands. "Why don't you two head to the bakery for a break? Hmm? I'll keep my eye on that lot in the garden."

"You just want juicy gossip to share with your friends at the bookshop." He grinned when she swatted him with a tea towel. "I'm right, aren't I?"

"Behave yourself, or I won't tell you what I find out. You're as nosy as I am, there's no use pretending you're not." She waved the towel at him, shooing him and Bishan out of the kitchen. "Go on. Reggie won't stop you with me here."

"He's scared of the towel," Bishan whispered to Valor, who snickered all the way out of the cottage.

Grabbing their bicycles from beside the cottage, they cycled the short distance through the village to the biscuit shop. The front of the business was relatively small. The majority of the building was taken up by the rather large kitchen.

How much room do you need to actually sell ginger biscuits?
Not much.

A crowd had already gathered inside with the shop assistants struggling to cope with all of them. They did steady business. Valor couldn't remember ever seeing so many people cramped inside at one time, particularly so early in the day.

"Right. How many of you are here for the biscuits?" Valor raised an eyebrow when they all claimed to be. "Of course, you all are. And how many of you want to know why Mr Spurling has so many police in our garden?"

"Told them I'd sent my Lottie over to find out." Wilfred stood head and shoulders above everyone in the shop. His long grey hair framed his face chaotically, making him seem like a wizard from one of the fantasy novels Bishan enjoyed reading. "Do they know who died?"

The entire crowd seemed to lean toward Valor in anticipation of the information they'd been hoping to get. He laughed at their complete artlessness. They didn't appreciate his gleeful refusal to answer.

He dragged Bishan through the crowd back into the kitchen. "They'll be torturing us to get information if we're not careful."

"Doubtful."

Valor shook his head, knowing from experience that sometimes Bishan completely misunderstood jokes. "Why don't we nick some biscuits to sustain us before Wilfred's interrogation begins?"

They grabbed a handful from one of the fresh stacks and retreated away from the door. Valor figured it would take a while for the shop to clear out. He'd usually have offered to help, but in this case, it might just make things worse.

"What's the point of it? All they do is run up and down a pitch, trying to kick a round ball." Bishan leaned against Valor's back to stare at the football match that he'd found on the tiny television Wilfred had hooked up in a corner of the kitchen. "Honestly. Why bother?"

"This from the man who was on the house cricket team every year at Harrow?" Valor reached up to tug lightly on Bishan's hair. "Isn't the point of the game to throw a small round ball back and forth?"

"More civilised."

"Why? Because you use your hands on the balls?" Valor snickered when Bishan shoved him on the shoulder. "Football is as civilised as cricket."

While Bishan spent thirty minutes detailing the many reasons cricket was more civilised, Valor's thoughts went back to the body in their garden. Detective Inspector Spurling had obviously expected him to know the man. He hadn't.

So why had Spurling seemed so surprised at his answer?

Or more importantly, why had the man been in their garden in the first place? Was he placed there before or after his death? And how had he died? Sudden heart attack or something more sinister?

Don't get involved, Valor.
It'll only get you in trouble.

CHAPTER 3

The body was gone from their garden when they returned home. Bishan disappeared into the library they used for a music room, needing to centre himself. He had a performance in London in a few days.

While Valor had spent his time post-university trying to build a business, Bishan had become a celebrated musician. He currently played with the London Symphony Orchestra and had turned into a bit of a YouTube sensation, creating classical covers of modern music. It was amazing.

The strains of piano filtered through the cottage. Bishan had decided to relax before he moved on to practicing for the upcoming concert. He played the violin, cello, oboe, and clarinet, depending on how the orchestra needed him to fill in.

Making a coffee for himself, Valor headed out into the garden to see the damage. The grass had been trampled badly, and the roses decimated as well. Caution tape still marked off a section of the backyard.

"Are you there, Valley of the Scots?"

Valor managed to contain his sigh of annoyance. He

turned to find his neighbour poking her head over the garden gate. "Mrs Harris. How are the frogs?"

Their neighbour kept frogs. *Everywhere.* Statutes, ceramics, a birdbath, and live ones all over. Bishan had wanted to dissect one. Valor thought it wouldn't endear them to the older woman.

It would've been a right laugh, though.

Until she called the police on us.

The frogs had grown on them. *Literally.* Valor often found them straying into their garden. He chucked them over the fence—gently.

"They're jumpy."

Only years of etiquette training kept Valor from busting out laughing. His lips barely twitched at the unintended joke. And it was unintended. They'd learned the hard way that Mrs Harris had next to no sense of humour.

"It's all that racket earlier. What've you two done now?" She whacked the gate with her walking stick. "What were you doing in the garden at three in the morning anyway?"

Valor found himself suddenly grateful for the old bat's annoying tendency to watch their every move from her house. "At three, you said?"

"Yes. Saw you stumbling around back there together. Looked as though you were holding Bishy up, then you went behind the bushes. Almost reported you to the authorities." She rattled on for a few minutes about how perverted behaviour should be kept behind closed doors. "You did seem quite a bit taller than normal. Do you wear heels?"

So, our killer was a tall bloke—or taller than me at least.

Why didn't she assume it was Bish, given the height?

Granted, she can't even see in the brilliant sunlight, so odds are she's blind as a bat at night as well.

So, the killer may or may not be a tall bloke.

"Did you tell the detectives what you saw?" Valor asked

curiously. He didn't think Spurling would have allowed them to head out if his neighbour had mentioned seeing them in the garden. "Did they talk to you at all?"

"No one listens to the frog lady." She lifted up her cane to point at him. "He had one of those hooded jackets that you wear. The ones with the sticks on the back. It's why I assumed it was you."

Sticks on the back? My Harrow hoodie? Is this all connected to school? We're in our thirties. How does that make any sense?

Not even bothering to excuse himself, Valor rushed into the house. He found his old lacrosse team hoodie hanging on the hook by the front door. It wasn't his original that had gotten too frayed over the years.

Still holding the hoodie, Valor stared at himself in the mirror on the wall to the left of the door. If the killer had been dressed in Harrow gear, the dumping of the body had been intentionally done and not a coincidence. *But why? And more importantly, will it make the police think we're involved?*

Another horrifying thought occurred to him. If the killer knew them, what kind of message was it supposed to send? "You're next," or "You're going to take the fall for me"?

Maybe I have been watching too much Poirot.

Valor dropped onto the bench against the wall with a thud. "This will *not* end well. I just know it."

The soothing sound of the oboe broke his moody silence. Bishan had obviously started to practice for his concert. Valor tapped his fingers against his leg, trying to decide the wisdom of telling Detective Spurling about what his neighbour had seen.

She might be the batty frog lady of Grasmere but she'd definitely seen something. Valor didn't think she'd hallucinated it. He didn't know if it was wise to share it with the police.

So much of it seemed like a coincidence, but he knew

from watching detective shows that there was no such thing. *Brilliant. Now I'm not only talking to myself, I've turned paranoid.* He didn't know if Spurling would believe him.

Why would he when I barely believe it myself?

CHAPTER 4

"How's Bish? Two whole days and neither of you can be bothered to tell us someone dumped a body in your garden." Sunesh Tamboli lived in Manchester, where he'd made a successful career out of the law. He also happened to be Bishan's elder brother. "Two days. Have you spoken to the authorities?"

"Listen, sunshine, they found a dead man in our garden. What do you think? We've obviously spoken to the detectives." Valor stepped back to allow Sunesh into the cottage. "You talk to your brother at least once a day via text. You know he's in London. So why are you here harassing me with all the questions?"

"Two questions does not equal harassing."

Valor grinned at the barrister over his shoulder before leading him toward the kitchen. "Coffee or tea?"

"Coffee. I've a case to prepare for tonight, and this drive hasn't helped." Sunesh perched on one of the kitchen stools. "But honestly, how do you not immediately call the family barrister? Do *not* play detective, Val. I know you two. You watch every single detective show on the telly. You're not bloody Poirot."

"I haven't done anything." Valor had always found Bishan's elder brother a bit intimidating. Sunesh had an intelligent, effortless authority to him, while Valor's own sibling was cold, calculating, and distant. "The detectives haven't been back since they finished in the garden."

Valor decided not to mention how Lottie had pumped her police officer niece for information. He hadn't asked her to do it. Not directly. It wasn't his fault the Grasmere villagers enjoyed gossiping in his biscuit shop.

"Don't muck around with the detectives. They might not take a second glance at you—all posh from Harrow with a title to your family name. Bishan won't be so lucky." Sunesh got straight to the point once the coffee had been made. He'd never been one to mince words. "They'll think his reactions are wrong. He hates making eye contact, so they'll think he's lying to them. He's cold. A bit detached emotionally."

"No, he's not. Bishan has all the same emotions as you or I. He doesn't always know how to express them." Valor had seen first-hand how his boyfriend struggled to decipher his feelings for himself, never mind trying to show others. "He's not a robot."

"Easy there, knight in shining armour. I'm not the enemy. I'm only saying what might happen. You can't stick your nose in because you've a fetish for investigations, and not expect there to be repercussions from it." Sunesh took a sip of coffee then stared pointedly at Valor. "I can't stay long, but you will keep me informed of any changes in the investigation. Also, Mum wants some of your biscuits." He grinned suddenly. "Can I get a packet or four?"

"For her and yourself?"

It had taken Valor a long time to get used to how the Tamboli clan interacted with one another. His family had

secrets built upon secrets intertwined with a healthy suspicion of one another. Closeness didn't come naturally to any
of them; he used to joke it had been bred out of them in
the 1800s.

It's probably true.

Ice in their veins was how his grandmother had described
both sides of their illustrious family tree. Valor had never fit
into the expected vision of a Scott scion. His parents had
privately written him off as a failure even before quite
publicly disowning him.

In contrast, the Tambolis were warm. They genuinely
cared for one another and were quite involved in each other's
lives. Valor had initially expected it to feel invasive in
contrast to the cold exclusion he'd experienced in his own
childhood.

"Val?"

He shook his head to clear it and found Sunesh watching
him with concern. "Stray thought. What were you saying?"

"Just be careful, yeah?" Sunesh might intimidate the hell
out of him, but Valor had a healthy respect and admiration
for the man. He'd lived with his parents, caring for them as
they grew older for a long while until they moved to Windermere to be closer to Bishan. "I don't want Mum or Dad to
find out and start worrying about Bish. They've only recently
come to terms with his independence."

"It's sweet."

"And annoying for him."

Valor grinned at Sunesh. "He'll be sad that he missed you.
Are you catching one of his performances this week?"

"Always." Sunesh, actually all of the Tambolis, made a
habit of going to as many of Bishan's performances as they
could. Valor had always been jealous of it at Harrow. "Try to
keep your tendency to involve yourself in check, please?"

"I'll do my best."

He meant it.

His best just wasn't enough when a tantalising clue had been dropped on him. They believed the dead man had been a Harrovian. *And that is definitely not a coincidence.*

And probably not going to make the police any less suspicious of us.

CHAPTER 5

few days later, Valor returned home from the shop
to find all the lights on in the cottage. He considered calling the police, but his curiosity got the
better of him. Bishan wasn't due back from his symphony
tour for another fortnight.

Entering cautiously after unlocking the front door, Valor
tiptoed into the cottage. He found Bishan sitting in the
corner by their small fireplace with a broken oboe in his lap
and Staccato perched on his shoulder. *So, not a brilliant end to
the concert. What the hell has happened?*

Valor tossed his jacket across the back of the sofa,
crouched in front of Bishan, and gingerly plucked the ruined
instrument out of his fingers. "Did they cancel the tour?"

"It was a nightmare. Nightmare of epic proportions.
Worse than the time I forgot how to walk on speech day.
Terrible." Bishan choked out the word. "My oboe was broken.
They sent me home."

Sitting back on the carpet, Valor rested his hands lightly
on Bishan's sock-covered feet. His Bish hated wearing shoes;
it was always a struggle to get him to put anything on his feet

even during frigidly cold winters. He claimed anything aside from fabric restricted his toes too much.

Valor chalked it up to another way being autistic made Bishan uniquely perfect. "How did your oboe get broken? I've never known you to even allow a scratch to any of your precious instruments."

Bishan flexed his fingers against his jeans. "Someone left a note—calling me names."

"Names?"

Bishan shrugged, earning himself an indignant hiss from Staccato, who slipped from his shoulder. "Ones you'd expect to hear on a playground."

It took a bit, but Valor got Bishan to explain what had happened. Someone had vandalised his oboe along with a number of other instruments. They'd gotten replacements in, but it had left Bishan shaken and unable to play.

"And they sent you home?"

"Sent myself home." Bishan's fingers trembled while he played with the seam of his trousers. "Sunny's going to talk to the director and the police in London about investigating. What's the point? People are always going to be cruel, whether it's about autism or the colour of my skin, or my choice of partner."

"Me? I'm too brilliant to annoy anyone enough to pick on you," Valor teased, only getting half a smile out of Bishan. "Why don't we have a *Doctor Who* marathon and eat some of the cottage pie Lottie brought over for me?"

Three hours into Tennant's doctor, Bishan had fallen into a fitful sleep on the couch in Valor's arms. His gaze drifted to the broken oboe. *Why smash it?*

Dragging his fingers gently through Bishan's silky hair, Valor pondered the mystery. He suspected the incidents were connected. Too many coincidences for there not to be a link.

It was hard to shake the feeling someone wanted to scare them—badly.

With one person dead, they had to consider that whoever was responsible wanted to do more than scare them. But who? And why? *Why us? Who could possibly hold a grudge against either of us this badly?*

I should stay out of it.

I should.

It'll only make things worse if I shove my nose in, won't it?

With a sleepily snuffling Staccato and Bishan pinning him to the sofa, Valor decided to join them in slumber. They'd probably all regret it in the morning. His back didn't take being all scrunched up as well as it had in his youth.

A sharp banging jolted him awake what seemed like a mere five seconds later. Valor struggled to work his way out from under Bishan; Staccato had already bolted from the sofa at the first thud. He tripped over a shoe, a bag, and a piece of oboe until he reached the door.

"Mr Scott."

Valor yawned widely and scratched his side absently. He rudely ignored the detective in front of him, giving himself a few seconds to wake up fully. "Sorry. We're not interested in whatever you're selling."

"Mr Scott. Is Mr Tamboli in this morning? We have a few more questions for him." Spurling appeared to be attempting to see over his shoulder into the cottage. "Could you get him for us? Or perhaps allow us inside to chat?"

To chat?

"What questions would those be?" Valor stood blocking the entrance and wished desperately that Sunesh lived closer than Manchester. The advice of a barrister would've been priceless to him. "Has there been a development in the case?"

"We've identified the deceased. You mentioned, both of

you, that you'd never met him." Spurling sounded as though the statement held a significance that Valor didn't understand. "If you don't mind, we'd prefer to come inside the cottage to discuss it further. It's a rather delicate matter to divulge on your welcome mat."

"Not sure you'll be all that welcome." Valor frowned at the detective. "And I'm fairly confident we both told you that while we didn't recognise the dead man, it was hard to tell given his face was distorted quite a bit."

Unable to think of a reason to say no, Valor stepped aside. He allowed the detective to head into the living room. Bishan had disappeared—from the sounds of the shower, to get ready for the day.

Making coffee for himself, Bishan, and the three police officers, Valor glanced out the window into the garden. Mrs Harris's head was just visible over the top of the fence; she appeared to be spying on them again. He had no doubts the detective's visit would spread rapidly through the Grasmere gossips.

We ought to charge by the hour for all the entertainment we're giving all the nosy neighbours.

He wasted time in the kitchen, trying to put off the inevitable. Cleaning the counters, he did everything but go speak with the detectives. He gathered up the coffee mugs when he heard Bishan's voice in the living room.

"If you could come with us...."

The mug shattered as Valor dropped it to the hard floor below. He tried to rush into the living room but was blocked by one of the detectives. They shoved him roughly into the kitchen, forcing him to leap to the side to avoid getting shards of ceramic in his foot.

"It's only for questioning. We're taking him in as a precaution only," Spurling offered to Valor before leading the group out of the cottage. "We'll be in touch."

You'll be in touch.

Sod you very, very much.

You've no idea what you've started.

The second the door slammed shut, Valor had his mobile glued to his ear. He called Sunesh while sending rapid-fire emails to anyone from the old boy network who might be in a position to help them. Harrovians, no matter how far removed from school, stood by one another. *For the most part.*

Sod everyone who says I shouldn't stick my nose into the investigation. They're looking at Bish. I'm not allowing them to screw him over.

Sunesh promised to drive out to Grasmere immediately, knowing Valor had next to no legal rights to get involved. In the eyes of the law, a boyfriend didn't have much of a reason to be kept informed. He didn't trust Spurling to keep his word.

I want him home.

I want him free.

I want the shit responsible for this to pay.

His first instinct had been to immediately follow them to the station. Sunesh, ever the thinking barrister, warned him to stay at the cottage to avoid adding to their problems.

The police questioning lasted for the several hours it took for Sunesh to drive from his office to Grasmere. He had a great deal of experience working criminal cases. Valor had no doubts the talented barrister would put all his efforts into ensuring the detectives left Bishan alone.

Valor stayed at the cottage, slowly losing his mind. Sunesh had worried, rightly, that Valor might be too volatile to be at the police station. *"Absolute wanker."*

Sunesh might've had a point.

The second Bishan returned to the cottage, he hid in the music room, in obvious need of time to himself. Sunesh ordered Valor to keep an eye on him. He intended to return to his office to begin drawing up some paperwork.

Right. What now?

Moving out into the garden, Valor wandered over to the fence separating their yard from Mrs Harris's. He crouched down slightly, then went up on his tiptoes. It took a bit of manoeuvring to find the right angle from what would've been his neighbour's perspective the night of the murder.

What did she actually see?

The batty old bint.

What are we all missing?

CHAPTER 6

Tensions rose over the next few days. Bishan refused to go outside. Valor split his time between the shop and helping his boyfriend cope with what seemed like a constant state of overload for him. Bishan didn't want to talk about it—or anything.

He'd had one of his rare bouts of being stressed to the breaking point and going nonverbal.

As much as Valor wanted to take Bishan away for a break, Sunesh had practically begged them to stay put and out of trouble. The detectives would be suspicious of them if they swanned off on vacation somewhere. Besides, his boyfriend needed the familiarity of home; all either of them could do was wait patiently.

In the meantime, Valor employed all the skills learned from years of watching *Poirot*. He spoke to all his neighbours. None of them had seen or heard anything.

His email to several of the other musicians with the orchestra didn't provide much insight either. They hadn't identified the vandal who'd damaged Bishan's instruments. Valor couldn't help wondering how hard they'd actually tried.

"*Oi*. Prince Valiant."

Valor glanced up to find Hugh Asheford, one of his old housemates at school who was a detective in Manchester, jogging to catch up to him on the pavement. "Hilarious, Ash, I'm laughing on the inside. Where've you been then?"

"London to see the queen."

Valor risked punching his friend in the arm. "You're really *not* funny."

"I am." Hugh blocked his second swat. "Stop assaulting an officer of the law."

"It's hard to take you seriously when I distinctly recall you slept with a purple bunny for the first year at Harrow." He danced out of reach of Hugh. "What can I do for you?"

Hugh took him by the arm to guide him toward a parked car down the street. "Can we talk?"

"We haven't exactly been miming for the last minute, have we?" Valor found himself bundled into the passenger seat, banging his head against the ceiling of the car. "What's going on then?"

"Remember Angus Williams?"

Valor had to think for a moment before he remembered. "Wasn't he the jerk in our shell group who got sent home for antisocial behaviour?"

In his first year at Harrow, one of their year mates had gone out of his way to make all their lives a misery. Bishan had been a particular target. Angus had gotten suspended, only for his parents to withdraw him from school.

"What about him?"

"Remember the body in your garden?"

"Bit hard to forget." Valor had a sudden moment of clarity. "You've got to be kidding."

"I haven't said anything yet." Hugh drove them through Grasmere, following Valor's directions. "You always were more clever than you looked. Do you have any idea why Bishan's childhood bully was found dead in your garden?"

"The opposite of divine intervention?"

"When was the last time you spoke to him?"

"First year at Harrow?" Valor wondered if this casual interrogation would lead to his turn at the police station. "Are you here in your official capacity?"

"I'm here as a friend. They think Bishan was involved." Hugh got straight to the point while parking in front of the cottage. "But not you."

"Not me? We live in the same cottage. I'm up later than he is most nights. And I'm not only stronger but also more likely to go outside in the dark." Valor tried to tamp down on his temper. He always struggled to control it when he believed Bishan might be under attack. "Is it because of my family? Because let's be honest, they wouldn't exactly be character references for their black sheep, would they?"

His sister might, but the rest of them would likely be thrilled to see him crash and burn. The majority of his family had been waiting with bated breath for him to fail for his refusal to fall in line with what they expected of a Scott. As if their name and title meant anything in the world; they all seemed obsessed with this idea of a time that no longer existed.

"Val?"

He shifted around in the seat, glaring at his old friend. "What?"

"You've got to get a handle on this now. I'm not even supposed to be talking to you about this. They're going to point fingers at Bishan. It doesn't look good—you know it. Bish's brother will do all he can; I've no doubts." Hugh paused to wave at Bishan, who had appeared in the cottage window. "He barely handled sharing a room in the first two years at Harrow unless it was you. He couldn't handle the one science course in the room without windows. How on earth will he handle being arrested?"

"You're not helping." Valor found his eyes drawn to the figure in the window. "What do we do?"

"Figure out who wants to bugger up Bishan's life. I'll do my best to put Spurling off, but I'm not even supposed to be here." Hugh dropped a hand on his shoulder, squeezing gently. "You're not alone, Val. Either of you."

The sound of vehicles drew Valor's attention away from the cottage. He tried to bolt from the car, but Hugh grabbed him firmly by the arm to keep him still. It took an intense amount of effort to yank himself free.

The struggle in the car had taken long enough for the detectives to get out of their vehicles and get to the cottage door. Seeing Bishan in cuffs with his head bowed enraged him. Valor made it a few feet before Hugh got his arms around him for a second time. The taller and stronger man lifted him away.

"You'll make it worse." Hugh kept his voice low while forcibly dragging Valor out of the way. "If you rush up, they'll restrain you."

"You're restraining me." Valor winced when Hugh tightened his grip. "Let me go."

"No. You can't help him if you're sitting in a cell across the hall from him." Hugh managed to get him to the side of the cottage near the garden gate. "You've got to think clearly."

"The long game." He fought to get away from Hugh. "We're not in *Sherlock*."

"The long game." Hugh nodded. He still refused to release Valor. "Spurling is a good detective. He'll follow the evidence, and Bishan will be set free."

"Yes, because men who look like him never get sandbagged by the system." Valor refused to simply sit back and wait. "This is the longest and most uncomfortable hug I've ever gotten."

"You're still an annoying twit." Hugh shoved Valor away from him. "I can hear them leaving. You'll want to get on the phone to—never mind."

"Sunesh? They've arrested Bishan." Valor spoke the second his almost-brother-in-law picked up on the other end. "No idea what the charges are. I'd imagine murder. They finally identified the body as one Angus Williams."

"Wasn't he the pillock who tormented Bishan?"

Valor snorted with laughter despite the seriousness of the situation. "Yes, the bullying twit from Harrow. That's the one. Though maybe call him something more respectful when you talk to the detectives. Let's not make Bish's case worse."

"If that's the goal, you should stay as far away from the detectives as possible," Sunesh retorted sharply. "I've asked one of the other barristers in our office to handle things. I don't want to risk the familial ties getting in the way."

"*Sunny.*"

"Trust me, Val."

He wanted to say it was easy for Sunesh to say, but it couldn't be easy for Bishan's family to sit back and do nothing as well. "I'll try."

And by try, I mean I'm going to solve this murder with or without anyone's help.

Right, new life motto, what would Poirot do?

CHAPTER 7

"Valor Tarquin Scott. Get out of the kitchen. I want to speak with you." His brother's voice lacked the authority and age of their father's, but it carried through the biscuit shop well enough. "Valor! Attend me."

Attend me?

Have we dropped into Downton Abbey *all of a sudden?*

And they wonder why I don't keep in touch with any of them.

Shoving the last of his lunch into his mouth, Valor left the sanctity of the little office off the side of the kitchen. He brushed the crumbs off his shirt before pushing through into the front of the shop. To his great surprise, his little sister stood beside his brother; she seemed a bit ill at ease beneath the mask of etiquette and manners.

The one lesson that had been drilled into all of them from a young age was never to show emotion. They'd been taught by a rather stern nanny to be miniature adults. It had been one reason Valor had been pleased to be shipped off to boarding school at eight; it offered him freedom to be himself —to be human.

"Penny. Bertie." He grinned when his brother tutted in

aggravated offense at the use of their childhood nicknames. *Pretentious twit.* "You're both a bit far from home and hearth. What brings you out to deal with the peasants?"

"We've missed you." Penelope placed a hand on their eldest sibling's arm, probably hoping to keep him calm. "You missed Christmas and New Year. Mother hoped you might join us for Easter dinner."

Valor stared stupidly at his sister for almost a full minute. "Is this some bizarre joke? You missed me at Christmas and New Year? Since when? When was the last time I was even invited to a family dinner?"

Not wanting to provide even more gossip to everyone pretending not to listen in the shop, Valor headed outside and down the pavement around the corner. His brother and sister followed him. He leaned against Wilfred's old battered van, glaring at his siblings.

"We *have* missed you." Penelope stretched an arm out toward him before letting it fall back to her side when Valor didn't move to take her hand. "We have."

"You might've. Bertie hasn't, have you?"

"It's Bertram." His eldest sibling frowned at him as much as etiquette would allow. "Stand up straight. For God's sake, must you slouch so? You're the son of an earl."

"You realise no one gives even the slightest bit of a shit about that anymore?" Valor merely raised his eyebrow at his older brother. "Is it Bertram? I can think of a few other more appropriate names for you. Why are you here? Penny's a dear, bit too caught up in being a Scott, but I know she's probably missed me. You, on the other hand, were thrilled when dear old Daddy disowned me. It's more money in the will for you. They have the heir, the spare really isn't required. Penny's good enough for it. So, again I ask, why are you here? Why now? After all these years?"

"Mother thought you might be more amenable now since

—" Penelope stopped abruptly when Valor shot a warning glare at her. "You should be with family. Can't we get beyond all this bitterness?"

I should be with family?

He mouthed the words several times, dumbstruck by the audacity of the ones who'd tossed him to the wolves. "I am with family. Wilfred, Lottie, my old schoolmates, and the Tambolis."

"You should distance yourself from him." Bertram didn't bother to hide his sneer of disdain. "As I predicted years ago, he'll only bring you trouble. I mean, murdering someone in your garden. What can you expect from someone like him?"

"From someone like him? Can't be bothered to actually articulate your posh brand of bigotry fully? Or use Bishan's name?" Valor hadn't backed down all those years ago, and he refused to do so now. "And my Bish didn't murder anyone."

His brother started to open his mouth, but Penelope tugged on the sleeve of his jacket. She shook her head then leaned up to whisper to him. Valor pinched the bridge of his nose, trying to stave off the headache that always came when he thought about his family.

Why are they even here? Not a peep out of them for ages, yet now they pop up out of nowhere the minute Bishan appears to be out of the picture. Bizarre even for them. Bertie hates slumming it, so why is he here? How much did Penny pay him to come with her?

The conversation between his siblings grew louder before Bertram stormed off, albeit politely. He strode down the alley, clucking his tongue. His arms swung at his side.

"Still walks as though Granddad's cane is right up his—"

"Don't be rude, Valor." Penelope stepped over to loop her arm around his. "Why don't we have a chat while we stroll down the lane to your cottage for tea?"

He glanced down at her slender hand that barely rested on his arm. "Why don't we cut through the fakery and you tell me what you two really want? And it's not tea in what I'm sure you think is my grubby little hovel."

"That's almost verbatim what Bertie called it." Penelope covered her mouth to laugh; she looked so much like their mother that Valor wanted to muss her hair up to break the perfect image. He'd forgotten how bizarrely restrained his entire family was. "We're worried about you. The police could consider you an accessory."

"Bishan didn't do it." He enunciated each word slowly.

"Valor."

The pity in his sister's voice angered him greatly. Valor failed to see why either of them had come to visit. He didn't believe for a second they genuinely wanted him back in the family fold.

"Is this damage control? Are the great Scotts concerned about how this might break their perfect image?" Valor watched his sister visibly wince and chuckled bitterly in response. "Go home, Penny. It's a longish drive, and you won't want to get stuck in traffic."

In an effort to avoid taking his temper out on his sister, Valor stormed away from her. He grabbed his bike from the rack at the back of the shop, cycling off toward home as quickly as possible. His family always brought the worst out in him.

The emptiness of the cottage made him want to turn around to cycle back to the shop. Bishan offered a quiet, warm comfort by merely being himself, and Valor ached to have him home. He wanted their easy cuddles in front of the telly.

He only went back to the cottage to ensure Staccato was cared for. If it hadn't been for the cat, he might've slept in his office chair at the shop. Being at home alone hurt far more than he imagined it would.

Empty.

It felt empty.

It reminded him of the time he'd gone back to West Acre, their boarding house at Harrow, during a break. He'd been the only one there. It felt almost post-apocalyptic; the vibrant energy of all his friends disappeared with their absence.

Falling into Bishan's favourite chair, Valor dropped his head into his hands. Staccato leapt up behind him, purring up a storm. The cat slipped down to curl up beside him.

"Not the same without Bish, is it?" Valor collapsed against the cushions, allowing Staccato to slither over into his lap. "I don't know what to do. It's beyond me. Sunesh won't tell me what's happening. I think he's worried about my reaction, which only stresses me out even more."

Staccato purred at him in response. Not helpful, but better than the awful silence of the cottage. Valor had taken to listening to recordings of Bishan's musical performances to keep from losing his mind completely.

Never realised how damn lonely I am without Bish.

CHAPTER 8

W*hat's this then?*
"Give it to me, you idiotic tree." Valor smacked the bark of the tree in raw frustration. "Give it."

The slip of paper mocked Valor from its spot at the base of the tree. He'd come into the garden to escape the silence of the cottage. A flash of something amidst the muted evening colours had drawn his attention.

After a fair bit of struggling, Valor finally managed to work it out from the tangle of roots to find a mere scrap of folded paper. How had the coppers missed it? He wondered if the detectives had somehow managed to push it deeper inside while going over the garden with a fine-toothed comb.

Brushing off the dirt and grass, Valor found himself staring at an old program from Churchhill Songs. It was specifically from the year both of them had attended. Bishan had even sung with the upper sixth choir. The concert was yet another one of those bizarre Harrow traditions.

Where on earth did this come from?

They kept all their photos, programs, and other Harrow

memories in a large album. Bishan's little sister had put it together for them as a Christmas present several years ago. They didn't have any loose papers floating around; this one definitely wasn't theirs.

So who had left it in the garden?

Valor instantly regretted touching it. His fingerprints would be all over the slip of paper. The Grasmere detectives weren't likely to be impressed by his explanation of having found it under a tree.

What did it even mean anyway?

He could just imagine the conversation now. *"Yes, Detective Spurling, I found an old school program. It could definitely crack the case."*

"No."

Heading into the cottage, Valor held the square of paper under one of the lamps in the kitchen. It seemed like any other program he'd seen in the past. They hadn't missed a Churchill Songs, which happened every five years, even as alumni.

Where did you come from, little piece of paper?

And why are you here?

He stared. And blinked. He twisted it around to see it from every angle. *I'm going cross-eyed with this thing.*

Hey, wait a second.

Valor leaned in even closer as he noticed certain letters appeared darker than others. He wandered into the living room, digging around in a wooden chest to find the album. It took a bit of flipping through pages until he located the exact same program.

He jolted in surprise, dropping the program and album when a hard knock sounded on the door. "Breathe. No need to jump at every single sound."

After picking up the program and album to place on a nearby shelf, Valor made his way to open the door. He found, to his surprise, three of their best friends. Cora and Daniel Zhou, brother and sister; the latter had been a year below him at Harrow. Nina Andoh had been Cora's roommate at university.

They'd all stayed good friends.

"When did you plan on calling in the reinforcements?" Nina shoved past him with a bottle of wine in one hand. "We brought food, alcohol, and our brains."

"And our brains will be useless after a glass or two of the stuff she brought." Daniel nudged by him as well, holding bags of something. "Mum made all your favourites. Cora insisted on picking up a cake as well."

"Let them eat cake?" She rushed forward to give him a hug, then followed her brother into the cottage. "Are you going to stand by the door all night?"

"It's safer." Valor shut the door, leaning against it. "Who told you?"

"Sunesh called Daniel. Reva phoned me. They were worried about you being alone at the cottage." Cora bent down to pluck Staccato up from the back of the sofa. "Why do you and Bishan always think you have to take on the world alone? You've got friends."

"Family, even." Nina leaned her head out of the kitchen. She collected four mismatched mugs to use as wine glasses. "I mean, us, not the blood relatives because they're rich wankers. No offense."

"You've met them. I never take offense at the truth." Valor feigned his brother's mannerisms for a moment. "Don't you all have jobs?"

"Impromptu vacation. We've a mystery to solve." Daniel lifted the various packets of food from the bag. "Besides, Cora and I are staying with our parents for the week. It's only twenty minutes away."

They noshed on the pork buns, dumplings, and crispy

onion pancakes Mrs Zhou had sent over. She'd also included her version of chicken fried rice. Valor stood firmly by his claim it was the best thing he'd ever eaten.

It didn't take long to bring the three up to date on the situation. Sunesh had told them about his progress, or lack thereof, in getting Bishan freed. They shared his outrage at the suggestion that the quiet musician could even be considered a murderer.

Somehow, knowing he wasn't alone made him feel so much better.

And in feeling better, Valor had an almost suffocating blanket of guilt overwhelm him. Bishan didn't have the luxury of support. He made a promise to himself to get Bishan free—no matter the personal cost.

Nina shuffled closer to him from where they all sat on the floor around his coffee table. She draped an arm around his shoulders. "We'll figure this out."

Valor had tried hard not to think the worst. He didn't trust a jury or judge to find Bishan not guilty even if there ended up being next to no evidence to prove him so. "And if we don't?"

"Prison break." She winked at him. "How hard can it be?"

"Very." Cora pointed at Nina with a spring roll. "How about we hope for the best? I'm not getting myself thrown into prison because Madame Revolutionary over there has watched one too many shows on the telly."

"Kids these days. No imagination at all," Nina scoffed.

"We're the same age."

"By the sound of your arguments, you're still both thirteen." Daniel interrupted the two women, who'd descended into a play fight over their level of maturity. "This is a serious matter."

By the end of the evening, they'd drunk the wine, eaten the food, and resolved nothing at all. Valor appreciated the company, but he thought they hadn't done much to help with the murder mystery. They'd meant well.

He kicked them out after a quick breakfast. Nina headed off to visit the police department. Daniel went home to check on their parents, and Cora stole Bishan's bike to ride into the village to visit the biscuit shop.

Finally.

Peace.

He'd lamented the quiet. And now missed it when it was gone.

Sipping coffee and ensuring Staccato's needs were handled, Valor's gaze wandered over the crumpled program. *Oh yes.* He shoved it in his pocket to investigate later. As the owner, he tried hard not to show up late to the shop.

And I fail most mornings.

Bad Valor.

"Mr Scott?"

Damn it.

He closed the cottage, locking the door before turning around to face Detective Spurling. "Here to arrest me?"

"Could we speak?"

Valor bit his tongue to keep from making the easy joke. He didn't think the man seemed in the mood for a laugh. "Go on then."

"All the evidence points to Bishan Tamboli as the murderer." Spurling apparently saw no reason for polite conversation. He went straight for slamming the knife into Valor's back. "We found nothing to indicate anyone else was involved."

"Is there a point to this?" Valor hadn't drunk enough coffee to be either as polite or patient as he probably should be.

"I don't believe he did it."

Valor barely managed to keep his jaw from hitting the ground. "Pardon?"

"My instincts tell me that he's innocent." Spurling stepped closer, his voice low. "I've no evidence to the contrary. My superiors want to throw the book at him. I'm doing my best, but if you've any ideas on who would do this to Mr Tamboli, now would be a good time to share it with me."

"Have I hit my head and woken up in an episode of *Poirot*?"

"Not that I'm aware. I'm not French, and neither are you." Spurling frowned at him in confusion. "Why?"

Valor decided not to point out that Mr Poirot was Belgian and not French. "I think someone's framing him."

"And?"

"I've no idea who." Valor thought about the program in his pocket but decided to keep it to himself for the moment. "Can I see him? I really need to see him."

CHAPTER 9

Over seventy-four randomly bolded letters.

Sitting at his desk at the shop, Valor arranged the letters in a blank document on the computer. He felt as though he'd been dropped into a high-risk game of Boggle. Or, they'd gotten themselves trapped into a spiral of someone's madness.

After a quick search on Google, Valor quickly realised the anagram, if it was one, contained too many letters to be solved by any of the free sites he found.

An hour had granted him nothing useful aside from the beginnings of a migraine. *And a whole lot of nonsense.* He'd never been especially gifted with anagrams or word games in general. Bishan did better, which was dead useful with him in jail.

The visit from Detective Inspector Spurling had been equal parts encouraging and discouraging. Bishan was innocent. *As if I needed him to tell me that.* They just had to find a way to prove it.

Thank you ever so much, Detective, you helped us out brilliantly.

I'll start calling him Detective Inspector Obvious.

"Val?" Wilfred set a cup of tea and a plate of biscuits on his desk. "My Lottie says your family's been sniffing around lately. She wanted me to make sure you're all right. She's in Windermere looking after a friend."

"I'm fine."

"Val?" Nina poked her head around the corner. She'd come into the shop to help out once again, and sneak a few free biscuits. "You'll never guess who just stepped out of a shiny Rolls Royce."

"Nina." He glared when she grinned unrepentantly; her dark eyes sparkled with mischief. "Unless it's Bishan, I'm not all that interested."

"A fancy chauffeur. He's stepped into the shop and asked me to inform Mr Scott that his father is here to see him." Nina adjusted her apron slightly. She'd actually worked at the shop over one summer after university. "Can I throw eggs at the Rolls Royce? I mean, what kind of father only visits his son now?"

Valor got slowly to his feet. He resisted the urge to straighten his shirt or run his hands through his slightly chaotic red hair. "I'm not his son. He made it quite clear years ago."

It took shoving his hands into the pockets of his trousers to keep from fidgeting with his clothing. Valor refused to do anything to make himself more presentable to a man who'd thrown his own child away for his sexual preferences.

"Valor." Wilfred rested a spotted, aged hand against the side of his face. "Any man would be proud to have you as a son. Why don't you let me run him off? He's not welcome here."

Because I'm an adult.

Because underneath it all, a part of me still wants my family to love me.

He opted not to tell the truth quite so baldly. "He's my

problem. I'll deal with him and his overgrown sense of self-worth."

And my own issues with being without family.

Here's hoping I can manage it without sounding like a petulant teenager.

It would certainly be an improvement on their last conversation, which had ended with him screaming obscenities in his father's face. Valor ignored the chauffer standing by one of the counters, leaving him to be pestered by Nina. He made his way outside to stand next to the Rolls.

"Get inside so we can speak as civilised adults." His father lowered the window briefly. "Do hurry up about it, Valor."

Valor leaned casually against the Rolls. He'd be polite, but he wouldn't kowtow to the man. "You want to chat, Father. Why don't you step outside?"

You know what?

Screw polite.

After several amusing minutes of a one-sided argument from his father, the man finally got out of the Rolls. The bright red flush on his cheeks was the only visible sign of his temper being tested to the maximum—an impressive display of how emotionally repressed his family was.

"Valor."

"Bertie Sr."

"You will address me with proper respect." His father folded his arms across his chest. "Are we clear?"

Valor needed a moment to take in how much his father had aged in the years they'd been apart. "I'd rather not address you at all, but we all have our disappointments to deal with."

"I'm here to offer my help."

"Seriously?" Valor couldn't stop his eyebrows going up in complete disbelief. "What sort of help are you offering? We've got the best barrister possible for Bishan."

"Not *him*." His father's feelings clearly hadn't changed. "I've had paperwork drawn up to bring you back into the family. There's a flat in London all set up for you."

"A flat in London?" He scratched his head for a second. "Why would I leave my shop, my friends, and the only people I claim as family?"

"He is *not* your family."

"And you are?" Valor held a hand up to stop his father from answering his rhetorical question. "I'm happy. Well, I will be once Bishan is free. We have our life here. Our *home* is here. Why can't you be pleased for me? Why do you feel the need to come here in your Rolls to try to bribe me into fitting into whatever image of a perfect son you have in your mind?"

"And you will always be nothing but a disappointment." His father gave a deep sigh of obvious disdain. "I have wasted my time."

"Yes." Valor pushed away from the Rolls and started toward the biscuit shop. A hand grabbed his arm to stop him. "Is there anything left to say?"

"Think about your mother."

Valor wrenched his arm away from his father. He shook his head with a bitter laugh. "Think about my mother? What about me? What about your son? You abandoned me with nothing. For what? Because I'm gay? Because the man I love happens to be Indian?"

His father sneered at him but tellingly didn't respond. "Don't be rude, Valor."

"Rude?" He rubbed his forehead roughly. "What part are you finding hard to swallow? Which bigotry are you most ashamed of? I'd wager none of it. Go home, Lord Scott."

Leaving his father by the Rolls, Valor strode purposefully into the shop. He refused to flee, cowering from the man who'd intimidated him as a child. Time had changed both of them; he no longer saw someone to admire in his father.

GRASMERE COTTAGE MYSTERY TRILOGY

In some ways, Valor found himself in the middle of a bit of an epiphany. For years, he had mourned the loss of his family. He finally realised they'd never truly been his loved ones.

They might be related, but blood meant very little to the Scotts if their standards weren't met. He waved off the concerned inquiries from both Wilfred and Nina. The chauffeur barely acknowledged his presence before answering the sharp call from the impatient earl waiting outside.

"Val?" Nina followed him through the kitchen into his little office alcove. "Do you want to talk about it?"

"Not really." He dropped into the chair with an exhausted groan, slouching down until his head rested on the back of the seat. "When are Daniel and Cora returning?"

"This evening. Their mum wanted them to have lunch with her." Nina perched on the edge of his desk. "How goes your word puzzle?"

Valor twisted his laptop slightly so she could see the screen as well. "It's gibberish."

"You can spell gibberish with the words." She swatted away his hand when he went to flick her arm. "There are computer programs you could use to decipher it."

"Are anagrams deciphered?" Valor knew underneath the mass of black, kinky curls lay a brilliant mind when it came to computer programs. He felt like a caveman in comparison to what Nina knew. "Could you create something?"

"It's not really in my realm of expertise." She tilted her head to glance up at the ceiling while considering. "My girlfriend's brother might know. He's more into this."

"Oooo."

"Don't be an idiot." Nina glared at him. "You've met Rose. She's lovely."

"She is lovely. How does she put up with you?" Valor grinned at her. He turned serious as his attention went back to the alphabet puzzle. "Do you think Rose's brother might help?"

"If he can't, he'll know who can." She offered him a hopeful grin. "Tell you what. Shoot this over to me in an email. I'll see if we can crack it for you."

"Nerds," he teased playfully.

"And if we solve your mystery?"

"Brilliant nerds I owe my life to."

"That's more like it."

CHAPTER 10

In the few days that had passed since Bishan's arrest, Valor felt as though an entire month had gone by. He'd stayed focused on keeping busy with both the shop and finding a way to get him out of jail. Sunesh continued to try to warn him off involving himself.

Sunesh meant well, but Valor couldn't stay out of it, not after his conversation with Spurling. His almost brother-in-law would get over it. He refused to just wait and hope for the best.

With Cora and Daniel off with their mother again, Nina had made the long drive to London to connect with some of her fellow computer nerds. Valor hoped they managed to work miracles with the anagram. *Well, we're assuming it's some sort of word scramble. What if it's nothing at all?*

He didn't want to expend everyone's efforts only for it to be a true red herring. *But honestly, who else could've shoved the program under our tree roots aside from the murderer?* He'd spent so much time starting at the letters, he'd started dreaming about Scrabble and Boggle.

It was the middle of the morning when Valor received a

text from Spurling asking if he could stop by the police station. *Great, am I getting arrested now?* He wasn't.

"Are you kidding?" Valor found himself shoved into a room with Bishan before he could get an answer from Spurling. "*Bish.*"

Bishan didn't move from his chair. He lifted his hand slightly to wave. "Hi."

Valor couldn't help grinning at him, remembering the first time they met at Harrow. A similarly hesitant Bishan had waved in the same way with an equally muted hello. "Hello, love."

Taking one of the empty chairs, Valor moved it around so it sat beside Bishan's. He dropped into it, close enough to touch if his boyfriend wanted. It didn't take a genius to see the autistic was perilously close to the edge.

"Hold?" Valor rested his hand on the table, leaving the decision up to Bishan, whose fingers wrapped around his almost desperately. His heart broke a little at the way they trembled. "I've missed you."

"Same."

"Are they being kind?" Valor wanted to wrap his arms around Bishan and drag him out of the building. He settled for simply holding his hand. "Is the tea decent?"

"It's warm. Too milky." Bishan shifted enough to allow him to rest his head on Valor's shoulder. "Sunny's been to see me. So have Mum and Dad. Reva might come tomorrow if I'm not free by then."

"We'll get you free," he promised.

"Reggie's nice."

"Is he?" Valor's opinion on the detective inspector improved greatly just on that alone. "They let me bring your sketchbook and pencils, so at least you can draw cartoons to make fun of the idiots who've locked you up."

"Be nice, Val." Bishan tilted his head to kiss Valor's neck.

"They'll be here in a minute. They don't let visitors stay for long."

They spent the last of their visit in silence. Bishan appeared to want to just be held. His arms clung to Valor, even after one of the detectives returned to take him out.

Dropping his head into his hands, Valor sat in the empty room for several seconds. It took all his strength to not race after them. He'd seen and felt the tension in his boyfriend; Bishan couldn't possibly manage under the strain for much longer without severe damage to his health.

"We've made him as comfortable as possible." Spurling waited for him by the door. "I'll walk you to your car."

"Bicycle." Valor had biked over from the shop, not seeing the point of cycling home to drive all the way back to the village. "Thanks for this."

From his texts with Sunesh, Valor knew they planned to petition for Bishan's immediate release. He tried not to get his hopes up. Then again, even if Bishan was let out, they still faced the uphill battle of proving him innocent.

Spurling followed him outside to where Valor had locked up his bicycle. "I know it's hard to imagine, but would any of your former schoolmates have a grudge against the two of you?"

"Why?"

"Who else but someone attached to Harrow would know about the incident in your first year? Someone picked this victim to provide a potential motive to make Bishan seem guilty." Spurling rubbed his eyes tiredly. "Think about it, will you?"

And Valor did. The thought consumed him all the way back to the shop. He'd yet to come up with the name of someone who'd hated either of them enough to do this.

Or is sick enough to do it.

"Valor?" Lottie called him over the moment he stepped

into the shop. She held out a folder to him. "Nancy from my gardening group has a son who works as a medical examiner. She managed to get a few of his notes for me from the autopsy of the poor lad found in your garden."

"Dame Lottie strikes again." Valor had no idea how her network of nans didn't completely rule the Lake District. "Does her son know she copied it?"

"Don't you worry about that." She patted him on the head. "Why don't you look it over in your office? Hmm? I'll bring you tea and a snack later."

Forget the Lake District, they can take over the world at this point.

Right, let's see what this says. Cause of death? Cinnamon.

What did I just read?

No matter how many times Valor read it, the cause of death didn't change. His old schoolmate had been killed by inhaling cinnamon. *How is that even possible? Death by spice?*

A quick search online informed him the body couldn't absorb it. The substance had clogged up his lungs. It sounded a dreadful and painful way to go.

Cinnamon?

It seemed highly unlikely. Two memories struck Valor at almost the exact moment. Bishan had spent virtually their entire lower sixth year having nothing but cinnamon toast for breakfast. The other was the challenge their whole house had done trying to eat a spoon of spice.

Someone's being a cheeky bastard.

And I'm fed up with it.

An additional note from one of the detectives indicated Bishan's fingerprints had been found on several objects inside the man's pocket. *No wonder they think it's Bish.* Valor would be hard pressed to prove them wrong.

Whoever did this is dead clever.

We're going to have to be even smarter.

CHAPTER 11

S eventy-four letters didn't seem all that difficult. Nina's friend had returned over seventy thousand potential results. Valor felt a bit overwhelmed by it.

He highly doubted it was any of them. For one, they didn't make any sense. None of the sentences did; he'd only gone through about thirty thousand of them.

With coffee and a sandwich, Valor sat on the living room floor with the coffee table completely covered in sheets of paper, photos, and programs. He'd split his time going over the suggested anagram solutions and searching through his old Harrow documents. One of the boys in the photos and old school papers had done this to them. *I just have to find him.*

Their five years of Harrow provided an overwhelming number of possibilities. Valor hesitated to include students outside his own house. With twelve boarding houses at the school, the pool of potential murderers felt almost as daunting as the anagram list. *I'll never get through this.*

After three hours of hunting through both his memories and all their old albums, Valor had distilled the hundreds of names down to fifteen boys—now grown men. He didn't honestly believe any of them capable of murder. Yet some-how, one of them had to have done it.

Bishan obviously hadn't.

Shifting gears a bit, Valor checked the online Harrow calendar for any upcoming events. He thought about giving his old housemaster, Mr Colin Clarke, a call even though he was no longer in charge of West Acre Boarding House. Valor knew he could trust the man to give him honest advice on how to proceed.

Wait a second.

Founder's Day.

They'd attended most of the Founder's Day events since graduating. In particular, they'd been at the one a month ago in February. Most of their year mates had attended. Bishan had taken hundreds of photos, using his camera as a buffer between the crowds and himself.

It took a bit of hunting, but Valor found the digital images on Bishan's laptop. He couldn't help wondering if perhaps the murderer had been triggered by seeing them at the Old Boys vs Upper Sixth Harrow Football match, a Founder's Day tradition. It irked him to know they'd likely been betrayed by one of their friends.

Face after face *after face.*

Using his list of fifteen for a guide, Valor checked off the ones within the photos. He created fifteen folders, separating all the images into files by name. It might help him to organise his thoughts.

In the end, Valor wound up with eight folders containing images. The others hadn't attended the event. Four of the old boys he knew well enough to have their current numbers and addresses. The others would require a bit more legwork.

His best bet would be to ask Mr Clarke. Valor made a quick call to set up a meeting with him in Blackpool, where his old housemaster had moved to after retiring from Harrow. He still kept in touch with the majority of the boys who'd been a part of West Acre during his time.

That done, Valor thought for a few minutes before picking the phone up again. He waited impatiently for Hugh to pick up. "C'mon, Ash. Answer your mobile."

"Asheford."

"Why can't you answer your mobile like a normal human being?"

"Hello. This is Detective Inspector Asheford of Manchester. How may I help?" Hugh paused for several seconds. "Is that better?"

"Much." Valor found something tight in his chest easing at the familiar humour. "Are you free tomorrow?"

"Might be. Why?"

It didn't take much convincing to get Hugh to meet him in Blackpool. If two heads were better than one, perhaps three would be even more so. He hoped.

Hope is all I'm running on at this point.

The hour and a half drive to Blackpool gave him enough time to think about how to explain things to Mr Clarke. Valor didn't want to spring it on the man. He was in his sixties; he might have a heart attack.

Valor couldn't help laughing at the ridiculous idea. Colin Clarke had always been incredibly fit. Both Bishan and Valor had developed crushes on the man who'd worked so hard to guide them through their years at Harrow.

Tall, dark, and handsome had described Mr Clarke perfectly. One of his classmates had described him as a slightly more posh version of Idris Elba. Even now, years after retiring, his greying hair had only added to his good looks.

In some ways, it reminded Valor of a simpler time when he and Bishan had bonded over their mutual crush. He smiled at the memory, only to tear up moments later. *God, I miss Bish.*

He shook his head to clear it then knocked on the door, smiling at the man who opened it. "Mr Clarke."

"Valor. Seeing as neither of us are at Harrow, perhaps you could call me Colin? I'd rather not feel even older than I am." Mr Clarke offered him a warm handshake and a friendly smile. "How's Bishan? I remain completely stunned at how any thinking person could believe the gentlest soul I've ever met capable of murder."

Valor struggled to control his suddenly overwhelming emotions. Tears filled his eyes again and clogged his throat. "Sorry. I'm being so stupid."

"It isn't." Mr Clarke wrapped strong arms around him. "You'll both be just fine. I've no doubts. Justice might not always be swift, but have faith in it. Why don't you come inside? My wife's made tea, and I baked flapjacks. Hugh arrived a few minutes ago. We'll have a cuppa while you tell us how we can help."

It took no time at all to get the photos and list spread across the Clarke's large kitchen table. They sat around it, arguing for or against each potential perpetrator. Valor had been surprised at how well Colin took the news that one of his old boys might be a murderer.

"Twelve years as the housemaster of a boarding school and a total of twenty-two years as a teacher. I've seen what all of us are capable of, whether young or old." Mr Clarke gathered three photos, setting them in a row in front of his coffee mug. "I'm saddened by the thought, and I hope we're all wrong in our suspicions. But...."

"But?" Valor prompted after a prolonged silence.

"My educated guess would be one of these three." He tapped a finger against the side of his mug. "Fletcher, Clayton, or Edwards. It can't be Jones or Black—they're both in

Australia, left a week after Founder's Day. Kim is in Canada. And I just don't think the other two are capable of this level of planning and patience."

"You're missing someone." Hugh spoke around a mouthful of flapjack, earning a glare from both Mr and Mrs Clarke. "Sorry. Didn't know Ms Manners was going to be judging me."

"Ash." Valor intervened before Hugh poked the sleeping dragon. "Who are we missing?"

"Harrison Smith."

"Harrison Smith?" Valor searched his memory for the familiar name. "Wait. The weedy little music scholar who was a shell in our final year?"

"The same."

"It can't be." Valor searched through everything on the table to find the report on the victim. "How would Smith have even known about Angus?"

"I've no idea, but I think his name should be on your list." Hugh shrugged. "He watched you—a lot. Just call it my police instinct. Might be wrong, but there's no harm in checking up on him."

"All right, then."

The group talked well into the afternoon. Hugh left early to get back to Manchester. He promised to see if he could find anything out on their four potential suspects.

After promising to keep the Clarkes updated, Valor made his way back to his cottage. He found a note from Reva, Bishan's sister, pinned to the door. She'd sweet-talked the detectives into letting her visit him, and promised to stop by in the morning for a chat with Valor.

"Where've you been then?"

Valor immediately regretted deciding to step out into the garden to enjoy the cool spring evening. "Good evening to you, Mrs Harris."

"You were gone all day, and you weren't at your shop." She had her bright green frog hat on, and it bobbed on her head. "Well?"

"I'm sorry. I hear the phone ringing. Excuse me." Valor ducked into the cottage, shutting the door and leaning against it with a tired groan. "Nosy old bat."

I hate this.

I hate every single moment of him not being here.

Above everything else, Valor longed for the calm and loving presence of Bishan. They'd never been overly tactile as a couple; even as young men, they'd appreciated their own personal space.

Valor had grown up deprived of touch in his restrained upper-crust family; Bishan could only handle so much before his hypersensitivity kicked in. They'd learned to show love in their own unique ways—and to ensure the moments of intimacy counted. Every touch mattered, meant something; it seemed to make Bishan's absence harder to bear.

His gaze drifted to the wall of photos, most from their adventures traveling around the Lake District. They loved finding out-of-the-way hiking spots and small villages. Anywhere there weren't a lot of people worked best for Bishan.

He stepped over to a photo taken not all that long ago of the two of them covered in snow. They'd had what felt like an absolute blizzard during an extraordinarily cold winter. Bishan had wanted to make snow angels—everywhere.

I'll bring you home, love.

I promise.

CHAPTER 12

"Val." Reva hopped on his bed at six in the morning, jolting him out of the blankets and onto the floor. "Good morning."

"What in God's name are you doing?" Valor yanked the duvet off the bed to cover himself. He thanked his lucky stars he'd fallen asleep in boxers. "I knew we'd regret letting you have a key to the cottage."

"I brought breakfast, coffee, and information." She snatched Staccato up from his perch on the foot of the bed. "We'll be in the kitchen. Hurry up, or I'll let the cat eat your bacon butty."

Grumbling to himself, Valor dressed quickly. He found his T-shirt on the floor and his jeans nearby. A shower could wait until the mischievous Reva had left to cause havoc somewhere else.

He grabbed half the bacon sandwich and coffee. "Well? What's this information you've got?"

Reva spun herself around on the kitchen stool by the counter. "My sources—"

Valor inhaled a crumb from his sandwich and coughed

violently for a minute while she glared at him for interrupting her grand moment. "Your sources?"

"I brought you food."

"And I'm grateful. What's this earth-shattering information you have for me?" Valor hid his grin behind his sandwich. Reva was younger than both of her brothers, sweet
and quite a bit spoiled due to being the baby of the close-
knit family. He blinked when his cat snagged a piece of the
sandwich and raced away with it. "Staccato thanks you
as well."

The sum total of her information revolved around the
gossip in Sunesh's office. She'd taken time off after university
to intern with him. Her family wanted her to have real world
work experience before she attempted her hand at anything
else.

A Tamboli tradition. Sunesh had worked at a few different
jobs before pursuing his qualification as a barrister. Bishan
had been the one exception. He completed university with an
excellent chance for continuing his career in music.

Turned out the detectives were also looking into former
Harrovians. Valor thanked Reva for the information. He
didn't want to dampen her spirits by telling her that he'd
already assumed the police would do their due diligence in
investigating every potential avenue.

"Well, I'm off to see Bishan again. Want to come with?
I'm sure they'd let you." Reva buried her face in Staccato's
fur. "Such a happy kitty. Are you feeding him enough?"

"No, I let him starve." Valor rolled his eyes. He and
Bishan both spoiled the cat rotten. "He's well fed, as you can
obviously see."

The visit with Bishan was short. Valor had thought seeing
him would make it better. It made everything worse; they'd
had to drag Valor out of the room.

He hadn't wanted to release Bishan's hand. The detectives

had gently but firmly pulled them apart. Valor didn't know how much more he could handle.

So short.

Every moment without him felt like complete agony. Valor didn't know where he'd find the strength to keep going. Then again, if Bishan could do it, so could he.

I've got the easy part.

I'm not stuck in a cell, going through what must be absolute hell.

Reva headed off to see her parents, leaving Valor to check in at the biscuit shop. He stepped inside to find it packed. Every day since Bishan's arrest, they'd done double their usual business.

Nosy bastards.

They all wanted a bit of gossip. He assumed they bought biscuits to feel less obvious about being nosy. Wilfred kept telling him not to stress about it; they wouldn't be complaining at the end of the year when they did the books.

A fair point.

"Reggie Spurling stopped by earlier. He said to give him a call," Wilfred whispered to Valor when he squeezed by to get into the kitchen. "You might want to take a few days off. Your presence only seems to make them act as though the Beatles popped by."

"The Beatles?" Valor grinned cheekily. "Not sure there are enough of them around to cause this much excitement."

"Young people." Wilfred waved an apron at him. "Off with you. Go find out what Spurling wants. I'm tired of you moping around."

Stepping outside, Valor placed a quick call to the detective. He offered to meet Spurling at the café not far from the biscuit shop, only for his walk over to be interrupted by a familiar Bentley pulling up beside him. *Not again.*

"Valor? Father asked me to speak with you again." His brother spoke through the open window. He reached out to open the door for Valor. "Well? What are you waiting for? I don't have all day."

"Go away." Valor continued walking down the pavement. His brother kept up a slow crawl in the vehicle beside him. "What do you want?"

"To talk some sense into you."

Valor roughly dragged his fingers through his hair. "Is this punishment for something I did in a past life? Why do you all continue to bother me? You made it quite clear you wanted no part in my life. Bishan being unjustly locked up hasn't changed my opinions on your nonsense. Go back to your father and tell him I'm quite happy being struck from the will. You can have all the money, Bertie. I don't want any of it."

Striding purposefully down the pavement, Valor jogged across the street toward the café. He had no interest in indulging his family's nonsense any further. His patience had come to a complete and abrupt end.

The more cynical part of him suspiciously wondered why the sudden aggressive need to bring him back into the fold. Valor made a mental note to do a bit of sniffing around to see what was going on with the Scotts. He'd have to be careful, or his family might take it the wrong way and assume he wanted to reconcile.

He didn't.

He took a few breaths before stepping into the café. No need to give Spurling the impression that he was flustered. He found the detective sitting in the far corner of the restaurant with a mug and a sandwich in front of him.

"Everything all right? You seem a bit haggard," Spurling commented after Valor had dropped into the seat across from him.

Valor placed his order for tea and yet another bacon butty

with extra bacon, then answered with a slightly sharper tone than intended, "I'm fine."

Spurling shook his head and chuckled quietly. "Saw that vehicle following you on the street. Something I should be worried about?"

"Unless you're involved in family counselling, no." Valor latched on to the mug of tea set before him. He drank slowly, trying to wipe away the frustration from dealing with his brother. "It's an annoyance, nothing more."

"Could your family be behind the murder? I've heard they don't particularly care for your choice in boyfriend." Spurling kept his voice low to avoid being overheard. "People with influence and money often believe they're above the law."

"Money? They definitely have it. Influence? Only in their minds." Valor leaned forward with his elbows on the table, ignoring his inner voice that sounded like his childhood tutor telling him to stop being an ill-mannered barbarian. "I doubt they'd resort to murder. I'm not that much of an addition to the family. I slouch. I don't care about etiquette. And I run my own business. Uncouth swine that I am."

"So, not your family?"

"Probably not." He took another bite of his sandwich. "What did you want to talk to me about?"

"Harrow."

"In general? Or something more specific?" Valor shifted further into his chair with a groan. "I can't help get your sprog into it if that's what you're hoping."

"I don't have any kids." Spurling glared at Valor, who grinned unapologetically. "Were you aware your name was vandalised at your old boarding house?"

"What?"

Name carvings were one of the many old traditions at Harrow. It went back to well before even Lord Byron's time at the school. All removes (a Harrow term for students in their second year) had their names etched onto a wooden plaque on a wall in their boarding house.

It had been a point of pride for them as young men. Bishan always made a habit of going to see his name whenever they visited the school. Valor didn't understand how or why someone would mess with his name.

"There are CCTV cameras all around the boarding house. Did they catch who did it?" Valor remembered when they'd been installed to ensure the safety of students and beaks—the Harrow term for teachers. "Or at least get a glimpse of them?"

"It apparently happened on the first day back after a term break. Too many people moving in and out; the cameras didn't pick up on anyone who shouldn't be there. Several former students were there that day; my gut says it was one of them." Spurling pulled printouts from a folder. "Do you know any of them?"

Valor made a quick scan of the twenty-odd sheets of paper containing multiple images per page. He eventually set aside six of them. "The short answer is yes. The longer one is I think it's one of these four men. You can follow them moving through the house toward the stairs where my name is carved."

And they're the only ones who are on my suspect list.

This is definitely starting to feel more like a pointed attack.

And I'm terrified.

Spurling glanced briefly at the images. "I'll take a closer look at them. And Valor?"

"Hmm?"

"We'll keep you and Bishan safe," he promised.

CHAPTER 13

T hat is a dead bird on my pillow.

And a smug cat sitting beside it.

"What have you done?" Valor inched away from the feathered carcass while glaring at Staccato. "I thought the cat ate the canary. You've left it as a present. Thank you. Is it my birthday? It's not, is it?"

As the dead bird wouldn't handle itself, Valor decided to get up. He dressed quickly, wanting to remove the temptation before Staccato chose to play with it. The cat usually brought them the occasional gift of a twig or leaf, maybe a mouse.

Never a bird.

"This is *not* how I want to wake up in the morning." Valor gingerly lifted the pillow to carry it and its passenger outside.

Dumping the entire pillow complete with befouled fowl in the rubbish bin outside, Valor froze when he turned back toward the cottage. Dead skylarks had been carefully placed along the posts of the fence—on every single one he could see from the front. He walked a few steps to look into the garden to find his guess had been correct.

Staccato didn't do this. He couldn't have. What is going on here?

Valor stared at them for almost two full minutes before grabbing his phone from his pocket and calling Detective Inspector Spurling. *Am I being paranoid?*

"Reggie." Spurling interrupted his internal debate. "Hello?"

"It's Valor." He hesitated for a second trying to determine how to explain. "I've a dead bird problem."

"Could you elaborate?"

"Dead skylarks on every post of the fence going around my garden." Valor scrubbed his fingers tiredly across his eyes. "Not sure what you could even do about it, but it seemed something you'd want to know about."

"Dead birds."

"Lots of them. My cat brought one and left it on my pillow."

Spurling coughed a few times, obviously trying to hide a laugh. "Are you sure the cat didn't do the rest?"

"Look. I'll take a video and text you." Valor hung up with an angry huff. He made sure to capture the birds in all their horrific glory. The detective called him back after a minute. "Well?"

"Don't touch them. We'll be out in under an hour. Maybe we can get prints from the gate." Spurling didn't wait for a response and disconnected the call.

Rude.

In the time it took the police to arrive, Valor managed to shower, get properly dressed for the day, and fix breakfast for himself. He'd poured his third mug of coffee when the first vehicle pulled up behind his little hatchback. The forensic team immediately moved towards the fence while Detective Inspector Spurling headed to him.

"Valor."

"Reggie." Valor lifted his mug in greeting to the man.

Spurling had insisted on first names during their meeting the previous day. "Want tea or coffee?"

"Why don't we step inside to talk?" Spurling followed Valor inside the house. "Assuming we find fingerprints that don't belong to either you or Bishan—"

"Or Mrs Harris," he interjected.

"Who?"

"Slightly bonkers and overly nosy frog lady who lives next door. You've probably seen her peeking over the fence." Valor pulled down several mugs and cups in case the other detectives wanted something to drink. "I'd wager her prints are everywhere."

"I'll have them eliminate hers from the list." Spurling seemed to be trying very hard not to laugh. "She's the one with the frogs?"

"Ribbit." Valor couldn't help himself. He leaned against the counter to let out a helpless burst of laughter. "What will it prove if you find prints that aren't ours?"

"Well, you obviously haven't gone on a vicious skylark murder spree. Bishan couldn't have done it. This might go quite a ways to proving the case that someone else is responsible." He held a hand up to stop Valor from speaking. "Don't get your hopes up yet. The killer left no prints on the body, yet managed to put your boyfriend's there. I'm not confident we'll find anything."

They collected over thirty birds. Valor stared at the collection in shock. He couldn't understand the cruelty or the point of it.

"Why would someone do this?" Valor shoved his hands into the pockets of his jeans. Spurling had stayed behind after the forensic team left. "To scare me?"

"My first partner once told me never try to apply reason to the acts of a killer. It's a waste of time." He placed a hand on Valor's shoulder. "I'll let you know what we find."

Sitting alone in his cottage, Valor jumped at every little sound. He considered grabbing Staccato and begging Wilfred and Lottie for space on their couch. *I will not let whoever this is take control of my life any further.*

He lasted an hour before contemplating calling in reinforcements. Nina, Cora, and Daniel planned to come over later in the evening. He wasn't sure his newly discovered anxiety could wait for them.

Valor called Hugh on his mobile. "I'm losing my mind."

"Interesting take on hello." Hugh chuckled.

The laugh helped Valor to settle down at least a little. He told Hugh about the birds and what the detective had said. They both agreed it was sick and twisted behaviour.

"If it is an old boy from Harrow, why do this? Why me? Why Bishan? What could we have possibly done to him? Neither of us were bullies at school. We protected others, if anything." Valor sank down into the sofa, letting Staccato leap onto his shoulder a second after. "I don't understand."

"Maybe they were jealous of you?"

"Jealous? Of me? If it is someone from Harrow, they'd know I literally lost everything. No inheritance, no immense cash flow, no estate in the countryside. I've a little cottage, and a small business, and a lovely boyfriend. Hell, we ride bicycles everywhere. What's to be envious of?" Valor reached a hand up to pet Staccato, who leaned into his fingers. "I'm not self-deprecating either."

"How about all the awards you won for our house in sport? Or being head boy? All the accolades both you and Bishan earned in school. You led West Acre in your lower and upper sixth years." Hugh ignored Valor's derisive snort. "Maybe you don't see yourself the way everyone else does. We admired you both—even more after everything that happened with your family."

"I don't understand."

"I've worked homicides for three years now. Trust me, Val, when I say jealousy can turn into a poison of the mind. People have done horrible things in the name of envy." Hugh paused to speak to someone away from the phone. "Listen, I've got to go. I'm at work. Don't sit by yourself and brood. Go to the shop. Walk Staccato in the park. Do something aside from worrying about the motivations of bad people."

"Walk Staccato in the park?" Valor laughed at the sudden visual of his fluffy orange cat on a leash. "Not sure I'm ready for that level of eccentricity."

"Have you thought about installing CCTV cameras around your place?" Hugh asked seriously.

"What? No." He thought about it for a second. "Not the worst idea you've ever had."

"You promised never to speak of that again." Hugh cut him off sharply. "You might give Olly a call."

"Which one?"

"The techie."

"Ah. That's right. He's got his own business doing security." Valor had known several Ollys in school. Oliver Smith had been technically savvy even in their first year at Harrow. "I'll give him a call later."

"Sooner rather than later." Hugh sounded worried.

"I'll be fine."

"For all of our sanity, call him now?"

"Yes, Mother." Valor tried to make light, even though they both knew Hugh had good reason to be concerned. "I'll let you know what the police say."

Even if it's not good news.

Valor needed it to be good news.

I t took two days for the fingerprint results to come back with nothing at all. *Useless.* Spurling encouraged him not to lose hope. He believed the absence of evidence, in this case, might actually prove their point even better.

Someone had clearly killed a load of skylarks. It wasn't Valor or Staccato. Bishan had an ironclad alibi involving multiple police officers. So, who had done it?

The murderer.

"Valor? Mrs Harris hasn't moved from watching her frogs in the pond. Stop glaring at her. It won't stop her from putting her nose in." Lottie had come over early with a large plate of his favourite scones. He'd been immediately suspicious that she had bad news for him. "You know my nephew works on your family estate managing the farm, right?"

"Yes." He drew the word out unnecessarily long. "Why? Were the scones to cushion the incoming blow?"

"Your grandfather included you in his will."

"I'm aware. He died years ago, though. What differences does it make now?" Valor topped up his coffee, grabbed another scone, and shifted over to sit next to her at the kitchen table. "Well? What bombshell do you have for me, Dame Lottie?"

"Do you know what your grandfather's will actually said?" She pulled a photocopied sheet of paper from her massive purse, ignoring his teasing about how much it weighed. "Take a read. Maybe young Sunny might want to have a go at it as well."

"I don't... understand. What am I seeing?" Valor sipped coffee and tried unsuccessfully to translate the legalese. "Why is this important?"

"Your grandfather, for all his faults, cared greatly about you. He worried." Lottie had begun her working life when his grandfather had been the earl. "The will should've protected you from what happened. They shouldn't have been allowed to take the money he left in trust for you."

Valor leaned back in his chair, balancing it on two legs. "I'm not surprised, but why does it even matter now?"

"My nephew claims your father is being investigated for potential tax fraud." Lottie pointed toward the paper in his hand. "I'd imagine somewhere in there, you'll find a reason for your family to suddenly want you back under their thumb."

Oh.

All the visits from his siblings and his father suddenly made sense to him. His family held their reputation and their money above everything else. Anything that might cause the loss of either wouldn't sit well with them.

They'd clearly become desperate.

How desperate?

His mind went right to the suspicions Spurling had shared with him. Could his family have committed murder? Valor didn't want to believe any of them capable of it.

"Maybe it's time for the prodigal child to pay a visit home? Ask a few pertinent questions?" She stood up, pressing a kiss to the top of his head. "And don't go alone either. You take young Reggie with you."

Young Reggie.

"You can't order a detective inspector around, Aunt Lottie." Valor wouldn't put it past her to try to badger Spurling into going with him. "I'll give Hugh a call. He'll know how to play nicely with the Scotts."

"You're a Scott, love," she reminded him.

And what if I wasn't?

He'd considered changing his name over the years. Now that gay marriage had been legalised, it would provide the perfect opportunity to not be a Scott. First, they had to get Bishan out from under the suspicion of murder.

"You can't change your blood or where you were born, Valor." She ruffled his red hair, then started toward the door. "They'll always be a part of you."

Not a good part of me, they won't.

After Lottie left him to his thoughts, Valor stared at the alleged copy of part of his grandfather's will. The idea his father or brother had been involved in the murder of a former Harrovian, any of his family really, drained him of all energy. He slouched further into his chair, letting the paper fall to the floor.

Was it worse to be betrayed by his family who'd already disowned him or by a former housemate?

CHAPTER 15

Though his family still owned their estate a mile or so from Dorset, they spent most of their time living in luxury in a large detached house in Kensington. Valor wasn't eagerly anticipating the drive—particularly with Hugh, who loved whinging about being stuck in a car for hours. It required a bit of negotiation to talk him into it, part of which required Valor not drive his little hatchback. He borrowed Daniel's SUV. That conversation led to him wanting to join them. Most of his friends wanted the chance to inconvenience Lord and Lady Scott. He'd wisely restricted it to Daniel and Hugh.

And Mr Clarke.

Hugh had narked on him to their former housemaster. Mr Clarke had wanted words with Valor's father for years. He was almost looking forward to it.

Two days later, they finally managed to get together to drive to London. Daniel and Valor started before the sun came up, stopping in Blackpool and Manchester to pick up the other two. Even with traffic in their favour, the journey would be over six hours.

"We're the weirdest boy band in history." Daniel glanced around his Range Rover at the four of them. "Unless Mr Clarke is our manager."

"Lead singer. Ladies love a silver fox." Hugh winced visibly when their former housemaster whacked him on the back of the head. "I retract my statement. You're hideously deformed, and no one could ever find you attractive."

Mr Clarke breathed a tired sigh. "Can I remind you three snickering fools that you're all in your thirties? Shouldn't you have outgrown this nonsense?"

"I hope we're never too old for a little nonsense in our lives." Hugh shifted in the seat; his overly tall frame didn't squash well in the back seat. "Val? How do you think the nobles will take the invasion of the peasants?"

"He's not a peasant," Daniel interjected.

"He's more peasant than noble." Hugh grinned at Valor when he glared at him. "Am I wrong?"

"They're not going to be pleased with any of us." Valor was suddenly grateful to have witnesses with him for this confrontation. He also thanked his lucky stars his family happened to be in London. The estate would've made it far too easy for his parents to simply ignore his presence. "Feel free to be as obnoxious as you possibly can be. Lick the wall if you like."

"There will be no licking of the walls." Mr Clarke leaned forward in the seat. "I had you boys for six years. I taught you to be men who had respect for themselves. No matter what Lord and Lady Scott choose to do or say, we won't disrespect ourselves in an attempt to upset them."

Though they might grumble, Valor couldn't argue with the words. Sunesh had given him similar advice when he'd called about the will. His suggestion had been to avoid giving the Scotts any ammunition to use against them.

They eventually arrived in London late in the afternoon,

after stopping for a quick bite to eat. Valor stood in front of the impressive house. He didn't want to go inside, but he wanted answers.

Not like they'll give them to me.

They'll lie like they always do.

"Valor." Mr Clarke stepped up beside him. He rested a strong hand on Valor's shoulder. "You're strong enough to stand up to them."

"I hope so." He walked up the three stairs to reach the door. He glanced briefly at the knocker before lifting his arm to bang his fist against the wood instead. "Showtime."

"Can I help you, sir?" A butler Valor had never met answered the door after a minute. "Are you expected?"

"I'm the prodigal son." Valor patted him on the arm, dodging past him into the house. "Are Mummy or Daddy home?"

Getting answers would require Valor walk a tightrope between getting information and not crossing any of the lines he'd set for himself. He had to unnerve his parents. They'd share more out of anger than anything else.

Just remember, it's not about them. This is for Bish. I'd cross an ocean of glass for him.

Chatting with my parents is the very least of the sacrifices I'd make for Bishan.

"Sir. If you could just wait...."

"Patience has never been a virtue of mine." Valor ignored the butler, who continued to call after him. He made his way through the familiar halls to find his parents sitting in their library having a late afternoon tea. *God. This really is pathetically* Downton Abbey. "Hello."

"Valor." His mother's hand trembled so much she almost dropped her teacup. "You've come home. *With friends.*"

The hope in his mother's eyes had been hard to bear.

Valor found it easier to deal with when disdain almost immediately followed. She clearly didn't approve.

"Mr Clarke. I wasn't aware you'd stayed in touch with our son." His father tried to stare him down, hard to do when he stood several inches shorter and a bit less fit. "Didn't they teach you about making appointments at Harrow?"

Valor pinched the bridge of his nose to stem the migraine that already threatened. "I'm sure they did, but as it was almost thirteen years ago, I don't recall the specific lesson that involved ensuring a warm welcome in my own home. Oh, wait; it's not my home, is it? You kicked me out of it."

Mr Clarke placed a hand on his shoulder. "Easy, lad."

"I haven't come here to fight." Valor found the lie an easy one to tell. He hadn't anticipated the old bitterness would come roaring back into him. It made it remarkably difficult to stick with his original plan. "Aren't you going to invite us to have tea?"

"Do we want tea?" Hugh muttered behind him. "I don't bloody want it. I'd break the cup."

"Wouldn't be the first time," Daniel leaned over to whisper.

Valor brought his hand up to cough through his laughter. He met the steady glare from his father without flinching. "How goes the tax fraud investigation? Have they found anything yet? Perhaps a will you hid?"

The flash of fear then anger that went across his father's face told Valor everything. If nothing else, his father had never had the right to steal his inheritance. He remembered the early years with Bishan after university, when without the Tambolis or their Harrow network they'd have struggled for food and a roof over their heads.

It had been good for him. Valor didn't know if he'd have grown into the same sort of person without the need to fight. *And I'm proud of the man I am.*

Even if they aren't.

"How dare you," his father shouted at him. "Get out of this house. I'd sue you for slander if you weren't my son."

"First, you disowned me. Second, you won't sue me for slander because you know it's the truth." Valor pulled a copy of the will to wave at him. "Grandfather wasn't as disapproving as you claimed. Is this why you've made such a concerted effort to reconnect with me? Are you afraid of what might happen if this comes out?"

"I believe he asked you to get out." His brother stepped out from the door behind his parents. "I'm sure you can find the exit."

"I'll go in a moment." Valor stood his ground. His friends stayed silent at his side, offering a strength he desperately needed. "Were you involved either directly or indirectly with Bishan being falsely accused of murder?"

"As if we'd sink so low." Lord Scott shook his head in amazement. He seemed genuinely surprised by the accusation. "You've called me a thief and a liar. Any other crimes you'd care to lay at my feet?"

Valor didn't fall for the sudden "woe is me; I've been wronged" façade. He'd seen his father use it one too many times to get his way. "What else would you call someone who stole their own son's inheritance?"

Bertie walked forward and placed his hand on their father's arm. He didn't seem quite so surprised by the questions. It made Valor wonder if his brother harboured more than just resentment toward him. "Leave."

Valor glanced briefly at each of the members of his estranged family, even his sister who'd hidden herself behind a bookshelf to eavesdrop on the argument. "You aren't Lord Scott just yet, Bertie."

The slight tightening around his brother's mouth worried Valor. Bertie had been the most spoiled out of the three Scott children. *The heir.* How far might he go to get what he evidently considered rightfully his?

"Careful, Bertie. Your avarice is showing." Valor smiled sharply at his brother, who took a step back from him. He turned his attention to his father. "We'll be going. You've no interest in being a family to me, and I've no energy left to waste. Oh, and if you're wondering or worrying about the inheritance, you can keep the money. I hope you choke on it."

Turning sharply on his heel, Valor strode from the library, down the hall, and out the door the butler held open for him. His friends followed quickly. They said nothing while he stood on the pavement with his head tilted up toward the sky to allow the falling rain to wash away any signs of tears.

"Why do I even let them get to me? It's been thirteen years." Valor shook his head violently, water flying everywhere. "Let's get out of the rain."

"Valor?"

He twisted around to find his mother on the steps in front of the house. He had to chuckle at the butler holding the large umbrella for her. "Lady Scott."

"We could be a family." She held her hand out to him.

A small part of him wanted to take her hand. Valor had never fully gotten over the loss of his family. It had taken until now for him to realise the truth.

He hadn't lost them.

He'd never had them in the first place.

Valor smiled sadly at her. "When were we ever a family in the first place? We shared blood and a last name. You never cared about who I am—my interests, my successes, my fears, or my failures. Go back inside, Lady Scott. Your tea is getting cold."

The silence stretched for what felt like an hour. It was really only a minute or two before his mother gracefully returned to the house without saying another word to him. *There's one door firmly closed on me.*

"Let's get out of the rain." Mr Clarke wrapped an arm around Valor's shoulders to guide him to the vehicle. They all clambered inside. "Let's find a pub. I'm sure we could all use something to warm us up for the long drive home."

"Right." Valor dropped his head against the seat with a groan. "Home."

"You've got family, Val," Hugh offered. "Maybe not by blood, but we're just as real."

After driving around for a while, Daniel found a cosy pub for them to warm up in. They had to race inside when the rain went from drizzling to a downpour. Valor slumped into the nearest chair at a table in the corner; he couldn't be bothered to do more than nod when Hugh ordered for him.

As long as the order was right, it didn't matter. Valor found himself immensely grateful for the men sitting with him. Once again, they'd circled around him to offer support.

"We've learned one important thing." Valor spoke after they'd received their food and drinks. "My parents weren't involved in the murder."

"They could've—"

Hugh held a hand up to stop Daniel. "I agree. Their surprise at being accused was genuine. Not so sure about your brother."

"Neither am I," Valor admitted. "In fact, he's moved further up my suspect list."

CHAPTER 16

"**W**ell, shit."

Literally.

And figuratively.

Valor stared at the paint and muck covering his living room. "Why? I can't even—"

One of the glass doors that led out into the garden had been shattered. Valor thought his heart might be in a similar state. Visiting his parents always left him a bit emotionally fragile; the attack on the cottage tipped him over the edge.

His knees went out from under him, dropping him to the ground in the middle of a puddle of blue paint. Valor couldn't find the energy to move—or care. He forced himself to retrieve his mobile from his pocket and give the police a call.

Detective Inspector Spurling arrived to find Valor still sitting on the floor. "Mind if I come in? The door is wide open."

"Our murderer believes in house pride." Valor gestured toward the red, white, and blue paint strewn across the room like a bizarre attempt at a Jackson Pollack painting. "They've matched West Acre's colours perfectly."

"Can I call someone?" Spurling hesitated near him as if he wasn't sure how to help. "I don't want you touching anything in the cottage. We might get lucky and find prints, but it might be best if you stepped outside."

Valor didn't budge from his spot in the paint. "Who hates us this much?"

Well, at least this proves it wasn't my family. Unless.... He genuinely believed his parents to be innocent. The fact that his brother might've had time to make the drive if Bertie had left immediately worried him.

They'd stopped for dinner and then in Blackpool and Manchester. The extended time to get home to Grasmere would've easily allowed Bertie to make the journey to the cottage and be gone well before Valor made it back. He tried to console himself with the idea that his brother hated manual labour enough not to mess around with paint or manure.

A slim hope was better than none at all.

Spurling knelt beside him, careful to avoid the paint. "There's a silver lining."

"Lining looks more red, white, and blue." Valor didn't appreciate having his living room covered in West Acre colours; no matter how much he loved his school and boarding house. "What's the up side to all of this?"

"Someone's done this. I'll be able to use this to get the investigation steered in another direction." Spurling grabbed his arm to help him get to his feet. "Do you have somewhere to stay?"

"I've a cottage." He took another glance around the room. "What gets paint out of fabric?"

The entire room would require a deeper clean than Valor knew how to do. He didn't object when the detective guided him out of the cottage. Only seconds later did a horrifying thought occur to him: he hadn't seen Staccato anywhere.

Pushing Spurling out of the way, Valor raced inside. He slipped and slid on the slick floor, but managed to get through the living room. His voice broke slightly while he called out to the cat.

Damn thing.

Why can't cats do what you want when you want?

His heart raced frantically. Valor ignored the detective telling him not to track paint everywhere. He couldn't stop, not yet, not without Staccato.

A muffled meow drew his attention to the laundry basket in the corner of their bathroom. Valor flung clothes across the room in an effort to find him. Staccato appeared at the bottom, underneath a blanket, his collar caught in the fabric.

"Oh my God. I thought we'd lost you." Valor carefully worked his cat free then lifted him up to crush him in his arms. "Will you quit wiggling? I can't set you down, you'll get covered in paint and shit."

"Ahh, the cat." Spurling stood in the doorway of the bathroom. "I've called the Wrights. Wilfred said for you to come over anytime. They've got the spare room all prepared for you. Are you safe to drive? Or should we give you a lift?"

Valor took a few slow breaths to calm his racing heart. "Can I pack a bag or would you prefer I leave everything behind?"

With a nod from Spurling, Valor cleaned up, changed into clean clothing, and then packed for a few days away for himself and Staccato. Lottie and Wilfred occasionally watched the cat for them so they'd have food and a litter box. He got it all into his vehicle, only to sit in it without moving for several minutes.

Well, now what?

The last few weeks had dragged on to a painfully long extent. Valor found it hard to believe it hadn't been a full year since they'd found the body in their garden. He didn't honestly know how much more he could withstand without shattering.

Driving usually helped him sort out his thoughts. Valor didn't believe it had done anything for him. The only comfort he found came from the soothing purring of Staccato, who loved being in the car.

He pulled in behind Wilfred's van and prepared himself for the inevitable. They'd want to smother him in care. He appreciated it, but he really wanted to be left alone to try to make sense of everything.

What sort of sense is there in madness?

"Val?" Wilfred knocked lightly against the window. "You coming inside, lad?"

"Sorry to wake you up so late." Valor didn't know what time it was, but he assumed they'd gone well past midnight. "Just give me a moment."

"I'll give you a hand with this while you sort yourself out." Wilfred opened the rear door to grab the bags and Staccato's carrier. "We'll get this little one somewhere comfortable. Kettle's on for tea, and there's some of Lottie's caramel apple loaf cake if you're hungry."

The appeal of Lottie's rather Moreish loaf cake drew Valor into the house. She gave him a gentle hug before drawing him over to the kitchen table. A cup of tea and a plate with a large slice waited for him.

Wilfred sat across from him with a cup of tea while Lottie headed off with a plate of tuna for Staccato. "And how are Lord and Lady Scott?"

"Disappointed."

He pushed the cake toward Valor, who'd practically inhaled his first slice. "Have another if you like. What did they want?"

"Capitulation." Valor cut two more slices for himself and one for Wilfred when he motioned for one. "I don't think they're involved in this mess, though, so the visit wasn't a complete waste of time."

"But?" Wilfred asked knowingly.

"Not so sure about Bertie." Valor had never been close to his brother, but the idea he'd been involved hurt something deep inside him. "I don't want to think him capable of murder."

"Could he have paid someone?"

"Yes." Valor paused to consider the idea. He had to admit Bertie had the funds to pay someone—and also knew enough about Harrow traditions to find a program for the anagram. "It's possible."

"But?"

"Bertie's always been hungry for money and power. I'm not sure he's capable of leaving dead birds or tossing paint around." Valor had a difficult time with the idea of his designer-suit-wearing brother stooping to that level. "Could it really be him?"

Wilfred shook his head slowly, pausing to swallow a mouthful of cake. "I've no idea. But I never believed they'd kick you from the family. It's not outside the realm of possibility."

Valor pushed the plate out of the way, then dropped his head to the table with a groan. "Why can't they just leave us alone?"

"Your family or the murderer?"

"Both." Valor hadn't felt this exhausted since his exams as an upper sixth when he'd also had a sports event, a play, and a few other commitments to contend with. "What am I going to do?"

"Sleep."

"Sleep?" Valor didn't know what going to bed would solve. "I've got to find out about getting the cottage cleaned up."

The to-do list to get their lives in order kept growing on him. Valor put getting security cameras installed close to the top of it, along with trying to salvage some of their belongings from the paint. The first item involved getting Bishan out of jail.

Everything else paled in comparison. And while everyone put on a brave face, Valor had no doubts being locked up would be incredibly traumatising for Bishan. No routine, no place to retreat to when overwhelmed, no control over anything; it might do irreparable harm to his emotional state.

"Get some rest. You can't figure anything out like this." Wilfred got to his feet and gathered up their plates. "Go on, you know the way. I'm sure Lottie's got everything laid out in the spare room. Have a sleep. We'll set things to right in the morning."

"Will we?"

Breakfast required choking down a full English. Lottie seemed wholly determined to feed Valor. "You can't handle the mess this hooligan made in your cottage on an empty stomach," she claimed.

And who's going to handle my mess if I can't hold this artery-clogging meal down?

He managed.

Valor eventually managed to escape, though he left Staccato in Lottie's loving care. The cat probably wouldn't want to come home with them after being spoilt rotten. *Well, let's see how bad the damage is in the bright light of day, shall we?*

Arriving at the cottage, Valor had to park a ways from it. Cars and SUVs blocked his drive and much of the side of the street. He raced inside to find Hugh organising what appeared to be a good twenty or more of his old Harrow schoolmates and their teachers as well.

Somehow, in the middle of the night after a message from Wilfred, Hugh had shown why he'd been a leader in their year by organising a cleaning party. He called everyone within driving distance of Grasmere. Many had to have gotten up well before dawn to arrive in the Lake District to help with cleaning up.

Valor grabbed the frame of the front door to keep from swaying on his feet. "I can't believe you drove all the way out here."

"Neither can we." Trevor walked by him with a bucket and a sponge. His twin brother, Trenton, followed after him. "Hours in a car, Val. *Hours*. I've suffered in the name of Harrow."

"Ignore the dramatic prat." Trenton shoved his brother toward a corner of the room. "Good to see you, Val."

"Morning." Hugh beamed at him, clearly proud of himself. "See you slept in a bit."

Valor honestly didn't know how to respond to their kindness. "Surprised you managed to convince so many to get out of bed so early for manual labour."

"So were we," Trevor called out from his corner. "Imagine if Matron could see us now, eh?"

Their group had been a particularly troublesome one for the West Acre house matron. Valor didn't know how she'd put up with six years of them. He'd sent her a thank you (and apology) letter when he heard she'd retired.

"*Oi*. How does this work?" Nick Wood, who'd been in the year above them, held up the vacuum with a cheeky grin.

Mr Clarke stood up from where he'd been working on stripping the paint from the wooden floors. "Behave yourselves."

"Why is his quiet disappointment still absolutely gut-wrenching? I'm thirty-three years old." Nick posed what was clearly a rhetorical question. He plugged in the vacuum and got to work. "*Follow up*."

With a chorus of *follow up*, a line from one of their school songs, echoing in his ears, Valor joined in the clean-up effort. The group worked well into the evening, stopping for lunch, and tea, and eventually a late supper. Pizzas and beer. His treat to thank them all for their effort.

They made a fair amount of progress. All the ruined bits had been thrown out. Hugh had spent much of his time supervising the installation of CCTV cameras all around the cottage; they'd now have a view from every aspect of their home.

No more shadowy figures sneaking in and out.

If the bastard comes here again, we'll catch him—at least on camera, if not in person.

Is it wrong to hope it's in person? I'd love a few minutes alone to pay in kind for trashing our cottage, and our lives, and Bishan. Mostly for Bish.

For the first time in a while, Valor had a house filled with Harrovians. They'd all opted to crash at his place. He had to pull out their camping supplies to find sleeping bags for them.

In the end, they all stayed up far too late watching the telly, reminiscing about schooldays, and finishing up the last of the pizza. Mr Clarke had declined the offer to stay overnight. He'd headed home along with Hugh, who had to work in the morning.

"Val?"

"Hmm?" He lifted his head off the floor with a groan. "I'm too old to sleep on the floor."

"There's an Indian family peeping through your front window." Trenton pointed toward the window. "Is that Lord Byron's sister?"

As a teen, Bishan had enjoyed writing poetry a fair bit. So much so their schoolmates took to calling him Lord Bryon, a nod to one of the most illustrious old boys attached to Harrow.

"Don't even think about it." Valor pointed a finger harshly at Trenton, the perpetual bachelor of their group. "Seriously."

Dragging himself upright, Valor picked his way across the room. He nudged or lightly kicked all the snoring helpers on the way to the door. The Tambolis stood in front of him, all grinning at him.

"What?" He glanced down at his rumpled and paint-covered clothing. "Something in my teeth?"

"Did you sleep in the shed?" Reva stood on her tiptoes to pick a piece of wood from his mussed-up hair. "We tried calling."

"Dropped my phone in a bucket. It's still drying off in a bag of rice." Valor heard fumbling, cursing, and crashing behind him. "Someone vandalised the cottage. I had some help with cleaning everything up."

"Vandalised?" Rana Tamboli, Bishan's mother, rushed forward to give him a warm hug. "Are you all right? Sunny, Sunny dear, why haven't you done anything about this?"

Sunesh rolled his eyes at Valor over her head. "I didn't know, Mum. Also, I'm sure Val called the police, who are more than capable of handling vandals."

"Well, yes. But you can help." She pushed by Valor into the house. "*Reva.*"

"You realise she's going to have the entire place redone by the time the day is over, right?" Reva groaned before trudging inside the cottage.

"How are you holding up?" Barnaby Tamboli, Bishan's father, offered Valor a tired but knowing smile. "Don't let Rana push you into anything."

"Is that advice you take as well, Dad?" Sunesh teased his father, who waved a finger at him in warning then disappeared into the house. "Tried to call to warn you, but you never answered. You know my parents; no answer from you had them panicking. Mum's a doctor, Dad's an accountant; you'd think they'd manage to think of a rational reason for you not picking up the phone."

"It's sweet." Valor always found it hard not to be envious of the warm, caring, and involved nature of the Tambolis. His family paled in comparison when it came to demonstrating their love for one another. "I'm grateful. Though, I'm glad you came this morning, not yesterday."

"That bad?"

"Worse." Valor glanced around Sunesh at the sound of a vehicle pulling in. He found Detective Inspector Spurling waving him over. "What now?"

With Sunesh close on his heels, Valor jogged over to the detective. His heart dropped into his stomach. He didn't know if he had the strength for more bad news.

"Pleasure to see you again, Detective." Sunesh held a hand out to the detective once he'd gotten out of his vehicle. "Have there been any developments in the case?"

Spurling leaned against the side of his vehicle. "Not as such. Mind if I speak with Valor in private?"

Valor nodded to Sunesh, who shrugged and strolled toward the house. He returned his attention to the detective. "Something wrong? Sunny's not a bad guy, even if he is a barrister."

"I'd prefer the family not know I'm encouraging your private investigation." Spurling probably hoped no one knew about it. Valor didn't think the police usually responded kindly to private citizens poking their noses into crimes, even if all the best telly detectives did it. "We found a few shoeprints that weren't yours or ours in your garden. No fingerprints in the house. We're trying to track down the source of the paint."

"And?"

"It takes time."

Valor massaged his forehead with a weary sigh. "Bishan doesn't have time."

"You might ask the frog queen. She seems to see everything, but refuses to speak with us." Spurling nodded toward Mrs Harris's cottage. They could see her peering at them through the curtains. "Absolute zero subtlety in that woman."

"Rumour has it that she won't talk to you because you once killed one of her frogs." Valor had gleaned that titbit from someone at the biscuit shop. "Is it on your permanent record?"

"I was ten." Spurling went from staid detective to slightly petulant in less than a second. "And it was an accident. He hopped in front of my bike."

Valor snorted loudly before collapsing into a fit of laughter. "Started young, did you? Was it tadpoles first, then you graduated to frogs?"

He pinched the bridge of his nose before glaring at Valor. "Will you talk to her?"

"I'll have a chat and see if I can't charm the information out of her. Maybe I can bribe her with a new frog statue to add to her collection." Valor made a note to see if Wilfred might make a batch of frog-shaped biscuits. "Oh, and Detective?"

Spurling paused in the process of getting into his vehicle. "Yes?"

"Ribbit."

CHAPTER 18

"You leave her to me." Rana had been waiting for Valor by the front door. She'd obviously overheard his conversation. "I'll see if she knows more than she wanted to tell the young detective."

Leaving Mrs Harris to Bishan's mum, Valor checked on the progress being made in the living room. He supposed they should be grateful the vandal didn't progress through the rest of the cottage. One area was better than their entire home.

"Your laptop keeps beeping." Reva handed it to him. "I didn't snoop. Sunny's going to pick up some new furniture for you. One of our aunties owns an antique shop an hour away. All we've got to do is get the rest of it out. The floor's all cleaned up."

"Why didn't you call us?" Barnaby wrapped an arm around his shoulders to lead him into the kitchen. "Have you eaten yet?"

"Call you over a bit of paint?" Valor tried to make light of it all.

"Not that—well not just the paint. You went to see your

parents." Barnaby handed him a plate with a few homemade *medu vada*, which were fried lentil dumplings shaped like doughnuts. They were brilliant for a portable breakfast. "We brought a bunch over for you and the other worker bees."

It took a great deal of self-control not to shove the entire dumpling into his mouth. *And not only to avoid the conversation.* They tasted absolutely delicious.

"Val?"

He found the concerned eyes of both Barnaby and Sunesh focused on him. "It went how visits to my family always go. A dismal failure of all parties involved to remain civil."

"Do you want to talk about it?" Barnaby pushed another two *medu vada* onto his plate. "You know we think of you as part of our family."

No.

I really, really don't want to talk about it.

Valor bit into another one of the doughnut-shaped dumplings and used the time spent chewing to think. "Not sure, in the end, there's anything to say. They haven't changed."

"Why don't you finish up here? We'll go make sure Reva doesn't decide your cottage needs to be her next project." Sunesh grabbed his father by the arm to drag him out of the kitchen. Valor could hear him whispering on the way out, "We promised Bishan that we wouldn't ask him about the Scotts."

"It was just a question," Bishan's dad protested.

With a quiet chuckle, Valor turned his attention to his laptop. He found an email from Nina with a new set of possibilities from the anagram. She'd highlighted ten of them she thought had potential.

Valor crossed out three of them right away for not making any sense at all. If the murderer had left this for him, he imagined they wanted him to know what it said. *Wait.* He read one of them out loud to himself. "Sh. The play has just begun. Tick-tock. Tick-tock. Lord Byron is struck down. How many more to go?"

Lord Bryon is struck down? Valor assumed it was a reference to Bishan. Another confirmation of the killer being a Harrovian. The nickname had been specific to the West Acre boys.

Grabbing the program from the drawer, Valor hoped having kept it in plastic meant the detective wouldn't get too angry with him. He regretted not giving it to Spurling sooner. It just seemed as though it might be another nail in the case against Bishan.

"How on earth do you live next to that woman without going insane?" Rana came in from the garden through the back door. "She talked about frogs so long I thought I might turn green. Goodness me."

Valor poured a cup of tea for her that she accepted gratefully. "Did she mention anything aside from the ribbiting creatures?"

"She claims to have seen someone carrying two buckets late in the evening. She assumed it was you." Rana sipped her tea for a moment. "Foolish woman. How could you be home when you were still traveling? Honestly. Also, she did ask if you'd dyed your hair a darker colour."

"Dyed my hair?" Valor blinked at her for a few seconds. "So, whoever it is was clearly pale like myself—and has dark hair."

Pale.

Dark hair.

That's at least one more off my list.

It took several hours to wrap up the clean-up of his living room. Furniture would arrive later in the evening. When the Tambolis left to visit Bishan, Valor used the time to check in at the shop with a slight ulterior motive; Spurling always stopped by to pick up biscuits for his grandmother late in the afternoon.

When the detective arrived, Valor had Wilfred guide him back into the small office. If Spurling was going to yell at him for withholding evidence, it would be better to do it in private. The gossips didn't need anything new from them.

"What's this then?" Spurling munched on a biscuit while checking out the program handed to him. "Where'd you find it?"

"Shoved between the roots of the tree in our garden." Valor continued quickly when the detective frowned at him. "I didn't know what I'd found at first. The bolded letters didn't seem out of the ordinary at first."

Spurling brushed his fingers clean then brought the paper up for a more precise view. "What about these letters then?"

After briefly mentioning about the anagram, Valor explained in detail what Nina had suggested. He covered the computer deciphering program, and all the possibilities spun out by it. And finally, he gave Spurling what they believed the correct solution to be.

"Lord Bryon?" Spurling questioned.

"Bishan's nickname. He went through a poetry phase— writing and reading it." Valor tapped his fingers against the desk nervously. He feared sharing with the detective had been a mistake. *What if he takes it as further proof Bishan did it? Damn. What have I done?* "What terrifies me is the 'how many more to go' bit. Is the dead body in our garden just the tip of what's to come?"

"Does 'the play has just begun' mean anything specifically to you?" Spurling plucked another biscuit from the package he'd bought. "Or is it our murderer wanting to sound posh?"

"Could be another Harrow reference? We have house and school plays quite frequently. Both Bishan and I were in a few, as were many other West Acrians." Valor went through his shortened list of suspects, only to find all three had participated in their school dramas. "I'm not sure if it means anything important."

"I doubt we'll find fingerprints aside from yours, which isn't brilliant, Valor." He sent a disapproving glare toward him. "Try not to do it again, will you? It doesn't make either of you appear innocent."

"How else was I supposed to retrieve it? I thought it was a bit of trash." Valor had no regrets at finding it. He didn't know if the detectives would've been able to figure it out. "I'm sorry."

"No, you really aren't." Spurling closed the biscuit packet and shoved it into his jacket pocket. "Not sure this does much for the case without more information. Did Mrs Harris offer anything useful?"

"Your suspect is dark-haired and Caucasian." Valor jotted down three names on a scrap of paper. "Given everything, unless we have some random killer with a Harrow obsession, I'd wager everything I own one of these three did it."

"You sure?"

No.

"Is anything sure in a murder like this one?" Valor didn't know much about gut instincts that all the telly detectives talked about, but his seemed to be saying he was right about the names. "Can I see Bishan? He might remember more."

"Come by later. I'll see if I can't work something out. He's seen his family." Spurling waved the program at him, then left.

"Everything all right?" Wilfred came in once the detective had left. "He seemed on a mission."

Valor dropped his head into his hands. "I've put forward the names of three schoolmates as potential murderers, and Bishan's still sitting in jail. None of this is all right."

He hoped it would be again. And soon.

CHAPTER 19

Sitting on the metal chair, Valor shivered slightly as he waited. They'd taken his jacket off him, and the room felt colder than it had previously. Each day that passed without Bishan seemed like a year.

He hated it.

After an agonisingly lengthy wait, Bishan entered the room. The dark shadows around his eyes spoke loudly of a lack of sleep and the heavy weight of stress on his shoulders. He stood by the chair, staring helplessly at Valor.

Valor ignored the guard, got to his feet, and held his arms open. And waited. Bishan sucked in his bottom lip then shuffled forward to collapse into his embrace. "It's all right, Bish. I've got you."

Bishan dropped his head against his shoulder. "I want to go home now."

"I know, love." Valor kept him close. His hand rubbed comfortingly at Bishan's back. "Sunny's working on it, and you know your brother finds it impossible to let go of anything until he's convinced everyone to agree with him."

"He's stubborn and strong." Bishan stepped back

abruptly. He wrapped his arms around himself and paced behind his chair. "I don't like this place. It's cold. And itchy."

By itchy, Valor immediately understood him to be struggling with his senses. When overwhelmed, Bishan often scratched at his fingertips and arms as though his skin was crawling. They'd learned over the years to find ways to deal with it to prevent him from actually harming himself.

The thirty-minute visit went far too quickly for both of them. Valor stared at the door long after Bishan had been led out of it. They had to bring an end to this nightmare, and sooner rather than later.

"C'mon, then. Let's get you some tea." Spurling found him in the hallway, unable to move. He took Valor by the arm and led him into a small kitchenette the officers used. "We're keeping him as comfortable as we possibly can."

Valor moved away from Spurling. He held on to his emotions by the slimmest of threads. "Fine."

"It's not, though, is it?" He held out a cup of tea to Valor. "It's really not."

The words didn't soothe Valor at all. His control slipped completely. He choked while trying to swallow down the tears, twisting away to avoid seeing the detective's pity.

He didn't want it.

He wanted Bishan free to go home.

Swallowing down the tea, Valor found the scalding to his throat helped bring his emotions under control. He scrubbed his eyes with his shirtsleeve. Spurling held out a napkin without comment.

"What do we do now?"

"Is there a way to get your potential suspects together that wouldn't involve the police? Something to keep the actual murderer from thinking we're on to them." Spurling leaned against the cabinet behind him. "I could just bring them all in for questioning, but the odds of them revealing themselves is slim to none. We've nothing tying any of them to the crime at the moment."

The only supposedly concrete evidence was Bishan's fingerprints. Valor knew they had a mountain to climb to prove him innocent. A police interrogation might do more harm than good initially.

"A house dinner."

"Pardon?" Spurling questioned.

"Old boys visit their houses all the time at Harrow. We have at least two or three events a year. It wouldn't raise suspicions for us to put together an event at West Acre. We might even manage to restrict the invites to people within our years of attendance. Less to sort out." Valor rubbed absently at the scruff on his jaw. "If he's so obsessed with Bish and me, he'll find it impossible to resist showing up."

"We'll post detectives—"

"I don't see how," Valor interrupted him. "We know each other, all of us. They'd spot you from a mile away. Hugh will be there; I'm sure the big lug can manage to protect me. I'm not exactly helpless either."

"Trained in martial arts and hand-to-hand combat, are we?"

"A master of the martial art of procrastination." Valor had probably earned a black belt in it over the years. "Where would you hide? If the objective is to simply gather information, the presence of police, whether uniformed or not, is going to stand out. Let me do it my way. It'll be fine."

"Famous last words."

They argued back and forth before Spurling finally agreed to his plan. Valor spent the rest of the day pulling his half-cocked plan together. Mr Clarke jumped on board to help convince the current housemaster and matron to the last-minute plan.

None of them were told why the sudden urge for a West

Acre reunion. Not wanting to risk the safety of any of the current boys living in the boarding house, Valor managed to get a last-minute booking at a hotel in London not far from the school.

In switching to the ballroom, they not only managed to invite a few more attendees but sneak in police officers as catering staff. Valor charmed and bribed his way into rushing everything to a week. He played off the last-minute dinner as a coming together to support Bishan.

Given the theme, it surprised no one when almost everyone invited RSVP'd yes, including their three suspects. Everyone who knew Bishan at Harrow had loved him, aside from the few prats who Valor refused to count. *And the murderer.* He only hoped the dinner provided them some sort of clue or evidence.

Anything at all.

A week after coming up with the mad idea, Valor stood outside the doors to the ballroom they'd rented out. Mr Clarke had already gone inside to mingle. It left him alone with Daniel, the twins, and Hugh, his closest mates from school outside of Bishan.

A few phone calls to former West Acre residents brought in enough funds to pay for the entire event. Hugh worked his own contacts along with Reggie to coordinate the police effort. The detectives were all more cooperative when they realised they wouldn't need to pay for anything.

Only Hugh and Daniel knew the truth of the evening. Trevor and Trenton weren't known for their ability to keep secrets. Valor hadn't told them the specifics. He still remembered the time they'd accidentally confessed to planning their upper sixth speech day prank before it had actually been completed.

"Ready?" Hugh asked while the other three stepped into the room. "They're all in there. I've already checked."

"No, I'm not ready." Valor straightened his jacket and tie, using it as armour in a way. "Right. Time to play Poirot and see if I can't suss out the murderer."

"Val?"

He froze with his hand on the door. "What?"

"You're not actually Poirot. Or Miss Marple. Or Father Brown. Or a police officer." Hugh moved up beside him, placing a hand on the door to keep it shut. "All I'm saying is try not to get so close to the mystery that you put yourself in danger."

"Oh, ye of little faith." Valor glared pointedly at the hand blocking him from opening the door. "It's a crowded ball-room. You're here. Spurling has his friends here. What could possibly go wrong? I won't eat or drink anything, so he can't poison me either."

Hugh let his hand fall away from the door. "I sometimes forget how arrogantly pig-headed you can be for someone who's so damned relaxed all the time."

Ignoring the pessimist, Valor stepped inside the ballroom. He had to stop to take in the number of men milling about in conversation with each other. His gaze went from face to face before eventually spotting one of his targets.

Harrison Smith.

The youngest on his list, Harrison didn't seem the type. He'd been shy and unremarkable at school. Valor only remembered him as it had been his job to help the new boys get settled in during the first month.

Now a grown-up, Harrison, from a distance, didn't appear to have changed much outside of gaining height. With a nod to Hugh, Valor made his way across the room. He stopped periodically to speak with friends who called out to him, until finally making it over to his quarry.

"Harry Smith? Right?" Valor held a hand out to him. He

offered a friendly smile to the clearly shy man. "It is Harry, or do you prefer Harrison now? I haven't seen you in ages."

"Harrison." He shook Valor's hand longer than required before yanking his arm back. "Bishan was kind to me at school. I wanted to offer my help if I can."

"Thank you." Valor had a brief but boring conversation before excusing himself. "Enjoy the dinner, Harrison."

Definitely not him.

Definitely.

Who was next?

Valor peered around the room before spotting Aubrey Fletcher. He started forward, only for someone to ram into him. They'd disappeared into the crowd before he could pick himself off the floor. "Well, that was rude."

Refocusing his attention, Valor continued on to Aubrey. He wanted at least one conversation with each of the three suspects before they sat down to dinner. It didn't leave him much time to dawdle.

He could do this.

He could—for Bishan.

Usually when Valor spent time with his former school-mates he enjoyed himself immensely. The absence of Bishan and the reason behind it made this one more torturous. He felt like an overly tightened bowstring, ready to snap at any moment.

Aubrey, it turned out, hadn't changed much since Harrow. He was as loud as Valor remembered. The more the conversation went along, the less Aubrey seemed capable of the subtleties of the murder. "*Oi!* Valiant. Aren't you listening?"

"One second. Just saw someone I needed to speak with." Valor ducked away from him to go find Hugh. His friend was observing the mingling crowd from a slightly elevated spot in the far corner of the room. "Anything interesting?"

"Clay." Hugh motioned with his head toward the opposite side of the room. "A bit odd for him to be here, isn't it?"

Clay, or Nick Clayton, had been a year below them. He generally avoided any and all Harrow events. They never knew if he merely hated thinking about schooldays—or preferred being antisocial.

"A bit."

"We'll keep an eye on him." Hugh's eyes lit up when they were signalled for supper. "Finally. I'm half-starved."

"Idiot." Valor allowed Hugh to lead him across the room to their table. He'd planned it so all three of their suspects sat with them, along with Mr Clarke, Daniel, and the twins. "Are you ready?"

"I was—"

"You were *not* born ready." Valor elbowed Hugh in the side. "Just find your seat."

CHAPTER 20

"What an absolute waste of an evening." Hugh slumped into one of the couches in the lobby of the hotel. "Did we learn anything aside from Aubrey is even more obnoxious as an adult?"

"Not really." Valor shoved his hands into his pockets, and his finger touched the edge of a paper. "What...."

"Val?" Hugh sat up, almost immediately on alert. "What did you find?"

"Let's get upstairs." Valor carefully eased his hands out of his pockets. He caught Hugh by the arm to drag him to his feet. They jogged through the lobby, then up a flight of stairs. "I want Reggie's help with it."

"With what? Val?" Hugh kept up with him as they rounded a corner to find the room where the detectives had set up the monitors for all the cameras placed around the hall for the dinner. "For God's sake, slow down."

"Don't they require you coppers keep fit?" Valor teased. He banged on the door, waiting impatiently for it to open. "There's something in my pocket."

"I'm not falling for that again." Hugh's grin disappeared

when Valor only stared at him. "You think the murderer left it?"

"Well, I didn't put anything in my pocket. And I doubt anyone in that room would slip me their number." Valor pushed into the room when the door opened, slipping off his jacket to hold it out to Spurling. "You might want someone with gloves to inspect the right pocket. It might be nothing, but I'd rather not screw the evidence up for a second time."

Pulling on a pair of gloves, Spurling used tweezers to extract a folded piece of paper from the pocket. Valor bent over to get a better view at it. He almost immediately recognised it as yet another Harrow program, one for one of the West Acre house plays.

"More bolded letters." Valor borrowed a glove from Spurling to get a closer look. "Can I write these down? I'll send them to Nina to see if she can run this one through the same program."

"We're going to want to scan through all the footage from the event to see if we can discover who specifically left it in your pocket." Spurling dropped the program into an evidence bag once Valor had copied the letters down. "Let's get some coffee. It's going to be a long night. Half the guests decided to spend the night at the hotel. If we can narrow it down quickly, we grab him before he checks out."

After texting Nina with the new anagram letters, Valor plopped down in front of a laptop to view the CCTV footage from the night. Hugh scooted up next to him. They went through hours of video from different angles and several pots of coffee.

"It's not wanking that makes you blind; it's police work." Valor dropped his head against the table. "I'm not even sure I know who anyone even is anymore. They're all blending together."

Poirot makes this seem so easy.

All their suspects had at one point or another come close enough to Valor to drop something into his pocket. He'd yet to find proof of it. They always seemed to be facing in the wrong direction.

"I'm so glad I didn't become a police officer." Valor leaned back into the chair while rubbing his eyes. "It seems way more exciting on the telly."

"Investigations aren't all flash and dramatics." Hugh stretched his arms up then glanced at his watch. "It's almost four in the morning. We should get some sleep. All of us."

"We'll wrap up here. You're not really supposed to be here anyway." Spurling had stood by the coffee machine. "Go on. I'll call you if we find anything."

They were so tired they accidentally went to the wrong floor of the hotel—twice. Hugh finally got the button on the elevator right. Valor collapsed on his bed completely clothed and was out within seconds.

Four hours of sleep made Valor feel a bit better, but not by much. He fell out of the hotel bed, literally, stumbled into a cold shower, and barely managed to remember how to put his clothes on. Room service kindly brought him breakfast with an extra-strong cup of coffee, which helped kick his brain into gear.

A quick check of his muted phone showed multiple messages from Nina. The computer had spat out a few answers to their new puzzle. One stopped him entirely in his tracks.

Shh. Not so cleverly done. Time's almost up. When the clock strikes one, whose name shall be crossed out?

Forwarding the message on to Hugh and Spurling, Valor haphazardly shoved all his stuff into the bag. He raced around the room checking to ensure he hadn't missed anything. His palms grew so sweaty his phone slipped out of his hand.

Had the supper been a bad idea?

Had they stupidly prodded him into action?

"Scott."

Valor skidded to a halt in the hallway leading from the elevators to the lobby. He found Nick Clayton waving to him. *Damn it.* "Nicki."

"*Nick.*" Clayton glared at him.

"Sorry." Valor waited for his former housemate to catch up to him. They continued toward the lobby. "Heading home?"

"Thought I might stay in London for a few days. I'm between jobs at the moment." Clayton grabbed Valor by the arm to drag him into a nearby alcove. "Listen, you—"

"Val? Where the hell are you?" Hugh poked his head around the corner. "Ahh. Nicki."

"It's *Nick.*" Clayton shoved Valor away from him, cursed them both out, and stormed off.

"What was that about?" Hugh stared after their former schoolmate.

"Not a clue. You interrupted us before he could tell me what he wanted." Valor dragged his fingers through his hair. He wondered if Nick Clayton was their murderer. "Did you see my message?"

"I did. Creepy. How certain are they it's the right unscrambled version?" Hugh led him toward the lobby where Mr Clarke waited for them. "Spurling decided to wait until all the Harrovians have cleared out. We don't want to give ourselves away yet. Nicki's certainly put himself higher on my list."

"Mine as well." Valor didn't know where they went with that information. "Now what do we do?"

"Let the police handle it," Hugh answered sternly.

"I have to agree with him." Mr Clarke added his own two cents.

"Of course." Valor had zero intentions of backing away from the investigation until Bishan was free. "Let the police handle it."

The drive home went quickly with his mind replaying everything from the previous night. Valor arrived back in Grasmere in time to check in with Wilfred and Lottie at the shop. They shared the news of the day, which translated to pointless gossip. He picked Staccato up from their house after having supper with them, and started home only to find the lane to his cottage blocked by the police.

Not again.

One of his neighbours waved him over to park in their drive. They told him a body had been found in the hedgerow. *Another one.* He breathed a sigh of relief that both he and Bishan had ironclad alibis for the last few days.

Knowing the police might take hours, Valor drove the loop around their area to approach from the opposite side of the road. The authorities had blocked off the lane a few yards from his cottage. He pulled into his own drive and headed inside to avoid the staring of his neighbours.

Please don't let it be a related crime.

Please God, let it not be someone I know.

With Staccato perched on his shoulder, Valor watched the police from his front window. It was impossible to figure out from a distance what had happened. The body had already been taken away by the time he'd arrived home.

He paced in front of the window. Staccato eventually grew tired of his moving and leapt off to find a more stable pillow. Spoiled creature. As the sun finally set completely, the police started to leave, one at a time.

Valor spotted Spurling walking up toward his cottage. He had the door open before the detective could even knock. "Am I under arrest?"

"Don't be daft." Spurling stepped inside when Valor

moved back to let him by. "We've already got time of death, and you were sitting with me in the hotel when it happened."

"Well, that's something. Is it connected?"

"Fancy making some tea?" Spurling flicked through pages of his little notebook. "I've a few questions for you."

With a sense of dread in the pit of his stomach, Valor went ahead to make tea for both of them. He even threw a few biscuits on a plate. Setting the tray on the coffee table with a thud, he flopped into his recliner with his legs dangling over the edge.

The tension in the room went up a few notches in the prolonged silence. Valor wondered what Spurling was building himself up to. He clutched at his cup of tea, praying for good news to anyone who might be listening.

"Well?" Valor prompted after an agonising wait. "What is it?"

"Does the name Lee Night ring a bell?"

"No?" Valor paused to consider the name. "Wait a second. He used to be the assistant housemaster at West Acre. He lives in Dublin, last I heard. Why on earth is he dead in a hedgerow outside my cottage?"

"We have no idea." Spurling seemed genuinely bewildered. "His family didn't know he planned to travel."

So they definitely had a serial killer on the loose. Someone, and Valor now had his money on Aubrey, had a list of names. And they'd undoubtedly come up with a bloody plan straight from a horror film.

"What about Bish? Shouldn't he be set free now?" Valor narrowed his eyes on the detective inspector. "It's obviously connected. This can't be a coincidence. And unless you think Bishan magically got out of prison and went back in after committing the murder, he should be free."

"I agree."

"And?" Valor shifted forward in his seat. "What are you doing here?"

"Found another anagram." Spurling lifted it out of his pocket in a clear evidence bag. "Could your friend see if they can decipher it?"

"What about Bishan?" Valor tentatively reached out for the bag. His gaze remained on the detective. "Well?"

"I'll work on it," Spurling promised.

Despite everyone advising him to be patient, Valor hadn't been able to listen. He'd driven over to the police station and parked outside not long after they'd finished up outside the cottage. They needed the motivation and reminder that Bishan mattered to his loved ones.

Hugh had joined him after making the drive up from Manchester to dissuade him. "I want Bishan free as much as you. Just not sure harassing the police is the way to go about it. They don't take kindly to being pushed."

"And I don't take kindly to my Bishan being locked up on the flimsiest amount of evidence." Valor leaned against his Fiat with Staccato sitting on his shoulder. His tail flipped into Valor's face every once in a while. "They've no reason to continue to hold him."

"Be patient."

Valor reached up to lower Staccato's orange-sherbet-coloured tail to allow him to glare more effectively at Hugh. "This is me being as patient as humanly possible."

"By standing outside?"

"I'm not inside, am I?" Valor crossed his arms then spluttered when Staccato covered his face with his fluffy tail again. "Damn it."

"Just try not to be a nuisance while I see where Sunesh and the detectives are, all right?" Hugh jogged up the steps into the building. He paused by the front doors. "Stay here."

CHAPTER 21

How sodding long does it take to spring someone from jail?

After almost an hour, Valor returned Staccato to the car. The cat curled up in the bed in the back seat. He'd have to take him over to Lottie until the killer had been found.

But not yet, not until he had Bishan in his arms.

Each time the door swung open, Valor anxiously stood up straight, only to relax against the vehicle again when it turned out to be someone else. *It feels like it's been eighty-four years. I'll be ancient by the time they wrap this up.* He roughly mussed up his hair with his fingers to release some of his frustration.

Closing his eyes, Valor tilted his head to soak up some of the sunlight. He knew even with Bishan's release, they hadn't heard the last of the murderer. It wouldn't end until the real killer had been locked up for good.

"Val?"

Valor kept his eyes closed for the briefest of seconds, soaking in the pleasure of the voice. He finally opened them to find Bishan waiting at the top of the steps, with Sunesh and Hugh just behind him. "Bish."

"Oh, honestly, you two. You've stood out here for hours like a numpty, get up here to say hello." Hugh rolled his eyes at them.

Valor chuckled at Hugh, though his gaze remained on Bishan. "Further proof of why you're still single. You've no appreciation for how deeply you can love someone."

"Yes, I do," Hugh muttered mulishly.

Ignoring Hugh, Valor pushed away from the Fiat to cross the distance toward them. Bishan hesitantly moved away from his brother. He offered a tentative smile to Valor.

"I can go home now." Bishan scrubbed his hands against his jeans repeatedly. "I want to go home. Don't like the police station. They use itchy soap."

"Do they?" Valor inched closer to him. He waited to see if Bishan even wanted physical touch after spending weeks teetering on the edge of constant sensory overload. "Home is ready for you. Lottie made a cottage pie for us, and Sunny probably mentioned your mum's made all your favourites as well."

"*Ladoo, ladoo, ladoo.*" Bishan bounced on his heels. "With coconut and almond. *Ladoo.*"

Ladoos were one of Bishan's favourite sweet. Round sweets made with flour, sugar, and different ingredients. He seemed to enjoy the coconut and almond ones the best.

"I've no doubts your mum will—" Valor was cut off when Bishan launched himself at him. He wrapped his arms tightly around him. "It's all right, Bish. Promise. We'll get you home. All comfortable and you can lock yourself in your music room."

"With you." Bishan's fingers gripped Valor's shirt firmly, holding him against him. "Hate it here. Hate it."

Sunesh stepped up beside them. "I'll get Mum, Dad, and Reva. We'll come over in a bit. That okay, Bishy?"

Bishan nodded against Valor's shirt. "*Ladoos. Ladoos. Ladoos. Ladoos.*"

Meeting Sunesh's gaze over Bishan's head, Valor knew they both realised it would take time for him to recover from losing his freedom—and his routine. They wanted to get him comfortable. He had a feeling they'd be watching the same shows on the telly for hours on end.

"Let's get you home, yeah?" Valor tried to get Bishan to look up, but he continued to clutch at his shirt. "We're apparently going to stay here."

"I'll go get the family." Sunesh patted his brother on the back and strode across the street toward his vehicle.

"I'll return to Manchester. Call me later." Hugh wandered off as well, leaving the two of them alone.

"Got you a present." Valor stroked Bishan's hair gently. "You're free, Bish. Free."

It was several more minutes before Bishan eased away from him. His fingers dropped away from Valor's shirt. He reached down to pull off his tennis shoes and wiggled his toes on the pavement.

"Freedom means no shoes?" Valor had to laugh when Bishan tossed the shoes at him. "Ready to go home?"

Bishan went immediately to the car. He glanced in the window, then yanked the back door open. "Staccato."

Getting Bishan into the Fiat required bribing him into it. Valor offered him a Rubik's cube. He immediately grabbed it then clambered into the back seat with Staccato in his lap.

The drive became increasingly difficult for him. Valor kept glancing over his shoulder to reassure himself Bishan hadn't disappeared. He'd dreamed of this moment so many times; it now seemed too good to be true.

"It's different." Bishan gripped the frame of the front door and peered inside the cottage. "Why's it changed?"

Valor mentally cursed his own stupidity. They'd forgotten to prepare Bishan for the new carpet and furniture. "The killer made a mess in the living room. We had to throw some stuff out."

"They were here?"

"We've added new locks and cameras outside as well," Valor assured him. "It's safe. They tried to match the furniture as closely as possible."

Bishan frowned at him and at the offending items. "Reva?"

"How'd you guess?"

"It feels like Reva." Bishan inched into the cottage until he reached the new recliner. He ran his fingers along the soft fabric covering the cushions. "Definitely my sister. She knows I don't like rough textures."

"Carpet's nice as well." Valor smiled through a sudden flood of tears while he watched Bishan test his bare feet on the plush rug. He'd held on to his emotions the entire time, and now the dam wanted to break. "You're free."

Bishan twisted around to stare at him while Staccato purred smugly from his shoulder. "Are you sad? Tears are the sad emotion. Why are you sad?"

"Not sad. I'm happy." Valor brushed the tears away impatiently. "Sometimes people cry when they're really, truly joyful."

"Why?"

"I've not even the slightest clue." He sat on the arm of the sofa to watch Bishan explore all the new things. Reva had done an amazing job of finding items her brother would enjoy owning—and touching. "Not sure how I'd manage without you, Bish. I fell apart in only a few weeks."

"You'd be fine."

Not taking offense at the blunt statement, Valor had to laugh instead. He'd missed how literal Bishan could be. It was part and parcel of being in a relationship with an autistic.

Romantic phrasing and gestures often went right over Bishan's head. Valor found it made the moments Bishan did grasp even more special. Weren't all relationships about compromise and learning to understand one another?

"I missed your toast." Bishan continued his inspection of the new paintings on their walls. "And how you make tea. Yours is the best."

Valor found his emotions threatening to take over him for a second time. "Do you want tea?"

"And your hugs. You squeeze right." Bishan ignored his question and reached up to take a pastoral painting off the wall. "Don't like this one. Makes me dizzy."

"We'll get a different one." He used the bottom of his shirt to wipe his eyes clean. "How about I make tea and cinnamon toast, then we can watch some *Poirot* until your family invades?"

"Season one. And two. Mostly one." Bishan pulled down a second painting, a smaller one of Grasmere. "Reva's not good with art."

Leaving Bishan to grumble about his sister's lack of taste, Valor put on season one of *Poirot*. The background noise would start the process of helping ease Bishan out of the constant state of stress from being jailed. He quickly got the kettle on and dropped a few slices of cinnamon-raisin bread into the toaster.

"Val?"

The slight tremble in Bishan's voice made him worry. Valor quickly turned the kettle off. He could always restart it.

He dashed out of the kitchen to find Bishan standing in the middle of the living room with a completely lost expression on his face. "What's the matter?"

"It's all wrong." Bishan appeared to be slipping quickly into a meltdown. "New and wrong."

In retrospect, Valor thought replacing the furniture, paintings, and carpet could've waited. Bishan tended to be quite particular about his surroundings. Home was his safe zone, the one place where he had complete control of his environment.

It was a compromise Valor had never begrudged Bishan. He'd readily allowed Bishan to take responsibility for setting up the cottage. Kicking himself for not thinking of it, though, could wait until things had calmed down.

"Why don't we go to the music room? Nothing has changed inside it." Valor guided Bishan down the hall with Staccato following closely. "I'm sure you've missed all your instruments."

It didn't take long for Bishan to get comfortable at the piano, beginning to pound away at the keys. Valor sat on the floor beside it with his back to the wall. Staccato curled up in his lap with a contented purr.

The feverish strains of Chopin's Prelude no. 15 in B Flat Minor slowly melded into the calmer waters of one of Mozart's piano sonatas. Each note played shifted the music from a roar to a gentle melodic flow. Valor closed his eyes to soak in the comforting familiarity that had been painfully absent for the past weeks.

When yet another sonata came to an end, Bishan stopped playing briefly. He tapped middle C over and over. Then after a brief run of the scales, his hands fell away from the keys altogether.

Slipping off the bench, Bishan stretched out on the worn-out rug they kept to deaden the sound slightly. He dropped his head on Valor's thigh. Valor stroked his fingers gently through Bishan's hair.

These were the quiet moments Valor had missed.

He knew family would eventually invade. The Tambolis had apparently decided to give them a moment to themselves. They'd show up soon enough, though.

Valor didn't want to think about them, or his own family, or the murderer. He had Bishan safely home; all the other nonsense faded away as it always did. "We'll fix the living room to your liking. I promise."

Bishan shrugged.

Grabbing the nearby remote, Valor switched on the music. He skipped to the playlist they'd put together to help soothe Bishan through meltdowns. It worked—seven times out of ten.

Thirty minutes, and a quarter of the way through the playlist, Valor's bum had gone completely numb. He tried to shift around without dislodging Bishan, who twisted onto his back. Bishan smiled up at him, the soft grin that always made his breath catch in his throat.

"I've missed you." Valor pressed a kiss to Bishan's forehead. "I've been thinking."

"Oh?" Bishan rolled over then sat up, narrowly avoiding bashing his head against the piano. "Where's the tea?"

Valor rubbed his fingers across his face and decided the romantic moment had to wait. "Tea is in the kitchen, where it belongs."

The doorbell rang midway through their tea.

Valor opened it to find Bishan's family smiling brightly at him. "He's in the kitchen. Don't crowd him."

Rana waited until the others had squeezed by him to head into the cottage. She dragged him into a tight hug. "You're a good boy. Always were. You're good for my Bishan. Now, we've brought food. And when are you going to marry him? Hmm?"

"I—"

She patted him gently on the chest, then stepped back.

"Now, now, I won't give the surprise away. Just do it soon, yes?"

"Yes." Valor sometimes hated how Bishan's mum saw straight through him. He'd never thought of himself as transparent; after all, Scotts were taught how to repress emotions practically from birth. "Once things calm down a bit."

"If you wait for calm waters, Valor, you might never get there." Rana carried her plate of food into the cottage, leaving him to stare stupidly at the open door.

He closed the door, locked it, and turned toward the living room only to have the doorbell go off for a second time. "Oh, honestly."

The next few hours dragged on for Valor. All their friends within easy driving distance had clearly decided a celebration was in order. Their cottage quickly filled up with their well-meaning but exhausting presence.

Valor watched the calmness Bishan had found slowly evaporate. His patience came to an end. "We love you all very much, but it's time to go now. Or I'll teach Staccato to deposit hairballs in your coat pockets."

"Rude." Reva flitted around gathering up the plates and cups from everyone.

It didn't take long for Bishan's parents to spot him attempting to hide in the corner with Staccato. He'd shrunken into himself in a chair with a blanket covering almost his entire body. Valor didn't care who he offended; they all needed to leave.

Bishan's dad stepped over to his son, leaning down to gently touch the top of his head. "Rest well, yes?"

While Rana said her goodbyes to her son, Barnaby moved over to Valor. He embraced him heartily, murmuring a thank you for taking care of Bishan. The words left both of them teary eyed.

Valor accepted hugs from everyone, not bothering to say

sorry. He refused to apologise for placing Bishan's needs first. "I'll text you all with how we're doing."

Lottie rested a hand on Valor's cheek before dragging Wilfred out of the cottage. "Come over in the morning for brekkie. I'll make a full English for you both."

The cottage eventually emptied out completely. Valor breathed a sigh of relief. It took almost thirty minutes of silence before Bishan stretched out from underneath the blanket and got to his feet.

"Want cottage pie for supper? Lottie left it for us." Valor followed Bishan into the kitchen. He watched him rummage around in the fridge and cabinets for several minutes, eventually coming out with milk and their box of Coco Shreddies. "Cereal for dinner, then?"

"Craved this for three weeks." Bishan grabbed the large mixing bowl, dumped first the cereal followed by milk into it, and then grinned at Valor who held up two spoons. "You can share with me."

"How kind."

They'd made it three-quarters of the way through the box when the doorbell went off once again. Bishan's shoulders drooped as he pushed the bowl away. Valor left him in the kitchen and stomped toward the front of the cottage, fully prepared for a good row with whoever'd interrupted them.

"Reggie?" Valor felt all his hopes sink into his stomach like a rock at the sight of the detective inspector. "You're not taking him back."

"No, I'm not. He's been completely cleared." Spurling gave him a weak smile. "Mind if I come in? I'd rather tell you both together."

If possible, Valor's stomach sank even further. He steeled himself for whatever bad news the detective had for them. They found Bishan waiting in the living room, anxiously clutching Staccato in his arms.

"You're not going back," Valor quickly reassured Bishan. He immediately relaxed into one of the chairs. "You're not. I'd take you to Timbuktu if they tried."

"I didn't hear that." Spurling sat on the edge of the sofa, waving off Valor's offer of tea. "We've been checking with the hotel for anyone registered the other night. Your brother was there."

"What?" Valor sat quickly to avoid his knees going out on him. "Really? Did we catch him on CCTV?"

"No, but that doesn't mean anything," Spurling acknowledged.

Valor narrowed his eyes on the detective when he hesitated. "There's something else, isn't there?"

"We've found another body." Spurling held up a Harrow program—one from a West Acre house play. "The victim was dumped in the pond down the road."

"Who?" Valor reached out a shaking hand to take the photo Spurling held out to him. He nearly dropped it a second later. "Oh no, no...."

"Val?"

He sent a horrified glance toward Bishan. "Mr Clarke."

DEAD IN THE POND

CHAPTER 1

"**M**ight need about three more cups of tea before any of this makes any sense to me." Valor rested his head on Bishan's shoulder briefly. "I am *so* glad you're home."

Everyone aside from Valor had been decidedly odd since Bishan's release from jail. He didn't like it. At all. Why couldn't their lives return to business as usual?

Well, probably not business as usual exactly.

Nothing could be quite normal after finding themselves smack dab in the midst of a mystery of the *Poirot* and *Father Brown* variety. The police had yet to figure out who'd begun the murderous campaign against former Harrovians; Bishan was only glad they'd stopped pursuing him for it.

He'd been freed from jail two days ago.

And sometimes it still felt as though he were there.

"It's not an anagram," Bishan insisted pedantically. And it wasn't. The creepy murder messages left via bolded letters in old Harrow play programs might be puzzles, but they weren't anagrams. "They're not already formed into words that you have to unscramble."

Valor had spread out the multiple not-anagrams across their kitchen table along with the two that had potentially been deciphered already. "So what are they?"

"Puzzles."

"Right." Valor grabbed his cup for more tea. "Do you think they got the first two correct?"

Bishan glanced at the two supposedly decoded messages with a critical eye. They both seemed plausible in the context of the victims and assuming the perpetrator was indeed a former schoolmate of theirs. He found the "Shh" or "Sh" at the beginning to be odd.

Shh. Not so cleverly done. Time's almost up. When the clock strikes one, whose name shall be crossed out?

Sh. The play has just begun. Tick-tock. Tick-tock. Lord Byron is struck down. How many more to go?

"I'm not the killer. I don't know." Bishan picked up one of the programs yet to be deciphered. He wrote down each bolded letter at the top of a plain sheet of paper. "They seem threatening enough to be accurate."

Valor plucked Staccato off the table and set the cat on his shoulder. "I know you're not the killer, Bish."

"I know you know." Bishan couldn't keep the slight sharpness out of his voice. He'd never doubted Valor's belief in him.

Valor stretched a hand out to rest on Bishan's shoulder. "I was agreeing."

"Oh." He deflated slightly. Non-autistics tended to agree by repeating what had been said, something he always found a bit confusing. "Of course."

Distracting himself with their puzzle, Bishan started to separate letters out into words. He went through almost ten versions with no success. Valor didn't press him to continue the conversation; he never did, which was something Bishan had always appreciated about his boyfriend.

"Let's assume sh or shh is going to be at the start of all of these." Bishan had separated the remaining unsolved programs and put the bolded ones at the top of individual sheets of paper. "If we go from there, it removes at least two to three of the letters straight away."

"We've been at this for ages. Why don't you take a break?" Valor stretched his arms over his head and yawned widely. "Let's go for a walk."

"It's been an hour. An hour isn't ages." He glanced briefly at the clock over the hob then back to his puzzle. He liked puzzles, but it felt wrong to enjoy this when it came from such an awful act of violence. "What if someone else dies?"

Valor visibly winced before shifting his chair around so he could wrap his arm around Bishan. "It won't be our fault. We're not the one with the gun."

"Cinnamon."

"You know what I meant."

Bishan had come out of jail with a mission: ensuring he didn't get dragged back. To him, it meant solving the crime, if the detectives couldn't do it themselves. "I can do this."

"Nina's got friends working on them as well. You going for a walk won't be the end of the world." Valor usually didn't want to go for walks in the morning. "What? Why are you frowning at me?"

"I don't understand why you want to walk so desperately." Bishan crossed his arms, twisting so the uneasiness at staring into Valor's face faded away. Eye contact always made him incredibly uncomfortable. "We can go later."

"You should be outside more."

"But why?" Bishan had never been much of an outdoorsy type of person. He enjoyed rambles in the woods on occasion, but not a walk through the village. Too many people tended to want to stop them for a chat. "Val?"

"Can we, please?"

"But why?" Bishan found it very difficult to force himself to do anything without understanding the reason.

Valor ran his fingers roughly through his already messy ginger hair, a sign Bishan had come to recognise as his boyfriend being unsure. "I keep seeing you locked up in a room without a window, and it makes me so sodding angry."

"It had windows." He noticed Valor appeared to truly be struggling and decided it didn't matter if he didn't entirely understand why. "Let's go for a walk."

Maybe I'll stop feeling so strange.

The uneasiness in the pit of his stomach hadn't gone away since they'd found a body in the garden over a month ago. Being home improved the feeling slightly. Bishan continued to struggle with it, though.

Dealing with emotions had never been his strong suit. It was hard to process them when first he had to identify them. Valor tried to help, but it usually only muddled it all up even further.

"Bish?" Valor stood by the door with his jacket already on. "Would you rather stay?"

Yes.

"Yes, but if I do it'll make leaving harder the next time." Bishan slowly got to his feet. He took a moment to run a comb through his silky black hair to straighten it a bit. They didn't both need to appear as if they'd only recently rolled out of bed. "Life can't be lived inside the cottage."

"Well, it can, but it'll be lonely. Is that another Barnaby-ism?" Valor teased.

"Maybe." Bishan enjoyed how his dad often coined what he called pearls of wisdom. "It's true, though."

"So, walk?" Valor prompted after Bishan had spent almost a full three minutes shuffling papers around, getting his jacket on, and finding shoes. "And yes, you have to wear trainers."

Bishan frequently went through a phase where he loathed wearing shoes; he felt like his toes were suffocating. In the summer, he almost never wore them. Valor had gotten quite stern about him putting something on his feet during colder months.

I only almost had frostbite one time.

They wandered down the lane to the walking path that led down to the pond. The police had already cleared the area. Valor had gone down once already to pay his respects to Mr Clarke.

Grief was strange.

Bishan had never been comfortable with it. He'd cried when Mr Clarke died, but he didn't want to attend the funeral. What was the point?

Mr Clarke wouldn't mind one way or the other. Funerals, as far as Bishan understood, meant more to the living. He wanted to find another way to demonstrate his admiration for their former housemaster.

Before allowing Bishan to attend the prestigious Harrow School, his parents had required more of him than just the multiple scholarships for music, maths, science, and English that he'd earned. They'd insisted on speaking at length with whoever would be the master of his boarding house. His father, in particular, had wanted to ensure they understood Bishan responded and approached life differently from the other boys.

Mr Clarke had been the perfect housemaster. He'd actively discouraged bullying of any sort while encouraging the boys to grow into strong individuals. Bishan had flourished at Harrow, and most of it came down to his time at West Acre Boarding House.

Going to a funeral didn't feel an adequate way to express his appreciation for what Mr Clarke had gifted him—a safe environment to grow, learn, and develop as a young autistic

Anglo-Indian man. It wasn't enough. Bishan wanted to do something more.

Even if it is only for myself as he's not actually around to see it.

"Do you think Mrs Clarke would mind if we had a dinner to celebrate Mr Clarke's life?" Bishan picked up a stone to skip across the pond. He dropped it in his pocket and continued down the path. "Something for us old boys who remember him?"

Harrow had numerous odd traditions. Bishan had enjoyed the structure of it. He'd fit in far better than anyone had expected, and even now, thirteen-plus years later, he missed some aspects of school.

"Why would she mind?"

"Allistics can be weird." Bishan shrugged. As much as non-autistics didn't understand him, he rarely grasped their thought processes either. "I know. We should have a Harrow football game in his honour. It was one of Mr Clarke's favourite things."

And maybe the murderer will show up.

They always do on Poirot, *just to see what's being said.*

"It's a brilliant idea." Valor held his hand out, waiting as always until Bishan decided if he wanted to hold it. "I'll start making calls to set it up when we get to the shop."

Bishan reached out to link his fingers with Valor's. He loved watching Valor's hazel eyes light up when they held hands. "It's a good idea? Really?"

"Promise."

"Good." Bishan darted forward to grab another flat stone to skip across the pond. He frowned at the sight of a loose bit of police caution tape stuck to a branch; it reminded him of why Mr Clarke had died. "Why does someone hate us so much? What did we do?"

It had been the thought going through Bishan's mind constantly. They hadn't been angels in school, particularly

Valor, but they'd never hurt anyone. He didn't get what drove a person to commit such evil acts.

And against Mr Clarke of all people. He'd been the best of men. The greatest housemaster in the entire school. No one had done more for the boys in his house. His death seemed so incredibly pointless.

Not that any of the other murders had been deserved.

"Nothing. You certainly didn't do any damn thing at all. Neither did Mr Clarke." Valor lifted their hands to brush a kiss against Bishan's. "Evil people do evil things. I'm sure whoever it is will have some twisted reasoning, but it doesn't make it true."

"I don't understand."

"Neither do I, really." Valor shook his head. "Let's skip some stones, then we can plan to honour Mr Clarke in a truly Harrovian fashion."

CHAPTER 2

Bishan loved Valor.

He loved his mum, his dad, Sunesh, and Reva.

He adored Wilfred and Lottie, who had once worked at Valor's family estate.

But sometimes Bishan preferred having the cottage to himself. In the three days since his release, they hadn't gotten much time alone. He hadn't.

And he was desperate for it.

With Valor and Hugh attending Mr Clarke's funeral that afternoon, Bishan had cried off to enjoy some peace and quiet on his own. His family were otherwise occupied with work. He felt for the first time that he could actually breathe.

Once Mrs Harris had gone on her daily jaunt into the village, Bishan made his way into the garden. He'd put his Brahms, Mozart, and Beethoven piano playlist on loud enough to hear it outside. Staccato explored the taller grasses along the edge while he painted and sipped tea.

In the peace of the garden, Bishan thought about Mr Clarke. He'd penned a letter with all his memories and how much the man had meant. Valor had promised to read it out at the service.

"Don't stalk frogs. You might get warts." Bishan leaned around his canvas and easel to watch Staccato slinking through a patch of flowers. "I warned you."

The watercolour began as a study of their garden and Staccato—one of his favourite subjects. It grew darker with each deft movement of his brush. Shadows filled in spots with deeper reds than he usually used.

His pent-up fears from his time in jail poured over into the painting. Bishan wanted to rip it apart or set it on fire. He simply sat and stared at the partially finished canvas.

Part of the reason Bishan had avoided unloading his emotions into music had been his fear of breaking an instrument. He'd never once struck out at another person in the midst of a meltdown. But at times, he'd bashed away at the keys of a piano when the world became impossible for him to process.

"Thought they'd locked you up."

Bishan jolted so sharply he upended his pot of paint-mucked brushes and water off the little portable table next to his chair. *Bother.* "Mrs Harris. Hello."

"I thought they locked you up," she repeated unnecessarily.

Not a question, a statement.

How do I respond to that?

Bishan focused on picking up the pot and brushes. He nudged Staccato away from the watery paint on the stones at his feet. "I'm not locked up now."

"So I see." Mrs Harris whacked her cane against the fence, causing him to flinch at the sound. "What's the racket you've got playing now?"

Bishan listened for a moment before recognising one of

his favourite pieces. "Mozart's Piano Concerto in A Minor. The Vienna State Opera Orchestra version."

"Not natural. How do you know from listening?"

"How?" He frowned at her in complete confusion. "I've studied music since I was four or five. It's quite calming. You should try it. I'm going inside now."

Leaving his canvas to dry, Bishan picked up Staccato to head into the cottage. He'd learned from experience not to engage Mrs Harris in conversation. Valor handled her far better; Bishan didn't really understand the point most of the time.

"You have to read between the lines, Bish" was what Valor always told him. Bishan didn't know how to do that. Why did words and sentences need double meanings?

Allistics are so confusing.

Setting the brushes and pot into the sink to rinse, Bishan switched off the music to avoid Mrs Harris deciding to come over to complain about it again. His phone beeped with a note from Valor to remember to eat lunch. He sometimes got distracted and forgot about food.

And water.

And sleep.

They hadn't restocked his cereal yet. Bishan didn't feel up to making something or going out. He stood in the kitchen, staring at the refrigerator in the hopes a meal might spontaneously appear.

It didn't.

Pity.

It took a frustratingly significant amount of effort to force himself into action. Bishan found a tin of spaghetti rings in one of the cabinets. He grabbed a spoon and proceeded to eat it straight out of the can.

He'd gotten halfway through the meal, which reminded

him of their university days, when the doorbell sounded. "Sodding people at the sodding door. Sod it all."

Sod. Sod. Sod.

Sod was one of his favourite words. Bishan had gone through a phase when it had been every other word. Valor accused him of trying to get away with cursing in front of his mum without getting in trouble.

It hadn't worked.

"You."

Bishan found himself face-to-face with one of his least favourite human beings in the entire world: Bertram Scott, the younger, Valor's older brother. "Yes?"

"I'm not here to speak to you." He scowled at Bishan, who stared pointedly at his nose for the appearance of eye contact. "Where is Valor?"

"Not here. Not interested in speaking with you." Bishan gripped the door handle firmly. "Go away now."

"Where is my brother?"

Bishan peered down at the foot blocking the door from closing. He opened it further then slammed it onto Bertram. "Not here."

Leaving Bertram to whinge about his broken foot that wasn't actually broken, Bishan calmly closed the door on his complaining. He'd found both the heir and Bertram Scott, the elder, Earl of nothing that mattered, to be feeble men. Their treatment of Valor proved it in his mind.

What kind of family completely abandoned one of their own?

Not a real one.

In their schooldays, Valor always returned from breaks a shadow of himself. It often took days for him to become his usual gregarious and confident self. The Scott family had a way of smothering his personality.

To Bishan, it seemed an utterly unforgivable sin. His family had gone out of their way to allow him to flourish in whatever way he wanted. He'd never understand how Valor's family hadn't been the same.

The doorbell rang again twenty minutes later. Bishan opened it to find Bertram and Detective Spurling, both glaring at each other. He lifted Staccato up into his arms to stop him from running out of the cottage and waited for the two men to realise the door was open.

"I brought you fish and double-fried chips." Spurling held up the bag in his hand. "Lottie thought you might want something, and I wanted to talk with you about the puzzles."

"What about my injury?" Bertram seemed outraged.

Spurling glanced down briefly at the scuffed-up shoe being held out toward him. "How did you injure it?"

"He slammed the door on me." Bertram seemed to realise at the last second how it sounded to the detective. "If you'd tell Valor I visited."

Bishan watched the spoiled, arrogant man stalk toward his Bentley. He had no intentions of mentioning his visit to Valor. "I don't like him."

"Not sure anyone does." Spurling held the bag up for the second time. "Do you know what my nan will do to me if I don't deliver this to you?"

"No. What?" Bishan asked seriously.

Spurling stared at him.

"Oh, a joke." Bishan kicked himself mentally for not catching it. He always missed when people were being facetious. Valor had been trying to help him get better at it. "What's wrong with the puzzles?"

After debating with himself, Bishan took the food then motioned for Spurling to follow him. They sat at the kitchen table. He noshed on the chips, listening to the difficulties the police had with deciphering what the solved riddles actually meant.

"Valor mentioned you were brilliant with word puzzles." Spurling ate from his own packet of food. "Have you made any progress with the most recent anagrams?"

"It's not an ana—" Bishan shoved a chip into his mouth to stop himself from repeating the argument he'd had four times in the last couple of days. "Not yet. My brain doesn't want to focus on it."

And it didn't.

He'd tried for hours.

"Give it time." Spurling unintentionally echoed Valor's thoughts on the matter. "How are you doing?"

"I don't know." Bishan had moved over to the fridge to find the ketchup, which he preferred cold to warm. He wanted Spurling to leave but didn't know how to ask him without being rude. "Is that all you wanted?"

Is that rude? It is rude. Damn it. I'm supposed to be getting the hang of casual conversation.

Spurling coughed through the bite of fish he'd inhaled. "Am I making you uncomfortable?"

"Yes," Bishan said bluntly. He groaned in embarrassment a moment later when Staccato leapt up onto Spurling's shoulder. "I'm so sorry. He likes you, though. He doesn't like everyone."

"Well, I'm glad someone is enjoying my uninvited presence." Spurling petted Staccato awkwardly before setting him down on the floor. "I'll get out of your hair."

"You're not in it." Bishan ran his fingers through his dark hair; it needed to be cut soon as it hung too far down into his eyes. "Why do you need to get out of it?"

"Figuratively speaking," Spurling continued without commenting on Bishan's remark. "Enjoy the chips. Let me know if you figure the puzzles out, all right?"

"Bye." Bishan dismissed the detective completely. He did follow him to the door to lock it, staring at the knob with a frown. "Not opening you again until Val's home."

CHAPTER 3

Morning coffee and toast had always been one of Bishan's favourite routines with Valor. They sat in the garden sometimes—or inside if Mrs Harris had woken up early. He read the music and art news for both of them while Valor read the sports, finance, and depressing current events.

Occasionally, if Valor happened to be in a particularly silly mood, they read them out loud together. Bishan didn't get the point, but it made Valor laugh. He liked that sound. A lot.

"Bish?"

Bishan lifted his eyes up from perusing a review of a recent symphony performance. "More toast."

"Not my question." Valor grabbed the toast rack to slide it closer to him. "As Harrow won't let us borrow one of their fields for a football match, how about we sing house songs instead? We can rent out a hall or conference room at a hotel close to us."

"For Mr Clarke?"

"Just think about it." Valor haphazardly shoved the loose newspaper pages together. "Are you coming into the shop with me? I've got to do the monthly books before Wilfred loses his patience with me."

Despite over a week having passed since his release, many of the Grasmere villagers had yet to find something else to gossip about. Bishan hadn't handled the whispers and stares well. He hated the extra attention.

He also knew spending another day hiding from them would only heighten the rumours. "Face it head-on" had been his father's advice. His mum had wanted him to come home to visit with them for a few weeks.

They both meant well.

How do I face head-on people who thought me capable of murder?

How can I show courage if I run home to Mum the moment I'm free?

Even if I want to do it.

"You pick the songs; I'll sort out when and where." Valor drew him out of his thoughts. He'd already carried the plates and cups over to the sink. "So? You coming with me?"

No.

"Yes." Bishan slowly stood up, dislodging Staccato from his shoulder. "I need a minute to change."

A minute turned into ten. Bishan sat on the corner of the bed, staring at the open wardrobe. He'd disrobed quickly but now struggled to find the gumption to pull on the jeans in his hand.

Why is this so hard?

I pulled my pyjamas off easily enough.

"Staying home doesn't make you weak, Bish." Valor leaned against the bedroom doorframe. "Be kind to yourself while you recover."

"It's not as though I were physically harmed. It's all in my head." Bishan picked at a loose thread on the seam of his jeans.

"And? I'd wager all the stuff going on in your head can be

as exhausting as running a marathon with a hangover." Valor stayed by the door but clearly wanted to offer his support. "Want a hug?"

Bishan patted the edge of the bed. He tilted his head to rest against Valor's shoulder once he'd sat beside him. "I'm not ready to deal with half the village that'll pack into the shop when they realise I'm there."

"Then don't."

Just like that.

It never ceased to amaze Bishan how cavalierly Valor handled certain aspects of being an adult. Where others worried about manners, Valor tended to shrug it all off, likely a result of snubbing his nose at his family heritage. He usually evoked a "why bother" sort of attitude.

"Stay home, watch *Poirot*, spoil Staccato, and solve this riddle." Valor plucked the copy of one of the programs off the nearby nightstand. "How about I bring lunch home once I've finished the accounting?"

"You don't mind?"

Valor looped his arm around Bishan's shoulders, easing him into a hug and pressing a gentle kiss to his lips. "Have I ever minded?"

"A couple of times," Bishan answered honestly.

"Rhetorical question, love." Valor chuckled before dropping another kiss on his lips. "Rhetorical. Question."

Oh.

Bishan lifted a hand up to stop Valor from coming in for a third kiss. He always felt a bit embarrassed by how he couldn't resist answering questions, even rhetorical ones. "Go away now."

"I'll text you when I'm getting lunch." Valor left with one last squeeze of his shoulders. "Love you, Bish."

Love you too.

For almost an hour, Bishan sat with the jeans in his

hands. He finally dragged himself off the bed to get dressed. Tossing the denim aside, he went for softer pyjama bottoms and an old T-shirt to help him relax even further.

You can do this. It's only a temporary exhaustion. You know it gets better.

By ten in the morning, Bishan had pep-talked himself into picking up his work on solving their puzzle. None of them believed the murderer was finished. They had to stop them before another body turned up.

They'd lost enough friends.

"I've got it," Bishan muttered to himself an hour later.

Several empty cups surrounded his many discarded sheets. Bishan grabbed a fresh piece of paper. He quickly transcribed down his latest, and most plausible, attempt.

Shh. Another and another and another and another. Who's next? Who will never follow up? Tick-Tock.

Bishan sent a text of it to both Valor and Detective Spurling, as they'd both likely want to discuss it with him. He repeated the phrasing in his head over and over, convinced it sounded right. "Why 'shh'? Is he trying to shush us? Is it his initials?"

A meow from Staccato broke Bishan out of his conversation with himself. He gathered up the dishes and let the cat into the garden, pausing to glare at the new CCTV cameras. They made him feel exposed in his own cottage.

And they'd be gone the minute the murderer had been captured.

He hated them almost as much as he hated cotton wool.

Almost.

Lunch arrived with Valor and Detective Inspector Spurling. Valor had texted first to ensure Bishan didn't mind. He liked the man who'd gone out of his way to make him comfortable under challenging circumstances.

"Twice-fried chips, fish, sticky toffee pudding with extra

sticky." Valor grinned as Bishan sent him a withering glare. "What else would you call a pudding with additional sauce on it?"

Bishan had to laugh with Valor. He grabbed plates for the three of them while Spurling helped to pull the food out of the bags. "I solved one of the riddles."

"And?" Spurling paused while pouring malt vinegar over his chips.

"It's not over." Bishan knew they'd all assumed it wasn't, but a chill still went up his spine. He toyed with one of his chips, suddenly not very hungry. "Who did we know heavily into drama and music at school?"

"All of us?" Valor handed Bishan several napkins.

He had a point. Their boarding house had always been known for a keen interest in music and drama. They took great pride in achievements in those areas.

"What about someone who didn't do so well?" Spurling interjected. "Well-adjusted individuals don't usually begin killing their classmates and teachers over a decade after leaving school."

"Fair point." Valor offered a bit of his fish to Staccato, who'd perched on his shoulder. "What about the 'shh'?"

"It's been in all three of them." Bishan switched to the page where he'd written the solved cyphers one on top of the other for easier comparison. "Not too far of a stretch to believe the fourth will start the same way."

"Shh or sh?" Valor tapped the odd one out. "Maybe the computer got it wrong, or we missed a bolded letter in the program?"

"Did we know anyone with those initials?" Bishan tried to run them through all the names he could remember from their Harrow days. He did recall something else it might fit. "Matron used to shush us for daily bill with 'shh.'"

"Bill?" Spurling frowned at him in confusion.

"Harrow-speak for registration. The roll-call we had in our boarding house three times a day," Bishan clarified. He turned his attention to his already cooling fish. "Either we've got a killer amongst the old boys, or the murderer is using Harrow traditions to throw the police off the scent."

Valor paused in the process of feeding Staccato. "A family member?"

"Or someone who hates what they see as tired old traditions?" Spurling offered his own thoughts. "None of this is really helping to eliminate suspects."

Bishan held the sheet of cyphers out to the detective. "It's one less mystery to solve."

CHAPTER 4

"I think *Poirot* lies." Bishan sat in the garden with Valor, Reva, and a few of their friends who'd come over to enjoy a bit of summer sun. They'd managed to slide into June without a peep from their killer; the police had also failed to make any real progress in their investigation into the three murders. "He solves all his mysteries in an hour; less than, actually."

He'd watched every single episode of *Poirot* in the past few months. None of it provided any useful sort of advice. It had soured him a little on his favourite detective.

Only a little.

I'll still watch him.

"*Poirot* is fictional." Reva flicked a blade of grass for Staccato to chase after. "It's easy to solve crimes when the author creates both the hero and the villain. Don't they say life is stranger than fiction? It makes sense this would be harder to solve than a murder mystery on the telly. Your Belgian bloke isn't that brilliant."

"Sacrilege." Valor tilted his head from where he'd stretched out to sunbathe. "Poirot is a genius."

"Still fictional," Nina added. She'd stopped by Daniel and Cora's again. "And I can't take anyone seriously with that moustache."

"Still brilliant." Bishan observed everyone from his quiet corner of the garden with a large canvas precariously perched on his easel to hide behind. It had been Valor's idea to help him cope with the influx of friends, all gathered to enjoy the rare spate of sunshine. "Why haven't the police solved it?"

"How? With what evidence? No fingerprints? No blood or hair or fibres? They've nothing to go on since it's been proven your prints were planted," Hugh answered. "Give 'em time, Lord Bryon. Crime isn't always solved quickly by flashy detectives."

"I don't write poetry anymore." Bishan returned to hiding behind the canvas. "And Spurling's a bit flashy."

"Don't tell him." Hugh laughed.

Leaving the others to their amusement, Bishan focused on his painting. He'd started to work on a portrait of Mr Clarke from his memories of the man at West Acre. It would be a lovely gift for his wife, hopefully, a pleasant surprise amidst all the tragedy.

Maybe she won't think too badly of us Harrovians.

"Bish?"

He peered down to find Valor had shifted his towel to stretch out beside him. "What?"

"You all right? Ready for them to leave?"

"I'm fine."

Valor rested his head on Bishan's bare foot, allowing the shadow from the canvas to shade his face. "On a scale of blush to tomato, how red have I gotten?"

"What's worse than a tomato?" Reva teased.

The comforting weight of Valor settled Bishan. He'd always found Valor helped ease some of his anxiety when it hadn't tipped over into overload. It was a closeness and a trust that he'd never found in any other relationship, not even with his beloved family.

"Weren't you all heading out for supper at some point?" Valor sat up after dozing for another hour. "Well?"

"It's three in the afternoon," Nina complained.

"Party is over." Hugh hustled the others out of the garden. "I'll text you later."

There was grumbling.

There was always grumbling. Bishan had noticed his friends and family often complained when Valor stepped in to kick them out of the cottage. He didn't think they meant to make him feel guilty, but they did.

Valor rolled over onto his back to peer up at Bishan. "Quiet evening in or a calm night out?"

"What's a calm night out?" He slowly started to pack up his paints and brushes.

"Picnic basket, books, Staccato, and watching the sunset over Loughrigg Fell. It's only twelve minutes. There's that one spot we can look over the lake that no one else visits." Valor sat up and laughed when their cat immediately leapt up on his shoulder. "Quiet evening in involves the same food, reading material, company, but telly instead of the vast outdoors."

"Is the lake the vast outdoors?"

"It's outside. And it's not tiny." Valor shrugged. "Well?"

Fear had kept Bishan from straying away from their cottage. It had become a massive struggle to go to the shops or to see his parents even though they lived only a short drive away in Windermere. He'd barely set foot in the Ginger's Bread, the biscuit shop Valor had started.

"Outside." Bishan had to force the words out. "Camera or sketching?"

"Cameras." Valor smiled brightly at him, and it made Bishan feel better. "We can compare our photos later.

When was the last time we went on a photography date?"

Ages.

Everything seemed ages ago. Bishan enjoyed photography because it put distance between the world and himself. Valor had discovered a talent for it at Harrow; some of their early dates had been brief adventures around the Lake District, usually at odd times to reduce the risk of running into throngs of people.

They cleaned up from their earlier guests, packed up sandwiches and biscuits, along with a thermos of tea, and drove the twelve minutes toward Ambleside. It provided the perfect place to park and walk up the hill overlooking the lake. Bishan kept Staccato on an extended leash to allow him to chase after butterflies and bugs.

Bishan spread out a blanket and sat on it, tugging Staccato closer. "Hungry?"

"Starved." Valor fell onto the blanket beside him, sneaking a bite out of Bishan's sandwich. "Have you ever thought about marrying?"

"No." Bishan continued to eat his sandwich, biting in a specific sequence. "Why?"

"No reason."

"Okay." He shrugged. "You know the last word puzzle from the killer?"

"The anagram?"

"Not. An. Anagram." Bishan glared at Valor, who grinned. "The incredibly long one that I've been struggling with?"

"Yes?"

"What if it's a quote or passage of something?" Bishan had been trying to figure out what the large sequence of letters could mean. "Could Nina's computer thing compare the letters specifically to plays, books, and poems? Maybe plays and songs specifically, given how all the programs were from those types of events."

"You think that's a hint?"

"Four programs—all music or drama related. It's not a coincidence." Bishan had spent weeks trying to solve the last of their riddles. "I don't think the puzzles are for the sole purpose of messing with us. It's not only about terror. It's a message. They have something to say."

And Bishan couldn't help wondering what the killer would do to get them to understand.

As the sun dipped down, uneasiness built within Bishan, making him increasingly restless. They packed up and returned to their little Fiat as darkness descended on the lake, intent on getting home quickly.

"Bish."

Bishan jolted up from where he'd been trying out breathing exercises to calm his mind down. His mum and sister swore meditation helped—he'd yet to find it accomplished anything. "What's wrong?"

"Did you hear that?" Valor had turned down the music and opened his window. "I thought I heard something."

Twisting around, Bishan tried to listen for anything out of the ordinary. All he heard was the rushing of the wind through the open window. Valor sped up to go around a van going well below the speed limit.

"Could you be more specific? What kind of something?" Bishan grabbed at Staccato, who had slipped out of his carrier. He didn't like having him loose in the vehicle. "Houdini cat. How does he always manage to sneak—"

A violent crunch interrupted Bishan, jolting the vehicle as they flew around a corner. The Fiat veered sharply then careened off the road. They rammed a straight stone wall, ricocheted down an embankment, and landed with a thud against a tree.

Bishan came to, hanging against the seat belt slightly with his arms still clutching Staccato to his chest. "Val? Valor?"

Blinking through the sharp pain in his head, Bishan found his senses wholly assaulted. Blood dripped down his face, making him want to scratch it. Staccato meowed frantically in time with the car's horn while in the distance he heard not only sirens but the lapping of the waves. They'd crashed near the lake.

"Valor?" Bishan tried for a second time to get his attention. He tried twisting his head to see, but his neck hurt too much. "*Val.*"

"It's all right, lad. I've called the ambulance. You'll be fine. Looks like your tyre might've popped off." A voice broke through all his panicked thoughts. "Can you hear me?"

He wanted to say yes.

He did, but his mind refused to cooperate with him and barely managed to get out one word past the impending shutdown. "Valor?"

CHAPTER 5

"Val?" Bishan shot up, only to collapse against the pillows behind him with a pained groan. He jumped again in surprise when a hand clasped his tightly. "Mum?"

"Oh, *pyaare bete.*" She shifted her chair closer, resting her cheek against his hand still clutched in hers. "My sweet boy."

"*Mum.*" Bishan groaned in embarrassment. "Mum. What's happened?"

"You had an accident—" She stopped when his father scoffed sharply. "Well, either way, your little Fiat went off the road into a wall and a tree."

"Staccato?" He didn't quite remember the accident, but a hazy vision of their cat sneaking out of his carrier teased at his memory. "Val? Oh, gods. Is Valor all right? Where is he?"

His mum turned a bit uneasily toward his dad, who stepped forward from where he'd been standing by the wall. "You stay right here. I'll go tell the doctor you're awake."

Bishan watched, bewildered and concerned when his mum bolted from the room. "He's not dead, is he? What's going on?"

Barnaby took the seat his wife had vacated and placed his own hand over Bishan's. "Staccato is perfectly fine. He's being spoiled rotten by your sister."

"And Val?"

"We don't know."

"How can you not know?" Bishan hated the slight trembling in his voice. "Where is he?"

"Calm, son. Stay calm." His dad patted his hand gently. "His parents showed up not long after you arrived at the hospital. They've refused to speak with us, and the doctors can't share anything with us. Hugh managed to find out a bit from the local detective inspector. Valor hasn't woken up yet. They don't know if he's suffered brain damage, but he's broken his nose from smashing into the airbag. We don't know about any of his other injuries."

"He'll hate his parents being here." Bishan had no doubts the second Valor woke up, he'd be screaming bloody murder at the Scott family being allowed to control any part of his recovery. "Was it an accident?"

"I...." His dad trailed off and seemed to be struggling with something. "Detective Inspector Spurling claims someone removed a few of the lug nuts on one of your tyres. It caused the tyre to fold under the strain and break off. You're both incredibly lucky you didn't go into the lake."

Bishan gathered his arms around himself with some difficulty from the various wires attached to him. He couldn't stop his body from shaking, and the roaring in his ears sounded like the engine of a train. "Can I go home now?"

"Not quite yet, Bish." His dad sounded completely apologetic. He picked up a bag from a nearby chair, dug into it, and a moment later handed him a stuffed bear in a West Acre shirt. "I've got your Rubik's here as well."

Taking his old bear, Bishan appreciated his father backing

off to allow him space to breathe and to process everything. He'd used both the bear and the Rubik's cube as ways to stim during times of extreme stress for years. The familiarity of it helped him to ease the chaotic whirling of his mind.

When his mum returned with two doctors, Bishan felt slightly more in control. He refused to be embarrassed about cuddling a stuffed animal. His fingers drew random geometric shapes into the soft fur while he listened to the list of injuries.

It was far shorter than Bishan had thought. Bruised, banged up, and concussed. By some miracle, he'd managed to avoid breaking or fracturing any bones. The doctors politely sidestepped his inquiry into Valor's current state.

Bishan frowned at the man and woman in white coats. "We arrived together. We've been together since our Harrow days. We're practically married."

"But you're not, and hospital policy dictates—"

"Go away." Bishan sharply cut off the doctor. He didn't quite know what the tone of the man's voice had been, but he didn't think it was positive. "I want to go home."

With distinctly ill humour, Bishan endured being checked over by the doctors. He logically understood Valor's family had tied the hospital's hands on the matter. It didn't mean he had to like it.

Or them.

"Here, Bishi." Reva offered him the reprieve of an iPod and headphones. "I put all your favourites on it. Sunesh went to get you chips—not sure the doctor will approve, but who cares. Staccato's staying with Lottie and Wilfred. Lottie made her extra-special scones that you love. I've got them hidden in my bag for you."

Latching on to the headphones, Bishan let himself sink into the familiar strains of a Mozart concerto. The ringing in his ears faded slowly, along with the trembling in his hands. He tuned everyone out, turning the volume up to keep the hospital sounds from interrupting his peace.

Once the doctors disappeared, Reva produced the promised scones—cherry and chocolate along with a cheddar one. He nibbled on them, careful of his lingering headache. His mum handed him a cup of her special tea blend that she'd brought from home in a thermos.

Music, nibbles, and tea.

Bishan went through thirty minutes of Mozart before feeling ready to face conversation again. His family had been whispering to themselves, wanting to stay close without disturbing him. "Is Hugh here?"

Hugh was indeed at the hospital and had been waiting outside for a while. He rushed in when Reva went to retrieve him. "Hello, Lord Bryon, good to see you awake."

"Valor?"

Hugh walked over to stand beside the bed. "Yes, hello, Hugh. It's lovely to see you. How've you been? I'm so sorry for worrying you."

"Why are you talking to yourself?" Bishan frowned at him in confusion.

"Never mind." Hugh laughed, though Bishan continued to stare at him. "The Scotts don't quite like me either because of how I've supported you and Val. I did manage to find out he's coming around as well. It wouldn't surprise me a bit if we heard him causing a fuss the second he's fully aware."

A fuss turned out to be an understatement.

Within an hour of waking, Valor had kicked his blood relatives out of the hospital. He'd managed to get them into a double room by claiming his recovery would rapidly increase if they were together. Bishan didn't know how anyone had believed that, but it didn't matter.

They were together.

A steady stream of visitors kept the two from enjoying a moment to themselves. Bishan found it hard to be satisfied with only being able to stretch his arm across the small gap between their beds to hold hands. A simple touch, but enough to assure him Valor hadn't died.

Of the two of them, Valor had undoubtedly come out the worst. His face was completely bruised up to match his broken nose. He'd suffered a hairline fracture on his right arm as well as a concussion.

They'd been lucky.

Incredibly lucky.

On the whole, Bishan couldn't recall the accident. He remembered their date by the lake. Bits and pieces filtered through the hazy moments, but nothing he could hold on to when Spurling came in and asked about it.

"Anything at all? Did you see a vehicle near yours? Someone hanging about?" Spurling pressed both of them for information. "There are no cameras where you parked the Fiat, so we've no footage of anyone in the area."

"My memory isn't any clearer than Bish's. Less so, actually. My father mentioned someone stopped to help us. Did they see anything?" Valor asked.

Spurling flipped through his notes. "Nothing pertinent. Several cars went by before the ambulance arrived. None of them stood out for any reason. We're hoping to find prints on the tyre itself—if the crash didn't make it impossible."

"Comforting." Valor rested his head against the pillow with a tired groan. "On another note, who on earth decided to allow my bloody parents to control anything in the hospital?"

"They're the only ones with the right." Hugh spoke from his corner of the room. "I tried. Sunny over there tried. They weren't interested in hearing from any of us. You've met your family. This shouldn't be a surprise."

"I'm surprised they showed up." Valor shook his head then immediately grunted in obvious pain. "In fact, how'd they even know?"

"Your brother contacted them, according to one of the nurses," Sunesh answered, before returning to his whispered conversation with his father.

With a weary sigh, Bishan settled tiredly against his pillows. They hadn't solved anything, and his head still hurt a little. He wanted them all to leave.

As always, Valor seemed able to read his mind. He began to complain of a massive headache. Their friends and family trailed out, leaving them to the relative quiet of the hospital room.

Valor twisted over on his uninjured side. "How are you really doing?"

"Hate hospitals. Smells weird in here—too clean. The beeping is incessant. The lighting is dreadful." Bishan twisted his Rubik's cube absently. "My head and neck hurt. I thought you died. No dying. Okay?"

"No dying sounds brilliant." Valor held his arm out toward Bishan, who eyed it before deciding to hold hands again. "Bish? Do you think it's odd my brother knew about the crash so soon? How? My family's in London. The drive isn't a short one. They hate making it. How'd he get in contact with my parents so quickly?"

"I don't know." Bishan closed his eyes against the oddly bright lights in the room. He couldn't wait until they were safely in their cottage. "Rest now. Questions later."

"All right." Valor squeezed his fingers before releasing his hand.

"Hate these sheets. They're scratchy." Bishan wanted to

twist around on the bed, but his body hurt enough to avoid it. "We almost died."

"I know."

"Val?" Bishan opened his eyes to meet Valor's gaze briefly. "Love you."

"I love you too." Valor smiled at him slightly. "Rest, Bish."

With strict orders from the doctor to rest, Bishan and Valor were sent home after being observed in the hospital for two additional days. They hadn't wanted to leave each other. The doctors had eventually agreed to allow them to go once their CT scans came back clear.

Of the two of them, Valor had it the worst. Bishan had sore, achy muscles and a diminishing headache. His recovery would be days—not weeks or months like Valor with his broken nose and hairline fracture.

They sat on their couch, warm and grumpy. The weather had turned hot. Bishan found it hard to find the energy to do more than lean against Valor to nap their way through the day.

"What kind of car do you want?" Valor broke the silence, waking Bishan from his doze. "Considering the Fiat was totalled. Insurance should cover the purchase—mostly. Do you want the exact same one or something different?"

"Small. Orange."

"That's our cat," Valor teased.

Bishan sat up slowly, scowling at Valor. "I like the Fiat."

"How about a—"

"I like the Fiat," Bishan interrupted. "They have the new 500x Cross. How about one of those?"

"I'm sensing we're not jumping to a new maker." Valor grabbed his laptop from the coffee table. They'd put everything they needed within easy reach to avoid moving. "How about I send an email to the place we got the last one? Yeah? See if they have one already in stock."

"Are you scared?" Bishan felt uneasiness eating away at him. He didn't quite know what it was or how to deal with it. "My stomach feels weird."

Valor twisted toward him, grunting in pain. "Is it the new car? Or the crash?"

Bishan shrugged.

He didn't know. They'd avoided talking about the crash. *It's not an accident when someone tries to kill you.* All his routines had been completely ruined in the past few months; he wanted normalcy in their lives.

"We can wait for a new car until this is resolved. Not like either of us has anywhere to go. I'm sure we'll have no end of people ready to give us a lift or bring things if we need them." Valor set his laptop on the table and allowed his uninjured hand to rest on the cushion. He smiled when Bishan stretched his own out to take it. "It's normal to be afraid, Bish. None of this situation is all right. We've a sick, twisted person out there who is trying to hurt us."

"But why?"

Valor appeared briefly at a loss for words. "I've no idea. I can't wrap my mind around someone doing such terrible things to innocent people. Mr Clarke certainly hadn't ever done anything to deserve being left in a pond. It's wicked. Evil."

Bishan tried to keep his body from tensing up. He already

hurt from the violence of the crash; no need to exacerbate the situation. "How do we stop them?"

"The detectives...." He trailed off with a shake of his head. "They'd done a rotten job thus far."

"Your brother." Bishan didn't quite know how to bring up his wariness about Bertie. "How did he know about the accident so quickly?"

"Something I intend to find out." Valor pulled his phone out of his pocket. "Time to focus on the weakest link—my baby sister."

Penelope Scott had always been a mystery to Bishan, more so than the rest of the stuck-up bunch. She occasionally showed the briefest glimpses of care toward Valor, then drew back into the family fold. He wondered if it would be yet another dead end.

He didn't understand any of them. They'd been cruel to Valor. Bishan couldn't and wouldn't forgive them for it; they'd crossed one too many lines in the sand.

Tuning out the stilted conversation between brother and sister, Bishan pushed himself to his feet. He wandered into the kitchen to make tea. Even with a killer on the hunt, he refused to spend another day without his usual routines.

They kept him steady and helped him to avoid meltdowns.

I will not allow them to steal my peace—the rare moments of it I find.

With the kettle on, Bishan found his favourite mug, one with piano keys on it. They'd have tea and biscuits from the basket Lottie brought over. And they'd take turns reading from their book of the week, another routine they'd skipped out on for months.

What were we reading? Oh, yeah, that new thriller. On second thought, maybe a different book, one that's lighter.

"Penny doesn't know how Bertie found out. She said he

texted her from Windermere." Valor joined him in the kitchen. He retrieved milk from the fridge for tea, and a plate of *Nan Khatai*, a treat Bishan's mum had brought for them. Her special recipe of cardamom-flavoured buttery biscuits. "She found it strange as well."

"Bertie was twenty minutes away when the accident happened." He paused in the process of pouring the boiling water into their piano-shaped teapot. "Strange isn't the word that comes to my mind."

"Suspicious?"

"He's your brother." Bishan didn't know how he'd respond if Sunesh ever appeared guilty of such a horrendous crime. "He's family."

Valor wrapped his uninjured arm around Bishan's shoulders. "*You* are my family. Lottie, Wilfred, all the Tambolis, all of you are my family. Bertie? He'd sooner throw me under a bus than help me or claim me as his brother."

Bishan leaned into Valor before stepping away. His shoulder and neck hurt enough that the weight of an arm caused them to twinge painfully. "What do we do?"

"The sensible thing would be to tell Reggie." Valor nibbled on a biscuit, taking smaller bites likely to avoid causing anything to pull on his healing nose. "Or we could invite Bertie over for tea. I'd love to poke at my big brother to see what he has to say for himself."

Bishan preferred the sensible route, especially since he hated strangers in the cottage. And the Scott family definitely fell into that category. "Why not let the detective inspector handle it? If Bertie is part of it, why would he waltz into the cottage for tea?"

"Curiosity." Valor continued eating the biscuit while Bishan returned to taking care of the tea. "How many times do killers return to the scene of the crime? Always. They can't help themselves."

He didn't exactly find it comforting to consider inviting a killer into their sanctuary. "Do we want to offer him a chance to finish the job?"

"We could invite Hugh and Nick or Daniel."

Bishan measured out the precise amount of milk and sugar for his tea. "They have jobs, Val."

"And?"

"I love you." Bishan stared intensely down at the teapot. "But, sometimes, the Scott in you rears its ugly head."

"Is this one of those laundry on the floor moments?" Valor asked.

Despite his differences from his family, Valor occasionally demonstrated how spoiled he'd been before Harrow. Bishan often wondered if Mr Clarke had roomed them together in their first two years to teach Valor a few lessons about how "the other half" lived. To his credit, his boyfriend had grown up and left much of his bad behaviour behind him.

"You can't expect people working regular jobs to take loads of time off for us. They've all spent so much time driving out to see us in the last few months." Bishan didn't know if he could ever repay Hugh, Daniel, Cora, and Nina especially for going above and beyond for them. "Tea, biscuits, book. Now."

"Yes." Valor offered him a playful salute. He grabbed his cup of tea and the plate of biscuits. "What are we reading?"

"Something light."

"*Lord of the Flies*?"

"You are not funny." Bishan followed Valor back over to their cosy space on the couch with all the windows open, a slight breeze wafted through to cool things off as the sun dropped behind clouds. "How about *The Secret Garden*?"

Valor set the tea and plate on the coffee table. He wandered over to the bookcase across the wall, running his fingers along the spines of their vast collection. "I've got it."

"Hmm?" Bishan dropped his gaze to his tea but lifted his head up when Valor began to read one of his favourite poems from their collection of romantic poets. "Well, it's definitely light reading."

"Exactly. Romance now. Murderers later."

"Well?" Bertie perched on the edge of the chair, looking like he thought it might dirty his trousers. "I'm here."

"We do clean the cottage. And Staccato's very good about not spraying anywhere." Bishan didn't understand why the man insisted on barely touching the cushion. He glanced over at a laughing Valor. "What? Maybe he doesn't know? Some people's cats mark their territory. Staccy's better than that."

Valor choked while trying to stop laughing. "Bertie's fine."

Bishan frowned over at Valor, realising he'd obviously said something funny but not understanding why. "The chair isn't dirty."

"Why am I here?" Bertie interrupted the conversation.

Bishan noticed he shifted ever so slightly back into the seat. "Why were you in Windermere?"

"*Bish.*" Valor groaned next to him. He covered his face with his hands and gave a strangled sort of laugh, muttering under his breath low enough Bishan had to lean forward to hear him. "Subtle. I said to be subtle."

"It's rude to whisper." Bertie folded his arms across his chest, peering down the distinct Scott nose at them. "And I fail to see how where I spend my time is any of your business."

"Bertie—"

"Will you *stop* calling me Bertie? We're not teenagers any longer, Valor," he interrupted his younger brother sharply. "You were taught better. It's his fault, isn't it? You used to be so well behaved and cultured."

"Cultured? Well behaved?" Bishan glanced between the two brothers. "Does he know you at all?"

"Not even a little." Valor rested his head back against the extra cushion they'd placed behind him for support. "None of them do."

Bishan adjusted the pillow slightly for Valor. He was inordinately grateful to his mum for teaching him so much about caring for the sick, something she knew intimately as a doctor. "Why were you in Windermere?"

The trouble with the subtle approach was Bishan didn't read tone or body language at all. He couldn't. Sunesh had dedicated almost an entire year to try to teach him—and it ended with him finally dumping a tub of yoghurt over his brother's head in frustration.

Yoghurt-gate had drawn the curtains on his siblings trying to "educate the autistic." They meant well, but some of the things they instinctually grasped would always remain a mystery to him. Bishan accepted it and chose to focus on learning how his brain worked and not how his siblings believed it did.

So Bishan decided to abandon playing subtle. It didn't work for him. And even with it, Bertie could be as slippery as an eel, with his carefully slicked hair and his smooth manners.

Bishan breathed in profoundly then forced himself to meet Bertie's cold gaze. "Well?"

Bertie ignored him, turning away to focus on Valor. "I only agreed to this to attempt to change your mind about returning to the family."

"You're lying." Valor sat up stiffly. "And badly."

"Right." Bertie got to his feet, making a show of brushing his suit trousers off. "I've wasted enough of my time on your childishness. I've no idea why you care so much about my trips to Windermere, but I'm seeing a young woman who lives there. And no, you can't meet her."

"Wouldn't want to." Valor grimaced. "I can only imagine she's as pleasant as you are."

"*Valor.* I've no desire to put up with your nonsense any further." Bertie tightened his jaw but showed no other signs of emotion. He strode quickly out of the cottage, leaving Bishan to stare at the door as it was slammed shut.

"Well, he obviously did it." Valor slowly lowered himself down to stretch out on the couch. He rested his head on a pillow and his legs across Bishan's lap. "I can't imagine anyone finding him attractive."

Bishan eased out from under Valor's legs to go lock the door. "Not sure that argument would stand up in court as a legitimate reason to accuse him of being a murderer."

"How about his smarmy smile?"

"No."

"Or maybe his inability to act and sound like anything other than a clone of my parents?" Valor asked with a chuckle.

"*No.*" Bishan covered him with a blanket, shifting Staccato from his shoulder down to curl up with Valor. "You rest. I'm going to practice my clarinet."

"Aren't you supposed to be resting as well?" Valor yawned, then had to spit out Staccato's tail. "Damn cat."

"Playing my clarinet is relaxing for me." Bishan brought his case into the living room, pulled the instrument out to practice, and had to hold in a laugh when not five minutes in Valor had fallen asleep. "And for you as well apparently."

With Valor snoring in time to Staccato's purring, Bishan continued his practice. His sore muscles eventually protested, forcing him to set aside his clarinet. He hadn't anticipated holding it up would be such a strain on his shoulders.

He headed into the kitchen to make a cup of tea for himself with one thought tugging at his mind. Why had Bertie even accepted their invitation? Did it do more for his guilt or his innocence that he'd come over?

Taking his tea, Bishan grabbed the last unsolved cypher. He (and the computer program) had yet to make any real progress on it. Nina had mentioned it might be difficult owing to the sheer number of letters, which equated to a vast number of possible solutions.

With a sip of tea, Bishan decided to take a different approach. He stopped focusing on the bolded letters and turned his attention to the program itself. *Wuthering Heights. Is that hint about a tragic romance?* It had been a school play—an adaptation of Emily Brontë's great work.

Bishan wandered over to one of their bookshelves, hunting for their copy of the original novel. It would be easier than trying to find a copy of their script. *I'll text Daniel, bet he still has a copy since he hoards everything from Harrow.*

"What've you found?" Valor's voice broke into his thoughts an hour later. "Bish?"

Bishan sat up slowly, stretching out his back. He'd definitely been hunched over too long while skimming through the novel. "I haven't found anything yet."

"But?"

"What if the clue to this puzzle is the story itself?" Bishan lifted up the book to show Valor the cover. "I'm finding it difficult to believe the programs themselves aren't part of some dark, twisted game being played."

"Maybe he thinks he's Heathcliff?" Valor shifted off the couch with a pained groan. "Who's Catherine then?"

"I think I've solved the puzzle." Bishan didn't know for certain, but the letters definitely fit. "Maybe."

"Well?"

Bishan read part of a quote from *Wuthering Heights*. Even without the script from their play. He did remember it being part of it:

"*Catherine Earnshaw, may you not rest as long as I am living. You said I killed you—haunt me then. The murdered do haunt their murderers. I believe—I know that ghosts have wandered the earth. Be with me always—take any form—drive me mad.*"

"Well, that's ominous." Valor came over to read over Bishan's shoulder.

"It goes on a bit." He pointed out where he'd double-checked each bolded letter, making sure it fit. "If he's Heathcliff, which one of us is Catherine?"

"I still think we're missing something." Valor glanced at the four solved riddles spread across their kitchen table. "None of these point to anyone I can think of."

"Yeah, we're missing the fact that we're not actually detectives." Bishan worried they'd progressed from keen interest to actual obsession. It was hard not to be when they were the potential victims. "Maybe Reggie is right? We should let the actual police handle it."

"They've done a bang-up job of it thus far." Valor

gestured to the bruise covering a large area of his face. "Not sure if that pun's intended or not."

He wasn't wrong.

Bishan didn't know if he was exactly right, either.

His recent experience with police investigation had taught him truth takes time. If the detectives had rushed, Bishan had no idea if he'd ever have found his freedom. He might've ended up going before a judge.

When all the evidence points at me, what else were they to believe?

"Bish?" Valor placed his hand on the table, palm up. "You all right?"

Bishan dragged his fingers over Valor's palm. "What if they try again? The crash wasn't an accident. I don't think the purpose was to scare us. They wanted us dead."

"But we're not." Valor clearly wanted to sound encouraging. "We're okay."

"But what if they try again?" he couldn't help repeating.

"We'll be fine."

And even Bishan could tell Valor wasn't wholly convinced.

CHAPTER 8

With Valor under doctor's orders to rest for another week to encourage his recovery, Bishan braved the village on his own for a bit of shopping. He'd started to feel better far more quickly than Valor. It would take weeks for him to return to something resembling full health.

He wouldn't have needed to go to the shop if his mum hadn't decided unhealthy foods might deter their recovery. She'd gone all doctor on them, throwing out their much-beloved junk food. His siblings had found it hilarious.

"Oh, *pyaare bete*, how can you heal with all this rubbish going into your bodies?" And with those words, she'd corralled his dad and brother into betraying him. Reva had simply snickered from the safety of the far corner of the room.

He hadn't found it amusing at all. It was a struggle just dealing with Valor moving things around in the cottage. One of the ways Bishan had learned to ease some of his stress involved having control over his environment at home.

All their comfort food being taken away tested his temper.

His mum meant well, and Bishan had learned to pick his battles. She'd at least left homemade snacks for them.

Thankfully, four days after they'd left the hospital, his parents had finally returned to their home. Bishan had made a list of everything that had been thrown out. He planned to head into the village to replace it; he couldn't see how crisps and biscuits, and maybe some custard would do anything worse than the accident had done.

Crash, not accident.

Stop calling it an accident, someone tried to murder us.

His basket at the shop amused the young woman who checked him out. Hobnobs, Hula Hoops, Jaffa Cakes, the list went on and on. Bishan smiled sheepishly when she raised her eyebrows at the sheer amount he'd gotten, including the multiple packs of frozen pizzas and ice cream.

"Hungry, love?"

"Pregnancy cravings." Bishan said the first thing that came to his mind. He grabbed the bags and rushed out of the shop.

Pregnancy cravings?

She knows us; she's going to think I've lost my mind.

Stowing the bags in the boot of their rental car, Bishan berated himself the entire way to the cottage. *Honestly. Pregnancy cravings.* He hated it when simple questions caught him off guard.

What the....

Bishan pulled into the drive to find shredded bits of paper strewn along the path toward the cottage. He bent down to pick a piece up and found it was a piece of a music sheet. It led him through the house into the garden where Valor sat on the wooden bench under their tree. "Did you lose your temper?"

"No?"

"Why is all the sheet music torn up?" Bishan bent down

to grab another handful of it. He tried to piece it together. "It's blank. Did you have an accident with scissors?"

"No." Valor sounded almost strangled. "I didn't have an accident. I didn't lose my temper. Scissors were involved, but completely on purpose."

Bishan flicked his gaze over to him in concern and then went back to staring at the shreds of paper. "Wind'll spread it all over. Where's the broom? Mrs Harris will scream if it gets into her garden. She'll go on about her frogs being poisoned by the ink."

"*Bish.*"

"You sound strange. Are you getting a cold?" Bishan bent down to gather up more of the paper. "You're supposed to be inside resting."

"I'm trying to do—"

"Oh, the ice cream. I've got to get it out of the boot. I got distracted by the paper." Bishan rushed through the cottage, ignoring Valor's slightly hysterical laughter. "It can't have gone bad in five minutes, can it?"

Grabbing all the bags, Bishan used his elbow to close the lid of the boot. He struggled into the cottage. Valor waited for him in the kitchen.

"I'm trying to be romantic."

Bishan paused with one hand holding the ice cream and his other on the handle to the freezer. "With shredded paper?"

"I…."

"Staccato likes it." Bishan pointed to where their cat had started diving through the winding trail. "Why is the paper romantic?"

"It isn't the paper."

"It is paper." Bishan had the feeling he'd missed something in translation. He quickly put the frozen food away then stowed the rest of the contraband into the cupboards.

Hopefully his mum wouldn't try to clean them out again. "Why are you trying to be romantic—with music sheets?"

Valor laughed helplessly before holding out a set of matching rings. "Will you marry me?"

Bishan grabbed one of the rings to twist the gold chain set inside a platinum band. "A fidget spinner."

"And engagement ring." Valor stepped over the cloth bags on the floor toward him. He clasped Bishan's hand tightly with his uninjured one. "I know we said we didn't see the point of marriage."

"I don't." Bishan couldn't wrap his mind around the proposal. "You hate marriage."

"I dislike my parents' idea of it." Valor lifted one of the rings between two of his fingers. "Hate is such a *strong* word."

"You said you did." Bishan remembered the conversation perfectly. "Why've you changed your mind?"

"I love you."

"Did you not love me before?" Bishan frowned at their clasped fingers. "You said you did."

"*Bish.*"

"I want to understand." He really did, as well. He knew Valor felt strongly about not marrying, so something important must've altered his perspective on the idea. In fact, Valor had once spoken quite eloquently about how marriage was brilliant for those who wanted it—but society shouldn't force it on everyone as the only way to express love. "Is it the murders?"

"No," Valor insisted. "Well, not exactly."

"Do you need to sit? You should." Bishan didn't think standing for an extended amount of time had been part of the doctor's instructions. "You can explain as easily on the couch as anywhere else. Why didn't the murders inspire your proposal?"

With bemused grumbling, Valor followed him into the living room. They had to dodge Staccato, who continued to skitter around in the paper. It was going to take them forever to get it all cleaned up.

"When did you get these?" Bishan held the ring loosely on the tip of his index finger. He didn't even hear the answer Valor gave him. "Are you actually asking me to marry you?"

"Is that a no?"

"Do you really want to get married?" He admired his own parents' marriage and others. It just wasn't something he'd wanted for himself. "Why? What's changed? Aren't we happy without papers?"

"Of course." Valor rested his head back against the sofa. "I'm not fussed about being married. I love you."

"Then?" Bishan held up the ring. He'd always been happy as they were. What was the point of paper? His parents had a perfect marriage, but he'd never wanted it, and Valor had always seemed to feel the same.

"You had no rights to me while I was in the hospital. My parents ran roughshod over everyone and had the law behind them to do it. I've no way to stop it, either." Valor slipped his ring onto his finger. "Maybe not for the ceremony, or the other stuff, but it's important to me that you're the one who gets to make decisions for me when I can't."

"Why don't we have Sunny draw up a next-of-kin agreement for us? It would solve the problem without you sacrificing your beliefs on marriage." Bishan had meant to mention it years ago; Sunesh had brought it up. As usual, it had gotten lost somewhere in his mind. "If you really want, I'll say yes. I'm happy with my ring being a fidget spinner that shows you love me—without the church or the law having anything to say about it."

"Not as romantic."

Bishan pointed to a paper-covered Staccato. "He disagrees."

"Will you *not* marry me?" Valor proposed for a second time.

Bishan tilted his head awkwardly to give Valor a gentle kiss without bumping into his sore nose. "I will definitely *not* marry you."

CHAPTER 9

"You took my son's family from him."

"I took his family from him?" Bishan tilted his head to stare at the red-faced earl screaming at him, focusing on his nose to avoid the pale blue eyes. "You should probably breathe. You've gone an alarming shade of pink."

"I beg your pardon." Valor's father glared down the Scott nose at Bishan. "Aren't you going to invite me inside? I'd prefer to have this conversation inside."

"No." Bishan refused to even open the door completely. "Val's resting. You'll disturb him."

"I have the right—"

"No, you don't. You abandoned him. Now you might lose money, and suddenly you want to play nice but only on your terms. *Of course.* Hypocrites." Bishan had tried hard for Valor's sake not to go off on his parents. "I think you should go away."

"I want to see my son." He tried to ease closer to the door, but Bishan refused to back down. "We are worried about his recovery."

"Are you?" Bishan didn't believe it for a second. "And it has nothing to do with the impending deadline? What happens to Valor's portion of the inheritance from his grandfather if you fail to reach a compromise with him?"

"That is none of your business." Lord Scott's mouth pressed into a thin line. "I'll ruin your family as you've ruined mine."

"Will you?" Bishan wasn't overly concerned. "Are you threatening us? Have you met my older brother, Sunesh? He's a barrister. He'd be quite interested in hearing about your visit. I'm sure he'd also love to assist Valor with his inheritance. I'll never understand you people. So obsessed with etiquette and perfection, yet you threw your son to the wolves. Why? I know you tried to ruin his relationships and stop others from supporting him. Wasn't it enough to abandon him?"

"We made a mistake. Time has passed. We should all move on." The earl didn't sound particularly contrite.

Bishan didn't buy the backhanded offer of reconciliation. "A mistake? Deliberate cruelty isn't an accident."

"What would you know about it?"

Bishan opened the door slightly. For Valor's sake, he could be brave and speak his mind plainly. "I propped him up when you broke his heart. So why don't you sod off back to London? I'll set the cat on you."

"The... what?"

Bishan slammed the door shut in his face. "*Bastard.*"

"You'll set the cat on him?" Valor was watching him from the couch, Staccato stretched out along the back of it. "Not sure he's an attack kitten."

"We could train him."

"Doubtful." Valor lowered himself down on the cushions again. "I'm proud of you."

"Don't be daft."

"I am. You told him off without having a meltdown." Valor lifted his good arm up to give Bishan a thumbs up. "You were brilliant."

"Only you would think me telling your dad to sod off was brilliant." Bishan felt a bit shaky. He checked on both the cat and the human on the sofa before heading into the kitchen to make tea. It would do wonders for his attack of nerves. "Hope they stay away this time."

"They won't." Valor followed him into the kitchen, sitting in the recliner that Bishan had dragged in from the living room to allow him to sit comfortably. "Money and status matter most to them. They'll do anything to maintain their status quo."

"Including murder?"

Neither of them really knew what to think. On the one hand, it seemed mostly like one of their former classmates was behind the killings. On the other, Valor's family appeared to have the more significant motive toward getting rid of Bishan by framing him for murders.

But if it is them, why all the drama? Why so many murders? It doesn't make any sense at all.

Over a week since their crash, their bruises had healed further. Valor was able to move around more as well. He was quieter about his aches and pains, though he still whined; he'd never been one to suffer in silence.

At school, Valor had once used a stubbed toe as an excuse to get out of their second Long Ducker, an annual Harrow charity ten-mile run from London to Harrow.

He'd used the flu to excuse himself from a singing event.

And a poetry reading.

"Bish?" Valor waved a hand toward the whistling kettle. "What's got you so deep in thought?"

"Your inability to handle any sort of injury." Bishan

grabbed the kettle to pour into their teapot. "You're a terrible patient."

"I'm delicate."

"As delicate as Reva's attempts to make biscuits." Bishan adored his baby sister, but her cookies tended to be harder than concrete. His thoughts returned to more serious matters. "Do you think your family is capable...."

He trailed off, not wanting to say the words.

"Capable of murder? With the right motivation? Yes." Valor ran his fingers through his mussed-up ginger hair. "Do I honestly believe they've done these monstrous crimes? I hope not. God, I hope not."

"I've been thinking about the cinnamon." Bishan busied himself by pouring the brewed tea. He opened one of the cabinets to hunt for honey to sweeten his. "It's strange, isn't it?"

Until they'd seen the reports and spoken with Detective Inspector Spurling, Bishan had found it hard to believe cinnamon might be anyone's weapon of choice. The killer had, in two of the cases, injected the victims with it, and in the others poured the spice down their throat, filling their lungs with it.

"Definitely ups the creep level." Valor nodded his thanks when Bishan handed him a cup of tea. "It also begs the question of why he chose to try to kill us in the car."

Bishan had wondered about it as well. "Do serial killers usually change up their pattern?"

"Why are you looking at me as though I have first-hand knowledge?" Valor slouched further into the cushioned chair. "They didn't leave a note either. No puzzle or clue to their involvement."

Bishan leaned against the counter. "It doesn't fit the pattern."

Even if watching all those detective shows didn't amount

to their genuine understanding of how investigations worked, Bishan thought they might've hit on something important. Valor grabbed his mobile to text Spurling. He would at least listen to them, even if he chose not to believe them.

"Reggie wants to come over for a chat." Valor waved his phone at him. "You up for a guest? He said he'd bring pizza for a late lunch."

He clutched his cup and considered it. "Just him?"

"Promise." Valor returned to texting, leaving Bishan to his thoughts.

The detective inspector arrived thirty minutes later with three small pizzas. Pepperoni for himself, chilli con carne-themed for Valor, and margherita for Bishan. They ate in silence, until about halfway through Spurling finally spoke up.

"We've managed to narrow the potential suspects in your crash down to a handful of vehicles. It's a lot of video footage to track. We'll find them, I promise." Spurling laid out several printed images in the middle of the table. "Are any of these familiar to you at all?"

While they inspected the ten cars, Valor mentioned their concerns about the seeming change of pattern. Bishan tuned out the conversation. His eyes focused on one of the vehicles that seemed familiar.

Standing up, Bishan made his way into the living room to find his magnifying glass. He'd used it when he went through his model-making phase. Their cottage had been filled with all sorts of ships and robots until he decided the smell of the glue bothered him too much to continue.

"Find something?" Valor asked when Bishan returned to peer more closely at the vehicle. "Do you recognise it?"

"I'm not sure." He turned and grabbed his phone to shine a light on the image. "It's familiar, but honestly, how many of these have I seen in my life? It doesn't necessarily mean anything."

Valor held his hand out to take the magnifying glass and paper from Bishan. "We see at least ten of them in the village through the week when the tourists are flocking to the Lake District. Any number of old Harrovians drive them as well. Hell, I think Bertie had one at...."

Bishan turned toward Valor as he trailed off. "Bertie."

Spurling sat up sharply in his seat, shoving his pizza away from him. "Your brother?"

Valor poked at the image with the magnifying glass. "He was driving a similar model. It's a bit blurry, so I can't say it's definitely him. He claims to have been in Windermere at the time."

Bishan moved over to wrap his arm around Valor, who seemed lost. "You won't just accuse him."

Spurling shook his head with a smile. "We won't jump to any conclusions."

"Like you did with me." Bishan liked the detective. He'd been over a few times since Bishan's release from custody. "Bertie's not a nice person, but no one deserves to be accused unjustly."

Not even Bertie.

CHAPTER 10

The London Symphony Orchestra had respectfully and somewhat gently declined his offer to return for their upcoming summer performance schedule. Bishan hadn't been overly surprised. The director couldn't afford to have his presence overshadow the entire group.

Maybe next year.

Despite Valor's claims of their being perfectly fine without his income from the orchestra, Bishan refused to be the one not contributing to their future. The biscuit shop did decent business, but he wanted to be an equal partner in their life. It mattered to him.

After agonising over opening his email for an hour, Bishan finally settled down to send a few messages out to former classmates. He focused specifically on the old Harrovians who'd gone into the world of film and telly. Several of them had begged him for years to work on their soundtracks and other projects.

It surprised him when two responded almost instantly.

"Well?" Valor set a mug of coffee and a plate of biscuits on the table in front of his laptop. "Any luck?"

"Ollie—"

"Which one?" Valor interrupted before he could continue. "Elder, younger, Ollie B., Oliver, Olive, or Oliver Twist?"

"Twist." Bishan grabbed the coffee and took a long drink. They'd gone to school with six Olivers, who'd gone by nicknames to avoid confusion. "He's working on a short film and wants help with the soundtrack."

"Oh?"

"He's invited me to London. He's apparently dying for a 'proper cellist.'" Bishan didn't know what qualified him as a "proper cellist," but he wasn't about to complain. "Will you be all right by yourself? Do you want to come with me?"

Most of the time, Bishan travelled up to London on his own for practices. Valor tended to hover when they went together. He meant well, but Bishan had always clung fiercely to his independence.

Being autistic didn't make him incapable of functioning as an adult in the world—though it did make it harder.

"What about—" Valor cut himself off and gestured to the solved riddles stuck to their kitchen cabinets. They'd put them up there while attempting to make sense of them. "Not sure either of us should travel anywhere alone right now."

Bishan paused in the middle of responding to Ollie's email to consider it. "I'll be fine."

"Bish."

"*What?*" His tone went even flatter than normal. "I'm in better shape than you are."

They argued.

Well, not really.

On the whole, Bishan avoided conflict with everyone—even the cat. He tried to argue, but words tended to evaporate off his tongue in the midst of making his point. His frustration levels grew to the point he lost his ability to think straight.

So, they argued with chalk.

It had been Valor's idea. He'd wanted to find a way for them to disagree without Bishan shutting down. One can of chalkboard spray paint and a section of their bedroom wall had provided him with a way to get his thoughts out clearly.

Stepping up with the piece of chalk clenched tightly in his fingers, Bishan wrote in bullet point all the reasons why he could make the trip on his own. Valor had a concise response: *The murderer has already tried to get rid of us once. I'd rather go together than spend a lifetime without you.*

Weird, true, and slightly romantic.

Wasn't that the perfect description for them anyway?

Bishan brushed the dust off his fingers and hesitantly walked over to wrap his arms around Valor. He hid his face against Valor's neck, tilted slightly to avoid the ginger stubble tickling his nose. "You've got chalk all over your fingers."

"Is it bothering you?"

Bishan dragged up his courage to broach one of the few subjects he'd always struggled with. "I could help you rinse it off in the shower."

"In the middle of the morning?" Valor's hazel eyes brightened.

Sex was a minefield for him. They always danced a careful line toward complete sensory overload. They'd experimented with so many things over the years, and nothing helped.

In his heart, Bishan knew Valor likely wanted more physically from their relationship. It had almost broken them apart in their early twenties. Their love and need for one another had been strong enough to bridge the gap.

And as always, Valor compromised to help him.

Bishan brought his fingers up to play with Valor's red hair. "Do you want to?"

Valor shifted back slightly and reached out to lift Bishan's chin, leaning forward for a kiss. "Always."

"Stop quoting Harry Potter." Bishan scowled at him.

"And now I'm thinking about Alan Rickman naked." Valor snickered at him and dragged him by the hand toward their small en suite. "I'd much rather see you than him."

CHAPTER 11

While London might've been calling, it turned out to be for all the wrong reasons. Penelope had called, asking Valor to drive to Windermere to check on their brother. Something both of them found to be odd in the extreme.

"Why does your family suddenly want to act as if they didn't abandon you?" Bishan found all the Scotts completely bewildering. They practised what his brother Sunesh called the subtle art of speaking with all the important bits hidden between the lines. He didn't really understand it. "We are closer. Maybe she doesn't want to drive to the Lake District again?"

"Penny can be lazy." Valor shrugged. He didn't seem worked up over it.

"I'll tell Ollie we'll be late." Bishan considered it before handing over his phone to Valor. "On second thought, you can text him since it's your sister causing the delay."

"And you hate all forms of communication, including text."

"I talk to you," Bishan insisted. He glanced through the

window into the garden to find binoculars resting on the top of their fence. "Mrs Harris is watching us again."

"Kiss?" Valor stepped over so they could both be seen by the nosy neighbour. "Maybe it's what she hopes to catch us doing."

"Doubtful." Bishan repeated the word a few times to himself. His fingers tapped out the rhythm against the window pane. "*Doubtful.*"

"No kiss then?"

Bishan allowed himself to be drawn into Valor's arms. He'd always loved the symmetry of their lips connecting. They kissed until Mrs Harris could be heard shouting over the fence at them. "Too much?"

"Don't see how. I only grabbed your arse once." Valor waved at the retreating Mrs Harris. "Fancy another shower?"

"We've only just gotten out." Bishan didn't see the point of washing twice in the morning. A glance at Valor suggested he'd missed something in translation. *Oh.* "Maybe later."

After a brief discussion, they decided to check on Bertie first then head to London. They dropped Staccato off with Wilfred and Lottie. Bishan sent a text to Reva to ask if she wanted to travel with them, as she'd been staying with their parents for a few weeks.

It took them an hour to get Reva. His parents insisted on feeding them, even though they'd had breakfast already. His mum made a packed lunch for them to have on the drive with thermoses of tea and soup.

"Does she think we're going to be travelling by foot to get to London?" Valor lifted the two bags of food while Bishan carried the thermoses. "We could eat for days on this lot."

"You've met our mum and dad, right?" Reva grabbed one of the coconut biscuits from the container she carried. "We can offer gifts of food to Ollie."

"Speaking of Ollie. Are your parents aware of the massive

crush you have on him?" Valor asked Reva once they'd gotten into the car. "Do they approve?"

"Bish. You promised not to tell anyone." Reva swatted him on the arm. "*Bugger*. You haven't told Sunny, have you? He'll want to do a background check on him."

Bishan brushed the powdered sugar from his sleeve. "Sunny knows because he's not blind. You went all weird when Ollie came to visit us last Christmas."

The trio chatted about Ollie for the short drive from the Tamboli cottage over to the slightly fancier place Bertie had been renting in Windermere. Bishan twisted in the seat to talk to Reva in the back. She pressed him for details about his old Harrow friend.

Bishan didn't want her to get her expectations up. Ollie hadn't dated anyone after getting his heart broken a few years back by his boyfriend at the time. He hadn't looked at a man or woman since.

Valor interrupted them by throwing his phone into Bishan's lap. "Call Reggie."

Bishan jolted forward against the seat belt when Valor slammed on the brakes and barely took the time to turn off the car before bolting out of it. "What is going on?"

"Bish? Isn't that—"

"Close your eyes," Bishan interrupted. He fumbled with Valor's phone; his fingers refused to cooperate. Reva reached between the seats to snatch it out of his hand. "Okay. You call the detective. Lock the doors when I get out until the police arrive. Don't let anyone inside with you."

With Reva contacting the authorities, Bishan rushed up the path. He eased around the Bentley that appeared as though someone had taken a cricket bat to it. Valor knelt in the grass beside his brother's lifeless body.

"Don't touch him." Bishan dropped to his knees behind Valor, wrapping his arms around him to stop him from reaching out. "We don't want our fingerprints confusing the police again. I'm so sorry, Val."

"I hated him."

"I'm so sorry," Bishan repeated. He could feel Valor trembling in his embrace.

"Hated his stuffed-up shite. Hated how he pretended you didn't exist even if you were right in front of him." Valor shook more violently, and Bishan clutched him tighter. "Hated the bastard and how money mattered more to him than his little brother did. Hated him. But he's still my brother, and he's dead."

Bishan rested his chin on Valor's shoulder. "I am so sorry."

"I hate him. But he's my only brother."

The words resonated painfully around them. Bishan knew Valor had missed his family—or more, what he wished they should've been. Dead on the ground wasn't how anyone should go.

Valor shuddered in Bishan's arms. "See the dust around his mouth? It has to be cinnamon. He wasn't our killer after all."

"No." Bishan wondered absently why their killer would go after Bertie. He hadn't been at Harrow during Valor's time. "I don't know how to help you."

They knelt in silence by Bertie until the police arrived. Reggie showed up minutes after the other detectives. He insisted on them waiting by the vehicles, away from the body and presumably any evidence left behind.

Reva waited for them by the car, sitting on the nearby curb with Valor's phone clutched in her hand. "I called Mum and Dad, and Sunny as well."

An hour went by before Detective Inspector Spurling came out to speak with them. He crouched down in front of them, raising an eyebrow at Reva. Bishan nudged her until with much grumbling, his little sister returned to sit in the car.

She's probably listening to everything from inside anyway.

"He's dead." Reggie held his hand up to stop whatever Valor had begun to say. "Cinnamon, more than likely. We'll have to wait for the coroner's report for certain. I found another program."

Bishan looped his arm around Valor's shoulders. He had to be strong for both of them like Valor usually was for him. "Is there anything else?"

"We'd planned to arrest him for your accident."

"What?" Valor sounded completely shocked.

"We pieced together CCTV footage and his mobile phone records. His girlfriend also provided a statement to us. We felt quite confident in our evidence." Reggie shook his head slightly. "It's possible the killer was angered by your brother's attack on you."

"A serial murderer angered by an attempt on our lives?" Bishan blinked at the idea. "Are you serious?"

Reggie only nodded in response.

Valor shrugged off Bishan's arm and got to his feet. He paced angrily for several minutes, then turned back to the detective inspector. "Why?"

"If the killer is as obsessed with you as we believe, it's possible Bertie's attempt angered them." Reggie stood up, waving to one of the detectives processing the scene. "I understand from Reva that you intend to head to London for a few days."

"We can stay." Bishan knew Ollie wouldn't mind postponing, given the situation.

"I'd prefer you go, but with one of our detectives along for the ride, if you don't mind." Reggie seemed to have a plan but appeared unwilling to share it. "Trust me."

"You locked me up when I was innocent," Bishan stated

bluntly. He'd lost his trust in the detectives after being confined for weeks. "Which detective?"

"Edwards."

"Oh." Bishan had liked Patrice Edwards. She'd made tea and chatted with him at night when he couldn't sleep. "She's fine."

Valor stepped over to take Bishan's hand, turning his attention to the detective. "You'll want to contact my parents."

"Don't you—"

"No." Valor heaved a heavy sigh. "They don't want to hear from me. And I'm sure bringing this news won't improve our relationship."

Bishan shifted slightly, so he stood in front of Valor. He couldn't shield him from all of this, though he wanted to try. "If the detective won't, I'll do it."

It would be worse than Valor calling them. Bishan didn't care. He might not know how to help with the anger and grief—or lack thereof—but he was capable of faking his way through a phone conversation.

Hopefully.

CHAPTER 12

The six-hour drive to Twickenham provided far too much time for all of them to think. Bishan usually loved silence. The quiet in the confined space of their rental car weighed heavily on him.

Reva and the detective inspector, who'd insisted they all call her Pattie, sat in the back seat. His sister spent much of the drive texting on her phone. Bishan wished they'd dropped her off at home; they'd all had a shock and perhaps a trip to London wasn't the best idea.

Not that Reva was delicate, but he couldn't recall ever seeing her quite so silent for such an extended period.

When they arrived at Ollie's semi-detached house in Twickenham, Bishan had never been so grateful to see his old friend waiting with cups of tea and a plate of fancy biscuits made by Ollie's nan who lived next door. She'd also been kind enough to send over supper for them, though no one really wanted to eat.

Pattie disappeared to make her report to someone. Bishan hadn't been paying any attention to her. He fully intended to drown himself in tea until the world seemed like a better place.

"*Oi*, Lord Byron." Ollie caught Bishan's attention with his old Harrow nickname. "Val's heading upstairs with your bags. Why don't we have a late supper after you've rested for a bit?"

Bishan narrowed his eyes suspiciously at his sister and Ollie, who'd been whispering to each other over their teacups. "Fine."

Trudging up the stairs after Valor, Bishan had to check a few doors before he found the right room. He found Valor sitting on the edge of the bed with his head in his hands. Neither of them was equipped to deal with this nightmare.

He sat on the bed next to him, uneasy with the intense emotions. "Do you want a hug?"

Valor sat up straight and eased his arm around Bishan's back. He tilted his head until it rested against Bishan's shoulder. "Is it wrong to not grieve for him?"

"I don't know." Bishan thought death and grief affected everyone differently, even if the person in question had been a terrible human being. "Will you miss him?"

"He tried to kill you." Valor didn't actually answer his question.

"And you." Bishan did find it odd that Bertie had risked causing their accident; he'd always seemed to prefer to keep his hands clean of dirty work. They'd probably never really get answers as to why he'd done it. "However you feel is valid. No one can judge you after everything your brother did to you over the years."

"I won't miss him."

"Good." Bishan certainly wouldn't. He had never liked Bertie, with his constant sneering and cruel arrogance. "I don't wish death on anyone, but I won't miss him either."

"Should I have been the one to inform Lord and Lady

Scott?" Valor collapsed onto the mattress, snagging a small decorative pillow to clutch to his chest. "Oh, damn it all. You realise this means I'm the heir, right? They're going to try to drag me into the fold even harder than before."

Bishan shifted up the bed, stretching out on his stomach and resting his chin on Valor's shoulder. "You don't owe them a phone call or anything else after being disowned. They've lost the right to ask."

Grabbing his phone and the coiled up headphones from his pocket, Bishan offered one set to Valor and kept one for himself, connecting both with a splitter. He scrolled through his playlists to select one comprised of relaxing classical piano pieces. They stayed on the bed on their backs, side by side, allowing the music to wash over them.

It was a familiar comfort. The tension eased out of Bishan's body with the gentle, fluid strains of a piano sonata. The pressure of being social had been hard to manage; his brain needed the brief respite to recover.

An hour of musical solitude brought them both some semblance of relief. Bishan knew they'd have to make a reappearance soon. Ollie would think them rude—or be spending a little too much time with his sister.

Valor bent forward to drop a gentle kiss on Bishan's nose before rolling off the bed and landing on his feet. "Up you get."

Bishan took his time stowing the earbuds and his phone. "Are you going to be all right?"

Reading emotions had never come easily to Bishan, not even his own. He second-guessed himself constantly. The smile on Valor's face seemed oddly frozen or forced.

Valor ignored his question to duck out of the room, and Bishan had to jog down the stairs to keep up with him. He slowly opened the door to the living room. "Well, it seems we can stop worrying about Ollie's broken heart."

Bishan had to agree when he peered over Valor's shoulder and spotted Ollie cuddled up on the sofa with Reva. "Break her heart, and she'll bury you in your own garden."

"*Bish.*"

"What? I grew up with her. She buried my first clarinet under Mum's roses." Bishan scowled at his laughing sister. "You still owe me an instrument."

"It was revenge for you taking all my pens apart." Reva slipped off the couch to give him a hug.

Bishan had gone through a phase as a teen when he took ballpoint pens apart, particularly the ones with small springs in them. "I put them back together."

"Without the springs."

"I liked the springs." Bishan still had a collection of them somewhere at the cottage, mixed in with their school memorabilia. "You didn't need to bury my clarinet."

Ollie and Valor burst into a rousing rendition of "Let It Go." Reva collapsed against Bishan in helpless laughter. He rolled his eyes and decided to feign a chuckle, as he didn't quite understand why it was so funny to his sister.

Leaving them to it, Bishan headed through the door leading into the kitchen. He glanced back to find Valor had followed him. It didn't surprise him Reva wanted to spend as much time with Ollie as possible.

She'd had a crush on him for a while. He had suspicions it went back to their days at school. She would've met him during speech day when the whole family came out to see him.

"Sorry." Valor held a hand out toward him.

Bishan took the hand, dragging Valor into a hug. They stood in the kitchen with arms wrapped around one another. "I like springs."

"I know."

"Let's see what Ollie has in his fridge." Valor danced him

over to the refrigerator. He yanked the door open so they could peer into it. "Oh, trifle."

"Shouldn't we have something savoury first?" Bishan asked while Valor grabbed the bowl and handed it over to him. "What are you doing?"

"Inspecting." Valor had crouched down to get a closer look. "There's half a banoffee pie in here."

Bishan exchanged the trifle for the pie. "Mine."

"What are you doing?" Reva asked when she stepped into the kitchen a few minutes later to find them sparring with large serving spoons.

Bishan put his fencing lessons to good use against Valor. "Winner gets the pie."

"I thought the winner got the trifle?"

Bishan used the distraction to disarm Valor and grab the plate with the banoffee pie. "Victory is mine."

"Cheater." Valor tried to sneak a spoonful of the pie, but Bishan twisted away from him. "One bite, please?"

The silliness gave all of them a reprieve from the heaviness that had settled around them. Ollie's nan interrupted their pudding feast midway through. She took one glance at all of them and strong-armed them to her house next door for a proper meal.

"You sent Florentines," Bishan blurted when he spotted a familiar tin. "We ate those every evening with tea while studying during sixth form."

"So I did." She patted his arm gently, guiding him toward the dining room and an antique table set for six. "And you play music beautifully. Ollie brought me a CD of yours."

"Thank you." Bishan rubbed the palms of his hands against his jeans uneasily. A quick glance at Valor had him deftly distracting her. He traced a finger across Valor's back, muttering to him, "And *thank you*."

CHAPTER 13

A light across the street flickered randomly through the window, despite the curtains. The caterwauling of a randy cat echoed in the distance, competing with traffic and the barking of a lone dog. Valor snored sporadically and audibly enough to be impossible to ignore.

Overwhelmed by everything, Bishan sat against the headboard with his legs stretched out in front of him. He had his earbuds in with Mozart blasting. His Rubik's cube lay on the duvet beside him, abandoned after two hours of fidgeting with it.

Bishan jerked in surprise when a hand covered his. "I wish you'd quit scaring me."

"I've literally been in bed with you the entire time. How could I possibly scare you?" Valor rolled over onto his side. "Have you slept at all?"

"Not much." Bishan didn't find it as amusing as Valor, who always managed to catch him off guard. "Too many strange sounds. Old houses creak and groan."

"Like the cottage?"

"I know our cottage." Bishan used a sound machine at

night to drown out the worst of the nighttime noises. They hadn't dared turn it on with a killer on the loose. He hadn't slept well in weeks. "I don't know these."

Valor shifted closer to him and threw an arm across Bishan's legs. "We'll sort it all out, Bish. We'll find our routine again."

"You can't promise though, can you? None of us knows who might be next. Why haven't the detectives caught him?" Bishan dropped his fingers into Valor's mussed-up ginger hair. "I've gone right off cinnamon toast."

Valor inhaled sharply in surprise then busted out laughing. "It's too early in the morning to make me choke on my own saliva."

"Gross."

"Body fluids are natural."

"And also disgusting." Bishan gave a full-body shudder. He didn't even like thinking about the texture of the aforementioned natural fluids. "Who do you think the killer is?"

"Aubrey."

"Really? Can he manage subtle?" Bishan questioned. "I mean, he might run us all over with a lorry, but cinnamon and puzzles?"

"Fair point. Clay might."

Clay, or Nick Clayton, had been in the year below them. A bit reclusive, but Bishan couldn't honestly begrudge him his privacy. He'd always had issues with Valor, but that didn't explain all the others.

Why do I get the terrifying feeling we're all missing something absolutely critical?

A quiet knock on the door broke into their conversation.

"You up, chaps? We've got an earl-sized problem." Ollie spoke from the other side of the door. "I can turn him away, but he'll only return later."

Bishan set his earphones on the nightstand with an aggravated huff while Valor reached for his silenced mobile. "How'd he find us?"

"Detective Inspector Spurling." Valor held out his phone a moment later to show a text to him. "The earl couldn't be bothered to go to Windermere for the body of his son, but he's plenty of time to harass us in the early hours of the morning."

"Chaps?" Ollie knocked on the door again. "Reva's decided to chat with the earl while you get ready."

Bugger.

"Bugger," Valor echoed Bishan's thought.

They bolted from the room, almost knocking Ollie over in their haste. While Valor kept him from falling, Bishan raced ahead to intercept Reva. His sister meant well but would likely exacerbate the situation.

Bishan sidestepped her to block her from view, focusing his attention on the earl's nose and gathering his courage. "Morning."

"Are you usually prone to greeting guests in Tardis pyjamas?" Lord Scott tapped his fingers against his side. "Where is my son?"

Bishan bristled at the dismissiveness he always felt from the man—the whole family, really. He tried to keep his words and tone polite. "My condolences on the loss of your son. You must all be heartbroken."

"Quite."

"Morning." Valor joined them, standing beside Bishan and reaching down to lace their fingers together. "Shouldn't you be on your way to the Lake District?"

"Despite our grave disappointment, you are now my heir. I'll expect you to—" He stopped short when Valor laughed at him. "Show some respect."

"You have some." Bishan squeezed Valor's hand tightly. He despised how the Scotts had treated their younger son; children shouldn't be disposable. "You've lost your heir, and now you want the spare back. Is that it? You're a disgrace to parenthood. Perhaps, *Lord Scott,* it might be time to focus on your daughter as the only child remaining who you claim as your own."

"Bravo." Valor chuckled.

Shushing Valor to stop his laughter, Bishan leaned against him. He'd never liked giving speeches, had avoided it at all costs at school. His sudden eloquent rush of courage failed him as quickly as it appeared.

"Why you little re—"

Valor flew forward to place a warning hand on his father's chest. "Time for you to leave now, Lord Scott. You threw one son away, and you've lost your other. Bish is right. Penny deserves your full focus."

Before the situation could devolve, Bishan dragged Valor back inside the house, and Reva slammed the door in Lord Scott's face. She gave him two thumbs up, a familiar sign of her approval for him. He shook slightly with the sound of his heartbeat booming in his ears.

"You okay?" Bishan searched Valor's face, unable to gauge his emotions. "Sorry I called you a spare."

Valor waved off his apology and looped his arms loosely around Bishan. "I love you. Never, ever change."

"Why would I change?"

"Not what I meant." Valor stole a quick kiss before taking both Bishan's and Reva's hands to lead them through the house. "Let's see about breakfast."

Breakfast quickly turned into toast and coffee in the studio Ollie had put together in what had once been a library on the second storey of the house. Reva and Valor stayed out of the way. It allowed Bishan to ignore their presence and focus on music.

For two days, Bishan played through the score Ollie

provided. Valor helped with some of the instrumentation and lent his voice to the project. They eventually got everything recorded to all of their likings.

While the three old schoolmates played with music, Reva had taken it upon herself to work her graphic art charm. She'd been playing around with the idea for a while. Ollie seemed pleased to let her turn her artistic eye to the posters for his project.

Ollie had been both awed and bemused by her forceful takeover. Bishan thought the mutual crush might be blossoming into something more. His parents would be thrilled with her artistic endeavours; maybe not so much with her potential romance.

Their detective escort joined them on the journey back to Cumbria. They took Reva to Windermere first and had an early supper when his parents refused to take no for an answer. The police station in Grasmere was their next stop to drop Pattie off.

Once inside the station, Bishan started to feel uneasy. He fidgeted. And again. Valor noticed, said their goodbyes, and followed him outside.

Reggie caught up with them at the vehicle. "Do you have a moment?"

"No." Bishan wanted to be home. He'd pushed himself too far in the past week. "What is it?"

The police had been investigating under the assumption Bertie's death was somehow connected to all the others. Grasmere didn't exactly have an extended history of murder, after all. Reggie explained they had yet to find anything concrete.

They had gotten answers to the accident. In Bertie's car, they'd found proof of his involvement. His internet search history also provided a wealth of information, along with emails to the private investigator hired to follow Bishan and Valor.

The investigator had reached out to Bertie the day of the crash when Valor and Bishan had gone on their picnic. Bertie had dismissed the PI and made the short drive over to their parked car. If he'd lived, the case against him would've been ironclad.

"I don't understand why he did this." Valor twisted away from them. "Why kill me? I'm not even in the family anymore. I wanted nothing from them."

Bishan decided Valor had definitely had enough for one day. He glared at the detective then opened the passenger door to push Valor into the car. "We're going home."

"Have you looked at the new anagram?"

"First, it's not an anagram." Bishan closed the door behind him. "Second, it's only been a few days. I'm not actually a police officer. No one is paying me to spend hours trying to decipher some twisted message. I'm not sleeping. Just leave me alone, and I'll get to it."

"Be careful, all right?" Reggie waved to both of them, then jogged up the stairs into the station.

Bishan quickly moved around the car to slide into the driver seat. He sat with his hands gripping the steering wheel while his fingers trembled slightly. "No more talking."

"Ever?" Valor tried for a smile, but Bishan thought it a bit forced. "I'll have to brush up on my charades skills. And you can have the entire day to yourself tomorrow."

An entire day to himself was quite possibly the best gift ever. Bishan loved Valor, their friends, and family. He did. But an empty cottage was pure bliss.

No expending energy being social.

No complaints about my being antisocial.

I can sit on the sofa and count the lines in our paintings without any concerned questions into my well-being.

With Valor recovered enough to return to the Ginger's Bread, Bishan had the cottage all to himself with only Staccato for company. Tea and toast with some of his mum's homemade jam provided the fuel required to tackle the latest message the police had found in Bertie's pocket.

The first few attempts included words Bishan undoubtedly wouldn't utter in front of his mum. He regularly checked them against the already solved puzzles. The killer had kept a similar thread in all his messages, aside from the direct quote.

Several hours later crumpled papers lay around him, covering much of the kitchen table. A few of his more plausible attempts had been set aside. In the end, all his solutions were little more than educated guesses.

If the police caught the killer, maybe then he'd know for sure. Bishan had grown less optimistic with each passing day. *How many more of us will die before they stop him?*

Well, this one seems more plausible than the others.

Sh. The peacock threatened me. He paid the price. Tick. Tock. The clock has been reset. Tick. Tock. Who will be next? Which of the *dynamic duo falls?*

The peacock had to be Bertie. Bishan assumed "me" either referred to Valor or the killer himself. He wondered if they'd had the wrong end of the stick all along. Maybe it had less to do with revenge and more about an unhealthy obsession.

Had one of their old schoolmates wanted to be with Valor (or with him) so badly that jealousy poisoned their minds to the point of twisting it beyond redemption?

CHAPTER 14

Two weeks passed without incident. Bishan's uneasiness grew with each day. They spent an increasing amount of time with both Reggie and Pattie in the guise of late suppers.

It didn't take a mind reader to see how concerned the detectives were. They had no concrete evidence leading them to a particular suspect. The myth of a perfect crime no longer seemed quite so unbelievable.

With all the drama, Valor had chosen not to attend his brother's funeral. Bishan understood his reasons. The Scotts wouldn't have left their son alone to show his respects.

And Bertie hadn't deserved his respect, in Bishan's opinion.

It was hard to mourn for someone who'd tried to hurt them—and almost succeeded in killing them.

"*Pyaare bete.*" His mum held his hand as they sat in his parents' garden with cups of her favourite blend of tea. "We worry about you both. Why don't you and Valor spend the week here? We've plenty of space for you even with Reva camped out in her old room."

No. No. No.

No.

Absolutely not.

On the whole, Bishan had been gifted the best family in the world. His parents had supported him every step of the way. Living with them as an adult had not felt like the best option for him.

He wanted and needed independence.

With Valor's occasional help.

His parents had always worried about him more than his siblings. The false accusation, jail time, and death threats had only made it worse for him—and them. Bishan knew they'd wrap him up in blankets if they could.

"Bishan." She patted his hand before releasing it and returning to her tea. "Promise me you'll be careful."

"Promise."

Picking up both their cups, his mum returned to the house, leaving him alone with his thoughts. Bishan allowed his mind to stray to the killer. The puzzles left behind continued to plague him.

"Bishan?"

He twisted around in the chair to find his dad stepping out of the house. "Fleeing the mum-soon?"

"A pun worthy of your dad." He lowered himself onto the seat beside Bishan. "Mum-soon. She won't appreciate it."

Bishan decided two hours of dithering was sufficient. He plucked a nearby flower to pick at the petals absently. "It's not time for a weekly supper or tea. Why'd you ask me over?"

Routine.

His entire life revolved around following routines created to reduce his stress levels. While Reva and Sunesh handled random visits with their parents, Bishan preferred set times to meet up with them. Even with family, he usually needed a day to prepare and time after to recover.

Preparation frequently involved practising conversations in his head. Valor had typed out a list of potential topics and sentences, sticking them on the inside of the doors of their wardrobe as a Valentine's present years ago. Bishan had gotten quite emotional over the gift, a demonstration of how much Valor worked to make the world an easier place for him.

His parents loved and supported him unconditionally but often failed to realise how differently Bishan saw the world. He appreciated how hard they tried. Valor, after all, had received nothing from his family that didn't come with strings attached.

Quid pro quo.

Bishan remembered the phrase from his Latin classes at school. It fit how Valor's parents treated all their children. *Do they even qualify as a family?*

Grubby, dishonest people.

"Bishan?"

He realised with a wave of embarrassment his thoughts had gotten away from him. "Sorry. Did you say something?"

"We've missed your company."

"You saw me three days ago." Bishan glanced up briefly from the decimated flower in his hand, a summer blossom. They'd begin the slow drift into his favourite song in a few weeks. "You've seen me more this month than you have in ages."

His father rubbed his forehead while chuckling. "Why is it that after thirty years plus of being your dad, I'm still surprised when you don't respond how I expect?"

"I don't know." Bishan shrugged.

A lie.

He did know why. His parents, like many of the wonderful

neurotypical people in his life, tended to forget about his differences. They saw his ability to script and mimic his way through social events as the norm and not the massive effort it was.

They forgot he wasn't "normal." It seemed cruel to point it out, though. And as usual, Bishan brushed the slight hurt off.

"I'm sorry." His father walked over to gently kiss the top of his head. "Your mum's been so worried about you. She's not slept well for weeks."

"The killer's not after her," Bishan protested. "You're retired. Aren't you supposed to be relaxing?"

"It's—" He cut himself off with another wry laugh. "Trust me when I say a parent never stops stressing about the health of their children."

"Okay." Bishan grabbed the mini Rubik's cube out of his pocket to play with. "Can I go home now? We've had lunch and tea."

"Yes."

Good.

His father handled his leaving before supper better than his mother. She frowned and lectured him about his not eating enough. Bishan eventually escaped to meet up with Valor at the Ginger's Bread.

"Rough day?" Valor asked when Bishan slumped into his office and collapsed on the floor behind his desk, resting his head on Valor's knee. "Parental overload?"

Bishan nodded.

"Right." Valor tapped out a few more things on his computer while Bishan enjoyed the smell of gingerbread and not being required to converse. "Let's pick up a pizza. We can have pizza and chips, your favourite, while we watch season one of *Poirot*."

"No puzzles?"

"No puzzles. No police. No family. Just us, the cat, and our bizarre taste in pizza." Valor shifted his chair away from the desk. He bent forward to offer his hands to Bishan, who allowed himself to be tugged into a hug. "I love you, Bish. I'm sorry your family visit stressed you out."

"It's okay."

"It's not really," Valor said firmly.

"You can't fight my mum and dad. They're lovely. And they love me. It's not their fault."

"Yes, they are lovely people who adore you. They're clever enough to learn what works best for you when you're already struggling in our world. Not adjusting is their fault." Valor embraced him tightly, moving in for a kiss before releasing Bishan. "What sort of pizza are we having?"

"Cheese."

"Just cheese?"

"We can add grilled tomatoes, chips, and fried eggs to it." Bishan loved a good breakfast pizza, especially when they added the toppings themselves. "And baked beans."

"We've got those lovely bangers from the butcher." Valor grabbed his hand to lead him out the back of the bakery, avoiding the customers gossiping with Wilfred in the front of the shop. "It'll be a brilliant evening."

"Clogging our arteries and watching a Belgian solve crimes." Bishan hoped by the end of the evening the fear crushing his chest lessened a bit. "Sounds perfect."

Their additions to the simple cheese pizza made the slices impossible to lift up. They made a complete mess of themselves in the attempt. Staccato managed to run off with several pieces of sausage, much to their amusement.

Four episodes and far too many slices of pizza later, Bishan found his shoulders slowly lowering. The tension sending his heartbeat racing lessened considerably until he breathed easier. *And Reva claims junk food is bad for you.*

They stretched out in bed together. Bishan didn't want physical contact, but he wanted the closeness of Valor beside him. He lay so their bodies had barely an inch separating them and he could feel Valor's warmth without the sensory overload of being touched.

"Do you ever wish I was—"

"Not even once." Valor cut him off before Bishan could voice the one fear that always haunted him. "You are who you are. I've never imagined you any other way. I love every single note that makes up the Bishan melody in my heart."

"Weird, but romantic."

Valor rolled onto his back, cackling with laughter. "Weird, but romantic. Our theme song."

"More of a motto."

"I refuse to allow your pedantic nature to ruin my romantic gesture." Valor winked at him. "And yes, I did rhyme on purpose."

"You worry me." Bishan knew Valor was going out of his way to boost their moods. "A lot. Lot. Lottie. A lot."

Lot.

He hated it when a word got stuck on repeat in his head. It had always embarrassed him in school, particularly when forced to give a presentation. Children weren't necessarily the kindest of souls.

"Lottie will appreciate the shout out." Valor, as always, managed to continue the conversation without disrupting him. "Did we save any pudding?"

"We just ate our weight in breakfast pizza." Bishan thought his entire body might float away on a sea of greasy delight.

"There is always room for pudding." Valor poked him in the stomach. "*Always.*"

CHAPTER 15

"Why are we staring at photos of old Harrovians?" Bishan had scowled at the six familiar faces for over an hour with an equally impatient and grumpy Valor while Reggie prodded them to focus. "I'm not a Hogwarts alumnus, divination isn't one of my talents. I've no idea which one, if any, did it."

"Nerd." Valor grunted when Bishan poked him in the side.

"It's your boxed set we watched the movies from over the weekend." He returned to the line-up of photos, most taken from the alumni events within the last few years. "Why are we doing this?"

"I thought maybe seeing them all lined up might jog something from your memories." Reggie had already explained how the detectives had decided to start at the beginning, assuming nothing, and put together a list of suspects based on a number of factors. He'd refused to go into details on what their criteria had been based upon. "Just try?"

"We've been *just trying* for an hour." Bishan shoved the

photos toward Valor with a frustrated huff. He hated being forced to stare at faces, particularly when he didn't fully understand why. "It's pointless if you won't give us any specifics as to why these six."

Three of the names had been the ones Bishan and Valor already suspected, Aubrey being at the top of their list. The others were men who'd attended Harrow but lived in other houses. Bishan hadn't known any of them well.

"What's your gut instinct?"

Bishan blinked for a second, trying to process the detective inspector's question. "Your stomach can't actually have an instinct. Instincts come from learned behaviour and your brain, things you observe. Why would your gut be involved?"

"I'm not actually sure." Reggie sounded bewildered.

"Right. Not literal." Bishan shuffled the photos around on the table, separating them into groups based on how well he'd known them. "This isn't helping."

"Of all the names we put together initially, these six are ones we can't account for during the various attacks. Before we approach them to see if they can provide a sufficient alibi, I'd hoped you might have some deeper background for me." Reggie seemed to have an infinite amount of patience. He hadn't gotten frustrated once, which Bishan found impressive. "Any odd moments with them? Maybe you saw them soon before the first murder?"

"Outside the usual alumni events most of us attend?" Valor asked, giving Bishan time to consider the images in a new light. "It's not out of the ordinary to see one another every year or two."

"Aubrey." Bishan eased one of the photos away from the group. He selected another after a moment of considering. "Stewart Hodge."

"Stewie." Valor shifted forward in his seat to poke at the

image. "Sh. Maybe the 'Shh' in the notes is a homage to his initials?"

"Why those two in particular?" Reggie took both photos, making a notation at the bottom of each.

"Aubrey came to see me at one of my performances with the orchestra. I didn't understand why at the time as we'd never been great friends or interacted much at school." Bishan tapped his finger against Stewart's image. He'd been one of the few boys from other houses who'd gone out of his way to pick at him, until their housemaster intervened. "Stewart emailed me out of the blue a week before the first killing to apologise for his behaviour."

"Weird but not evil." Valor added Nick Clayton's photo. "Clay and Aubrey are my two picks."

Bishan didn't want to see the photos any longer. Couldn't. He'd had enough for one day, for a year even. "I don't know."

Getting to his feet, Bishan fled the room, disappearing down the hall into their music room. Valor could deal with seeing Reggie out. He honestly had no further insights to provide.

As much as Bishan loved mysteries, he lacked the excitement and drive Valor had to solve their own nightmare, though he believed part of Valor's enthusiasm came from fear. All his favourite shows on the telly made investigations seem easy. Procedurals lasted an hour or two at the maximum with everything wrapped up neatly at the end.

Nothing about the cinnamon killings qualified as simple or straightforward. Bishan found his joy in mysteries beginning to dim. For Valor, it appeared to be the exact opposite; he'd developed an obsessive desire to solve this, with or without help.

Bishan didn't understand why.

Sunesh had tried to explain it to him. Bishan didn't understand what him having been locked up had to do with

Valor's obsession. His brother had given up after a circular conversation where both of them wound up frustrated.

Sitting on the bench in front of his piano, Bishan ran through a few scales. He rubbed his hands together, trying to warm up his fingers. They'd had a few rainy days, and late summer had turned cool all of a sudden.

I will not let this take my joy.

I can't allow a killer to make me live in fear.

He sat up straighter, transitioning from scales into a sonata by Carl Vine. It was a piece that had always evoked strength to him. He soaked in courage from playing it.

One musical masterpiece flowed into another. Bishan played until his fingertips began to numb a little. He twisted around on the bench to stare at the large painting on the opposite wall, a landscape he'd done of one of his favourite spots in the Lake District near Lake Windermere.

In the farthest corner of the lake, Bishan had hidden an ode to the Loch Ness monster. They'd gone hunting Nessie on a break from university with a group of friends once because Hugh had become obsessed with the myth. They came home from Scotland with bad colds and no photographic evidence.

And that's why Hugh isn't allowed to plan our vacations ever again.

"Bish?" Valor knocked softly on the closed door. "Want some tea?"

"With cheese toast?"

"One of those days?" Valor asked. He opened the door and leaned against the frame. "The rain finally stopped. Want to sit in the garden?"

"With Mrs Harris watching our every move? Not likely." Bishan caught Staccato when he leapt up into his lap. "Did you leave poor Wilfred to do all the work again?"

"Don't mock the man who makes your toast."

"Why?" Bishan followed him through the cottage into the kitchen. "Will you eat my toast?"

"No."

"Then why shouldn't I mock you?" Bishan allowed Staccato to clamber up onto his shoulder.

"It was rhetorical."

"It wasn't a question." Bishan blinked in surprise when Valor threw a piece of bread in his face. "It's not toasted yet. Can statements be rhetorical? I don't want cheese now. Just toast."

"I just made one. Right. No cheese." Valor dropped a new slice of bread into the toaster. "Butter? Jam? Lemon curd? Marmite?"

"Marmite? Why do we even keep it?"

"For Sunny."

"Sunesh hates Marmite." Bishan pointed to the jar of homemade lemon curd. Lottie brought it over to them whenever she made up a fresh batch for Wilfred. He refused to have his breakfast without it, apparently. "How did I miss Marmite in our kitchen?"

"I hide it and trick Sunny into eating it." Valor waggled his eyebrows before showing off the Marmite. "Serves him right for lying about the curry."

"One time." Bishan remembered the time his older brother had tricked Valor into eating the spiciest curry his auntie made. "He did it once. Ages ago."

"I have a long memory." Valor returned the Marmite to its hiding place in the back of the cupboard.

CHAPTER 16

The beginning of September brought changes in Grasmere. Hugh moved from Manchester to a cottage across the street from them. Bishan found it strange, despite their old friend insisting he'd applied for the promotion ages ago.

He hadn't.

There was zero chance of him wanting to live in Grasmere. Hugh loved living in the city. He'd mentioned it repeatedly, enjoyed being single in Manchester.

Why move now?

And why was he over at their house constantly if he'd moved for work?

Neither Bishan nor Valor believed their friend's reasoning. They chalked it up to him being concerned over their safety. Bishan wouldn't put it past their local detectives wanting any help they could get either.

The weeks had gone swiftly, with his days spent recording pieces for Oliver. Reva stopped by on Fridays to retrieve his work to drive up to Oliver in London to drop it off. Bishan didn't mention he could easily email it.

Who am I to get in the way of true puppy love?
They're so adorable.

Somehow in the midst of everything, Bishan found time to start a new project of his own—composing his first symphony. He heavily relied on his cello and piano for it. One of his dreams from Harrow days had been to create a masterpiece of his own.

He'd never tried because of crippling self-doubt, but something had changed within him.

Day after day was spent locked in the music room. He lost himself in the drama of it. The first bars took forever to get perfect.

Composing had never come naturally to him, but the struggle drew his mind away from the fear and upheaval that had been brought into their lives. Bishan etched out the emotions in the music. With each added note though, the tone of the piece grew darker and far more sinister than he'd initially intended.

In Harrow, Bishan had earned himself not only a music scholarship but a coveted spot in the Guild for his achievements. He adored every aspect of orchestral magic except one. *I hate composing.*

We hates it. Hates it.

Right.

I'm not Gollum.

"Bish?" Valor's muffled inquiry drew his attention away from the piano.

Bishan eased off his headphones and twisted around on the bench to face Valor. He had just enough time to lower his hands to catch the custard doughnut tossed gently to him. "You went by Lucia's. Did you get sausage rolls as well?"

"Of course." Valor took a massive bite of his own doughnut. "I thought you might want some brain fuel. I've tea as well. Lottie sent over your favourite blend. She also made some sort of casserole for us. Between her and your mum, do they think we never shop or cook?"

"We admittedly do takeaways a lot." Bishan knew they both could cook, but usually laziness found them turning to picking food up. "More than we should."

Valor licked his fingers clean from sugar and custard. "About Hugh."

Bishan held his hand up while he finished inhaling his own sugary treat. He waited until his mouth was cleared and his brain had processed the change of subject. "Are we going to talk about how Hugh definitely didn't apply for a transfer to Grasmere ages ago?"

"Yes, yes we are." Valor plonked himself down on the floor, leaning against Bishan's leg. He held up a paper bag. "Sausage roll?"

Bishan grabbed one and bumped it against the one in Valor's hand. "Cheers."

Valor took a bite of the roll, sending flakes of pastry everywhere that Staccato chose to chase after. "Was Hugh asked to come by Reggie? Or did Hugh bring it up himself?"

"They colluded." Bishan had gotten the sense from the detective inspector recently that his stress levels had gone up for some reason. Something had caused him to fear an imminent attack. Why else would Hugh randomly move in across from them? "Collude. From the Latin *colludere*, meaning to have a secret agreement."

"They definitely colluded," Valor readily agreed.

Bishan was grateful Valor, as usual, didn't focus on his sudden transformation into a dictionary. "Why didn't they just tell us?"

"I'm sure they wanted to avoid making us uneasy." Valor flicked a piece of his sausage to allow Staccato to race after it. "Want some of this tea?"

"They've failed at their mission. His presence makes me

more afraid than I was previously." He got to his feet, laughing when Valor fell over dramatically without the support of his leg. "Tea."

The casserole turned out to be more of a vegetable stew with dumplings. Valor ate all the latter while Bishan stuffed himself with the perfectly soft potatoes. They fought over the orzo pasta and tomatoes, leaving the carrots behind.

"Cheddar and thyme make the best dumplings." Valor slouched into the chair with a contented sigh. "So, about Hugh."

"We did that already."

"No, I mean, how should we punish him for breaking the code?"

"You realise we're not actually at Harrow, right? We're adults in our thirties?" Bishan shook his head at Valor. "We can't invoke our rules for lying to each other over beaks. Reggie isn't one of our teachers. He's our age."

"Are we not punishing him then?" Valor tilted his chair back and balanced it on two legs. "We could dump cat litter in his garden."

"No, if I wouldn't let you do that to Mrs Harris, you can't do it to Hugh either." Bishan didn't really understand Valor's desire to poke at their nosy neighbour. She was an annoyance, but he could think of far worse people to deal with than a frog-obsessed elderly woman. "We could ask him."

"Boring." Valor dropped the chair legs back to the floor. "Let's go now. We can raid his fridge for pudding."

"We have pudding."

"It's always better when it's stolen." Valor shot out of his seat, grabbing Bishan to lead him toward the door. "I saw Detective Inspector Spurling's car parked outside Hugh's cottage. What say we surprise them?"

"Who says pudding is better stolen?"

"Benedict Cumberbatch in school." Valor grinned at

Bishan when he nudged him in the side. He paused to allow Staccato to climb up to his shoulder. "Well, he probably did."

"Pudding is pudding. Theft not required." Bishan threaded his fingers with Valor's as they made the short walk across the street to Hugh's cottage. "And you didn't even know Benedict."

"Details, details." Valor rang the doorbell, knocked on the door, and kicked the frame lightly. "Think I have their attention?"

"I think I should've stayed at home." Bishan released Valor's hand and stepped behind him. He glanced around Valor when the door opened to reveal Hugh. "Hi."

"Do you have pudding?" Valor pushed by Hugh into the cottage, dragging Bishan along for the ride. "Well, hello Detective Inspector Spurling, what a surprise to find you here. With all those case files on the table as well. Have you eaten? We have some mangled carrots left in a casserole."

With an embarrassed groan, Bishan tugged his hand free from Valor's. His chest tightened as they walked through the cramped hallway, and he darted into the kitchen to stand by the sink to stare out the window. Hugh needed to do some work in the garden; it looked pitiful.

"Have you even stepped into the garden?" Bishan couldn't help asking.

"No. Did you see my flat in Manchester? The closest thing I had to a plant was mould growing on an old block of cheese in the back of my fridge." Hugh joined him in the kitchen, staying on the opposite side to give him space. "What's this about pudding?"

Bishan couldn't help a full-body shudder. "After hearing about your cheese? I'll skip the pudding if it's in your refrigerator. What is wrong with you?"

"I work long hours." Hugh moved over to grab his kettle to fill it with water. "Does everyone want tea?"

"Is there mould on the tea?"

"No, Lord Bryon, I've left the mould off the tea just for you." Hugh levelled a glare at him that Bishan ignored completely. "Did you two want something?"

"You hate the countryside." Bishan got straight to the point, talking over Valor's sigh of obvious exasperation. "And Grasmere. And the Lake District. You *love* Manchester. And I wager you've kept your flat while renting this place."

"Bish." Hugh glanced from Bishan to Valor. "I...."

Bishan waited impatiently after Hugh's voice trailed off. "Well? You what? We already know our lives are in danger. Why've you suddenly moved across the street from us?"

"Are you always this welcoming to new neighbours?"

"*Hugh*." Bishan refused to let the conversation go. He knew Valor probably would've found a more subtle way to handle the conversation. "What changed?"

"We found another body." Reggie spoke up before Hugh could answer. "And another puzzle."

Bishan grabbed hold of the counter to keep from stumbling. It felt like the words smacked him hard in the chest. "Who?"

"Ollie B."

"Oliver Best?" Valor sounded as stunned as Bishan felt. "Why the hell would someone kill Ollie B? Everyone loved him; he loved everyone."

Bishan remembered one bit of information Valor had probably forgotten. "Didn't Ollie kiss you under the mistletoe at the Christmas party a few years ago?"

Valor cringed at the memory. "He smelled of wine, Marmite, and old coffee grounds. A vile mixture."

"Could it have been enough for the killer to be jealous or angry?" Bishan believed the murders all connected through some misguided obsession with Valor.

"We need to rethink our list of potential victims." Reggie

grabbed a notebook from the table with all the files. "I think we're going to want coffee—and tea. It's going to be a long evening."

Coffee, tea, pudding, and a miracle.

Not that either of us believes in miracles.

We're screwed.

"Pudding. First pudding."

As they progressed into the evening, Staccato grew restless. Or at least, that was the excuse Bishan used to go home. Hugh and Valor had gotten too boisterous for him to handle.

With Staccato running free in the garden chasing after one of Mrs Harris's stray amphibians, Bishan wrapped up in a blanket to sit outside, enjoying the last of twilight. He didn't need the duvet for warmth, but the familiar weight helped soothe him. Thinking up names of potential victims had seemed a thousand times more painful than coming up with suspects.

And how do we ignore that my name is probably at the top of the list?

If it's an obsession with Valor that started this, surely getting rid of me is paramount?

If we're right.

If. If. If.

I'm so tired of not knowing what's going on.

He preferred to focus on the new anagram that wasn't actually an anagram. The program used this time was one from their last year at Harrow. It had been a performance by the school's symphony orchestra, one in which both Bishan and Valor had played.

Should I be terrified for myself or for Valor?

Bishan wondered if he should review all the previous programs found to see if a connection could be made between the show or performance and the victim. Lifting up Staccato, he headed into the cottage. He made tea, set out a treat for the cat, and sat at the kitchen table to get to work.

Picking up his notebook, Bishan turned to a blank page. He quickly scoured the program and jotted down all the bolded letters. Only twenty-five. The lowest number he'd seen so far across all the puzzles found during their nightmarish spring and summer.

He hoped the shorter pool of letters made it easier to solve.

Gong?

Why on earth would he use the world gong?

Doubtful.

An hour later his tea had gone cold. Bishan emptied it out and made a fresh cup. Staccato purred contentedly from his spot on the blanket on the chair beside him. He'd gone through multiple versions before finally finding a plausible one.

Wrong. Wrong. The poet falls. Shh.

Ollie B had not been a poet. He'd played sports a lot and split the rest of his attention between the Harrow Farm and the horse-racing society, the Turf Club. *I wrote poetry, gobs of it.*

Pushing the notebook away from him, Bishan leaned back in the chair. He stared blankly at the words written on paper by his favourite pen in his favourite bright green ink. Staccato leapt into his lap, the sudden movement jolting Bishan to his feet.

He stood, Staccato now on the ground; the chair had been knocked over as well. "Okay. Breathe, Bishan. The cat isn't a serial killer unless frogs are involved."

And I'm not a frog.

Staccato scolded him in several loud meows before prancing off to hide in his favourite spot on one of their bookshelves. Bishan righted the chair and collapsed into it, pressing his hand to his chest.

It couldn't be, could it? All the previous riddles seemed to reference the deceased victim in some manner. Bishan feared this one changed things, and it chilled him to his core, causing him to reach over to grab the duvet Staccato had used as a bed to wrap around himself.

He sat in a deceptively cosy silence in the cottage. Was the mystery going to end with his life hanging in the balance? He didn't know what to do—or how to process the raw fear.

I don't know if I can do this.

CHAPTER 17

"Why are we doing this?" Bishan asked for the twentieth time. Not nineteenth, or twenty-first; he'd kept track as a way to distract himself. Valor had woken up a few days after the latest murder and decided they should "see Cumbria in all its glory." It basically amounted to them playing tourists. "We've managed to avoid all this nonsense for years. Why are you torturing me with it now?"

"Romance isn't torture." Valor grabbed his hand to continue leading him through the Holehird Gardens. "We're being romantic."

"No, romance is when we have a *Poirot* marathon with all our favourite puddings and chips because a balanced diet is important. Or when we hide away in the music room and play for hours." Bishan found the entire exercise of forced normalcy pointless. They did love in their own way. "Why've we spent the entire day in public?"

"It's a date."

"Bit out of the usual for us, though, isn't it?" Bishan had

raced through the museum, grumbled through two galleries, and dragged his feet through the garden. He was about ready to shove Valor into the nearest pond or lake. "When was the last time we voluntarily went to a museum?"

Valor scratched his jaw, clearly thinking. "Lower sixth. We wanted to avoid playing Harrow Football during that horrid stormy week, so we volunteered to visit the National Maritime Museums. It was riveting." He snickered with Bishan for a second. "I love you."

"Yes. What does that have to do with your sudden desire to play explorer?" Bishan shifted behind Valor slightly when a loud group of tourists went by. "And I love you too. Still, don't know why you've dragged me from one end of our corner of Cumbria to the other."

"Hardly." Valor had to push onto a different path when yet another bunch of people went by.

Bishan bit the inside of his cheek when a rush of intense emotion went through him. He knew they'd both missed the signs of sensory overload. "Can we be romantic at home?"

As yet another boisterous group strolled by them, Valor finally caught on to his distress. They exited the gardens quickly. Bishan slipped into the passenger side of their car, taking his headphones out and immediately scrolling on his phone to find his high-anxiety playlist.

Tired of a rental, they'd finally gotten a new vehicle to replace their totalled one. Bishan had held to his desire for another Fiat; Valor had wanted something more substantial. They'd gone back and forth, test driving a few models until settling on a Ford Ecosport.

It had been hard to argue with Valor's reasons. He'd wanted something larger—more substantial after the devastation caused by their accident. Bishan had readily agreed; he could deal with not getting another small hatchback.

"I'm so sorry, Bish." Valor kept his voice low. He grabbed the quilt they kept in the back seat and carefully laid it across Bishan. They had an emergency stress kit stored in the vehicle for just such purposes. "I'll drop you at the cottage then pick up some of the sticky toffee pudding and treacle tart from Lewis's. Maybe grab chips as well?"

With a grunt of acknowledgement, Bishan breathed through the quiet chaos running through him. His mind was blank. Worse than. He couldn't fully form thoughts or words even as his brain felt full of ever-expanding cotton.

Angry cotton.

They drove the long way home, avoiding the curve where they'd crashed. Valor thankfully stayed quiet. It allowed Bishan to bleed off the raw energy with slow, deep breaths.

He was exhausted.

His head ached like it had grown to weigh a ton. Bishan tilted back to rest against the seat. They had definitely overdone it.

After dropping him off, Valor headed out to pick up the treats. By the time he returned, Bishan had spent much-needed time in the blissfully peaceful embrace of music. He knew it would take hours, maybe even a day to return to his version of normal.

Staccato had snuggled up with him, purring deeply. He added a comforting presence. It helped reduce his stress even further.

The weather hadn't grown cold enough to need the fire, but Bishan still had multiple blankets draped around him. He found the weight helped to centre him. His mind floated between the musical melody, the vibration from Staccato's purring, and the warmth of the quilts.

When Valor brought in the food, they formed the blankets into a nest in front of the telly. They turned off all the lights and indulged their sweet tooth under the watchful eye of their favourite Belgian detective. Three episodes into their marathon, the pudding feast turned into a food coma that saw both of them drifting off.

"Valor!"

"Bish?" Valor's sleepy voice came from the kitchen. "Got coffee on. You all right? Did Staccato try to smother you?"

It took him a moment to register what Valor had said. The dream had been something straight from a horror film. He'd woken up staring at his hands, fully expecting them to be covered in blood.

Valor's blood.

Bishan had suffered through various versions of the nightmare since the killings began. They all ended the same, with Valor's death. He wished his subconscious would stop torturing him.

"Fine. I'm fine. Perfectly fine," Bishan lied. He trembled under the blankets and tried to shake off the nightmare. It had seemed so real. "I'm fine."

Valor walked into the living room with their tin of ground coffee in his hand. He crouched down in front of Bishan, reaching out to brush the sleep-mussed hair out of Bishan's eyes. "Have a *bête noir*?"

"Is that all the French you remember from school?"

"Oui." Valor shifted around to sit on the floor beside him. "Don't change the subject."

It wasn't entirely changing the subject. Bishan had done slightly better in languages. Their entire year had done better than Valor, which made it even more entertaining to him when Valor trotted out the few words he remembered.

Maybe I am changing the subject, if only to allow the dream to slip away.

"It's slipped away." Bishan leant over to rest his head on Valor's shoulder. "Do you think Reggie can stop *him*?"

"Eventually." Valor stared at the tin in his hand. "Eventually."

And the question I can't bring myself to ask is whether we'll be alive to see it?

CHAPTER 18

With everything else going on, Bishan had known the issue of the Scott family had only been put off temporarily. He was proved right two weeks into September. After much needling from Penny, Valor had caved and agreed to head to London to speak with them—and their solicitor.

In the middle of working on his symphony and Ollie's project, Bishan had begged off going. He'd had enough of London for one year. And his presence would only serve to antagonise Valor's family even further, so he opted to stay home.

The peace and quiet of the cottage hadn't lasted for long. Reva and Sunesh crashed his party of one by inviting themselves over for lunch. Bishan decided to endure their presence with a grace he didn't feel.

"Bishy. Oh, Bishy." Reva smiled her sweetest smile while dishing up the rajma masala one of his aunts had made for them at her restaurant. "Are you going to London anytime soon?"

Their auntie and her wife on their father's side owned a

restaurant in Windermere, and they lived close to his parents. His mum occasionally helped out in the kitchen since she'd retired. They had family suppers there at least a few times a month.

"Artless isn't a trait we usually associate with you." Sunesh sat across the table from them; he'd gotten time off from work to visit the family for the entire week. "Why does Bishan have to travel to London so you can visit Oliver?"

"Brothers." She flipped her hair over her shoulder with an annoyed huff.

While his brother and sister verbally sparred, Bishan grabbed a handful of the deep fried onion fritters that had been packed with the bean curry. He hid a smile when Staccato deftly snuck onto the couch to curl up on Sunesh's suit jacket. His smile faded when he spotted familiar eyes peering over the fence.

Speaking of artless.

Does she not know we can see her?

Mrs Harris had begun to monitor their moves constantly —more than usual. Reggie said she'd even started to send reports to the police. The woman obviously still believed one of them had committed the murders. If Bishan hadn't loved their cottage and garden so much, he'd seriously consider moving to avoid her.

"Bish?"

Bishan shifted his gaze back to his sister. "What?"

"London?"

"Not if I can avoid it." He shook his head firmly, even when Reva tried to use her sad eyes on him. "Sunny's right. You don't need an excuse. Ollie would love to see you."

Reva flicked a kidney bean at Sunesh when he laughed. "You are both completely useless."

"Only when we say no to your demands," Sunesh retorted.

Unlike some of the other middle children he'd known, Bishan enjoyed having both an elder and a younger sibling to distract others. He hadn't wanted to draw attention to himself. Sunesh and Reva had both managed to shine in all the right ways in their childhood, leaving him to enjoy the quiet bliss of his world of music.

They'd been the perfect foils for him. Sunesh had often purposely distracted the attention of their extended family at gatherings, deftly moving between Bishan and overly affectionate aunties. Reva had always been the apple of everyone's eye.

"No food fights. Staccato might try to eat curry, and you're cleaning up the mess if he does." Bishan pointed his fork at Reva when she went to throw another bean. "Are you staying all day?"

"You don't love us." Reva faux sobbed into her curry. She clutched dramatically at her chest. "Oh, the pain. The misery. The overwhelming heartache."

"It's indigestion. You'll be fine." Sunesh cut her off in the middle of her rant. "Are you sure graphic design is where you want to go? I can see overacting as a fine skill for you."

"Ha. Ha. *Ha.*" She added unnecessary emphasis to the last "ha," in Bishan's opinion. "Did you hear Dad's going to unretire?"

"How do you unretire? Is that even a word?" Sunesh seemed as surprised as Bishan by the news. Both of their parents had decided to retire in their sixties, once their children had all completed their education and begun to work. They'd spent a bit of time travelling before settling back in Windermere. "Did he get bored?"

"Being an accountant is boring," Reva interjected. "He decided to take up being a tour guide."

"Our father is going to play tour guide." Sunesh inhaled a bean, choking violently.

"Ha! Your face is a picture." Reva was far too pleased with herself. "He's writing a column on finance for some online magazine, which sounds as boring as accounting."

It did.

While Reva and Sunesh bickered playfully about their parents' post-retirement lives, Bishan finished up his lunch. He'd intended to spend the day working on his symphony. His sister had brought over a CD collection from their auntie of her favourite Hindustani classical music, particular the sitar and veena focused ones.

He'd had the idea to include some of his family's culture into his symphony. Stringed instruments would blend in perfectly with what he'd already composed. He hadn't asked for the CDs, but his auntie wanted to help.

She was apparently not aware he could search for any music he wanted online. It was his auntie's way of being supportive. Reva called it sweet; Bishan thought it was point-less and a waste of energy.

He'd learned over the years allistics frequently made impractical gestures in an effort to be helpful. It had taken a while for him to appreciate them. Valor usually pointed out to him that sometimes it was more important to recognize the effort over the actual usefulness.

"Bish?"

Bishan glanced up to find both his siblings watching him. "What?"

"You went quiet."

"I go quiet frequently." Bishan didn't believe that was his sister's point, and he'd prefer it if she said what she meant.

Clearly sensing his unease, Sunesh ended the visit after another hour. Bishan waited until they'd pulled away from the drive before carefully locking the door and checking the back one as well. He'd grown obsessive about it in the past few months; he also spent an unhealthy amount of time making sure their security cameras worked.

Time slipped away while Bishan stared at the live feed from the CCTV cameras. *Nothing. No one. Not even a stray frog. Maybe now I can do something other than go cross-eyed watching the garden?* He tried to drag himself away but struggled as his anxiety levels rose. The worrywart in his mind whispered the killer might show up if he even dared to glance away for a second.

With immense effort, Bishan forced himself out of the chair and room. He shut the door firmly on their office. It became easier to walk away with a wooden barrier between him and the cameras.

Still, every gust of wind, or sound from the cottage, or bump from Staccato playing with a toy, and Bishan leapt from the piano bench with his pulse racing. Every cell of his body hummed with fear on the edge of panic. Never mind the cinnamon, a heart attack would be the death of him before the killer actually got there.

Why did I kick Reva and Sunny out?

Why is Valor in London with his family who don't even care about him?

As the afternoon progressed, Bishan gave up on composing anything useful. He couldn't settle down even to read or watch the telly. Thoughts flew through his mind uncontrolled and far too fast for him to register.

Grabbing his head, Bishan tried to find his centre. His mom had worked so hard to teach him yoga and meditation. Deep breathing helped a little.

Or, it did.

Until someone started banging on his front door so violently it rattled on the hinges.

Bishan hesitantly inched to the door, opening just enough to see through the crack. He glared when he spotted Hugh.

"What? Is it Val? Is he okay? Did someone else die? Please. Please say it's not Val. What's wrong?"

"He's fine." Hugh held a hand out to stop Bishan in the midst of his panicked rambling. "The feed from your CCTV cameras has gone down. Olly Smith messaged me to say someone was interfering with them."

And there goes my pulse rate again.

"To what end? And how many times has it been messed with?" Bishan wondered what the point of a security system was if anyone could hack into it. "How easy is it to get into?"

"We'll find out," Hugh promised.

Before or after he kills us?

CHAPTER 19

When a bouquet of cinnamon sticks was delivered to the Ginger's Bread, Bishan had reached the end of his tether. The killer had dicked with their CCTV cameras, paid someone to head to their shop; they were being toyed with. It was a twisted game, and Bishan didn't want to play anymore.

The police wanted him to go into hiding. Bishan refused. He'd already been locked up once because of the killer; he refused to allow it to happen for a second time, even for his own safety.

He couldn't.

It wouldn't be the same this time, obviously. He just couldn't. It would seem too much like a concession to the killer.

Valor had insisted on coming home immediately when Bishan called him. Bishan put him off. He knew Valor needed resolution with his family, and heading back to Grasmere early wouldn't help anyone.

Me included.

Some mornings, Bishan woke up convinced he'd see the

stark jail walls. They closed in on him. So he chose to ignore the advice from Reggie, Hugh, and Pattie when they argued with him about the need for him to go to a safe house.

I am not in a damned procedural on the telly.

Do they even use safe houses in real life?

Absurd.

It's a fancy term for a new form of jail, and I'm not having it. Not again.

Valor couldn't return soon enough for Bishan. He would, at least, understand. And go to bat for him.

Needing to get away from the cottage, Bishan bugged Reva to pick him up. They drove to Windermere to his auntie's restaurant. It was closed while she, her wife, and his mum prepared for a wedding reception later in the day.

He adored his auntie, Aashi Tamboli, who had come to London in her early twenties. She'd met and fallen in love with a young Spanish woman, Luna. They'd been together ever since, moving to Windermere to be closer to the rest of his family, opening an Indian and Spanish fusion restaurant.

They served Indian inspired tapas. Aashi pulled from all the regions of her country for vibrant flavours, while Luna brought her own tastes and culture into the mix. It had become incredibly successful over the last few years.

Bishan was proud of his aunties. They'd followed their dreams and found true happiness together. He'd been inspired by their courage to never hide their joy in each other.

It hadn't been easy for them. The two women had been a pillar of support for him and Valor, knowing how painful family rejection could be. He adored them even more for their courage.

"Oh, Bish. My poor dear." His auntie Aashi patted his cheeks with flour-covered hands, hugging him in a cloud of saffron. "Come, come. You'll help with the chiroti. The bride wants dozens of the crunchy sweets. You'll help roll out the roti, yes? Good boy. You've such a deft hand with them. Not like my Luna. She never manages to make them delicately."

Reva snickered behind him. "Be a good boy, Bishy."

"No teasing your brother." Aashi grabbed her by the hand to drag her through the restaurant toward the kitchen. "Now, what's this I hear about this Oliver boy? Hmm? How did you meet him? Is he treating you well?"

Her wife, his auntie Luna, smiled brightly at Bishan before holding out her arm to wait for him to take it. "How is your Valor doing? Is he surviving the torture of playing nicely in London?"

"Surviving? Yes. I'm not certain you can play nicely with the Scotts." Bishan had constantly been texting with Valor, who'd already had several verbal clashes with his father. His mother and sister appeared genuinely interested in some form of reconciliation. "The earl isn't inclined to be kind no matter how Val behaves."

"We'll be extra *kind* to him when he returns home." Luna squeezed his hand. She knew first-hand how cruel family could be; hers had abandoned her once she'd officially married Aashi. The Tambolis had welcomed her with open arms. "Poor dear. You'll both be fine."

"Why can I never get service in your kitchen?" Reva's grumbling interrupted them. She waved her mobile around, trying to find a corner for a signal. "It's always in here. The dining room doesn't have this problem."

"Perhaps a sign to focus on food and family? And not your new boyfriend?" Luna teased her, releasing Bishan's hand to move over to the large stainless steel table in the centre of the room. "These appetisers won't prepare themselves."

While his aunties and mum lectured Reva about her phone obsession, Bishan went over to wash his hands. He'd already formed six chiroti before they noticed. His sister teased him for being a goody two shoes.

The conversation quite pointedly avoided the murders. Bishan appreciated their attempt to distract him. It worked until his auntie pulled out a hoard of spices, including cinnamon.

Twisting away from the table, Bishan decided to make tea for everyone. They'd been at it for over an hour already. All the dough and fillings made him hungry for lunch, and he scrounged around in the cupboards for something to eat.

"Bish?" Luna waved him over to one of the commercial refrigerators. She plucked out a plate with a large slice of cake. "We've experimented to create a cardamom, coconut, and saffron spiced *tres leches* cake."

"Pudding." Bishan happily accepted the plate, handing over the tin of tea in exchange. "How'd it go over?"

"Good enough to go on our autumn menu permanently." She nudged him away to pull down several cups for tea. "How are you and Valor doing with all the stress?"

Bishan lifted his shoulders helplessly. "Fine."

"A mild-mannered word for barely managing to cope under it all?" Luna made everyone's tea just how they liked it. Bishan had no idea how she always managed to remember. "Whatever happens, however long it takes for the police to find them, none of this is your fault."

Bishan shrugged again.

His aunt stepped over to wrap her arms around him. She gave soft hugs that made him feel better. "Eat your cake. It makes everything better."

"Share." Reva snuck over with her own spoon, sending the flour covering her hands and arms flying. "Sharing is caring, Bish."

"No." He dodged out of the way of her spoon. "Get your own pudding."

"Reva." His mum intervened after another minute of his sister's teasing. She always enjoyed filching from other people's plates; Bishan found it a distressing habit of hers. "I'm sure your auntie can find another treat for you to have with tea. Leave your brother alone."

After a round of tea and leftover sweets from the previous night, they all got back to work. Reva periodically complained about not being able to get her phone to connect. Bishan grew tired of the whinging and shoved her toward the door that led out into the dining room.

Reva crashed straight into the unmoving door with a painful cry. "What the— It's locked."

"That's not possible." Aashi brushed her hands on her apron, rushing over to the door. She pushed hard on it with no luck, twisting the knob. "It's like someone put something against it. The knob is unlocked, but it won't budge at all."

Bishan exchanged a worried glance with his sister. He twisted around to try the rear exit, the only other door in the kitchen, which led out to the back of the restaurant. "It's blocked as well. The knob turns, though."

"Bish?" Reva walked over to him, keeping her voice low once she reached him. "Is it him?"

He avoided his sister's wide, worried eyes. "I've no idea. Can you get a text out?"

"I'll try."

Grabbing his own phone, Bishan sent messages to anyone he could think of without a one connecting. He tried every angle in the kitchen, trying to find some spot with even the tiniest amount of signal. They only needed a single person to know, who could then reach out to the police.

They all repeatedly tried to place calls or get a text message out. Nothing worked. Bishan pushed away at the panic bubbling up inside him; he had to keep a cool head if they had any chance of surviving.

0

 DAHLIA DONOVAN

"Try Hugh. Anyone." Bishan couldn't get his mobile to connect. He glanced around for the landline, only to realise it was in the front of the restaurant—not the kitchen. They'd been trapped. *But why?*

"Why don't we have a phone in the kitchen?" Luna asked. "We're fixing that."

"When we get out," Aashi agreed readily.

If, not when.

And how the hell do I get all of us out of here?

CHAPTER 20

A minute went by but seemed more like an hour. Bishan's mind had completely frozen. He couldn't quite grasp what was happening.

He wanted to bang his head against the nearest wall. Anything to jolt his brain into gear. Now was not the time to fall into a shutdown. *Come on, Bishan, get your autistic self together, you can do this.*

"The first thing to do is not panic." Reva sounded quite freaked out to Bishan. She'd gone a rather splotchy colour as well. "We're locked in the kitchen. We have knives so we can protect ourselves."

The terror in his sister's voice brought him out of his own panic. Bishan knew they'd only have a short amount of time to attempt to ensure they survived. And even then, the odds were probably not stacked in their favour.

"*Bish.* What do we do?"

Ignoring his clearly panicked sister, Bishan checked both doors, testing to see if either of them would budge. They wouldn't. And he only succeeded in badly bruising his arm in the process.

His aunties and mum kept alternating between shouting for help and attempting to find some corner of the kitchen where their mobiles would work. Bishan made his way to the interior door, pressing his ear against it to see what he could hear. *Nothing.* The shrieking behind him made it impossible.

How was he supposed to think with their arguing?

"Will you all please shut up?"

Nothing.

"Shut. UP," Bishan shouted at his family. They fell silent instantly, likely stunned by his actually raising his voice at them. He pushed his ear to the door again to listen for any sound of movement. *What is that noise? What's he doing out there? And why has he trapped us?* "Can anyone hear anything at all?"

All the killings thus far had involved an up close and personal encounter; this was definitely going to be different. Bishan doubted cinnamon would be the weapon of choice with numbers on their side. Locking them inside the kitchen meant the killer had another method in mind.

But what?

Fire?

An explosion?

A gas leak would provide both, but he'd have to be in the kitchen, wouldn't he?

He didn't smell gas. Bishan's mind readily threw about several equally horrifying suggestions. *I am not sitting around and waiting.*

No matter what happened, Bishan intended to fight until his last breath. His gaze flitted around the room, trying to assess their best options. He refused to surrender to the inevitable and turn into a terrified bowl of jelly.

Nothing is ever set in stone.

I am not dying.

And no one is touching my family.

His gaze kept coming back to the table, covered in ingredients and half-done appetizers. Pushing everything off it, Bishan shouted at the others to help him drag it across the kitchen. They pressed it between a tall shelf and the wall by the rear exit.

Bishan had no idea if it would hold up under much weight, but it was better than nothing. The position of the table provided protection from walls on two sides and the shelf. He practically shoved his mum, sister, and aunties into the small space underneath the table.

Okay.

What now?

If it's fire, we're the farthest away from the interior of the restaurant we can get.

Towels.

Grabbing every available towel, Bishan dumped them in the sink and turned the tap on. He placed a bunch of them by the interior door to hopefully keep the smoke out. The remaining five would work to cover their faces.

That's what they do in movies, right?

If it's fire, we just have to survive until someone notices the smoke, calls emergency, and the fire brigade shows up.

His mum waved anxiously at him, trying to get him to squeeze down underneath the table with them. "What's happening?"

Urging her to stay there, Bishan remained by the interior door trying to listen. He thought he'd heard movement on the other side of the door. His sister had been scrunched up behind their aunts, and disrupted his listening with a triumphant shout—she'd managed to get a text out to Sunesh.

"And you couldn't have sent a text out to the police instead?" Luna muttered.

"Sunny will call the police for us." His mum silenced his

aunt and sister, who'd started to bicker slightly. "Bishan? Come here, please?"

"I'll—"

An explosion cut him off before Bishan could get another word out. He had barely a second to process the screaming from his family. A sharp pain struck his head, then everything around him went dark.

"Bish? Bishan? C'mon, now. No sleeping on the job."

A familiar voice drew Bishan into a painful awareness. His body from the chest down felt as though an elephant had sat on him. A cacophony of sound echoed all around, dulled only slightly by the constant ringing in his ears.

"Bish?"

He managed to force his eyes open, only to close them a second later to avoid dust particles. He tried to speak but had to clear his throat repeatedly. "Mum?"

"Safe. She's safe. Reva and your nutty aunties. They're all alive." Hugh bent forward slightly until Bishan could almost feel his breath with each word. "They're terrified. A bit of smoke inhalation from the fire caused by the explosion. Quick thinking with the table. It kept the ceiling off them when it collapsed." Hugh grabbed his mobile when it went off. "Hang on. I've been trying to reach Valor." He held it out with the screen facing Bishan. "I've got Val on Facetime for you."

"Bish." Valor seemed visibly shaken. "I'm on my way home. The earl's letting me borrow the helicopter. I know, he's being nice for once. Penny's giving me a lift over to it; Ollie's going to drive the car back to Grasmere for us. Listen. You stay awake for Hugh. I'll be there. I'll be there before you know. Just keep your eyes open."

"Val." Bishan tried to lift his head, but the weight of whatever had fallen on him made it impossible. "I love—"

"No. Don't you sodding say it." Valor cut him off. "Don't."

Bishan knew despite Valor's insistence that they might not get another chance. "I *love* you. Even if you don't want me to say it."

"We're almost at the helicopter. I've got to go; I won't be able to hear you on the flight." Valor appeared to be getting out of a car then walking while carrying his phone. He hesitated for a few minutes. "I love you."

The chat window closed and Hugh pulled his phone back. He shifted again so Bishan could see his face instead. All around them, emergency personnel worked at a frantic pace, trying to clear enough rubble to get to him.

Dust and smoke forced him to close his eyes again. Bishan wheezed slightly as the weight on his body continued to press into him. He repeatedly blinked before peering up at Hugh, who poked him in the cheek.

"Quit pecking at me. You're not a chicken." Bishan wanted to bat away Hugh's finger, but his arms were pinned by a section of wall. "Did you get my family out?"

"They're already on the way to the hospital," Hugh assured him quickly. "I doubt they'll even be there overnight. They're fine. Can you tell me what you remember?"

"Boom."

Hugh gave a forced chuckle. "Aside from the actual explosion? Talk me through what you remember."

"Why?"

"I'm bored." Hugh grabbed a cloth one of the paramedics handed to him. He gently wiped some of the muck from Bishan's face. "You hit your head fairly hard."

"I didn't hit anything," Bishan corrected sharply. He wanted to rest. *Why couldn't Hugh let him nap?* "The wall hit me."

"Does it matter?"

"You said it like I intentionally dropped a wall and ceiling onto my head. I didn't." He hurt worse than when they'd had the car crash. It hadn't been so difficult to catch a full breath then either. "Reva and I came to spend time with my aunties. We noticed both the doors were blocked. I got them under the table and—boom."

From what Hugh told him, Reva's text to Sunesh had gone through. He'd immediately contacted Reggie and Hugh; the latter had already been on his way to check on them. They found the rear door blocked by a dumpster that had been shoved up against it using a lorry.

To Hugh and Bishan's amusement, it seemed Reggie had a bit of a misspent youth. He'd managed to break into the lorry and get it moving up. They got the door open, immediately finding the four shell-shocked women with damp towels covering their faces.

As ambulances and fire engines arrived, his family had been taken care of. Hugh and Reggie had attempted to make their way to him. It had required extensive work to shift the remnants of the ceiling, walls, and other kitchen equipment to get to him.

"Bish?" Hugh lightly flicked him on the arm. "Stay awake. Val's on his way, remember?"

"Right." Bishan forced his eyes open once again. "How long does it take to fly to Cumbria?"

"No clue. An hour? Maybe? I suppose it depends on if they have to stop for fuel." Hugh snapped his fingers next to Bishan's ear. "No drifting off."

They nattered about stupid things. Staccato's favourite toy. The best pudding served at Harrow. Hugh tried to keep his mind active.

In the midst of the chaos, paramedics checked on him, assessing his breathing. They all agreed their efforts were hampered by the rubble. Bishan noticed Hugh turned rather serious after a whispered conversation with one of the fire-fighters.

"What's wrong?"

Hugh knelt beside him, taking the cloth to wipe again at Bishan's forehead. "You're bleeding."

"Thought it was water from them putting the fire out." Bishan winced when the rough cloth hit a sore spot along his hairline. "What did he say?"

"They're about to shift the wall resting on your legs." Hugh turned around when the same firefighter called him over. "Hang on."

It took a great effort not to snark at him. Bishan didn't exactly have any options at the moment. He strained to hear the whispered conversation without luck.

"Well?" Bishan prompted when Hugh returned only to stay silent. "What's happening?"

"The greatest concern we have is that by shifting the wall we'll dislodge the rest of the ceiling." Hugh pointed overhead to a large section that hadn't fallen. "We don't want to injure you further."

"But?"

"The longer we wait, the more your body could be damaged by the weight already on you." Hugh rested a hand gently on Bishan's shoulder. "I'll be here the entire way. You tell me the second it hurts worse. I'll get you out safely."

Promises.

Everything already hurt. How much worse could it get? Bishan didn't want to worry Hugh further.

"Valor called." Reggie stepped up beside Hugh. "They've stopped for fuel. It'll be another thirty minutes or more until they're here. I've already got an officer waiting to rush him here."

Waiting became pure agony for Bishan. Each breath was

harder than the last. They came shallower no matter how he tried.

His rescuers made steady progress. They'd decided to shift the bits of the ceiling directly over him. Hugh and Reggie held a sheet over him to keep any stray rubble from hitting his face.

With the danger from the ceiling mostly removed, their efforts shifted to the wall covering the majority of his lower half. The second it lifted off him, immense relief turned to intense pain. Bishan cried out at the sharp return of sensation.

Paramedics rushed over with an inhaler. They told him to breathe deeply. He tried.

"We're almost there," Hugh promised. "Be brave for us. You'll get to see Valor and your family. I'm sure the doctors will fix you right up."

Hugh's voice had a bit of a panicked edge to it. Bishan tried to tilt his head to glance at him but couldn't. The whooshing in his ears returned.

Shouldn't the ringing have stopped now?

"Follow up. Remember? We'll do it together, like in school." Hugh had clearly become desperate if he wanted to sing. "Bish?"

Adrenaline had honestly been the only thing keeping Bishan going. All the noise—everything was so incredibly overwhelming. He wanted his blanket, his music, his cat, and his Valor.

Bishan tried to stay awake for Valor, but his eyes drifted shut. It took a herculean effort to force them open. *Why am I so tired? What's taking so long? Can't they let me nap? It's so noisy.*

"Bishan? *Oi.* Don't ignore me. C'mon. Bish? *Bish.*" Hugh's voice sounded incredibly panicked as it slowly faded away along with everything else in the room.

Why's it so cold all of a sudden?

DEAD IN THE SHOP

CHAPTER 1

Go faster.
Go faster.
Go. Sodding. Faster

Valor tapped his foot impatiently, trying to ignore the periodic glares from the helicopter pilot. "Can this go any faster?"

Silence.

That's a no, then?

The second Valor stepped off the helicopter, he reached for his mobile. He tried Bishan first, hoping against all the odds his beloved Bish would be conscious and able to pick up. *No answer. Right.*

He tried Detective Inspector Spurling next with no luck. He called Hugh, but his old schoolmate didn't answer either. *No news might be good news. I hope.*

A friendly police officer met him once he'd gotten away from the helicopter and refused to give him any information while driving him through Windermere. Valor sat, frozen, unable to get his hands to stop shaking. Visions of Bishan covered in dust and blood kept flashing in front of his eyes.

All day an uneasy sensation had gnawed at his stomach. He'd ignored it, assuming all his family drama had caused his inner turmoil. Hugh's call had brought all the nightmares of the last six months rushing back to him.

As they swerved around a corner, Valor got his first view of what had happened to the beautiful little restaurant. Smoke drifted above a partially collapsed building. The fire was clearly put out, though the firefighters continued to mill about outside.

How had any of his family survived?

Valor stumbled out of the vehicle when it finally came to a stop. "Bish?"

"Val?"

He barely heard Reggie, who stopped him from ducking under the caution tape. "I have to—"

"Bishan isn't in there. They managed to extract him safely from underneath a collapsed wall. We've sealed it off to investigate for arson and attempted murder, and your presence will only muddy the waters for us." Reggie grabbed him firmly by the shoulder and led him over to one of the unmarked SUVs. "Let's get you over to the hospital to see him."

A hundred questions raced through Valor's mind, but he couldn't summon the courage to ask any of them. He spent the drive to the hospital trying to dig holes into Reggie's leather seat with his clenched fingers. *Why can't he tell me how Bishan is?*

Attempted murder means he's okay, right?

Bit singed, but alive?

Singed, but alive. Valor couldn't help thinking it perfectly described their entire experience thus far. In the beginning, when they'd found the first body in their garden, he'd almost enjoyed the mystery, playing detective like his favourite,

Poirot. Now the novelty had certainly worn off as death piled up around them.

Friends, mentors, and his Bishan had been harmed.

The killer had to be stopped. Valor refused to call them a monster. The murderer was a person, not some faceless and brainless fiend. A human being who'd taken it upon themselves to destroy the lives of others, and no matter what the reason, he intended to dedicate all his energy in seeing them brought to justice.

"We're here."

Valor blinked in surprise when he realised they'd not only arrived but parked directly outside the hospital entrance. *Perks of being a copper?* "You coming in?"

He wasn't. After letting Valor out, the detective inspector swiftly pulled away. He apparently intended to return to the restaurant to help with the investigation.

Racing up the steps and into the hospital, Valor finally found Bishan's father, Barnaby, midconversation with his oldest child, Sunesh. Both men turned towards him as he skidded to a halt beside them.

In all his years of knowing Bishan and his family, Valor had never seen Barnaby quite so shaken. And Sunesh was usually the rock of the family, but his hands shook visibly while signing forms for a nurse. Valor's stomach dropped at the obvious concern.

"Is he—" Valor winced at the pain in his jaw when he snapped his mouth shut on the question, fearful of what the answer might be. He gathered his nerve and tried again. "How is he?"

"We don't know." Barnaby wrapped an arm around Valor's shoulders, guiding him away from the nurses' station. "He's in surgery. The doctor hasn't told us anything yet. The others are being treated for smoke inhalation. My Rana has a few abrasions and burns on her back and shoulders from protecting Reva."

They wandered down the hall into a room where Rana was in a hospital bed. Reva, Bishan's sister, along with his auntie Asha and her wife Luna, all sat comfortably with oxygen masks on. Valor breathed a small sigh of relief at seeing them doing relatively well; his mind continued to race fearfully at the possibilities for Bishan.

"Val." Reva waved him over. Her voice sounded painfully hoarse. "Sit. Sit."

He sat on the chair next to hers, smiling when she rested her head against his arm. "Am I playing surrogate brother, Rev Rev?"

"Shut up." She pinched his side, coughing through an attempted snicker. "He saved us."

"Bish?"

"Couldn't get out. Pushed us under a table, then it all went badly." Reva disregarded her father's insistence on her resting her voice. "Said to tell you he loves you."

"Reva." Valor's chest constricted painfully, and suddenly it seemed impossible to breathe even without the excuse of smoke inhalation. "He's going to be fine."

"He wanted you to know he loves you," she repeated insistently. "He said you'd been his best friend since Harrow and—"

"Stop." Valor wanted to plug his ears to block out Bishan's declarations. He hurt. Tears clogged up his throat, and he blinked rapidly to clear his eyes. *"Please."*

Reva ignored his hushed whisper. "He loves you."

"Reva, love." Barnaby stepped in before she could continue. He sat on her other side, easing her into a hug. "Bishan will be fine. Save your voice."

Silence descended on the cramped room. None of them wanted to consider the odds of Bishan's survival. They'd already had the miracle of his mum, sister, auntie, and auntie-in-law making it out of the destruction safely.

So they waited.

Over the next hour or so, Valor's mobile exploded with messages. One text followed another from their network of friends, all asking about Bishan. Wilfred and Lottie promised to keep an eye on the Ginger's Bread, his biscuit shop in Grasmere, and on their cat, Staccato.

He ignored all the other messages. It seemed pointless to text his friends back when he had no idea how Bishan was doing. His faith in no news being good news was rapidly fading away with the harsh reality of the sterile hospital environment.

Nurses wandered in periodically to check on the four women. None of them had answers about Bishan. And Valor wanted to scream at them.

He didn't.

Because I'm not a spoiled, rude arse.

"Val?" Sunesh snapped his fingers in front of Valor's face. "Let's find some tea."

"I don't want any bloody tea." Valor glared at Sunesh, who grabbed him by the arm to yank him out of the chair. He let himself be ushered out of the room. "Apparently, I do want some."

They eventually found tea and biscuits. Neither of them had eaten since breakfast. Valor had to choke down the dry cookies, burning his throat with the hot liquid to help.

"You made him brave," Sunesh commented offhandedly.

"What?" Valor brushed crumbs from his shirt, staring blankly at Sunesh.

"Bishan was timid. I used to think Reva had gotten the rambunctious playfulness that I'd always wanted my brother to have. He went to Harrow scared of his shadow in many ways, though he'll never admit to it." Sunesh crumbled a biscuit absently on his plate. "The first year I saw a difference in him. You helped him so much even as just a friend. You never laughed at him."

"Sunny." Valor didn't quite know how to respond. He'd always believed their relationship had brought out the best in himself and Bishan. They'd made each other better people. "He was already brave; he just didn't know it."

"I laughed at him."

Valor didn't want to sit through a confessional of what Sunesh had done to his little brother. "Sunny. He's going to be fine."

Sunesh shoved his plate away, all his biscuits crumbled into nothing. "He might not be."

"He will be."

Sunesh met Valor's gaze steadily. "I know it's hard, Val, but you have to prepare yourself in case he isn't."

"Don't." He couldn't.

"I pray he's fine." Sunesh stretched a hand across the small table to grip Valor's hand painfully hard. "But if we aren't ready for bad news, it'll crush us."

Valor thought he'd be crushed no matter how prepared they pretended to be for it. "He has to be fine."

He has to be.

Not sure I can survive in the world without my Bish.

CHAPTER 2

"Valor?"

He jolted awake, almost slipping off the chair. He turned to glare half-heartedly at a snickering Reva. "Something wrong? Or are you feeling well enough to pester me like usual?"

"Sunny and Dad are speaking with the doctor in the hall." Reva kept her voice low to protect her voice. "Bishan's apparently out of surgery."

"Why apparently?" Valor sat up quickly. "Well?"

"I don't know." Reva shrugged despondently. "They stepped out of the room to chat since Mum's sleeping."

"Mum can't sleep for all the nattering you're doing." Rana eased up on the bed, shifting a pillow behind her. "Valor. Go bring them here, please? I want to know how my son is doing."

Valor patted Reva's hand and hopped up to retrieve Barnaby for his wife. He found Sunesh and his father around a corner in conference with two doctors. They headed away just as he joined the others. "Something I said?"

His attempt to lighten the mood fell short as he spotted

the unshed tears in Sunesh's eyes. Valor wondered if his heart might explode from anxiety. Barnaby grabbed his arm when he started to sway on his feet.

"Easy, Valor." Sunesh added his own hand for support. "Bishan is in the ICU. He has burns and smoke inhalation. It's the damage to his lungs and leg that will require a lengthy recovery."

"He'll—" Valor didn't quite know how to ask the question that had haunted him every single second since the call had come about the explosion. "He's going to live."

He found himself squashed in a Tamboli crush. Barnaby and Sunesh wrapped their arms around him. Tears fell despite his best efforts to smother them.

When his mobile had rung, Valor had been in the middle of a tense argument with his father. His mother and sister had pushed for reconciliation. He'd honestly had no idea if their wish could come true with all the painful history between them.

And then his phone rang.

And rang.

Both Reggie and Hugh had called. He'd panicked. His greatest fear had been to arrive far too late; the journey from London to Windermere would take six to seven hours on a good day, never mind the traffic.

To his immense surprise, his family had immediately jumped in with offers to help. Valor hadn't initially believed his father when he suggested the helicopter. Penny had bundled him into her car before he could argue with them.

Seeing the restaurant reduced partially to smoking rubble, Valor hadn't expected Bishan to survive, not after learning how he'd been found. Tears flowed without his permission for what felt like an embarrassingly long time to him.

"I'll go tell Mum the good news." Sunesh ducked out of the hug to wander down the hall.

Barnaby squeezed Valor one last time before releasing him. "Why don't we make our way to the ICU? They likely won't let us sit with him, but we can probably see him from a distance."

They had to wash up carefully and put masks on, but the doctors allowed them into intensive care. Valor stood by the bed, afraid to touch Bishan at all. He winced at the various scrapes and bandage-covered burns.

"You'll wake up. And you'll hurt, but I'll take care of you. I promise." Valor gently brushed his fingertips across Bishan's knuckles. "We'll stop the bastard who did this as well. He won't touch you again—or any of us."

But especially Bishan.

With restrictions on the number of visitors, Valor bowed out to allow Reva to see her brother. She grabbed his hand when he walked by. They shared a quick hug before she made her way over to Bishan.

Her tearful exclamation chased Valor out of the ward. Valor had witnessed his own emotional breakdown. He didn't know if his heart was strong enough to see Reva's.

The walls of the hospital seemed to close in on him. Valor took turn after turn until eventually, he stepped out into the cool, foggy early evening. He found a nearby bench and sat on it with a groan.

Grabbing his mobile out of his pocket, he sent out a mass text to their friends. He kept it short and simple, enough to relieve their worries. After a bit of thought, he called Wilfred to pick him up to take him home.

He wanted to check on the cottage, shower and change, and grab a set of pyjamas as well as clothes for Bishan. "And maybe we'll both find a smidge of normalcy."

Wilfred had other plans. He drove them straight to his own house where Lottie had made a cottage pie for him. Valor had no choice but to sit and eat under their watchful eye. Even Staccato had clambered up on his shoulder and refused to move.

The older couple offered him the comfort Valor had never found with his parents. They only took him to the cottage after they'd seen him perk up a little. Staccato yowled at him when he left the cat in Lottie's capable hands.

With the killer striking ever closer to home, Valor refused to leave their beloved Staccato in the cottage alone. The furry monster would be safe with Lottie and Wilfred. Spoiled, but alive and well.

Valor had only just stepped out of the shower when his doorbell went off. He grabbed a bathrobe to wrap around himself and went to the door to find Hugh on the other side. "Shouldn't you be in Windermere with the detective inspector?"

"Where's your phone?"

"Not on me." Valor gestured to his robe. "Why?"

"Inside." Hugh pushed by him.

"Welcome." Valor rolled his eyes at his friend. "My phone is on the kitchen counter. Why?"

"We've wondered how they tracked your moves this whole time without being caught on the cameras." Hugh grabbed the phone and quickly removed the battery from it. "Ollie thought the phone might've been cloned—both yours and Bishan's. We know the killer left the body in your garden without you hearing him. What if he crept into the cottage and got a hold of your iPhones at the same time?"

"It wouldn't have been overly difficult." Valor knew the music Bishan required to sleep might've drowned out any slight noise. "And if our phones were cloned? Is it like Dolly?"

"No, you're not getting a sheep." Hugh rolled his eyes. "The killer has access to your messages and other aspects of your phone. We don't know for certain until they check."

"And if so?"

"We use this against them." Hugh pocketed the phone and handed Valor a different one. "New number. For now, hold off on telling anyone. We don't want to tip our hand just yet."

"Tip our hand? I just texted everyone with an update on Bishan. The killer knows he survived." Valor grabbed the counter when his vision swam for a second. He reminded himself to breathe; panicking or a heart attack wouldn't help anyone. "Does Reggie have anyone at the hospital?"

"Not yet."

"What do you mean not yet?" Valor wanted someone to be irate at, and the detective inspector made an attractive target. "Shouldn't he?"

Hugh held a hand up. "The hospital has security."

"It's Bish."

"So, we'll add a few officers to the security." Hugh grabbed his phone and started to dial. "Go get dressed. You're dripping all over your floor. We can ride to the hospital together."

Valor resisted the urge to offer his thoughts to Hugh in rude limerick. His old friend had won that house competition at Harrow in any case. He trudged through the cottage into his bedroom to finish drying off and dressing. "We'll get through this. Somehow."

"And stop talking to yourself," Hugh yelled after him.

"Stop listening to me talking to myself. Nosy bugger." Valor closed the bedroom door so the pillow Hugh launched at him bounced off it. He leaned against the door, covering his face with his hands; the buoyant mood feigned for his friend fell away in an instant. *Is this nightmare ever going to end?*

CHAPTER 3

S tretched out on an uncomfortable bed, Valor and Bishan perused CCTV images. The police investigation had revealed a glimpse of the suspect. A bad, blurry glimpse. The figure appeared to be male, blond with longish hair, and a dark hoodie that prevented them from getting a good look at any features.

"It's Aubrey," Valor insisted. He wasn't completely convinced, but none of their other potential suspects had that particular shade of hair. "Has to be."

"Maybe." Bishan peered closer at the image Valor held up for him. "Hard to tell. It's too blurry. How do we know how tall he is? We'd need something to compare him to within the photo. The hair is right, but anyone could use dye or wear a wig."

Three days after the fire, Bishan hadn't been released from the hospital but had been moved into a room outside the ICU. Valor had spent almost every moment with him. Today he lay in bed next to him, looking over CCTV stills Reggie had given them.

Despite the underlying current of stress and fear, Valor

found comfort from being snuggled up with Bishan, even if it had to be in a hospital bed. They'd clung tightly to one another since the explosion. It had been a staggeringly lucky escape for all the Tambolis.

The four women who'd been at the restaurant had all been released from the hospital. Rana was the only one to have lasting scars. She'd used her body to shield the others and had a few burns and abrasions to show for it.

The entire family made frequent visits to the hospital. Reva practically lived there. Valor thought she might be holding on to guilt about Bishan's injuries; he'd suggested her parents get her to a psychotherapist to help deal with the mental trauma.

He hoped they did; maybe the haunted shadows in her eyes would disappear.

How long will our luck hold?

We've had so many close calls.

And God knows we've not escaped unscathed.

Bishan smacked him on the head with one of the printed images. "You've gone all gloomy again. Stop it."

"Sorry." Valor knew Bishan wanted them all to attempt to keep a brave and positive face. He didn't want to think about almost dying, but Valor struggled with it constantly. "I'll try."

"What if it's someone playing on our belief it's Aubrey?" Bishan drew his attention to one of the less obscured images. "If our phones were cloned, they'd have seen our texts to Hugh about potential suspects. Aubrey was on the list. What if the killer is simply using it against us?"

"A red herring?"

"Yes." Bishan nodded. "I'm tired again."

After being released from the ICU, Bishan continued to require lots of rest. Valor had worried at the constant napping until doctors assured the family he'd need plenty of sleep to recover. The peaceful look on Bishan's face as he drifted off eased some of the tightness in Valor's chest. *We'll be all right. Somehow.*

Helping Bishan settle more comfortably against the pillows, Valor watched him doze for several minutes. The stack of printed images caught his attention after a while. He flicked through them slowly.

Is it Aubrey?

Grabbing his laptop from a nearby table, Valor logged into the Harrow alumni site. He searched through numerous archived newsletters and photos. A few group images from an event at West Acre two years ago drew his attention; he could almost convince himself a picture of Aubrey matched the killer.

Almost.

The main difference between the two photos was Aubrey's short hair. He'd grown it long in school; they'd teasingly referred to him as Goldilocks in sixth form. As an adult, Aubrey kept it closely shorn.

Could he have grown it out to distract us?

Or is the killer unaware of the change?

It seemed unlikely. If anything, the murderer had shown an eye for detail. Would he miss a haircut?

They couldn't refute the killer was clever. The police had yet to find any significant evidence to point toward a specific person. Valor hoped they wouldn't be living in fear for years on end.

Then again, with the victims all attached to Valor, the pool of potentials wasn't limitless. *Why is he doing this? Why me?*

He'd asked himself the same question over and over. Maybe he'd eventually find an answer.

"I can't nap with you thinking so much," Bishan grumbled. He gingerly shifted on the bed until his head rested on Valor's shoulder. They were already practically on top of one other with the size of the bed, but Bishan had insisted he get in with him. "We won't solve this from the hospital."

"We might."

"Shh. Less talky." Bishan's eyes drifted shut. "Less talky."

"Go to sleep," Valor retorted.

With Bishan practically snoring in his ear, Valor had no choice but to lie back on the bed. His mind refused to allow him to join in the nap. He couldn't shake the gnawing suspicion they'd missed something obvious.

But what?

The next few days were spent pondering that question. Valor didn't stray far from Bishan's hospital bed, occasionally popping over to the Tambolis' for a shower or to the cottage for extra clothes. He managed the website, orders, and finances of the biscuit shop straight from his laptop and trusted Wilfred and Lottie to handle the rest.

A few days later, a surprise visitor stunned them all. Valor couldn't quite believe his eyes when his little sister strolled into the room with a box under one arm; Penelope appeared completely immune to the bewildered stares being sent her direction. *What is she doing here?*

She set the box on the table at the end of the bed. "I've brought mini Bakewell tarts. They used to be your favourite."

Valor glanced between the box and his sister a few times. He decided to channel Bishan's abruptness and get straight to the point. "Why are you here?"

Penelope drew herself up in her delicately fashionable dress. "I want to apologise to you, Bishan, and his family by extension."

"Why?" Valor pressed her. He refused to relent until she'd demonstrated her apology came without a "but." "Why now?"

"Family—"

Valor wanted to give his little sister the benefit of the

doubt, but she'd toed the Scott line far too well in the past. "I'm grateful the earl bent far enough to lend me the helicopter. It's a stretch to think you've all suddenly changed your minds about Bish and everything else."

"It's not about Mother or Father. It's not about Bertie either." Penelope shifted uneasily in front of them. "I *am* dreadfully sorry that I didn't say anything in your defence. I might not have joined in, but it's about the same to sit by the side. Worse."

"We accept your apology on our family's behalf." Rana held a hand up to stop Valor from responding. She moved over to wrap an arm around Penelope. "We'll let your brother think about things. Why don't you show us what you brought?"

The awkward Penelope visit ended quickly. Rana wanted them to embrace, and disappointing her made him feel bad. Valor simply wasn't ready to open his arms to the Scotts, not even his baby sister.

Valor hadn't shut the door on her either literally or figuratively. Not as they'd done to him. He thought a bit of patience from Penelope was due.

From watching her interactions with the Tambolis, Penelope's change of heart appeared genuine. She wasn't a talented enough actress to fake her way through a relaxed conversation. Bishan surprised him by offering an open invitation to lunch when they'd gotten free from the hospital.

Not long after Penelope left, the doctors came in for Bishan's daily check-up. His lungs had begun to heal along with the burns. His leg would take the longest. They wanted him in the hospital for another day but believed he could then return home.

The doctors had laid out a detailed plan for his recovery. They wanted him to have frequent check-ups along with physical therapy. His breathing, in particular, needed to be monitored to ensure healing continued without issue.

When the doctor mentioned weekly visits, Valor had internally cringed. Bishan hated going to medical offices of any sort. It would be a nightmare to convince him to keep up with such a frequent schedule.

"Home." Bishan repeated the word happily with a definite hint of relief in his voice. "Home. I get to go home."

Valor grabbed the box with the tarts, offering one to Bishan but yanking it out of reach of Sunesh, who glared at both of them. "Yes, home. How does a *Poirot* marathon with Lottie's cottage pie sound?"

"Brilliant."

"Bad timing?" Reggie was waiting by his parked vehicle outside the cottage. "Do you have a minute?"

Valor hopped out of his car and motioned the detective over. "Give me a hand with this? Bishan's aunties decided we're incapable of fixing food for ourselves. They've channelled their trauma into fixing meals for everyone in their extended family. Keeps them busy."

"Keeps their mind off their ruined restaurant and how close they all came to dying," Reggie commented astutely. "Is Bishan inside? I didn't want to unnerve him by knocking on the door unannounced."

"Good." Valor knew the last thing Bishan needed was to deal with anyone without a buffer. "No, he's not here. Sunny and Reva took him for his first physical therapy session. I apparently made him anxious, so I ran errands instead. Help me carry this lot inside, will you?"

After Bishan's aunties loaded him up, Valor had made a quick stop for other necessities at the shop. He'd planned on spending the afternoon going over his options for avoiding his family's plans to make him the Scott heir. Reggie had thrown a not entirely welcome spanner into the works by showing up.

"What can we do for you, Detective?" Valor put all the perishable items away and then filled the electric kettle to get it going. Reggie's serious expression told him a few cups of tea were going to be required. "It's not another body, is it? Oh, God, it's not, is it? Can't it be over?"

"Not quite." Reggie eased his mobile out of his pocket, pulling up a video and twisting the screen toward Valor. "The crime scene had a visitor after we'd left."

He watched a hooded figure slipping under the caution tape and moving toward the restaurant. They stayed only long enough to retrieve an object from a crack in a brick wall behind the building. Or, at least, that's what he thought they did. "I'm not sure what I'm seeing."

"I've a theory." Reggie set his phone down on the table. "What if the killer decided since no one died this time, his puzzle no longer fit the situation?"

"What if he's saving it for a second attempt?" Valor absentmindedly dropped teabags into their grand piano shaped teapot before pouring in the boiled water. "Do you find that thought as terrifying as I do?"

"I do. I know you won't go into protective custody in a place we provide. But I'd like to have an officer with you at all times until we find the bastard responsible." Reggie accepted the tea Valor poured for him, dropping a few cubes of sugar into it. "And Hugh will keep close as well. I'm sure he'll make Bishan more comfortable with the situation."

Over tea and ginger biscuits, Valor and Reggie watched the video footage a few more times. He tried to guess at the height. The killer seemed shorter than Valor, based on where the top of the wall came to on his own body.

"Are you certain it isn't Aubrey?"

"As sure as I can be," Valor hedged his bet. "I haven't felt confident about any of this mess, but I'd wager you anything it's not Aubrey. He's taller than me."

And I'm staking my life and Bishan's on it.

Once again, the detective inspector tried to convince him to move into a hotel or with Hugh. Valor refused. Bishan was being pushed to the edge of overload with the constant chaos; his health would suffer without the comforts of a familiar space that he had complete control over.

"What about the cloned phones?" Valor dunked his biscuit, pondering the matter. "Couldn't we use them to our advantage? Make them think we've gone to a particular place, and you detective types can make yourselves useful in setting a trap."

"Are you saying we're not useful?"

"Drink your tea." Valor had grown to appreciate Reggie's wry sense of humour. He didn't take himself too seriously. "Have you looked into our frog lady?"

Reggie choked on his sip of tea. "She accused you of stealing tadpoles again."

"We haven't even been home." He tried to find amusement in Mrs Harris, but his laugh came out bitter. "How does one steal tadpoles? And more importantly, why? It's not Staccato, as the poor feline has been with Lottie and Wilfred. They've spoiled him rotten. He'll never want to come home with us."

"Right." Reggie blinked at him over the rim of his teacup. "It's a cat."

"Are you a dog person?" Valor narrowed his eyes at the detective inspector. "I'm reassessing my thoughts on your intelligence."

"Cat lover."

Valor snickered at the ridiculous turn of their conversation. "Is there a fine for interference of an amphibious nature?"

"You're not nearly as hilarious as you think you are." Reggie gulped down the rest of the tea before pocketing both his phone and a few biscuits. "The protective detail should be here within the hour. Hugh's at his cottage."

"We'll manage." Valor didn't want to be dismissive of the danger, but he'd already repeated himself multiple times. "Get out of here before I report you for biscuit theft."

It took a bit more convincing, but Reggie finally left. Valor didn't think it a coincidence that a police car pulled up in front of the cottage as the detective inspector was driving off. *All this trouble for what? I'll never understand the motivation behind all the death and pain. Ever.*

With the cottage to himself, Valor hurried to clean up and do several loads of laundry. It had been one of the first things he taught himself after leaving Harrow. He'd had no one to do it for him.

Well, I didn't teach myself. Lottie might've gone out of her way to ensure I knew how to clean the house and keep my pants clean.

This was what his family would never understand. Valor had changed from who they believed their middle son to be, had gone through a slow, painful metamorphosis. There would be no returning to their lifestyle.

He couldn't.

Would it be more convenient to have not only a title but wealth behind him? Definitely. Valor had had all that as a child and teen. He'd never been as happy as he was with Bishan, with their little cottage and his biscuit shop.

Would he welcome Penelope into his life? Maybe. Probably. Did he honestly believe his parents might follow her lead with a genuine apology of their own? Not in a million years.

Lord and Lady Scott would never lower themselves to get to know his life or respect it. Valor had given up on trying to convince himself they would. He refused to risk being hurt— and worse, having Bishan humiliated again.

Valor made another cup of tea while waiting for the washer to finish up. "That's enough mental moaning about things I can't change," he muttered to himself. "Bish will want comfort after the trauma of dealing with strangers and a new doctor's office."

Comfort called for their softest and heaviest quilt. As the weather had grown cooler, Valor got the fireplace going as well. Some evenings in late autumn and winter, Bishan would sit and listen to the crackling flames; it seemed to soothe him.

They had the paella from Bishan's aunties Luna and Aashi. Valor had picked up several of their favourite puddings as well while he'd been out. They had a few seasons of *Poirot* to finish up their binge-watching.

He added their *Miss Fisher's Murder Mysteries* DVDs to the stack by the telly as well. Bishan might want a change of scene. They both enjoyed the Australian series quite a bit.

They'd even attempted her fan dance themselves. Bishan had managed it better than Valor, much to both of their surprise. He'd done it as a present on their last anniversary— completely starkers with just a fan.

Shaking his head to clear it, Valor made a mental note to take a cold shower. *Time to focus.* Given Bishan's injuries, it would be months before they'd be up for any of that sort of fun.

Valor glanced around the room with everything set up. He waved cheerily to Mrs Harris, who he spotted staring over the fence. For the hundredth time. "I don't have your bloody tadpoles."

Right.

Don't yell at the batty old lady next door, Val.

Bad Val.

CHAPTER 5

Knock.
  Knock.
  Knock.

Jolting awake out of a nightmare, Valor blinked blearily in the dimly lit bedroom. He glanced over at the alarm clock to check the time. A chill went through him almost instantly—nothing good happened before sunrise.

Valor strode grumpily through the cottage to answer the insistent banging on the door. He found Hugh waiting for him on the other side. "*Oi.* Do you know what time it is?"

Hugh pushed by him into the cottage, grabbing Valor by the arm to drag him along. "Get dressed. Both of you. We've got to get to the shop."

"Why do we need to go to the shop when it's not even open? What's wrong?" Bishan wavered on his crutches in the doorway of their bedroom. With his shirt off, the bruises, bandages, and healing burns stood out against his skin. "Why are we up so early? Hello, Hugh. Did you know your buttons are done up wrong?"

Leaving Hugh to sort himself out, Valor helped Bishan

return to their bedroom. Dressing had gotten slightly complicated for him with his injuries. They went with easy to put on and take off clothes that didn't strain Bish too severely.

Once clothed, Valor ignored the impatient Hugh. He grabbed a basket of muffins Lottie had brought over. Bishan required a few different prescriptions and having them on an empty stomach had proved to be a terrible idea. Hugh pushed the two of them out the door, snatching one of the baked goods for himself.

Muffin in hand, Hugh hurried them out to his Range Rover. They helped Bishan into the back seat where he could stretch his legs out comfortably. Valor tucked a cushion behind his back for support, draping his favourite quilt over him and offering him a Rubik's cube.

Valor paused before shutting the door. He leaned in to gently kiss along the scarred skin on Bishan's neck, stopping at his ear to whisper, "Whatever has happened, we'll handle it together. We'll be all right."

"Hugh's huffing impatiently at us." Bishan offered him a grin. "Together."

"Could you two save your declarations for later? We need to get to the Ginger's Bread." Hugh twisted around to glare at them.

"Keep your shirt on." Valor rolled his eyes but did step back from Bishan.

"Why would he take his shirt off?" Bishan asked around a mouthful of muffin. "Right. Joke? Definitely a joke."

"All comfy, then?" Valor finally closed the door carefully and got inside the front passenger seat. "Why are we going to the biscuit shop? It's too early."

Hugh shook his head, refusing to answer. Valor couldn't help the second chill of icy fingers dancing along his spine. It wasn't like their old Harrow schoolmate to keep information so tightly to his chest.

Who would be at the shop this early in the morning anyway?

Oh, God.

"Hugh?" Valor dumped his muffin in the basket, his appetite suddenly gone. "Is it Wilfred? Say it isn't Wilfred. You listen to me, Detective Inspector Hugh Asheford. Did they find a body?"

Hugh gripped the steering wheel so tightly Valor heard the leather squeak. "They did."

Valor choked on air as his heart threatened to shatter. "Is it Wilf?"

"No."

Valor managed to find the will to breathe again. "Then who?"

"Let's get to the shop so Detective Inspector Spurling can speak with you directly." Hugh turned into the professional officer almost immediately. "I don't know the details."

Valor could usually tell when Hugh lied to him. Today his old friend was giving him nothing at all. *"Fine."*

"Val." Bishan leaned up and reached out to squeeze Valor's arm. "Hugh isn't the enemy. Don't be cross with him."

Offering an apology to both of them, Valor settled into the seat for the short drive through Grasmere. His mind raced with who the victim might be. Why the hesitation on Hugh's part to tell them?

It had to be someone more closely connected to them than a random former classmate. If not Lottie or Wilfred.... Valor found himself glancing over his shoulder at Bishan. His few bites of breakfast threatened to come back up. *Is it one of the Tambolis? Is that why?*

The police presence outside the shop had already started to draw attention. Valor pushed through the small crowd of villagers gathered outside the caution tape already blocking off the entrance. He'd left Hugh at the vehicle with Bishan, on the off chance the victim was a member of his family.

Valor followed one of the detectives into his shop where he found several officers and crime scene investigators milling about. Reggie immediately moved over to intercept him before he got to the covered body on the floor. "Who is it?"

Reggie tried to guide Valor toward the door leading to the kitchen and his office. "Let's allow the CSI to complete their work."

"Who is it?" Valor held his ground. He wanted to know who'd been dumped in his shop like nothing more than a piece of garbage. "Is it Sunny? Or Reva?"

"No." Reggie placed a firm hand on Valor's shoulder as though he expected a violent reaction. "We've found Lord Scott."

Valor swayed on his feet while trying to breathe through the sudden tunnelling of his vision. He almost gagged on the smell of death and cinnamon. "Lord Scott? What do you mean you've found Lord Scott? My father? What…."

God help me.

Reggie took advantage of Valor's shock to ease him away from the body and into the kitchen. "The killer broke in through the rear exit. We should have them on CCTV footage throughout the village. We'll find them."

"And this is different from all the other murders?"

"He's an earl." Reggie shrugged. "I'll have all the resources I want practically shoved into my lap to solve the crime."

"And Mr Clarke didn't? All the others don't deserve the best help the police can offer?" Valor dragged his fingers roughly through his messy red hair. He didn't know how to process his father's death, though screaming outrage at

Reggie probably wouldn't help anyone. "Have my sister and mother been informed?"

"I imagine they'll have someone a lot posher and higher up tell them." Reggie leaned against the stainless steel table in the kitchen. "You realise you're Lord Scott now, right?"

"Sod it all." Valor locked his knees to keep from dropping to the floor. "Is this nightmare ever going to end?"

How do I grieve for a man who never honestly cared about me beyond whether or not he controlled my inheritance?

Wandering outside for some much-needed air, Valor stood alone at the rear of the shop by the back exit. He'd stepped out for a brief reprieve from the stares of the police but more so the gossipy villagers peering in through the large windows. "What the devil happens now?"

He didn't want to be an earl. At all. Ever. He'd make a dreadful mess of it. His sister made a far better choice; she'd learnt more about estate management than he had.

Then again, Staccato probably knows more about estate management than I do.

Even if it would be brilliant to swan around with Bishan on his arm as the perfect rebuttal to all their bigoted behaviour. He thought it better to let Penny have it. Or perhaps allow the title to die out with the death of his father.

"Val?"

He twisted around to find Bishan hobbling towards him. "You should've stayed in the car."

"Not a car." Bishan frowned at him, moving carefully to avoid tripping over the cobblestones. "Do you want me to go away? Hugh said you'd gotten bad news. Was it Wilfred?"

"No. He's alive and well with Lottie at their cottage." Valor helped Bishan over to the bench under a tree across from the shop. He sat beside him, reaching down to grasp Bishan's hand gently. "I'm temporarily an earl."

"Your father?" Bishan squeezed Valor's hand. "We didn't

like him. You had more of a reason than I did. I'm still sorry he's gone."

Valor nodded absently but wondered if tears might come later. Mr Clarke's death had left him far more emotionally devastated. *My father's dead. Lord Scott is dead. My father's been murdered. Nope, still nothing. Is something wrong with me?* "I'm not sure how to feel about it."

"Welcome to my world. I'm never confident about how I'm feeling about anything." Bishan leaned against Valor slightly. "Was that wrong? Too soon?"

Valor grinned at him, hoping to allay his worries. "Do you ever wish emotions were easier for you?"

"Sometimes." Bishan squeezed Valor's hand once again. "Then I see you getting all twisted up and think maybe I've got it easier."

"Hilarious."

"Like everything, there are pros and cons for both of us." Bishan shrugged. "Do you want to talk about it?"

Valor didn't bother pretending he didn't know what Bishan meant. "Not sure there's anything to say. My father was murdered. It's as confusing as when Bertie died. How do I reconcile myself to family passing away when I didn't want them in my life anymore to begin with?"

"I don't know." Bishan scratched his head with his free hand. "I've never been able to understand your family. Not even sure we should call them *your family.*"

Valor ran his fingers through his hair absently. "I don't know if we should either."

How did he even begin to process any of the past six months or more?

They sat in silence with only the bustling of all the detectives for background noise. Valor sighed in resignation when his phone buzzed in his pocket. He fished it out and checked to find an incoming call from his sister.

He considered ignoring it, but his sister had every reason to grieve for their father. She'd enjoyed an entirely different relationship with the man. "Penny."

A full minute of sniffling tried Valor's patience. He decided to consider things from her point of view, because she wouldn't appreciate or understand his hanging up on her.

"Penny." Valor pinched the bridge of his nose. "Did you call to say something? Or weep quietly into my ear?"

Okay.

Maybe I should work on my patience a bit more?

Penny had been the first to reach out to him, but she certainly wasn't the last. Valor's mobile buzzed non-stop for the entire day with texts of condolence and calls of support. He attempted to take all of it in the spirit it was meant.

Old schoolmates reached out to him; ones who'd blatantly reached out for the sole purpose of reconnecting with the new earl. News, good or bad, travelled quickly in their circle of Harrow alumni. Valor snarked about his appreciation of their support during this difficult time and hung up on them.

Transparent, self-important twits.

He genuinely appreciated the friends who understood the conflict his father's death would cause for him.

Falling asleep had been next to impossible with so much weighing on his mind. Valor had eventually managed it. He woke up before the sun came up, expecting to find Bishan snoring blissfully beside him.

Valor glanced up to find Bishan working on the latest not-an-anagram anagram. "Couldn't sleep?"

Bishan blinked at him in the low light of the room. "Not really."

Valor stretched a hand out to flip the lamp on. "You'll hurt your eyes doing that in the dark."

"Won't." Bishan lifted up the small reading light that he'd used at school to study after they'd been told to go to sleep. "Still works."

"I thought I threw it out the window." Valor had hated the small book light. Bishan had often read late into the night. "I could've sworn I did."

"You did." Bishan poked him in the side with it. "Next morning, you had a guilty conscience and retrieved it for me, remember?"

He flopped beside Bishan's outstretched legs, careful of the broken one. "How can you ever forgive me?"

Bishan shoved him off the papers he'd strewn about. "What time are we heading up to London?"

Valor collapsed back into the pillows with a tired groan. "Never."

"Val."

He didn't want to deal with his mother or his sister. "Why don't we stay here? Staccato needs us."

"Staccato is staying with his Auntie Lottie and Uncle Wilf." Bishan gathered up the papers surrounding him with his attempts to solve the puzzle. "I don't want to go either. I hate funerals."

Valor took courage from Bishan reaching out to grab his hand to hold it. "Right. Off to London we go. Are we picking up Sunny on the way?"

They'd gotten a call from Sunesh with ideas on how Valor could avoid being forced into accepting his inheritance. He hadn't wanted any of it, particularly not after how they'd thrown him away. The Scott legacy had never mattered to him.

Why should it now?

And as always, Sunesh had a brilliant plan to help him. If the earl's will hadn't been changed, the title and everything attached to it should technically belong to Penny. His sister might not deserve it, but she'd certainly do more with it than Valor.

The days of inheritance being unable to pass to a woman had long since changed. Sunesh believed it a matter easy to resolve. Success hinged on whether his mother and sister wanted to cooperate with him.

"Is it sacrilegious to pray for my stuck-up family to play nicely for once?" Valor had more choice adjectives for them, but decided to practice discretion. Sunesh had warned him to do his best not to antagonise them. He frowned when Bishan's fingers tightened on his hand. "What's wrong?"

"Why did the killer go after your father?" Bishan motioned toward all his notes on the various puzzles. "He left him like a gift in the bakery—for you. Why?"

"I've no clue." Valor shifted up on the bed, resting against the headboard. "I hadn't thought about the reasons. But you're right, why drag him all the way down to Grasmere? He risked being found with a body."

"So, why?" Bishan fished around in his papers until he waved one in particular at Valor.

"That's an empty sheet of paper."

"I know." Bishan whacked him on the head with it. "I have no idea why they did this to your father—and I'm terrified of the implications."

Valor wrapped his arms around Bishan, carefully shifting him closer. "We'll handle this together."

And hope to God we're not dying together.

A mellow classical tune from their alarm clock signalled it was time for them to get up. Valor cheered up significantly while helping Bishan into the shower. They took their time washing up, enjoying what had become a rare stress-free moment for them.

In many ways, they'd had to work hard to avoid their relationship suffering from the constant turmoil of the past few months. Valor admired Bishan's courage greatly. He'd shown immense strength dealing with the nightmare of a false arrest and the aftermath of the explosion.

Valor admired Bishan—and tried to emulate his strength.

He knew, somehow, they'd need as much courage as possible to survive this hellish nightmare.

"**B**ut, Valor." His mother gripped his arm painfully, her elegant nails and extravagant rings digging in. "You must take up the running of the estate."

The shrill pleading from his mother had begun the second Valor stepped inside the family's London home. He'd tried to greet her civilly. She'd clung to him as though he were the only available life raft.

Valor pinched the bridge of his nose, trying to swallow down all the inappropriate comments that popped into his mind. "You disowned me."

"Never officially."

Valor pierced her with a glare that silenced her briefly. "Keep the money, the estate, the title, all of it. Give it to Penny. She'll do brilliantly as the new lady of the manor. She practically inhales Edwardian romances and *Downton Abbey*."

"Valor Tarquin Scott," his sister snapped at him sharply. "If I take up the title, I'm doing it to make our family name proud. Not to swan around in jewels and dresses."

"You'd swan a bit." Valor dodged the swing of her foot. "Am I wrong?"

"Yes." She glared when he tutted at her. "Maybe a small amount of swannage," she admitted.

"That's not a word," he interjected.

"I said it. Therefore it's a word."

Valor held a hand up to stop her from devolving into an argument over semantics. His mother tapped her foot impatiently on the floor. "Please. Lady Scott would like us to focus."

Spinning around on her heel, his mother rushed off in a flounce of elegance. A posh tantrum. Penelope heaved a huge sigh and started to follow her. Valor grabbed her arm to stop her.

"I should—"

"No, you shouldn't. Let her sulk." Valor refused to give any ground to his mother. He released his sister's arm. "If you really want the title and responsibility, you're going to need to learn how to not give in to her."

"You don't understand." Penelope paced in front of him, heels echoing against the marble floor. "It's all falling apart for her. She banked on Bertie taking up after father. All her energy went into creating the perfect heir for the Scott name."

"And you?" Valor knew exactly where he'd featured on his mother's list of priorities. "You always seemed thick as thieves."

"Appearances, Val, as you well know, were critically important to her—and Father." Penelope sniffled a little and delicately wiped non-existent tears from her eyes. "He'd have been proud to see you as his heir."

"You'll want to learn how to be a better liar." Valor leaned against the wall; they'd yet to make it out of the imposing foyer. "I'm half-starved. Why don't we scrounge something up out of the kitchen? Plotting requires energy."

"Plotting?" Penelope reluctantly followed Valor down the hall. "*Val.*"

He ignored his sister, suddenly glad Bishan had remained behind at Oliver's house to work on music. The drive up to London had been hard enough on his leg and still-healing body in general. *Poor Bish. He'll never manage all the stairs and hallways in this useless mansion.*

As a child, Valor had spent much of his time in the kitchen with Lottie or out on the estate with Wilfred. They'd offered him the love and attention he craved. They'd played the part of parents more than his own.

Valor ignored his mother's chef and assistant. And honestly, who required a chef and a sous chef for a household of three people? *Ridiculous.* He dug around in the refrigerator to find the makings of a decent early supper. "How hungry are you?"

Penelope stood awkwardly beside him. "The chef—"

"He's a lovely bloke, I'm sure. I can manage a sandwich without any help." Valor had laid out a selection of cheese and meats. "Remember when we used to sneak into the kitchen in the middle of the night for a snack without Bertie? He'd get cross and tell on us."

"He got cross because you kept sneaking bits of butter into his pyjamas. He'd wake up with his clothes and bed all greasy." Penelope eventually caved to his staring and joined him in putting a sandwich together. "You were a rotten child."

"Me?" Valor snorted. "Who pranced around with all the family diamonds at her third birthday? Hmm? If I recall correctly, it was you."

"I was precocious."

"Posh speak for spoiled rotten." He hopped up on the counter and grabbed the plate with his sandwich, grinning at the horrified glares from the chef and his sister.

"What? Never seen someone get comfortable in the kitchen?"

"Not in this kitchen." Penelope swatted his leg. "Get down. You're not in your grubby little cottage."

Valor stubbornly refused to get off the counter but did manage to bite his tongue to avoid snapping at his sister. "Grubby little cottage? It's quite clean, even the kitchen, even without the help of a butler, maid, or chef."

She went a bright shade of red, twisting away from him. "Sorry."

Valor was too tired to even roll his eyes at her. "Do you want to inherit the title and estate?"

Penelope choked on a tiny bite of her egg and cress sandwich. She dabbed at her lips with a napkin the sous chef had laid out for her. "Someone must."

"Someone must?" Valor wished the polite façade could be physically stripped away from his sister. He wanted an open and honest conversation. "I'd let it all fade away into history if I had my way."

"Our name? Our legacy?"

Her lack of insight blew Valor's mind. How did she not see their family had offered zero value to the world? Their name meant nothing; they had no legacy beyond the money they threw around.

His mother flirted with the concept of working with charities. "Diana was such an inspiration to me," fell from her lips often. Valor hoped his sister didn't fall into the same trap as their mother.

"Think mother dearest realises she's now the dowager countess?" Valor grinned cheekily as Penelope hid her smile behind the napkin. "I'm serious, Penny. What would you do as the countess? Shop? Or do something good in the world?"

"I've no idea."

"Good." He turned his attention to the chef who hadn't

bothered to pretend he wasn't eavesdropping. "*Oi.* Think you can rustle up chips and custard?"

"*Valor.*"

"What? Bish deserves a treat." Valor smiled winningly at his sister, who shook her head. "Why don't you come with me? Leave the dowager to enjoy her mansion. See how the grubby folks live."

"I am sorry I insulted your cottage."

Valor hopped off the counter and turned slightly to face her. "You didn't. The cottage doesn't have feelings. You insulted my choices. I know you're trying, Penny, but luxury has gifted you a twisted view of the rest of the world."

Penelope couldn't seem to meet his gaze. "I don't want to be a carbon copy of Mother."

"Mum."

"*Mother.*"

"Try it. Say, mum," he teased her. "Actually, she's not really a mum sort of woman, is she?"

Dropping the subject for the moment, Valor decided they both needed to escape the stifling atmosphere of the mansion. Any conversation with their mother would be pointless until she'd calmed her nerves. They had no reason to torture themselves waiting.

With a little cajoling, Valor managed to get Penelope to change into a more casual outfit. They snuck out with the custard, chips, and a plate of fancy cakes. He considered this a test of how genuine his sister's claims of wanting to change actually were.

Was she going to handle Oliver, Bish, and Reva without sneering at them in their natural habitat? Valor wanted to help his sister and be there for her. He refused to subject his loved ones to anyone sneering at them.

I should narrate it like David Attenborough.

We've secretly switched the posh princess's normal environment with that of a lowly peasant. Let's watch her reaction.

She appears not to be amused.

"I can sense you mocking me." Penelope narrowed her eyes on him while they waited for Oliver to open his door. "I can be friendly."

"Actually friendly? Or the Scott version of it?" Valor planned to etch away at the shell around her to find the real Penelope that he'd occasionally spotted. "Just enjoy yourself."

"Valiant the Brave." Oliver yanked his door open. His attention immediately went to the food. "Oh, you brought fancy fare."

"Chips and custard?"

"On fancy plates. Can we sell them on eBay?" Oliver grinned wickedly at Penelope's horrified gasp. "What? I bet I could get a few hundred quid for these."

"No." Valor glanced down at the family crest on the large platter in his arms. "A few hundred? More like a thousand or more. Pretty sure these are centuries old. Maybe even further back than that."

"And they let you carry them? And take them out of the house?"

CHAPTER 8

The evening had gone mostly without a hitch. Penelope had surprised him by taking their antics in stride. Reva had kindly offered her a respite from the "idiot boys," as she called them.

It had only taken a few hours for Penelope to call her driver to pick her up. Valor had to laugh when she made certain to take the Scott platters back with her. He appreciated her stepping so far outside her comfort zone.

Though, honestly, how difficult was it to eat chips with custard and debate the subtle differences between the ninth, tenth, and eleventh Doctors?

"Val."

He lifted his head from the pillow to find Bishan watching him in the darkness of the room. "Bish?"

"About the funeral...."

Valor sat up when Bishan stammered to a halt, struggling to finish his thought. "You should stay here with Reva. Oliver Twist is more than enough company for anyone."

"True." Bishan grimaced when he tried to twist on his

side. "Stupid leg. Sunny texted Reva. He's bringing Mum and Dad up to London."

"What? Why?"

"They want to be here—for you," Bishan answered simply.

Emotions Valor had swallowed down while dealing with his mother threatened to overwhelm him. He grabbed a pillow and covered his face with it. His heart swelled with gratitude toward the Tambolis, who'd always welcomed him with open and loving arms.

Valor blinked when the pillow lifted away from his face, and he smiled at Bishan. "Hello."

"You don't have to attend." Bishan absently ran his fingers across Valor's bare chest, playing out whatever tune happened to be in his mind. "He didn't do anything to deserve you paying your respects to him."

"Reggie did ask me to go." Valor had initially planned to settle matters with his mother and sister but avoid the funeral circus. "He hopes my attendance will draw out the killer."

"The detective inspector is a skilled investigator. If the police can't find this monster without you torturing yourself emotionally, then what good are they?" Bishan continued to play Valor's skin like piano keys. "Let the ghost of Lord Scott rest on someone else's shoulders. You standing at his grave won't make your memories of him any less painful."

Valor had learned over the years to pay close attention when Bishan felt so strongly about a particular decision. "It's not the end of the world if I skip the funeral."

Well, it might be to my mother.

"Good. Sleep now." Bishan dropped back onto the pillow, grunting when his leg bumped into Valor's.

The following morning the suit hanging from the closet door seemed to mock Valor. He'd worn it to Mr Clarke's service, a man who'd deserved every ounce of respect paid to him with tears, speeches, and a thousand schoolboy memories.

What had the late Lord Scott deserved?

Derision.

"Breakfast." Bishan eased out of bed, grabbing for his crutches and slowly getting to his feet. "Ollie's Keurig awaits."

"You're obsessed." Valor enjoyed Bishan's sudden fascination with the buttons and the sounds the Keurig made. "We're still not getting one."

"Technophobe."

"I am not." Valor held up his mobile by way of demonstration. "I just know Staccy would break it within ten minutes."

And he would.

With their usual room upstairs out of the question, Oliver had kindly offered them the larger space on the first floor. It had another great advantage: proximity to the kitchen. Valor had raided the fridge for leftovers in the middle of the night when they'd struggled to get to sleep.

"Hello, lovelies."

Valor offered Oliver's nan a broad smile and a kiss on the cheek. He went to get Bishan situated in a chair but got a whack to his shins for his efforts. "I'm only trying to help."

"I've a broken leg. I'm not an invalid." Bishan glared at him. "You can help with coffee."

Valor maturely stuck his tongue out at Bishan, who did the same in return. He turned to Oliver's nan. "How about you? Can I help you with anything?"

"I've got a lovely French toast casserole out of the oven. If you make up coffee for yourselves, I'll leave Ollie to plate it up." She waved cheerily at them before heading out of the kitchen.

Deciding not to wait for Oliver and Reva, Valor grabbed some of the casserole for them. They'd made it through their first portion by the time the scruffy and sheepish duo stumbled into the kitchen. Bishan snickered at his sister from behind his coffee mug.

"I'm suddenly glad we slept downstairs." Valor dodged the spoon Reva flung in his direction. "Violent woman."

They teased each other through breakfast. Valor almost managed to forget the reason behind his London visit. He wanted to pretend they'd come up to spend time with friends, and not to deal with yet another murder plus all the emotional baggage his family carried.

After cleaning up their breakfast, Oliver and Reva disappeared to work on graphics for his project. *Right. We'll stay in the kitchen to avoid any awkwardness.* Bishan had brought out his little file with all their attempts to solve the word puzzles.

"I solved it." Bishan shoved the pad of paper across the table to Valor after an hour of working in silence together. "I think. It's as close to correct as all the others, considering I'm only guessing."

"Brilliant guesses." Valor refused to allow Bishan to dismiss his hard work. "And more accurate than our illustrious detectives had managed."

Turning to the notebook, Valor read the short but ominous statement. *Tick-tock. Shh. Mine before the clock strikes nine.* A shiver went through him as an iceberg of fear settled in the pit of his stomach. He had no doubt of the accuracy of Bishan's solution.

Or of his own interpretation of the meaning behind it. The killer had turned his eyes toward Valor. *I'm his prize. And he's tired of waiting.* He suddenly wondered if Bishan had been right about skipping the funeral.

Valor flipped the notebook over to hide the words. "I wonder what nine means."

"Nine victims?"

"Dead victims? Or nine people he's attacked?" Valor didn't know the answer for himself. He decided they'd spent too much time trying to get inside the mind of their nightmare. "You know what they say about the abyss?"

"It's a long way down?" Bishan asked with the barest hint of a smile. He tapped his pencil against the back of the notebook. "Doesn't this terrify you?"

It did terrify Valor. He admitted as much to Bishan. They simply couldn't allow themselves to be frozen by the fear of potential catastrophe.

They talked for several minutes about their options before Reva returned with the news Sunny had called. The rest of the Tamboli clan would be invading in an hour or so. They'd arrive in time to go to the dinner Valor's mother intended to host at the mansion.

They'd skipped the funeral, but Penelope had begged him not to leave her alone to face the dinner as well. Valor agreed to attend on his terms. He refused to get all dressed up or go without a few friends for moral support.

He hoped the Tambolis and Oliver provided a sufficient buffer against his mother. Penelope had gotten better— slightly. Reva had suggested getting her out more often, away from the people she'd grown up around.

"She needs her horizons expanded," Reva had commented the night before after Penelope left.

How?

How did one expand the horizons of a young woman who'd already travelled the world? Penelope had managed to visit other cultures while locked in her privileged bubble. Valor knew more than going out would be required to soften the hard edges created by his family's luxurious lifestyle; he hoped Penelope had more to her than the spoiled princess façade.

In the hour or so it took the others to arrive, Valor texted with their detective inspector about the potential puzzle solution. He found out the police had watched the funeral, but none of their suspects had shown their faces. Reggie also mentioned investigators from London had been ordered to assist the Grasmere officers.

Now it's an earl who's died, they're all anxious to be the one to solve the case.

I almost feel sorry for Reggie, except they did falsely arrest my Bish.

Bastards.

"Oh, Valor." Rana Tamboli rushed into the kitchen, surprising Valor who hadn't even heard the doorbell. She hugged him tightly then gave her son the same treatment, though more gently. "How are you both? Have you all eaten enough?"

"Mum." Reva caught up to her with a hesitant Oliver behind her. "We had a light lunch, but remember we're eating with the Scotts this evening."

"Have you ever dined with their sort? They'll never feed you enough. It's all fiddly bits of overpriced nonsense like caviar." Rana waved off her daughter's concern. "What's in the fridge?"

Valor choked violently while trying to breathe and laugh at the same time. "This is going to be the best supper I've *ever* had with my mother. *Ever.*"

A few hours later, when they'd pulled up to park their vehicles, Valor didn't quite feel the same way about it. The idea of sitting at the antique table worth more than their cottage exhausted him.

Valor stood by his vehicle, staring up at the ornate door of his family's London mansion. "No."

"Val?" Bishan finally managed to get himself out of the back seat. He'd refused any help from Valor or Oliver, who'd ridden with them. The Tambolis had followed in Sunesh's vehicle. "No, what?"

"I refuse to subject myself and my real family to this exercise in pointlessness." Valor turned around to help Bishan reseat himself in the vehicle. "I don't owe them my presence or my grief. Penny making strides to better herself doesn't mean my mother and her grubby friends have changed one iota."

"Grubby?" Oliver leaned against the vehicle, waiting for Sunesh to jog over to them. "Are posh people grubby? I bet their grubbiness is diamond encrusted."

"Are we going inside?" Sunesh tapped the window and waved at Bishan, who rolled his eyes in response. "He's cheerful."

"His leg hurts." Valor knew Bishan required more rest than he'd gotten in the last few days. "And no, we're not going inside. I'd rather not force indigestion on all of us."

After a brief discussion between the three men, they agreed on a quiet meal elsewhere. Valor rang up another old friend of theirs, Cyril Kerr, who'd become an executive chef at a pretentious gastropub. They teased him endlessly about it.

With a promise from Cyril to set a table up for them, the two-vehicle convoy quickly made its way through traffic to the restaurant. Valor hung back when they arrived, and everyone raced inside to avoid the impending rain. He wondered if leaving had been the right decision.

Have I thrown Penny to the wolves?

Barnaby stepped up beside him, looped an arm around Valor's shoulders, and held an umbrella up over both of them. "I'm proud of all my sons."

Valor didn't quite know where Bishan's father was going with this. "You've every right to be. Sunny's all right for a solicitor. And Bish is the most brilliant man in the world."

Am I too biased?

Probably.

"I'm proud of you as well." Barnaby tightened his arm around Valor. "Maybe you'll never marry my son, but you're part of our family. And we love you."

He bit back his instinctual response of "thank you" because he refused to be as repressed as his mother or sister. "Best family I've ever had the honour to be part of."

Stepping inside the restaurant, they discovered Cyril had set them up inside a private room. Valor appreciated the consideration. He wasn't quite up to trying to block out the sounds of other people's conversation.

For Valor and Bishan, Cyril proved he remembered them well from school. He brought out a dessert plate of chocolate truffles first. They fell on them like ravenous beasts, to everyone's amusement, except Rana who seemed completely unimpressed by their indulging.

"It'd be rude not to eat them since the chef brought them for us especially." Reva grabbed a handful before Valor or Bishan could. "Besides, chocolate chases off dementors."

Sunesh rubbed his forehead, though Valor thought he should've been used to their casual mentioning of the Harry Potter world by now. "Dementors aren't real."

"Muggle," Bishan muttered.

Their actual first course shut down the conversation. Valor ignored the mushroom croquettes and inhaled the salt cod fritters. His phone started to buzz in his pocket in the middle of the lamb entrée.

Reggie?

Bugger.

Valor stepped over to the corner of the room and answered the call from the detective inspector with a sense of dread that made him regret those six fritters. "You've reached the AI response system for Valor Tarquin Scott, temporary Earl of Narnia. How can I be of assistance?"

"Val."

"You have reached the—"

"Valor." Reggie cut him off with a clear edge of impatience. "CCTV cameras captured a man placing a bouquet of cinnamon sticks on the steps of your family's mansion."

"Did you catch him?"

"No."

Valor tried to keep his fear from morphing into anger. "With all the CCTV cameras in London, how'd the police manage to bugger this up?"

"I've no idea. I'm only a village detective. We're only getting bits and pieces of what the senior detectives from the Met police are doing." Reggie sounded nearly as frustrated as Valor felt. "I've done my best, but the death of a peer of the realm catapulted this beyond my reach."

There was no point in taking out his frustrations on Reggie. Valor had come to greatly respect the detective inspector, who'd gone above and beyond to try to solve the case. He ended the call and found everyone else in the room staring intently at him.

"Someone left a present at the mansion." Valor slid back into his seat between Bishan and Sunesh. He pushed his plate of half-eaten lamb away; the smell no longer enticed but nauseated. "They didn't manage to catch the bastard."

"What sort of present?" Bishan leaned against him slightly while folding and unfolding his napkin into a hat.

"A bouquet of cinnamon sticks." Valor grabbed Oliver's glass of wine and chugged it down. "Anyone else ready to get off the merry-go-round?"

CHAPTER 9

Tired of dancing around the issues, Valor asked Sunesh to put him in contact with a solicitor in London who focused solely on wills, contracts, and estates. He'd made his decision during a sleepless night after their supper at Cyril's restaurant. For better or worse, Penelope would inherit all of it.

They'd returned from London immediately after Valor signed a few documents. His mother hadn't attempted to reach out to him once. He had no doubt the now dowager had latched on to Penelope to ensure her lifestyle didn't change.

And I want no part in any of it.

Home in Grasmere.

Days and weeks went by in an uneasy calm. Valor found himself at the start of December with a mostly recovered Bishan and no idea why their killer had gone silent. He wondered if they'd wind up dying from the agonising stress and pressure of waiting for the next horror to hit.

"We found him."

Valor bolted out of his chair in his tiny office at the

bakery. He glanced over to find a bemused detective in the doorway. "Maybe knock next time?"

Reggie lifted a hand up to knock lightly against the doorframe. "Wilfred said you were here. Going to open up again soon? I've missed the biscuits."

Valor slumped into his chair with a groan, waving Reggie toward the one across from him usually reserved for Wilfred. "We're renovating the front of the shop. I'm hoping it erases the memory of seeing the earl dead."

"Your father."

"Was he?" Valor met the detective inspector's steady gaze with one of his own. He'd come to terms with all the emotional turmoil of his father dying and had no desire to even attempt to justify himself. "What can I do for you? You're not here for biscuits. Dame Lottie told me about the basket she sent over to you."

Wait.

Valor sat up suddenly. "Did you say you'd found him?"

"Not the killer," Reggie quickly clarified. He'd obviously read the hope in Valor's expression. "Detectives in London worked extensively to track down the hooded figure who left the cinnamon bouquet. It's taken a while, but we found him."

"And it wasn't the killer?" Valor hazarded a safe guess. He reached over to grab a tin of biscuits.

"No." Reggie grabbed a few of the biscuits when Valor held the tin toward him. "We found a young teenager who was offered a hundred quid to place it on the doorstep. He never saw the killer's face."

"Did you get any useful information at all from the kid?" Valor hadn't honestly believed their killer idiotic enough to get caught playing one of his cruel tricks. "How'd he transfer the money to him?"

"In cash. Dropped it off after an advertisement on a

website. We're hoping to track him either through the cash or the website." Reggie grabbed a handful of biscuits and got to his feet. "It's been a few weeks. Be careful, all right?"

"Why?"

"Just an uneasy feeling I've had." He waved a thank you for the biscuits and disappeared out of the kitchen.

"Brilliant." Valor slouched further into the chair with a sigh. "How am I supposed to be careful if I don't know how or why?"

The Tambolis had descended on them early in the morning. Valor had insisted on heading into the shop, mostly because Rana and Reva had hinted at him needing a haircut. He didn't trust them not to grab scissors and have at his ginger locks.

Pulling himself away from the accounts, Valor headed into the kitchen. They'd closed the shop temporarily to visitors while maintaining their online orders and local deliveries; it meant he had the place to himself in the afternoons.

The Ginger's Bread did brilliant business during the last few months of the year. Valor hated being closed any time at all in November. They'd risk their books going close to the red if they were forced to remain shut through December.

People tended to buy a lot of ginger biscuits at Christmastime.

His plans for the renovations weren't overly complex. Valor had called in a favour with yet another old Harrovian who now worked in construction. The front of the shop would be sparkling and ready in another week or two, in time for the start of the holiday rush.

In the mornings, Wilfred, Valor, Bishan, and the other employees quickly worked through their internet orders. By lunch, they'd all left but Valor and Bishan, who enjoyed time together while managing mundane administration tasks.

Quiet moments were the ones they always tried to make the most of.

Right.

I've cruelly left Bish on his own with his family for long enough.

I should rescue him.

Maybe bring pudding, so he doesn't make me sleep on the sofa by myself.

Locking up the shop, Valor pocketed his keys as his mobile buzzed. *Perfect timing. What's Penny want?* He'd heard from his sister several times in the past week. She had truly taken the reins and dedicated herself to attempting to change the public view of the Scotts, much to his amusement and their mother's horror.

"Countess." Valor leaned against the back door. "How can your pauper brother help you today? Is the dowager behaving herself?"

"Pauper?" Penelope scoffed. "And Mother is pouting at a villa in the south of France."

"True suffering."

"Torture. Do you have a moment to chat?" Penelope's tone changed slightly as she spoke, but in a way he recognised immediately.

"No." Valor had washed his hands of it all, and while he wasn't opposed to a relationship with his sister he had no intentions of getting involved. "I'm not corralling her for you, Little Lady Fauntleroy. You got the money, mansion, and title; you get to deal with the baggage as well."

"Did you just call our mother baggage?" Penelope giggled quietly. "I haven't asked you anything yet."

"You were going to. I've known you since you were an ugly, wrinkly baby. And stop sulking, you sound like her." Valor chuckled when his sister cursed at him and disconnected the call. "Like mother, a bit like daughter as well."

After a few minutes without a return call, Valor pushed

away from the door to head home. He'd driven instead of riding his bicycle to avoid the rain. But also, Rana had lectured him about not getting sick by playing around in the damp and cold morning air.

"Valor."

He stopped in the process of opening the car door to find a familiar man standing behind him. "Harry?"

"*Harrison*," he corrected sharply. "You remember me."

Valor frowned at the sudden emotional tone of Harrison's voice. He bumped into the car door trying to back away. "I haven't seen you in ages."

"I've seen you."

"What—"

Before Valor could get away from him, Harrison lifted a Taser and fired two prongs into his chest. Valor slammed into his car, toppling to the ground in a flash of electrified pain. It felt as though it lasted for an eternity before a prick to his neck made the world go dark.

CHAPTER 10

The bite of freezing cold brought Valor out of a deep yet uneasy sleep. He shifted around on the bed, grimacing when his back rubbed against a bare wooden floor. With immense effort, he managed to force himself to open his eyes.

Why does it feel like I drank three bottles of Wilf's homemade brandy on an empty stomach?

And why am I bloody naked?

Valor shivered in the cold, damp darkness. He brought his hands up to wipe his face, confused by his inability to separate his wrists. "Bish?"

Silence.

And wind, lots of wind.

Sitting up slowly, Valor shifted toward the small bit of light coming from the moon through a window. He found his hands bound with a plastic tie. It was almost impossible to think clearly with his head pounding.

Valor leaned against the wall underneath the window. He pulled his legs up to his chest, resting his head on his knees. "Hello?"

Harrison Smith.

After a few slow, deep breaths, Valor managed to clear his mind enough to remember snippets from earlier in the day. *Is it the evening? How long have I been out?* He'd stood outside the shop, spoken with Harrison, and then his memory went fuzzy on him.

He had flashes of being on the floorboard of a car with a heavy blanket over him. His neck and arm seemed unusually painful, as though he'd had multiple injections. *And where are my bloody clothes?*

Bastard could've at least put me on the bed, I'm too old to be passed out on a floor.

For the first time in his life, Valor was thankful for all the annoying training he'd suffered through during his time with the Harrow Combined Cadet Force. He'd learned how to escape bindings, including zip ties. It had been one lesson he always assumed would be unnecessary.

Carefully twisting his wrists, Valor worked slowly to free one of his hands. The tie was tight enough his fingers had gone numb, but he ignored it. He rotated one way then the other, and inch by inch managed to get out of the plastic binding.

After working his wrists free, Valor rubbed them vigorously to get feeling into his fingers. He slowly got to his feet to search for clothes. The one-room cottage barely had the basics of a bed, a small kitchen area with no food or drink, and a toilet in the corner.

No clothes.

And no food.

No phone.

The way the wind bashed against the thin cottage walls made Valor desperately wish for clothes. He managed to find a worn blanket shoved into a cupboard along with a set of dirty sheets. It was better to be warm and dusty than clean and hypothermic.

Valor curled up on the lumpy mattress and considered his options. *Do I wait for daylight to try to escape? Or do I risk running into the freezing night air in the hopes Harrison doesn't come back?*

With daylight, if the weather cooperated, sunlight might prevent him dying from hypothermia. He didn't fancy running around starkers with a blanket toga to cover his bits in the howling wind. *Is it better than waiting for death?*

As his mind cleared more and feeling returned to his fingers, Valor gingerly traced the swollen spots on his neck and arm. He wondered if Harrison had used a tranquiliser to keep him knocked out. The injection obviously hadn't been cinnamon—not this time.

Not yet.

Another search of the room provided him with a pair of socks that had been lost behind an empty bookcase. Valor shook them out multiple times to ensure no stray spiders had made a nest in them. He slipped them on his feet to offer additional warmth.

"I've socks, a blanket, and a sheet." Valor scrubbed his hands across his face with a tired groan. "And I'm talking to myself."

After sitting for what seemed like hours, Valor grew bored of it. He wandered around the cramped space, trying the front door and finding it locked from the outside. *Of course it is. I suppose I'll be clambering out the window somehow.*

As the sun came up outside, Valor got a clearer view of his prison. He found a note he'd missed pinned to one of the walls. His heart hammered in his chest while he reached up to grasp the paper.

G one to handle business. I'll return. It's time we have a chat, isn't it? H.S.

W hat business had Harrison left to take care of? Valor crumpled the paper, ripping it to shreds and allowing them to flutter to the floor. He had to get himself far away from the cottage as quickly as possible.

"They don't know." Valor had no idea if Reggie had checked the CCTV cameras around the shop. "They don't know it's weedy little Harry Smith. *Bugger*."

A sudden sense of urgency overtook Valor. He went over to the window and managed with a fair bit of force to slide it open. His body hurt enough to keep him from easily lifting himself up out of it, though.

Unwrapping the blanket and sheet, Valor shoved them through the opening. He used the single chair in the cottage as a stepping stool. Though a tight fit, he managed to squeeze himself through the window and out into the frigid air.

Valor landed with a thud on the mass of blanket and sheet. He quickly wrapped himself up in both to block some of the wind. "Where in God's name am I?"

It was definitely *not* Grasmere or anywhere in the Lake District. Valor stumbled around the side of the cottage and found himself staring out at a dock with no moored boat and the choppiest of seas. *Am I on an island?*

With the blanket and sheet clutched tightly around him, Valor walked along the coastline. He discovered the small shed-like cottage was the only structure on the island. No boats, no way to tell how far he was from civilisation. His swimming definitely wasn't strong enough to keep him alive in the choppy, freezing waters.

Death by drowning?
Or death by cinnamon?

Rescue seemed unlikely to him. Escape seemed equally impossible. The bleak cottage in the distance offered him slight protection, but he wondered if his sanctuary might transform into his tomb.

Though the wind continued to batter him on his hunt around the island, the sky cleared of cloud and the fog abated. Valor managed to spot another shoreline in the distance, either an island or the mainland. The sea hadn't calmed at all, and swimming didn't feel a safe option to him.

How do I draw attention to the island?
What would Bear Grylls do?
Fire.
They always use smoke to signal for rescue on those survival shows Hugh watches.
Bugger.
He'll be insufferable if this works and his crap telly saves my life.

Glancing over at the cottage, Valor weighed his options. With no shelter, dying of exposure became a terrifying possibility. On the other hand, Harrison might return at any moment.

Would I rather die of exposure or suffer through whatever the weedy Harry has planned?

In his multiple inspections of the cottage, Valor had spied a box of matches above the empty fireplace. He gathered driftwood from all around the island. Anything even slightly flammable went onto a growing pile beside the structure.

Much of it was damp, but Valor figured once the cottage went up in flames it wouldn't matter. If the fire burned hot enough, the dampness might even help to increase the visibility of the smoke. He hoped.

His entire body shook from the cold. Valor found it increasingly difficult to wrap his fingers around branches along the coastline. He decided to start the fire while still capable of working the matches.

For several minutes, Valor attempted to dry off and warm up. He considered the options for ensuring the fire burned for an extended period rather than fizzling out. *Poirot certainly never taught me anything about this. Maybe I should've watched more survival shows with Hugh.*

Here goes nothing.

Opening up the mattress on the bed, Valor dug out a wad of the dry stuffing inside. He set it on the floor beside the best of the kindling. There'd only be one chance to get this right.

Is a slow start better than a quick spread?

What am I doing?

What the hell am I doing?

I'm trying not to die so I can get back to Bish before Harrison finds him.

The thought of Bishan steeled the thread of panic boiling up inside him. Valor refused to cower in the cold, not trying to discover a way to escape. He found the courage to get to his feet.

After careful consideration, Valor made two initial fires. One in the corner of the cottage near the kitchen and the other underneath the bed. He hoped both areas would prove flammable enough to take the entire structure. He stayed inside while the flames began to spread, long enough to warm up, until the oppressive heat chased him out into the cold.

Valor found a spot nearby to sit and watch for any potential rescue. He felt some of the warmth from the fire but mostly shivered in the wind. *What if no one sees the smoke?*

Frozen.

His fingers struggled to hold the blanket closed around his body. Valor considered inching closer to the now out-of-control fire but worried about being unable to see any approaching boats. He struggled to take deep breaths.

Valor tried to get to his feet to move closer to the fire for warmth but crashed to the ground in a painful tangle of the blanket. He curled up on the bitterly cold ground, unable to force himself to sit up. "Tired. Why...."

CHAPTER 11

Valor woke up with a strange, disorienting sense of déjà vu. He found himself comfortably situated on a bed with an IV in one arm and covered in multiple blankets. *Well, I'm not dead.*

Yet.

"Are you all right?"

Valor forced himself to sit up in what was clearly a hospital bed. He found his hands wrapped loosely in sheets, and glanced over at the kindly woman in a crisp white coat standing nearby. "I've been better. Where am I?"

"Can you tell me your name?" She held a clipboard in her hands.

"Valor Tarquin Scott." He frowned at the doctor who continued to pepper him with questions. "There are probably a lot of people searching for me in the area. I went missing from Grasmere yesterday. Well, I'm not actually sure how long it's been. It's possible it's been a few days."

"Grasmere?" She lowered the clipboard and moved closer to him. "You're from Cumbria?"

"Yes." Valor realised slowly that her accent definitely

didn't match those of most of the doctors from the hospital near Windermere. "How far have I travelled?"

"You're in Scotland."

"Bugger."

"You were found on an uninhabited island used for grazing sheep in the spring. They had to resuscitate you when you stopped breathing." The doctor checked his blood pressure while she chatted with him. "You've been out for a day and a half. Can you tell me how you got in such a state?"

Valor tried to think back but his memories seemed fuzzy at best. "I woke up without my clothes. I tried setting a fire in the hopes someone spotted the smoke. I'll pay for the damage."

She waved off his concerns. "I'm Dr Paterson. Everyone calls me Maggie. You've found yourself in North Uist. A long way from Cumbria."

"North Uist?" Valor wondered how Harrison had managed to sneak an unconscious man so far north without anyone the wiser. "Is it Thursday?"

"Monday."

Monday?

He'd been gone five days. Bishan had to be out of his mind with worry. "I'm not sure how I got to Scotland."

The doctor did a thorough check up on him. She checked on his fingers and toes, which had suffered from mild frost-bite. They'd found him in time to prevent serious permanent damage, but she wanted to keep a close eye on his feet in particular before removing the loose bandages completely.

A nurse brought him a thick stew. It tasted better than any hospital food he had ever experienced. She explained the mother of his brave rescuers had brought it up to the clinic for, in her words, "the poor wee frozen lamb."

Valor ate slowly with one of his hands still carefully

wrapped, taking in the warmth of the stew. "Is there a phone I can use?"

If Harrison had his mobile, he likely knew they'd discovered the cloned phones. Valor wanted to warn the detective. But more importantly, he wanted to hear Bishan's voice to remind himself why he had to survive.

With one hand inconveniently bandaged, Valor relied on the nurse to dial Hugh's mobile. Bishan wouldn't answer an unknown number. His Bish hated being on the phone, never mind an unexpected call from a stranger.

"Asheford."

"Hugh?"

Silence.

"Can you hear me?" Valor prompted when the prolonged quiet continued. "Are you there? *Oi.* Ash."

"Prince Valiant." Hugh cleared his throat loudly. "You all right, Valor? We thought…."

Valor teared up as Hugh couldn't finish his sentence. He had no doubts they'd all feared they were searching for his body. "I've a small case of frostbite. I'm in Scotland."

"Scotland."

Valor heard the slamming of a door followed by running footsteps on the other end. Hugh likely wanted to find Bishan quickly. "North Uist, apparently. Hugh. I've no idea what you've all found, but the killer is—"

"Harrison Smith." Hugh cut him off. "We caught him attacking you on CCTV footage from behind your shop."

"He's got my mobile."

"No, he doesn't. You dropped it." Hugh had started to breathe heavily, sounding as though he was running. Valor heard his footsteps stop and then pounding on a door. "Wilfred found your mobile and keys underneath your car. He notified the police. Hang on a second, Val."

Taking advantage of the break, Valor finished his last bite

of stew, thanking the nurse who whisked the dish away. He shifted slightly, careful not to dislodge the phone propped up on his chest. His body felt blissfully free of pain, likely due more to pain medication than anything else.

"Val."

His eyes did flood with tears at the hesitance in the beautifully familiar voice. "Bish."

"Wilf found blood. Blood." Bishan cleared his throat a few times. "Blood, your mobile, and car, but no you."

"Bish."

"Thought you died," Bishan continued, despite Valor trying to interrupt. "He hasn't left anyone else alive."

Valor closed his eyes against the obvious pain in Bishan's voice. He ached to reach through to hold him tightly. "I'm alive, Bish. We're going to be okay. I promise."

I hope.

"Val?"

He was jolted out of his thoughts at the sudden ageing of the voice over the phone. "Wilf?"

"Your Bishan's not quite able to natter at the moment." Wilfred sounded as cheerfully gruff as always. "How's Scotland?"

"Cold. Damp. Windy."

"Little Reginald plans to head up to bring you home safely."

"Little Reginald is a grown man who happens to also be a detective inspector." Valor wondered if Reggie ever regretted choosing to remain in Grasmere, where every villager over a certain age remembered him as a young boy. "Is Bish okay?"

"Not sure he'll believe you're alive until he sees you." Wilfred went silent for several excruciating seconds. "He broke a little when we told him about finding your car and the blood. He did that quiet thing, you know, and waved his hands around. It took both his mum and dad to get him out of his music room to eat or sleep while the police tried to find you."

Valor, once again, found talking almost impossible. He tried to breathe through the desire to collapse into tears. "I'll be home soon."

And I'll get home to him safely.

Ending the call, Valor sank into the pillow with a weary groan. He wiped his arm across his eyes. *What are we going to do?*

Weather and abduction aside, the people in Scotland were lovely. Valor appreciated the care from the doctor and nurses. His rescuers (and their family) came to spend time with him; their mother brought him a change of clothing since he was making do with a borrowed set of scrubs.

Stuck in a hospital bed, Valor had nothing to do but turn his mind to their partially solved mystery. Harrison Smith was their killer. He honestly found it hard to reconcile his memories of the young boy in his first year at Harrow with the man who'd viciously attacked him.

When had Harrison become so twisted and why?

What had set him off?

Despite what the others believed, Valor no longer accepted the theory of Harrison being in love with him. Something about the note left in the cottage pulled at Valor's mind. He had a terrifying feeling they'd find a more profound and darker motive at the bottom of the abyss.

And hopefully, the abyss doesn't stare too deeply back at us.

CHAPTER 12

"**A**re you going inside?" Reggie prodded Valor, who found it difficult to move now that they'd finally parked outside the cottage. "As much as I enjoyed the ten hours trapped in a vehicle with you, I'd think you'd be anxious to get inside."

Valor dropped his head against the seat and gave Reggie a nod. "Cheers for the clothes and the ride."

In total, between the abduction, rescue, and recovery time at the hospital, Valor had been gone from Grasmere for over a week. He'd mostly recovered from his ordeal. His frostbite required a few more sessions of heat therapy for his toes, and the injection sites were still a bit sore.

Nerves had built up inside him over the last hour of the drive. Irrational, but there nonetheless. He hadn't faced the truth of how close he'd actually come to death. *The crash, the fire, and being dragged off to Scotland. How much more can we survive?*

Forcing himself out of the vehicle, Valor had to take a few breaths to settle himself. He started up the walk toward the door, which swung open almost immediately. Reva stared at him for several seconds.

She flew down the walk and pounced on him, ignoring his pained grunt when her shoe bumped into his. "You're alive."

Valor gave her a tight hug but released her when Bishan hobbled down toward him on one crutch. "Bish."

Ducking around them, Reva disappeared into the cottage. Valor didn't even pay attention to her; he focused his attention on the man held tightly against him. Bishan had looped his free arm around Valor.

"Val. *Val.* Val." Bishan grabbed onto Valor's shirt so tightly he worried the buttons on the front might pop. "Val."

He waited patiently, despite the rain beginning to pelt them, while Bishan continued to murmur his name over and over. "I'm here. I'm all right—didn't even lose a finger or toe in the process. They're a wonky pink colour, though."

"Not funny." Bishan's fingers dug into his back a bit more firmly as he pressed closer to Valor. "Mum said to stay hopeful. I made Sunny take me to the shop. Saw the blood. Your blood. I thought he'd finally gotten you."

Valor decided not to offer fake platitudes; none of them knew if they'd escape alive. He'd been incredibly lucky in Scotland, as had Bishan in the explosion. "I did my best to get home, Bish. I'll always fight with everything I am to stay safe for you."

The increasing rain drove them into the cottage. Valor helped Bishan through the crowd inside, who immediately tried to get their own hugs. He managed to embrace each of them with Bishan still clutching his hand.

While Valor appreciated their vigil in Grasmere for him, their presence had to be overwhelming for Bishan. *I'm tired of them already, and I just got here. Is it rude to toss them all out on their ear? Probably.*

I just want a moment to myself with Bishan without an audience of hundreds.

Not hundreds, but it's more than I want to deal with.

Lottie and Rana joined forces with Bishan's auntie and her wife to whip up an early supper for the group. Valor was amazed they'd managed it in the small kitchen. Food temporarily stemmed the endless flow of questions from their gathered friends.

After a break in the eating and conversation, Daniel Zhou, one of his Harrow friends, dragged off his sister along with Nina and several of their other old schoolmates. Valor thought they'd realised Bishan was treading close to snapping from the strain. The rest slowly trickled out after them, catching the hint.

"We'll bring a late brunch for you in the morning." Lottie patted his cheeks with her hands and dragged her grumbling husband after her.

"Oh, how we worried." Rana pulled them both into hugs before taking Reva and Sunesh out.

Barnaby held Valor in a strong embrace, longer than the others had. "My Bishan. He didn't do so well without you. We're all thrilled to find you safe and whole."

Valor stammered for a response and eventually mumbled a simple, "Thank you."

With a wry chuckle, Barnaby released him and made his way to the door. He took the remaining stragglers out with him. Valor collapsed on the sofa beside Bishan and enjoyed the silence for a moment.

Bishan adjusted his cast-covered leg, a cast that would be coming off in a few days, and leaned against Valor's shoulder. "Music room needs cleaning."

"Why?"

"I had a meltdown," Bishan said sheepishly.

Valor wrapped his arm around Bishan, adjusting him more comfortably on the couch. "We'll sort it out."

They stayed on the sofa for almost an hour. Valor hadn't wanted to move. He'd feared for so long he'd never see Bishan again—and cuddling up in the peace of their cottage settled him.

"Val?"

Valor shifted up to glance at him. "Yes?"

"Did you think about dying?" Bishan's eyes focused on his nose.

Valor closed his eyes and rested his head against the cushion. He didn't have to think hard for the torturous thoughts of the past few days to come rushing back to him. "I tried to focus on not dying."

"He's not going to stop."

"No, probably not." Valor opened his eyes to stare up at the ceiling. "What do we do?"

"We stop him." Bishan tilted his chin up and met Valor's gaze. "We've got to try to find a way to stop him. I'm not sitting at home waiting for the inevitable as if I've no choice in the matter. Not again."

"How?" Valor knew the detectives were doing their best, particularly after the death of a peer. "I barely managed to escape with all my fingers and toes."

Bishan dropped his gaze and stared down at his forcefully clenched fists. "I've no idea."

Sleep didn't come easily for either of them. They wound up curling up under the duvet and watching one of their favourite shows on a laptop. Bishan eventually drifted off four episodes into the marathon; Valor had no such luck.

He sat up in bed with his back resting against the headboard and Bishan's head on a pillow on his lap. His fingers played absently with the inky, wavy mass of hair. "We're going to make it through this, Bish."

The strain of the past few days was evident in the dark circles around Bishan's eyes. Valor had peeked into the music room before going to bed. The meltdown had apparently been a bad one. Sheet music and pieces from a stand were strewn all over—definitely not a good day.

December usually meant happy moments for both men. Valor decided they needed a break from the awful nightmare. Tackling the killer could wait a few days.

Valor desperately needed a spark of joy, if only briefly, to remind himself that he'd survived.

CHAPTER 13

V alor awoke to trails of kisses being left on his chest. He tilted his head to get a better view. "Bish?"

"You're not a dream."

"Thanks." Valor chuckled. "Are you complaining or complimenting?"

"I had a nightmare." Bishan pressed his forehead against Valor's side. "Reggie brought you home in one of those black bags. He propped you up in the garden like a gnome."

"Rude bastard."

"*Val.*"

He tried not to snicker but failed miserably. "Should I commission someone to make a me-shaped garden gnome for you?"

Bishan glared at him for a second then collapsed into helpless laughter. "We should get one for each of us and put them in the garden. Can you imagine Mrs Harris's face when she peeks over the fence to find our gnome-selves staring at her?"

"That's holiday gifts for each other sorted." Valor had no doubts they'd hear about Mrs Harris's disapproval if they managed to get the gnomes. "I vote for an entire family of them."

"Gnomes?"

Valor sat up in bed, dislodging Bishan. "Let's do a pudding crawl."

On rare occasions when Bishan decided to brave going to a restaurant instead of having takeaway, they'd indulged in pudding crawls. They picked out several specific places to eat and tried desserts at each one. It had been ages since their last one.

Nothing cheered Bishan up like copious amounts of pudding. *Maybe Staccy, but he's being spoilt by Lottie. I'm starting to worry we'll never see our cat again.*

"Isn't it too early in the day for a pudding crawl?"

Valor twisted over to grab his phone off the nightstand. "It's almost eleven. We apparently needed sleep. And honestly, is it ever too early for pudding?"

"I—"

"No, the appropriate response would be no. It is *never* too early for pudding." Valor flopped back onto his pillow. He sent two quick texts out: one to Penelope to make sure she knew he'd made it home safely and the second to Hugh to see if the detectives had discovered anything new. "So, what do you say?"

"Just us or a group?"

A group meant safety, but Valor wanted to retain some semblance of normalcy. He didn't know how date-like it would feel with an entourage of friends. As much as he refused to let Harrison change their lives, how could the imminent danger not alter their decisions?

"Small group." Bishan tried to roll off the bed without success. "Damn it."

"You forgot about your leg, didn't you?" Valor crawled

over to the edge of the mattress to check on him. "You okay?"

Bishan adjusted his leg slightly to allow him to stretch out between the bed and the wall. "I'm all right."

"How do you forget about a broken leg in a cast?" He got up and bent down to carefully help Bishan to his feet. "Who should we invite in our small group?"

"Staccy."

"Pretty sure Staccato isn't allowed in restaurants." Valor looped his arm around Bishan's waist to lead him toward the bath. "How about we see if Hugh wants to play the third wheel?"

Given the recent abduction, Hugh and Reggie would likely insist on an officer tagging along with them. They'd spotted the police car parked outside their cottage. It had been there through the night.

And they'll probably follow us until they catch Harrison.

A quick shower devolved into carefully washing each other. Valor had to help Bishan with his cast. They managed to get clean, dried off, and dressed without falling over each other in the small bath.

Valor stared down at some of the bruises and cuts on his upper body, his shirt still held in his hand. *How close to death by hypothermia did I come?* The doctor had tried to spare him those details.

"Do you want to talk about it?" Bishan asked. He sat on the edge of the bed with his crutch leaning against the wall.

He dragged his long-sleeved shirt over his head and sat beside Bishan. "I slept through most of it."

"Does it bother you? Not knowing what happened while he had you tranquilised?" Bishan tugged on Valor's sleeve when he went silent. "Val?"

"It does." Valor tried not to dwell on those hours or days

when he had no memory of what happened. "It's maddening."

Neither of them had anything to say. Valor had already made the decision to not think about it. He'd likely never know for certain. Why drive himself into a pit of misery with maybes?

With a plethora of sweets on the menu, Valor insisted on toast and tea before leaving. Their stomachs might be less likely to rebel from the onslaught of sugar. He grinned as Bishan cut his buttered bread into squares before eating it.

"Ready?" Valor led Bishan across the street to cajole Hugh into joining their excursion. He banged loudly on the door until it swung open. "Morning. Ready for a pudding crawl?"

Hugh glanced bewilderedly between the two of them. "You want to—now? We only just got you back safely. And you honestly want to swan around the Lake District? Fine. *Fine*. You're paying."

"Cheap sod." Valor grinned at him. "If we're paying, you have to drive."

"Only because you plan on getting drunk on sugar." Hugh retrieved his jacket and stepped outside between them with his keys dangling in his left hand. He made quick work of locking up. "Wasn't Mrs Tamboli or Lottie bringing you lot brunch?"

Bishan lifted up his phone. "Texted Mum to say Valor wasn't ready for another family invasion. He's delicate."

"Delicate?" Hugh brought both arms up to guide the two of them toward his SUV. "He's as delicate as a rampaging sheep."

"Do sheep rampage?" Bishan asked seriously. "They jump a bit. Not that chaotic or violent."

"Maybe it's just the cloned ones." Valor dodged out of the way of Hugh, who swung a playful punch at him. "What? You brought up the rampaging ewes."

With more good-natured teasing, they clambered into Hugh's vehicle. Bishan had already jotted down a list of potential restaurants within easy driving distance. They'd chosen ones with a decent lunch menu that had interesting desserts.

Their first stop happened to be at one of Valor's favourite Grasmere cafés. Situated across from the Ginger's Bread, they stopped there frequently. He particularly loved their salted caramel and chocolate cheesecake.

"Do you know how much running I'll do to work all this off?" Hugh grumbled after making a dent in his sticky toffee pudding. "I won't fit into my trousers."

"And yet you ordered dessert anyway." Valor traded bites with Bishan, who'd gotten the chocolate cake. "Aren't designated drivers supposed to abstain?"

"On pub crawls, definitely." Hugh spoon duelled with Valor for a bit of his cheesecake. "Pudding ones have no such requirements."

Pudding crawls had become one of their traditions after one of their many Olivers had given up drinking. They'd supported him through Alcoholics Anonymous, and decided to create a way to celebrate without alcohol. Instead of reunions spent in one pub after the other, they gorged on sweets instead.

Their livers thanked them, but their stomachs had risked expanding.

After finishing up their first stop, they walked down the street to yet another café. Valor drooled over the sticky gingerbread pudding. From the smile on Bishan's face, he knew it had been the perfect way to spend the day.

Despite Hugh moaning about not being a chauffeur, Valor clambered into the back seat with Bishan. They cuddled up together, mostly to avoid the cast getting in the way of sitting comfortably. By their fourth restaurant, their appetite for pudding had only slowed a little.

"*Oi*. What did I say about snogging in the back seat?" Hugh twisted around while stopped at a light.

"Nothing, actually."

Hugh glared at him before turning the right way round as the car behind them honked impatiently. "Have you heard from Penny today?"

Valor exchanged a look with Bishan at the change in tone and subject. *Penny?* "I confirmed her fears of being an only child were no longer a concern. Why?"

"Just wondering."

"You haven't." Valor leaned forward to rest his elbows against the sides of the front seats. "Are you trying to seduce my little sister? Not after her money and title, are you?"

"*Val*."

He snickered at the flush on Hugh's neck. "Oh my God. You've got a crush on Penny. Since when?"

"Always," Bishan piped up. "Perhaps not *always*, but he's definitely been a lot more attentive since she displayed she has a personality of her own—and is not a clone of your mother."

"Has he?" Valor had no idea how he'd missed this development. "Hugh? Something to share with the rest of us?"

"Stop distracting me while I'm driving." Hugh refused to respond further, much to Valor's amusement.

Settling into his seat again, Valor wondered how his sister would respond to Hugh. She'd grown up in the past few months. If nothing else, it would be entertaining to watch the drama unfold.

As the vehicle went over a bump, Valor found himself jolted back to days ago. His nose filled with the scent of a different car's interior. Memories from being bounced around while stretched out and restrained on the floorboard hit him hard.

I should've sat in the front.

"Val?"

"I'm fine." He waved off Bishan's concerned whisper. "Just remembering something."

Bishan rested a hand gently on Valor's knee. "Sometimes I can smell the smoke from the fire as though I'm still crushed under the wall."

Brilliant.

We're both suffering from flashbacks.

Determined not to allow their "cheer ourselves up" moment to be ruined, Valor pushed the memories out of his mind for now. Dwelling on them wouldn't bring him answers. For now, he'd focus on healthier pursuits like eating his feelings.

Six hours of hopping from one village to the other left them all too full to do anything other than moan about their own stupidity. Valor didn't know if it had been a brilliant or idiotic idea. They'd definitely eaten way too many sweets.

Their last stop had been to a holiday-themed festival. Bishan had immediately baulked at the large number of shoppers. They grabbed a few fig puddings and frosted biscuits and made a hasty retreat.

"Try to not get abducted again." Hugh laughed when Valor slammed the door shut in his face.

Valor stared around their living room, which showed the touch of Bishan's father, who tended to straighten when stressed. He hadn't noticed it the day before, too busy revelling in the joy of being safe and having Bishan in his arms. "Shall we laze by the fire and watch telly? Or clean up the music room disaster?"

"I'll set the fire."

"Laze by the fire it is." Valor collected the remote and

collapsed on the couch. "Bish?"

"Hmm?" Bishan glanced over with the box of long matches in his hand. "Something wrong?"

Valor found himself unable to voice his fears that had bubbled inside him since being rescued—an ever-present sense of doom. "*Poirot*? Or, shall we be a bit adventurous and watch something new?"

"*Poirot*."

They both fell asleep before the credits of the first episode. Valor woke up to a still darkened living room thanks to their thick curtains. He dragged himself up and into the kitchen to get the kettle on for coffee.

Stumbling around in the kitchen, Valor wandered over to the sink to splash cold water on his face. He shook his head, sending drops flying. While he got the mugs ready with their favourite instant coffee, Bishan grumbled loudly in the living room over the rudeness of morning in general.

"What's wrong with Hugh?" Bishan's voice broke into his thoughts a few minutes later.

Valor leaned out of the kitchen to find Bishan standing by the front windows with the curtains partially opened. "Define wrong?"

"Something's going on out there." Bishan shrugged.

"Give me a second." Valor quickly grabbed the kettle once it started to whistle and poured the boiling water into the mugs, along with cream and sugar.

Grabbing the two mugs of coffee, Valor headed over to stand beside him. He offered Bishan one of the cups. They sipped their morning wake-up juice and watched with growing concern the activity across the street.

A chaotic grouping of vehicles had parked haphazardly in the street and on their front lawn as well as Hugh's. Valor spotted an ambulance with an obviously alive Hugh sitting on the rear bumper. *Thank God, he's not badly hurt.*

Hope they plan on fixing our grass now they've driven all over it.

"Shall we stick our noses in?" Valor took another sip of coffee, then set the mug down on the table by the door. "Not coming?"

"No." Bishan was understandably uneasy around some of the detectives.

Valor darted in for a lingering kiss, then rushed out the door. He chose to ignore Bishan's parting remark of his becoming more like their nosy neighbour. "It's not morbid curiosity. I'm worried about my friend."

It's a bit of morbid curiosity.

Who wouldn't want to investigate with all this activity?

"Curiosity killed the cat, Val." Hugh didn't buy the inno-cent concern when Valor sidled up to him.

"Yes, but as satisfaction brought it back, I'm not overly worried." He didn't see any visible marks on Hugh. "What happened?"

"Harrison tried to sneak into my cottage." Hugh got to his feet and pushed away from the ambulance. "I'm fine. Not a scratch on me."

The detectives outside the cottage didn't bat an eyelid at Valor following Hugh inside. He noticed the scuff marks on the door. Harrison had obviously not expected a struggle.

Murderous idiot.

"Did you catch him?"

"He sprayed me in the face with something that burned my eyes." Hugh seemed angry about letting Harrison get away. "I'm pretty sure I broke his arm with my cricket bat."

None of the local clinics had gotten a visit from Harrison. Reggie apparently had an officer calling any hospital or doctor within driving range to see if anyone had shown up with a broken arm. Valor didn't believe they'd find him that way.

And thus far, they hadn't.

CHAPTER 14

"Phone."

Valor threw a hand out to grab the phone being chucked at him. "Why am I always answering your calls?"

"You like talking." Bishan disappeared down the hall to clean up their music room.

He frowned at the strange number on the screen. "Bishan's phone. His loveable rogue of an answering machine speaking."

"Is this Bishan Tamboli?" a woman asked after a few seconds of silence.

"No." Valor drew out the word while trying to place the unfamiliar voice. "Who's this?"

"Hannah Smith." Her voice was so soft that Valor had to jack the volume up on the phone. "Harrison's sister?"

Bugger.

"Are you still there?"

Valor stopped massaging his forehead and returned his attention to the call. "I'm here. It's not Bishan. I'm Valor. What do you want, Hannah?"

"I'm not sure why I'm calling you." She went quiet for so long Valor wondered if the connection had dropped. "It's about my older brother, Harrison."

Valor leaned his head against the fridge, resting his arm against the handle. "What about him?"

Hang up.

You don't owe her anything. She might not be her brother, but that doesn't mean you've got to be nice to her.

Just hang up the sodding phone.

Curiosity once again got the better of Valor. *And this is why I get along so well with Staccato.* He had to know why Hannah had called, so he waited patiently while she gathered her thoughts.

Hannah sniffled on the other end. "I don't know what he's doing. I've been to France on an exchange program with my uni. My parents are missing. He left a bunch of notes in our home, which included your name and Bishan's. I remember him mentioning both of you as well. I knew Bishan's sister, she gave me the number. What's going on? Have you seen him?"

"Hannah." Valor reached into his pocket to grab his own mobile. He sent a text to Reggie and Hugh. "Don't touch anything else in the house. Can you do that for me?"

"What's going on? Where are my mum and dad?" Hannah sniffled a little louder.

"Just breathe deeply for me. It's going to be all right," Valor lied. He knew without a doubt the poor girl's entire life had changed dramatically forever, but she couldn't afford to fall apart just yet. "When did you hear from your brother last?"

"A month ago, maybe. We don't get along."

Valor instantly liked her even more. "What about your mum and dad?"

"A week. They usually check in on me every evening.

After missing three days, I decided to come home to see if they were all right." Hannah sounded young—and distressed. "What has he done?"

Valor refused to be the person to break her heart. He didn't believe the odds of her parents being alive were high. "My good friend Reggie is a detective where I live. I've texted him about your situation along with your number. When I hang up, he's going to give you a call to see if he can't help you. Okay?"

"We waited too long."

"Pardon?" Valor paused at those oddly chosen whispered words. "What do you mean?"

"Mum said early in the year that Harrison had grown more combative when she tried to take him for his monthly visit to the psychotherapist," Hannah answered hesitantly. "He has a number of issues, but he genuinely seemed to want to get better. My parents were worried."

Valor breathed through the urge to shout at her. *How many lives could've been saved if they'd spoken to someone about their concerns?* He refused to take his anger out on this young woman who was clearly distraught. "No point in worrying about it now."

"Oh, I've another call." She disconnected before he could say goodbye.

Valor set the phone on the kitchen counter and kicked the cabinet in raw frustration. "Damn it."

Not wanting to overwhelm Bishan, Valor stayed in the kitchen until he had control of his emotions. He threw his energy into putting together a late lunch. By the time he had tea, sandwiches, and cake put together, his mood had improved.

Two days had passed since the failed attempt on Hugh. Valor had woken up with the energy and drive to finally tackle the wrecked music room. Bishan had, of course, refused to allow him to do it himself, despite his still healing leg.

My Bish is a stubborn Bish.

He gathered up the mugs and plates on a tray and carried it down the hall into the room where he found Bishan seated at the piano picking at random notes. "Tired?"

"Frustrated." Bishan punctuated each syllable with a hard middle C. "Why is answering the phone so hard?"

"Phones are evil." Valor set the tray on the nearby bookcase and joined Bishan on the bench. He brought his fingers up to start a simple duet with Bishan on the piano. "No one enjoys answering them."

"Sunny doesn't struggle with the phone."

"Sunny argues for a living. Of course he enjoys conversations of all kinds. They're all a chance to debate someone into capitulating." Valor found immense satisfaction in Bishan's quiet laugh. "I've heard your brother try to convince a telemarketer that they were selling the wrong way."

"Tea's going cold." Bishan shifted beside him.

Valor lifted a hand from the keys to cover Bishan's hand. "There's nothing wrong with you, Bish."

"I couldn't answer the phone." Bishan banged his free hand against the piano keys.

Valor hated moments when Bishan beat himself up for not being able to do something. "Bish."

"Who was it?" Bishan never liked to dwell on what he considered his bad moments. Valor did his best to respect those wishes and not press him. "You chatted for a while."

"Harrison's sister."

"Pardon?" Bishan turned on the bench to face him. "His sister? Did you know he had one? Wait. I remember. Didn't she come to Speech Day in our last year at Harrow?"

"You want me to remember our last Speech Day? I was too busy trying to fill Mr Clarke's office with rubber ducks."

Valor had been tasked with coming up with the best upper sixth form prank—a proud Harrow tradition. He'd managed it but wound up sleeping through much of the rest of the day. "Whatever. Yes. His younger sister, Hannah, called. Her parents are missing. She also found some disturbing journals and other papers at their house."

"Poor girl."

"Sure." Valor nodded absently. He frankly found it more concerning that the Smith family hadn't actively done more to seek help for Harrison. "You ready for tea now?"

"Tea's gone cold." Bishan glanced over at the tray. "Cold tea is cold. Cold."

"Why don't we head into the kitchen and get not-cold tea?" Valor snorted in amusement while Bishan spent a good minute ranting about lukewarm hot drinks. "Is that a yes or a no?"

They made their way into the kitchen with Bishan rambling about the perfect temperature for tea. Valor nodded at the important parts and quickly got the kettle going for the second time. He'd heard this particular monologue at least ten times over the years; Bishan took his tea seriously.

"We should investigate." Bishan grabbed one of the sandwiches Valor had made earlier. He peeled one of the bread halves off and ate it a corner at a time. "I've got a notebook filled with notes plus a map of Cumbria with all the pertinent locations. We can start with the restaurant; the contractors haven't started to fix it up yet."

"We know who the—"

"We should investigate," Bishan repeated insistently. He frowned at the cheese in his sandwich. "Do we have cheddar?"

"We should investigate." Valor rummaged around in the fridge and found the cheddar. He exchanged several slices for the gouda that Bishan held out to him as though it were the most disgusting food on the planet. "Why don't I call Hugh to see if he wants to come with us? We can use his expertise."

And we can make him drive.

I am brilliant.

"Stop congratulating yourself." Bishan pointed a bag of crisps at him. "Is Harrison's sister safe?"

"I'm sure she will be." Valor had no doubts a throng of detectives would descend on the Smith residence in the hopes of finding detailed information on where he might be. He was honestly surprised they hadn't already done so. "Going to share the crisps?"

"No."

CHAPTER 15

"I am not your personal chauffeur, Lord Byron and Prince Valiant." Hugh glowered at both of them from the driver seat. "Why am I doing this? I should kick you two out and make you do it yourselves."

"I'll tell Penny about the time you had an accident during a rugby scrum at school." Valor snickered after getting Bishan better situated. "It might put a dampener on your attempts at being suave and seductive."

"I will turn this car around," Hugh threatened.

"It's not actually a car." Bishan glanced up from where he'd been obsessively going through his investigation note-book. He poked Valor with his pen. "Stop being mean to Hugh."

Hugh grinned at Bishan, who ignored both of them to go back to his notes. "At least one of you has sense."

"I'll show you sense." Valor reached up to flick Hugh on the arm.

Bishan glared pointedly at the two of them and slipped on his headphones. "If you two are quite finished?"

They made the trip to Windermere easily. Valor kept up a

quiet conversation with Hugh, allowing Bishan to relax into his music. He never handled raised voices well, even when the argument was completely in jest.

Even with Bishan's meticulous plan, Valor wasn't certain why they'd returned to the scene of the explosion. *Why are we here? What is Bish hoping to find?*

"I'm going over here." Bishan wandered away from them, leaning on his crutch with a notebook in his other hand. "Don't be loud."

Allowing Bishan to take the lead, Valor and Hugh moved away from him toward the half wall along the edge of the parking lot. They waited patiently as their intrepid investigator carefully retraced Harrison's path based on the CCTV footage. He obviously wanted to view the area specifically from that perspective.

Valor hopped up to sit on the brick wall. He had no idea how long Bishan would be lost in his own world. "Hugh."

"Hmm?" Hugh joined him.

"Quit staring at Bish." Valor gestured to the empty space beside him. "He doesn't want a Watson to his Sherlock just yet."

"What's that make you, Mrs Hudson?"

Valor shoved Hugh off the wall. "Penny is only a call away."

"We're not dating."

"Yet." Valor actually believed the two might be exceptionally good for one another, though he had zero intention of telling Hugh. "Have you always lusted after my baby sister?"

"Oh for—" Hugh lunged at Valor, who launched off the wall and raced off laughing. "Quit running, you prat."

Valor skidded to a halt, putting Bishan between them. "Save me, Bish."

"No."

Valor collapsed dramatically on the ground in front of

Bishan. "Oh, the betrayal. Right in the heart. How can I ever go on?"

"Val." Bishan held up the printed image from CCTV of where the hooded Harrison had stood for quite a while watching the restaurant. "Can you go stand over by the front doors?"

"Okay." Valor wandered over to the general spot Bishan had pointed out. "Here?"

After two minutes of back and forth, Valor eventually found the right spot. He stood for what felt like ages—doing nothing. Bishan seemed to be simply watching him, and the image, and him.

Why?

What's he learning from this?

Why am I so whiny?

Despite his inner frustration, Valor worked hard to give the appearance of patience at least. Bishan had a way of seeing problems from a unique perspective. It generally paid to give him space to think his way through.

"He waited."

"What?" Valor asked, blinking a few times in the rare December sun. "Harrison?"

"He waited." Bishan waved the photo at them. "He *waited*."

Valor glanced over at Hugh, who seemed equally lost. Neither of them followed Bishan's train of thought. "Why is that important?"

"Reva and I were late. He didn't follow us. He was already here." Bishan plucked his mobile out of his pocket, almost teetering over while resting on his crutch. "He knew we'd be here because of the trackers on our old phones."

"And?" Hugh promoted. He looked as curious as Valor felt. "How does it help us?"

"He doesn't know we don't have the phones anymore."

Bishan turned toward the vehicle, clomping over to it. "Harrison waited to ensure we arrived before entering the restaurant. He didn't care about the collateral damage of my mum, aunts, or sister. But I'd wager he'd been inside it before. How else did he know how the doors worked and the best place to set an explosion? He didn't want the blast to kill us. It would've been too fast; the fire and smoke was what he intended to take us out."

Valor hated the casual way Bishan spoke of it. "Harrison's a psychopath."

"Maybe." Bishan shrugged. "It's too easy to wash him with that brush. Didn't Reggie say Hannah claimed her brother had been diagnosed with Narcissistic Personality Disorder when he spoke with her earlier? That doesn't make him psychopathic. And does it matter? Debating his neuropathy won't get us any closer to catching him. I'm more focused on the methodical nature of his planning."

That's my Bish, always finds words when he's done his research.

"Why?" Valor grabbed the crutch and offered a steadying hand to help Bishan into the back seat. "How will it help us find Harrison?"

"He's not finished, is he? If it's not about love, but some twisted revenge related to Harrow, we're clearly still on his list." Bishan got comfortable and started sifting through his notes before pointing to one of his many puzzle solutions. "I had a thought. What if the non-bolded letters meant something as well? I asked Nina to put the ones from the first one into her computer program."

"And?"

Bishan shifted further into the seat as Valor climbed in next to him. "They spelt out the names of a significant number of our old housemates, Mr Clarke, the matron, and the other West Acre staff."

"And us?" Valor asked.

"And us." Bishan showed Valor and Hugh a computer printout. "He's not done."

"Well, isn't that a terrifying thought." Valor grabbed Bishan's hand, easing closer to rest his head on his shoulder. "What struck you about the waiting?"

"What if he's waiting now for us to use our phones?"

Valor glanced from Bishan to Hugh. "Reggie has them."

While Hugh drove them quickly toward Grasmere, Valor texted their detective inspector to fill him in. They made it to the police station in record time. Reggie waved them into his tiny office, shutting the door on his curious colleagues.

"I'm not using you as bait." Reggie didn't even wait for them to offer their arguments. He'd obviously grasped Bishan's idea faster than Valor had. "It's too dangerous. You've both been hurt already."

"Hurt, but not dead. Not sure about Bish, but I'd definitely rather work to ensure it stays that way." Valor knew instinctively they might not find a better angle toward catching Harrison. "Even with CCTV and the fancy London detectives, you're not any closer to finding him."

"We'll use the phones but not you." Reggie tapped his fingers against his desk.

"You've already tried it. Harrison won't be caught easily." Bishan pulled his headphones off and entered the conversation. "He won't reveal himself without spotting us first. Why risk it when the police have his name?"

"Bish is right." Valor agreed completely. He only hoped they weren't setting themselves up for yet another close call. "Surely there's a way to do this safely?"

I've no intentions of this near miss being my last.

None.

"We're not running headlong into this without careful planning." Reggie stared intently at each of them, though Valor noticed he avoided forcing eye contact on Bishan. "I've no idea if I can convince everyone on the brilliance of your plan, but it's worth a shot."

"And suddenly I feel like Gimli before they all rushed out to meet the horde." Valor had no doubts the certainty of his death had been greatly elevated ever since Harrison reentered their lives. "I vote we avoid dying."

"Good plan." Reggie rubbed his forehead roughly. "Go home. It'll take time to set up. Try not to do anything irrational."

"Us?" Valor thought they'd gone out of their way to be careful. "I'm the picture of—"

"No, you aren't, but Lord Byron will keep you out of trouble." Hugh gave Bishan a thumbs up. "Right, Bish?"

Bishan pulled out one of his earplugs. "Pardon?"

"We're all going to die," Hugh groaned.

"Ribbit." Valor glared at the new frog ornaments strung along the top of their fence. He lifted his mug for another sip of coffee only to find it empty. "Damn it."

The past two weeks had dragged by excruciatingly slowly. Valor had begun to wonder if Bishan had been wrong. They'd made plans multiple times, showed up with an entourage of detectives who blended in badly, and never once spotted Harrison. Anywhere. The police hadn't appreciated what they considered to be a massive waste of time and resources.

Valor watched from the kitchen window as small birds flitted around in the cold mid-December morning. "Could you feathered creatures find it in your hearts to poop on all the frog statues? That would be brilliant."

I should probably stop talking to the birds.

Today would be their last attempt to con the killer. Reggie had refused to set up another expensive sting operation. He and Hugh would be the only detectives attending the Windermere Holiday Fair with them.

Truthfully, Valor was dreading the entire day. He'd woken

at five in the morning, unable to sleep or calm his racing heart. His dreams had been haunted with every worst-case scenario imaginable.

Instead of waking Bishan, Valor had gotten out of bed. He'd made two pots of coffee already. Mornings like this, he found himself missing Staccato, who'd usually keep him company.

Yet another reason to end the Harrison drama once and for all, though Staccy might not want to come home with us after being spoilt rotten by Dame Lottie.

Obvious danger aside, Valor also worried about the toll the frequent outings to crowded spaces was taking on Bishan. It troubled him. But Bishan refused to stay at home.

Grabbing the French press, Valor topped up his coffee. He didn't necessarily need another cup, though hopefully the caffeine would keep his mind alert and clear through the long day ahead.

Was there such a thing as too much coffee?

"Couldn't sleep again?"

Valor grinned at the image Bishan made, standing barefoot in his hooded panda pyjama onesie. Reva had gotten it for him as a joke gift for his birthday. He loved the soft texture of the fabric so much it usually made an appearance every winter. "Morning."

"Coffee," Bishan grunted. He hobbled over to the cabinet to grab his usual Tardis mug. "Did you leave any coffee for me?"

"I did. And some of those apple bread rolls your mum brought yesterday." Valor nudged one of the chairs away from their little kitchen table with his foot for Bish to sit. "How's the leg this morning?"

"Itchy." Bishan rested his head against the table with a groan. "I don't want to human today. Can I not human?"

"Sure." Valor set the container of apple rolls within easy

reach before topping off his coffee and pouring Bishan a mug. "Why don't we cancel?"

He lifted his head only enough to drink some of the coffee by tipping the mug. "Can't."

"We can." Valor had no qualms at calling the entire operation off, even if it angered Reggie. Hugh had already offered his reservations about how stressed Bishan had appeared the last time. "Have an apple roll and think about it."

Bishan dragged his arm up and slowly reached a hand out to snag one of the sweet breads from the plate. "Can't cancel. Not today. We've set everything up."

Valor wished Bishan wasn't quite so stubbornly insistent on pushing himself. "We might have fun at the fair. Food should be good. It was last year."

They'd been dragged to the annual Christmas-themed festival in Windermere by Reva. None of them really celebrated, but she loved the atmosphere and music. Bishan had lasted an hour before deciding the noise and crowd were too overwhelming.

"The fair might be fun," Valor repeated.

It will not be fun, and I'm already exhausted.

From his grimace, Bishan agreed completely with him. Valor knew Barnaby and Rana would likely have tried to step in and cancel despite their son's wishes. He refused to even consider taking away the decision.

They mean well, but Bish's an adult and fully capable of making mistakes like we all do.

And I'll always help him face things—even crowd-induced melt-downs we could've avoided.

Valor moved away from the table to inspect the contents of the fridge. "These rolls need bacon."

"Bacon-wrapped bread?"

"Maybe not wrapped."

They intended to be in Windermere before noon; there

would be plenty of snacks and treats to enjoy for lunch. The Tambolis planned to meet up with them. Bishan had reasoned perhaps Harrison hadn't believed their previous texts because they'd always shown up alone.

Just a normal family outing.

An ordinary outing with a side of intrigue and death.

We're all going to die, but at least we'll be listening to crap music as it happens.

"Val?"

He paused in the process of grabbing the bacon to find Bishan had managed to finally sit up straight. "Changed your mind? Not in the mood for the most perfect meat in the world?"

Bishan coughed violently on his coffee.

"Having naughty thoughts, Bish?" Valor snickered then easily caught the bread roll Bishan threw at him. "*Mine.*"

"I licked it."

"I—" Valor's dirty joke was interrupted by a banging from the garden. He stood up to glance out the window to find Mrs Harris braving the cold. "What is she doing?"

"Populating the world with ugly frogs."

"You're not wrong." Valor watched as their neighbour dragged one of her marble frogs from one end of her garden path until it rested by the fence. "Is it like a salt line? Does she believe lining them all up will protect her from the demons next door?"

What is she doing?

Mrs Harris appeared intent on shifting all forty of her frogs so they grouped together facing their cottage. Valor wondered if they should be worried for their safety. *Is death by amphibian a legitimate phobia?*

Bishan stood up and hopped over to stand next to him. "We should definitely buy a lot of gnomes."

"Gnomes?"

"Lots of garden gnomes. Paint them in rainbow colours and decorate the garden with them." Bishan grinned at him. "Where do we find twenty ugly statues?"

"The ugly gnome store?"

CHAPTER 17

The festival had already gotten underway by the time they arrived. Valor had no idea where Reggie or Hugh had hidden. They'd likely only make their presence known as necessary.

In an attempt to avoid being spotted, the detectives had shown up several hours before the festival opened to the public. They knew Harrison would be watching. He'd shown his ability to be patient over his months of terror.

The Tambolis had always intended to spend at least a few days at the festival. Barnaby and Rana stayed active in the local community—even for holidays they didn't necessarily celebrate. Valor couldn't help wishing they'd stayed home.

We're giving him far too many targets to pick from, especially with only Hugh and Reggie mingling with the crowds.

Please let us all make it out of this alive.

"Forget Hugh and Reggie. My mum and auntie will sort Harrison out." Reva sidled up to Valor, who'd been watching the two women organise their booth. She looped her arm around his. "Dad knew the people in charge and begged them to give us a spot."

"It'll be good for keeping up business while the restaurant is being fixed. Ollie not here? I'm surprised he missed this chance to charm his future in-laws." Valor danced away from Reva's swinging fist. He wandered over to rescue Bishan, who'd gotten trapped behind the booth with his mum and aunt. "Mind if I borrow Bish?" he asked.

Not giving them time to debate, Valor caught Bishan by the hand to lead him away. He'd switched to a cane earlier in the week as his leg continued to heal. They meandered slowly through the crowd toward the Ginger's Bread booth that Lottie and Wilfred were in charge of.

The Ginger's Bread did good business during holiday festivals. Free treats brought in a lot of people who often signed up to order from their website. Valor found it challenging to focus on business with the looming threat of Harrison weighing down on him.

"Hello, lovelies." Lottie waved them over with a bright smile. She offered them up some of her special mulled wine to go with mince pies and ginger biscuits. "Grab a few while we've got them. There are more people than last year. The girls are bringing more treats up in a few hours as I'm sure we're going to run out in no time at all."

"Shouldn't we save them?" Bishan only ate his after Lottie had assured him it would be fine. "Do you have tea?"

"I made some up just for you." Lottie set aside the mulled wine and grabbed a thermos Wilfred handed to her. "Eat up."

Valor forced himself to inhale the mince pies with his usual enthusiasm. "I'm going to find Bish a spot to sit for a few minutes to rest his leg."

While Lottie gave him an easy, understanding smile, Wilfred's steady gaze seemed to bore into him. He knew how close to the edge Bishan was. Valor knew Wilfred had been keeping a careful watch over both of them.

"Don't stray too far from view." Wilfred clearly didn't buy into Valor's façade of normalcy. "No disappearing on us again."

Snatching a handful of mince pies for the road, Valor laughed when Bishan shoved a few into his pocket then clutched the thermos of tea to his chest. He winked at Lottie, who waved them off. They made their way through the clusters of tourists to find an unoccupied bench on the edge of the cordoned-off street.

Bishan immediately collapsed on it, and his fingers began to tap against the edge of the thermos. "Why is it so crowded already?"

I've got to get him out of here.

He'll hate having a meltdown in public.

Valor searched his pockets for the mini stress ball he'd shoved into it on the way out the door. He always tried to carry some form of fidget toy for Bishan. "Bish? Here."

"Earplugs?"

Valor fished into his other pocket to untangle the noise-cancelling earbuds from his keys. "Are you sure we can't go home? I don't give a damn if Reggie gets ticked off at us."

"Not yet." Bishan immediately pushed the plugs into his ears. "Tea, though. We should've had tea."

Valor grabbed the thermos to pour out some of the tea into a cup. "We can leave, Bish."

Instead of answering, Bishan began to kick the side of the bench with his uninjured leg. Again and again. The heel of his shoe connected with the concrete repeatedly. Valor stayed silent, waiting for Bishan to ride the wave of overwhelming sensations from his meltdown.

Years at Harrow had forced Bishan to develop methods to release the pent-up energy from his meltdowns. He hadn't wanted to draw attention to himself. Valor, along with a few of their other year mates, had usually gone out of their way to distract the beaks to keep him from getting in trouble.

They'd also pummelled anyone who made fun of Bishan. Valor and Hugh had been the ones to lead that particular charge. Their rugby skills frequently came in handy.

Valor couldn't do anything but patiently sit beside Bishan. He popped a mince pie into his mouth then froze when movement caught his attention. *What's the opposite of good luck?* His heart pounded in his ears louder than any of the noise from the milling crowds. "Harry."

"Will you stop calling me Harry. My name is Harrison," Harrison snapped at him.

Valor wasn't overly concerned about the tantrum, but the needle in Harrison's right hand and the Taser in his left absolutely terrified him. "Sorry about the cabin. Scotland didn't agree with me."

Harrison moved closer until he stood almost on top of Bishan. "Jokes. It's always a joke. Would you find it funny watching your *special* friend die?"

"No." Valor clenched his jaw tightly to keep from ripping into Harrison for mocking Bishan. *Priority, Val, worry about the ableist shit after we're not in a life-or-death situation.* "I don't find you or anything about this situation humorous."

"Val." Bishan dropped his hand on Valor's leg when Harrison brought the point of the needle up to hover against his neck.

"Why are you doing this?" Valor wanted the needle away from Bishan's neck. *Immediately.* "Why now?"

"Weedy little Smith." Harrison turned a hardened gaze toward Valor. "You ignored me. All of you. I was nothing to the entire house. To the school. *Nothing.* What of my achievements? You always outshone me. All of you. *All. Of. You.*"

"Told you," Bishan muttered.

"Not helpful, Bish." Valor crushed the inappropriate

urged to snicker. "Harrison wants our full attention while he unloads his trials and tribulations."

"Do you ever stop mocking anyone?" Harrison clearly didn't approve of how they'd interrupted his dramatic moment. "Would you trade places with him?"

"In a heartbeat." Valor would inject himself with the cinnamon if it kept Bishan alive. "In a heartbeat."

Where the hell are Hugh and Reggie?

As Harrison rambled with his endless complaints, Bishan seemed to be coming out of his meltdown. Valor cringed every time Harrison's arm shifted at all. He couldn't risk any accidental movement causing the needle to go in.

Dying is not an option.

I am not losing Bish.

"Is this an example of your brilliantly evil plans for all of us?" Bishan sounded remarkably calm and narky with death a hair's breadth away from his jugular. "Honestly, our cat could've done better. What will you do with all these people milling about? There are police all over. So you either intend to die with us, or you are working under the mistaken belief you can vanish into thin air. Plan on waving a magic wand? It won't work. If you did manage to end my life, you won't make it far."

"You…." Harrison stammered.

"Yes, me."

Valor wished Bishan wasn't so cavalier with the needle so close to his throat. "Bish has a point. What's your end goal? Killing us in the middle of a festival with hundreds of witnesses?"

As Harrison twisted toward Valor to respond, Bishan fell backwards off the bench. His foot swung up to catch Harrison between the legs with impressive force. Their killer dropped to his knees instantly with a pained groan.

"Bish?" Valor shouted while crushing the dropped needle

under his foot and then kicking the Taser out of Harrison's hand. "Bish? Are you all right?"

"Easy does it, Prince Valiant." Hugh caught him by the shirt to drag him away from Harrison, who Reggie was already working to restrain. "Calm down."

"Get off me." Valor shoved Hugh away and leapt over the bench to reach Bishan. "Bish? Did you hurt yourself?"

"Not dead," Bishan grunted. He'd fallen straight on his back but managed to catch his foot on the bench on the way down. "Harrison?"

"Reggie has him well in hand." Valor helped him sit up. His fingers trembled when he reached out to check Bishan's neck. "Did the needle—"

The adrenaline rush that had allowed him to stay calm evaporated. His nail trailed across the faintest abrasion where the needle had grazed Bishan's neck. Valor breathed through the range of emotions while wanting to clutch Bishan in his arms yet simultaneously resisting the urge to launch himself at Harrison.

"He's not worth it." Bishan had clearly read his mind. "Not worth the trouble."

"But you are." Valor slid his hands up to rest along the sides of Bishan's neck, gently rubbing at the red mark. He kissed him desperately, all the fear he could still taste bled through their prolonged embrace. "You saved us."

"My mince pies are mashed." Bishan brought a hand out of his pocket. "I wanted those."

"Priorities, Bish." Valor rested his forehead against Bishan's, chuckling with a bit of hysterical relief mixed with genuine amusement. "We'll get you more pies."

Utter chaos.

If Valor had to pick a word to describe the moments after Harrison's final attack, pure chaos fit perfectly. Reggie had dragged the ranting man away from the gathering crowd. Paramedics had rushed in to check on Bishan, who grew grumpier by the second, wanting his mince pies replaced and some peace from all the questions and well-intentioned medical prodding.

Valor knew any chance at peace and quiet had already flown out the window. "I'm fine, Hugh. Quit hovering and do something useful."

"Do something useful?"

"Well, you didn't actually manage to stop the criminal, did you? Brave officers that you are. Bish saved us." He grinned at the scowling detective. "Am I wrong?"

"Why are we friends?" Hugh sighed heavily.

"The bond of old Harrovians." Valor dragged Hugh into a hug, slapping him on the back. They'd always joked with each other, but he didn't want one of his oldest friends to think him ungrateful. "Thank you… for shifting your entire life around to move to Grasmere to try and keep us safe."

"Go rescue Bish." Hugh shoved him away. "Twit."

"Twit? Here I am being all appreciative." He released Hugh and made his way over to the obviously exasperated Bishan. "Right. I think he's had enough medical treatment."

"He could—"

"He's autistic and already been through a traumatic experience. How about we give him some space." Valor reached between the paramedics to extract Bishan, who glared at him. "What?"

"You abandoned me to the wolves."

He held up a non-smashed mince pie. "Truce?"

"I won't be bought."

Valor retrieved the second one that he'd been holding on to for himself. "Oh?"

"I forgive you." Bishan crammed one of the mince pies

into his mouth. He glanced around while chewing and struggling to swallow. "Lost my cane."

They found it under the bench—slightly bent.

A metaphor for how we all feel? A bit bent, but mostly okay. God, I hope this is the end of it.

"**B**ish."

Bishan shifted to hide behind Valor. "Save me."

Valor found himself the recipient of a smothering group embrace from the Tambolis. "Are you going to save me when I'm smothered to death by your family?"

"It's fine," he mumbled.

"Quit eating the mince pie and rescue me." Valor eventually extracted himself from Bishan's family. "We're both perfectly all right with only the slightest scratch to show for the anticlimactic end of our nightmare."

Perfectly all right was a tiny lie. Valor knew they were both holding on to their emotions by the skin of their teeth. No amount of hugs or mince pies could bury the relief so intense it made him want to sleep for a month.

To his surprise, Bishan lasted through hugs from each member of his family along with Lottie and Wilfred. When he started to wilt slightly, Valor decided to intervene. *Bish saved me; least I can do is keep his family from thrusting him into another meltdown.*

Using Bishan's leg and falling from the bench for an

excuse, Valor managed to extract him from amidst their loving family. They got a head start on heading home. He had no doubts the others intended to eventually follow.

And the detectives.

At some point, Reggie or the London detectives would want to question them about what exactly had happened with Harrison. Valor planned to put them off as long as possible. They finally had time to catch their breath, and he refused to be rushed.

Bishan had survived.

He had survived.

Everything else could wait.

The drive to Grasmere went quietly. Neither of them felt like talking much. Bishan spent the entire ride with his head resting against the window, staring blankly out; he was so out of it Valor had to guide him into the cottage.

Bishan took one step inside the cottage and froze.

"Bish." Valor kicked the door shut and wrapped his arms around him. "We're home. We're safe. He can't hurt anyone else."

Bishan twisted around, stumbling slightly in his arms. He rested his head on Valor's shoulder. "He hurt enough."

And wasn't that the painful truth.

With his arms still wrapped around Bishan, Valor helped him over to the couch. They collapsed on it with mutual exhausted sighs. Their nightmare was over.

"It's a bit like exams." Bishan had stretched out on the sofa to give his leg a rest and had his upper body leaning against Valor. "Isn't it? The massive amount of stress and when it's over, the relief is almost worse than the antic-ipation."

Almost.

I think I'd rather have the painfully exhausting relief.

A knock at the door jolted both of them out of their

thoughts. Valor carefully eased out from under Bishan to answer. He wasn't surprised to find Barnaby and Rana waiting patiently on the other side.

"We brought mince pies." Rana shoved the plate into Valor's arms and pushed by him. "Where's my son?"

Barnaby offered Valor an apologetic smile. "I tried to give you two more time. She's his mum—and we've all been terrified of losing you both."

Nodding in understanding, Valor decided not to mention his own mother hadn't been concerned. Then again, her maternal instincts had never truly kicked in when it came to her middle child. *I wonder if she's enjoying the south of France.*

"Hugh wanted me to tell you that he contacted your sister. She's on her way up from London." Barnaby eased Valor into a hug. "I'm so pleased you're both safe, and this awful nightmare is over."

"Val?"

He turned around to find Rana wringing her hands and glancing at him. "Something wrong?"

"He's retreated to the music room." She put on a cheerful smile that he knew she didn't feel. "We'll head to the shop to pick up some groceries. I'll whip up a feast as I'm sure everyone will want to celebrate."

With the house to themselves again, Valor made his way through the cottage to the music room. He found Bishan sitting on the floor in front of his piano. *Maybe we can take a holiday on some remote island?*

Not Scotland, though.

Anywhere but Scotland.

Maybe not an island either.

Valor plopped down beside Bishan, stretching his legs out and leaning against the wall. "What happened to the plate of mince pies?"

"I ate them."

"All of them?"

Bishan shrugged.

"We don't eat our emotions."

"Mince pies aren't emotions." Bishan grabbed the plate from the bench behind him. "Saved one for you."

Valor glanced at the single pie. "Did you lick it?"

"Once."

Valor tossed it into his mouth, grinning at Bishan. "Lottie's bringing Staccy home."

"Can we hide in here?"

"You can," he promised firmly. "I'll fight them off for you."

They sat in silence for a while, leaning on each other.

Valor glanced over at Bishan when the quiet became too much, to find tears in his eyes. "Bish?"

"It's over. Over. All over. Over," Bishan repeated helplessly. "Over."

"It is."

Somehow the weight of fear being gone left a void of weary relief. Valor was too tired to be happy. He'd thought the capture might bring joy, but all the pointless loss seemed even more vividly stark to him.

"We owe them a celebration." Bishan dragged an arm across his face to wipe away tears. "My family, our friends. They worried nearly as much as we did."

Valor saw the same exhaustion in Bishan's eyes. "No, we don't really."

"Val?"

"We don't owe anyone a celebration." Valor leaned in for a quick kiss, then got to his feet. "They'll understand."

Or they're not really family.

And honestly, Valor didn't care one way or the other if feelings were hurt. The past months had been a nightmare.

They finally had time to breathe and grieve without the weight of imminent death bearing down on them.

Leaving Bishan to sort himself out, Valor made his way over to the bookshelf to find a scrap of paper. He scrawled a brief message and stuck it to the front door. *Enjoying not being dead. Bugger off until tomorrow. Knock before then, and I'll set the frogs on you.*

Hopefully that would do the trick.

Aside from the police, Valor thought his note would deter everyone. Maybe not Penelope, but his sister might take hours to get to Grasmere, and Hugh was undoubtedly capable of entertaining her. *Oh. Bad thoughts, bad thoughts.*

Where's the mind bleach when I need it?

"Now what?" Valor scratched his head absently and gazed blankly at the empty room. "Is it too early for a full-on pudding feast?"

They needed normal, their brand of it.

Pudding it was.

Pudding and Poirot—*until whatever this feeling is fades away.*

It didn't fade, not completely. Valor slept uneasily. He mostly watched Bishan, who drifted off relatively quickly.

How close had they come to dying?

The world crashed in on them eventually. Valor woke to find a tangle of Tambolis waiting outside their front door the following morning. Breakfast ended up being a boisterous affair. Bishan hovered on the edges with his earplugs blocking out the extra noise.

Halfway through the pancakes Rana had made, his sister arrived with Hugh on her heels. Valor found their flirtatious glances amusing. He wondered where their growing attraction might go.

And I have all the time in the world to watch it.

"You okay?" Bishan joined him by the front door. "Cora and Daniel just pulled in."

"Good news spreads fast." Valor knew their nearest and dearest would all be making their way to Grasmere. "It's getting colder out."

"I love you."

Valor glanced suspiciously at Bishan. "I'm not hiding you from your mum again. Not yet. But I love you too."

"Prat."

CHAPTER 19

Under police questioning, Harrison had revealed his hatred of Harrow and how it slowly began to centre on his old mentor—Valor. He'd wanted to ruin his life, starting with Bishan. The bizarre riddles had been a ploy to throw them off.

Valor didn't buy it, not entirely. He told Reggie as much. They'd been called in for their own interviews with several detectives.

"I know it's frustrating, but even small details can be important during the trial. Can you talk me through what happened at the holiday festival in Windermere?" Detective Roberts from London had driven to Grasmere for the sole purpose of interviewing Valor and Bishan. Neither had been thrilled at the prospect of being separated for a supposedly friendly conversation at the police station. "When did the suspect approach you?"

"When we least expected it." Valor had to admit that he hadn't exactly been as cooperative as he could've been. He was glad Reggie had taken over the questioning of Bishan.

"Mr Scott." Roberts frowned disapprovingly at him. "We'd appreciate it if you'd take this seriously."

"Detective." Valor leaned forward in his chair and ran his fingers through his hair. "You have CCTV footage and witness statements. I've already described in great detail what I can remember. But sure, why don't you ask me the same question in a different way for the tenth time and I'll try to get more imaginative with my answers."

One question had followed another. They all sounded like the same words scrambled into a different version of the same query. Why did he have to waste another minute on Harrison? Hadn't enough of their lives been stolen by him?

The killer had been caught red-handed.

Wasn't that sufficient?

Valor took comfort in knowing Reggie wouldn't allow anyone to run roughshod over Bishan. It didn't mean he wasn't ready for this to be over. "I hope you're being this thorough in your continuing interrogation of the serial killer we caught for you."

"Your father often spoke about how difficult his youngest son could be." Roberts seemed to be waiting for a reaction from him.

He eyed the London detective for a moment before deciding he'd played the game enough. "He's dead. You have the man responsible for it in custody. And I've given enough of my life to both Lord Scott and Harrison Smith. I'm finished."

Getting to his feet, Valor exited the room without giving the detective an opportunity to respond. He thought they'd earned a break. It wasn't his job to wrap up the investigation into a nice package.

"Well, I am surprised it took you this long to lose your temper." Reggie greeted him with a smile. He appeared to have been enjoying a cup of tea with Bishan. "Go on. Get out of here."

"Home?" Bishan asked when they'd safely made it outside.

"Not quite yet." Valor had an idea of how to celebrate and lighten the mood.

After a quick stop at the cottage for blankets, a thermos of tea, and snacks, Valor drove out to one of their favourite spots to visit during the winter on Lake Windermere. It required only a short walk from the car park, and Bishan easily managed to reach it. A triple layer of quilts offered a soft cushion to sit on the ground.

"Duck, duck, goose?" Bishan cheered when Valor retrieved two sets of binoculars and a battered notebook from his bag. "We haven't played bird watchers in ages."

"You cheat."

"How can you cheat watching birds on a lake?" Bishan flipped through their scorebook to find a blank page. They'd used it to keep track of their silly game for years. "Are we going with most accurately named or most spotted overall?"

"Quality over quantity." Valor knew his odds of winning weren't brilliant. He simply craved the normalcy of being themselves—however quirky that might be to others. "I win, I pick the pudding. You win, and I'll probably still select it because you can never decide."

Draping an extra quilt over Bishan's shoulders, Valor settled down to enjoy their silly game. Bishan had invented it when they'd first moved to Grasmere. Money had been tight, and watching birds didn't cost anything when Wilfred gifted binoculars to them.

They competed to see who spotted the most birds or made the most accurate identification of said fowl. Bishan always won. Valor rarely tried to; his fun came from how enthusiastic Bishan grew with each one.

"Duck."

"Is it?" Valor grabbed the thermos to pour some tea. He grinned at Bishan, who'd already started to mark his finds in the notebook. "Hey, Bish?"

"Hmm?" He didn't turn away from scanning the lake. "What?"

"Your symphony."

"Yeah?" Bishan lowered the binoculars. "I've a ways to go before I finish it."

"With Sunny's help, Penny's managed to sort out my inheritance from my grandfather. I want to put some into the Ginger's Bread, fix up the cottage with a proper soundproof music room for you, save some, and lastly, get your symphony out there." Valor had thought long and hard about what to do with the money. He'd initially considered burning it; Sunesh had quickly talked sense into him. "You've put your heart and soul into this musical masterpiece. Why not see it performed?"

"Maybe."

Valor offered Bishan the plastic cup of tea. "I'm proud of you. You're bloody brilliant."

Bishan glowered at the tea. "Thanks."

"And maybe, one day, you'll learn how to take a compliment." Valor rolled away when Bishan went to smack him with the notebook. "Look, it's a goldeneye."

"Don't scare it." Bishan grabbed the binoculars to find the easily spooked duck. "And Val?"

"Yeah?"

"I'm proud of you as well."

EPILOGUE

Two years to the day after Mr Clarke's murder, his boys, the boys of West Acre, gathered at their old boarding house at Harrow-on-the-Hill. They'd sung his favourite school songs, drank a toast to him, and helped the school to honour him with a plaque on the wall. Over a hundred men had returned from all over the world—a tribute to their housemaster who'd helped form their youth.

A group of the best musicians had come together to repeat a performance Mr Clarke had loved. Valor was amazed they remembered all the words. They weren't completely in tune, but it didn't matter; it had been the perfect way to celebrate and say goodbye to the heart of their West Acre memories.

"He'd be proud of us." Hugh draped an arm around Valor's and Bishan's shoulders. "His boys come together in his honour. Nice portrait, Lord Byron. I'm glad Mrs Clarke wanted it to hang in the house. He should be remembered by more than our generation."

Valor watched Bishan jog across the field to a few of the other former music scholars he'd been especially close with.

He glanced over at Hugh. "Any word on Harrison's petition to be transferred to a psychiatric hospital?"

Hugh glanced over at him. "Do you honestly want to know?"

"I do." He'd claimed disinterest the week before since Bishan hadn't wanted to hear about it. "Bish doesn't."

"Ahh. Well, Hannah asked the court to deny his request to be transferred. She hasn't quite forgiven him for murdering their parents. I think she's terrified he'd escape more easily from a hospital." Hugh stared across the field where they'd gone to play a rousing game of Harrow football after the more fancy ceremony. "Surprised you didn't send a letter of your own."

"Why bother?" Valor had gotten his sister to send one instead. People listened to Lady Scott more than they did a Mr Scott, even if he had once had a claim to the title. "Penny managed just fine—as you well know. How is she doing?"

"*Val.*"

"You date my sister, you live with me periodically choosing to mock you." Valor hadn't been overly surprised when Hugh moved to London, or when they'd announced their engagement after a year and a half of dating. "When's the wedding?"

"Next year. Don't want to steal Ollie and Reva's thunder." Hugh dodged out of the way when several players went by completely covered in mud. "Your mum is threatening to boycott our nuptials."

"Good. She'd only ruin the day for Penny." Valor had already spoken to his sister about the wedding. She'd asked him to walk her down the aisle, mostly to prevent their mother's new husband from trying to stick his nose in where it wasn't wanted. None of them liked the new Mr Dowager. "Picked a best man yet?"

"Lord Byron said no."

"Bish hates attention. And giving speeches. And doesn't understand the point of weddings." Valor had tried to talk Bishan into at least considering marriage. He just didn't get them. "We love each other; it's enough for me. Why isn't it enough for you? Paper is weird. Weddings are weird. And crowded. And mostly weird," had been Bishan's exact words. Valor turned toward Hugh. "Who'd you ask instead?"

"Reggie."

"Well, at least you know he won't muck up the speech." He was pleased the detective would be at the wedding. They'd become good friends with Reggie since the arrest and trial. "You realise the entire event will be a circus, right? Lady Scott marrying… you."

"What's wrong with me?" Hugh shoved him, and Valor immediately pushed him back.

"Can we go home now?" Bishan wandered over, interrupting their mock fight. He had a gnome painted like Poirot clutched in his arms. "See? Jaime made it for me. He's added garden statues to his pottery store."

"Ah, yes. How is your gnome legion doing?" Hugh asked.

"Annoying Mrs Harris. We move them around into different formations. We've started dressing them up. Bish's mum and Lottie have gotten together to make all sorts of outfits for them." Valor enjoyed their game of one-upmanship with their neighbour. She'd actually resorted to calling the police a few times when they put the gnomes in compromising positions. "Reggie brought a policeman's helmet for one of them. We're calling him the mini-Reg."

"Sergeant Gnome." Bishan grinned over the head of the garden Poirot. "He's my favourite."

"How often do you play gnome wars with the sergeant in charge?" Hugh snickered. "Why don't you two head out? You've enough time to get at least halfway home before dark."

After a lengthy series of goodbyes, they escaped to their vehicle. Valor had booked a room at Crewe Hall for them in Stoke-on-Trent. They intended to visit Chatsworth Garden in the morning before continuing on to Grasmere.

With his symphony almost finished, Bishan had wanted to visit the gardens. He hoped to find the last inspiration to wrap up his musical masterpiece. It had taken him all this time to get it almost perfect.

Once the upcoming weddings were out of the way, Valor intended to make setting up the perfect orchestra performance his pet project. It would be his gift to Bishan. He'd already made tentative plans with the director at the London Symphony Orchestra.

The director had regretted losing Bishan's talent. Valor thought performing his symphony would be the least they could do for not standing by him more vocally. *Not that my Bish holds grudges; he's got me to do it for him.*

"I said goodbye."

"To whom?" Valor continued manoeuvring through traffic; he hoped to avoid the worst of the usual jams on the way to Stoke-on-Trent. "We both said bye to the old boys."

"No. To Mr Clarke." Bishan peered over his shoulder to check on gnome Poirot, who they'd strapped carefully into the back seat. "I couldn't really do this before. It didn't seem right with Harrison Smith on the loose. Now, though, he's resting in peace. I wanted to say goodbye at school. Do you think he's been reborn?"

"As a gnome?"

"Mum believes in reincarnation." Bishan fiddled with the radio, hopping from one station to the next. "Mr Clarke might be out there somewhere."

"As a gnome."

"*Val.*" Bishan tried to glare, but his chuckles gave him

away. "I heard the end of my symphony on the pitch today. It's hope. I'd forgotten."

"You'd forgotten hope? The word or the concept?"

"Forgotten to end on a hopeful note. Need quiet now. No talking." Bishan put earplugs in, leaving Valor to enjoy whatever nonsense was on the radio.

Right.

Their day had been filled with a lot of people and noise. Valor wasn't surprised Bishan wanted time to decompress. He focused on traffic and not getting lost.

Stoke-on-Trent turned out to be a bust. Bishan spent the evening and morning in the hotel under a duvet watching the telly. Valor gave him space, hunting around by himself for treats to take home with them. They left after a light lunch and managed to arrive at their cottage in time for tea in the garden with Staccato stalking a stray frog who'd managed to sneak through their line of defence.

"Are you ready for the wedding?" Valor had put off asking Bishan, who'd been dreading his sister's ceremony since agreeing to be her man of honour. "Have your mum and Reva reached an agreement yet?"

"No." Bishan snorted into his cup of tea. "Mum's gone a bit weird. Food has always been how she honoured our family, right? But now, all of a sudden, for Reva's wedding, she wants all this stuff that she and Dad missed out on. Reva's all about having a modern, fashionable ceremony."

"Your mum wants Reva to have a traditional wedding?" Valor was surprised. Rana was the most modern woman, from her career choices to everything else. "What do you think?"

"Not my wedding." Bishan shrugged. "Not Mum's either."

"True."

"Don't get it really." Bishan set his cup on the arm of the

chair. "They didn't raise us with my grandparents' traditions. Mum went through so much drama with her family when she married Dad. And then with everything my auntie suffered, they always said they wanted us to create our own paths. Why change that now?"

"Maybe she wants to honour the family who can't be here." Valor had zero experience with what Rana and Reva were going through. And he didn't honestly think it was any of their business. "Let them sort it out, Bish. They'll find a compromise."

"Or they'll have a massive argument and Dad'll talk Mum into letting his princess have her way." Bishan grabbed his cup to keep Staccato from knocking it over when he leapt up onto his shoulder. "I created a little piece of piano music for Reva to walk down the aisle. It's inspired by Mum and Dad's favourite song."

Well, that explains the delay on his symphony.

He's a better big brother than I am.

My gift to Penny will likely be getting Hugh drunk the night before.

"I won't take this a second longer." Mrs Harris slammed her cane against the fence, jolting both Valor and Bishan. "You've added another hideous creature."

"The Great Gnome Poirot," Bishan offered helpfully. "He's best friends with the sergeant."

"Not sure you're helping." Valor tried not to laugh while Mrs Harris ranted at them, waving her cane wildly and walking quickly toward her cottage. "I bet you the last custard tart that she's going to phone Reggie."

"I'll make another pot of tea. He'll want a reward for dealing with our gnome wars again." Bishan teased Staccato with a strand of hair, then got up to head inside. "Want another cake?"

"Always."

With Bishan inside, Valor leaned back to enjoy the beautiful summer weather. They'd had a good year. The last month had been the first time neither of them woke up with nightmares that had plagued them.

Post-traumatic stress had been the official explanation from the therapist they both saw—together and separately. Valor didn't care about fancy names. He wanted the memories to stop haunting him.

Most of their physical scars had faded away. Bishan had a few from being burnt that would likely never disappear. Valor's were marked on his heart and soul and were no less painful.

Harrison had left an indelible mark on them whether they liked it or not. Valor knew they both looked more suspiciously on people than they had in the past. It saddened him to know in many ways their innocence had been lost.

His nightmares all revolved around losing Bishan. The last two months had been the first time Valor hadn't woken up in a cold sweat, convinced the explosion had taken the love of his life away.

Those nights or mornings, Valor went into the garden and cried until he thought his body would run dry. He'd slowly gotten better, as had Bishan. The memories faded with each passing day and eventually, he knew, they'd be nothing more than a fleeting ghost in the corner of his mind.

"You back there?" Reggie tapped on the garden fence.

Valor jogged over to open it for him. "Bishan's topping up the tea. Want some?"

"Did you really need another gnome?" Reggie followed him into the garden then crouched down to inspect their latest addition. "Poirot?"

"He was a gift." Valor grinned unrepentantly. "It could be worse."

"How?"

"He could be naked."

"If you put naked gnomes in your garden…." Reggie trailed off, seeming completely at a loss for how to finish his sentence. "Can you not antagonise the woman?"

"I could." Valor had no intentions of stopping their gnome wars. He thought it a perfectly passive-aggressive punishment for their nosy and bigoted neighbour. She disliked them because of their relationship and Bishan's ethnicity. "But I won't. Not going to apologise either."

"Fine." Reggie shook his head and chuckled. "I've already spoken to her about it. I did point out the gnomes are in your garden."

Valor reached down to grab a stray frog, tossing it over the fence. "Unlike her amphibians."

"What are you doing?"

"Making it rain?" Valor snickered with the detective. "Sorry."

"Don't lie to the police." Reggie laughed. "She'll send another complaint, and I have better things to do than write reports about flying frogs."

"Really?" Valor wondered if he could get a copy of one of those reports to frame and put on the wall. "Could I—"

"No, I'm not making copies for you." Reggie glared at him, proving how well he'd gotten to know them. "Why don't we have tea inside? Prevent Mrs Harris from pelting you with frogs."

"Will rivers of blood be next?" Valor wandered into the cottage with Staccato and Reggie following close. "Bish?"

"Made tea." Bishan waved at Reggie and plucked Staccato off the floor. "Did you chuck another frog over the fence?"

"Who, me?"

Over tea and cakes, they caught up with the detective. Reggie left after an hour or so. They returned to the garden with Bishan hefting out his easel.

"New project?" Valor stretched out on one of the lounge chairs closest to Bishan.

"Us." Bishan pulled out his supplies.

"Us?"

Bishan held up a photo of the two of them with Staccato. They were curled up on a blanket staring out at Lake Windermere; Valor had set up the camera behind them to get the shot. "I want to turn it into a painting to go in the living room."

"Us?"

"Us. Happy, loved, safe." Bishan clipped the photo to the top of the easel. "The therapist asked me what I learned from everything we survived."

"And?" Valor hadn't known how to answer the question. He'd given a slightly flippant response about knowing how to deal with hypothermia and starting fires. "What did you learn?"

"I'm brave and strong. I'm capable of brilliant things. And I love you." Bishan fumbled around in one of his art supply bags, finally pulling out a pencil to make his initial sketch. "Us. I love us. Together."

Better than my answer.

Valor tried to speak around the lump in his throat but failed.

A beautifully honest answer. Bishan had definitely grown stronger in the aftermath. He put his foot down more as well. If he didn't want to go, Valor no longer had to create excuses for them, Bishan simply said no—firmly.

It was telling in some ways that Valor had been the only one not surprised at Bishan being the one to bring Harrison down. Even two years later, some of their friends continued to exclaim in surprise at his bravery. *In spite of everything.* It didn't take a genius or a degree in psychology to figure out what they meant.

The usually quiet Bishan had taken to calling them out for it. They'd lost friends. Valor had told Bishan not to worry about it.

Would a true friend be surprised at Bishan being capable of bravery?

No, they wouldn't.

"What did you learn?" Bishan asked when he didn't respond.

"You're brave. You're strong. You are brilliant. And I love you." Valor grunted when Staccato jumped onto his stomach. "We should frame the photo as well, put them up side by side."

"Why?"

"We're better together."

The End

ABOUT THE AUTHOR

Thanks for reading *The Grasmere Trilogy*. I hope you enjoy the rollercoaster ride that I make Bishan and Valor endure (and I hope you forgive me for the tiny cliffhanger in book two.) I appreciate your help in spreading the word, including telling a friend. Before you go, it would mean so much to me if you would take a few minutes to write a review and share how you feel about my story so others may find my work. Reviews really do help readers find books. Please leave a review on your favorite book site.

Don't miss out on New Releases, Exclusive Giveaways and much more!

Join my newsletter: http://eepurl.com/Q0n0X
Like me on Facebook: Join my reader group:
https://www.facebook.com/groups/1326515147425106/
Visit my website for my current booklist:
http://dahliadonovan.com/
I'd love to hear from you directly, too. Please feel free to e-mail me at dahlia@dahliadonovan.com or check out my website www.dahliadonovan.com for updates.

facebook.com/dahliadonovan

twitter.com/DahliaDonovan

instagram.com/dahliadonovanauthor

pinterest.com/dahliadonovan

ACKNOWLEDGMENTS

Writing is simultaneously a solo and group activity. I put the words on paper, but turning that into a novel requires people far more talented than I.

My thanks to my brilliant betas for this trilogy Meg, Renee, Pen, & Debbie. And also to the fantastic women in my writing pub who help keep me motivated.

The second set of people who make my stories brilliant are the amazing women at Hot Tree Publishing. Becky, Olivia, and everyone else, I heart you so much.

Thanks to my hubby and Bacon the Wonder Chihuahua, who didn't complain when I binge-watched Poirot and Miss Fisher's Murder Mysteries for four months.

And lastly, to all my readers, thank you for following me on my writing journey while I play genre magpie. I hope you love my cosy mystery trilogy. Bishan and Valor hold a special place in my heart.

ABOUT THE PUBLISHER

Hot Tree Publishing opened its doors in 2015 with an aspiration to bring quality fiction to the world of readers. With the initial focus on romance and a wide spread of romance subgenres, we envision opening up to alternative genres in the near future.

Firmly seated in the industry as a leading editing provider to independent authors and small publishing houses, Hot Tree Publishing is the sister company to Hot Tree Editing, founded in 2012. Having established in-house editing and promotions, plus having a well-respected market presence, Hot Tree Publishing endeavors to be a leader in bringing quality stories to the world of readers.

Interested in discovering more amazing reads brought to you by Hot Tree Publishing? Head over to the website for information:

www.hottreepublishing.com

facebook.com/hottreepublishing

twitter.com/hottreepubs

instagram.com/hottreepubs

Ingram Content Group UK Ltd.
Milton Keynes UK
UKHW010831190423
420422UK00001B/173

9 781925 853100